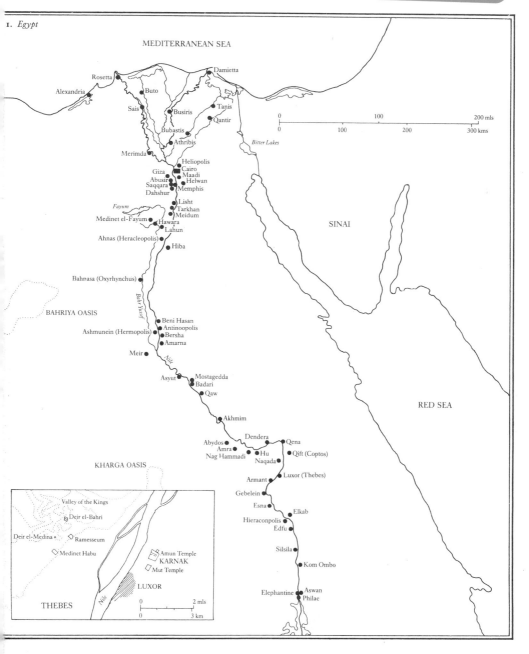

1. *Egypt*

MEDITERRANEAN SEA

Rosetta
Damietta
Alexandria
Buto
Sais
Busiris
Tanis
Qantir
Bubastis
Athribis
Merimda
Heliopolis
Cairo
Giza
Maadi
Abusir
Helwan
Saqqara
Memphis
Dahshur
Lisht
Tarkhan
Meidum
Fayum
Medinet el-Fayum
Hawara
Lahun
Ahnas (Heracleopolis)
Hiba

Bitter Lakes

SINAI

Bahnasa (Oxyrhynchus)

Bahr Yusuf

BAHRIYA OASIS

Beni Hasan
Antinoopolis
Ashmunein (Hermopolis)
Bersha
Amarna
Meir

Nile

Asyut
Mostagedda
Badari
Qaw

RED SEA

Akhmim

Dendera
Abydos
Qena
Amra
Hu
Qift (Coptos)
Nag Hammadi
Naqada

KHARGA OASIS

Luxor (Thebes)
Armant
Gebelein
Esna
Elkab
Hieraconpolis
Edfu

Silsila

Kom Ombo

Elephantine
Aswan
Philae

Valley of the Kings
Deir el-Bahri
Deir el-Medina
Ramesseum
Medinet Habu

Amun Temple
KARNAK
Mut Temple

LUXOR

Nile

THEBES

0   2 mls
0   3 km

0   100   200 mls
0   100   200   300 kms

THE THIRD TRANSLATION

❧ THE THIRD TRANSLATION

Matt Bondurant

NEW YORK

Library of Congress Cataloging-in-Publication Data

Bondurant, Matt.
    The third translation / Matt Bondurant.—1st ed.
      p. cm.
    ISBN 1-4013-0181-9
    1. Americans—England—Fiction. 2. Archaeological thefts—
Fiction. 3. London (England)—Fiction. 4. British Museum—
Fiction. 5. Egyptologists—Fiction. I. Title.

PS3602.O657T48 2005
813'.6—dc22

                                2004054112

FIRST EDITION

10 9 8 7 6 5 4 3 2 1

For the Beautiful Angelic Geniuses of
438 Collicello Street

Who does not regard with reverence an aged tree, which a thousand years ago, beheld generations long since passed from the earth, sitting in its shade? . . . Who can pass without emotion through the silent streets of Pompeii, which once resounded with the bustle of the forum and the song of sailors?

. . . It cannot be denied, that every man regards whatever is ancient, with a certain interest and reverence. And why does he do so? These ancient things, be they beautiful or ugly, complete or fragmentary, lustrous or encrusted with filth, *speak* to every one that beholds them. Ay, antiquities *speak*. We hear their language distinctly, not with the outward ear, but with an inner sense, with which the Creator has endowed us . . . And what is it, that these monuments of antiquity have to say to us?

Their language is: Consider, how young you are compared with those bygone generations, whose contemporaries we have been! Bethink you, how soon you will disappear from the series of living things, without leaving behind you any such monuments of your existence! A different world has been on earth before you!

—GUSTAVUS SEYFFARTH, *Summary of Recent Discoveries in
Biblical Chronology, Universal History, and Egyptian Archeology*

The wisest sages of Egypt [...] in order to designate things with wisdom do not use designs of letters, which develop into courses and propositions, and which represent sounds and words; instead they use designs of images, each of which stands for a distinct thing; and it is these that they sculpt onto their temples [...] Every incised sign is thus, at once, knowledge, wisdom, a real entity captured in one stroke.

—PLOTINUS, in the *Enneads* (V. 8 5–6)

The discovery that, by combining different hieroglyphs, evocative visual emblems might be created inspired these last scribes to experiment with increasingly complicated and abstruse combinations. In short, these scribes began to formulate a sort of kabbalistic play, based, however, on images rather than on letters. Around the term represented by a sign (which was given an initial phonetic reading) there formed a halo of visual connotations and secondary sense, a sort of chord of associated meanings which served to amplify the original semantic range of the term. The more the sacred text was enhanced by its exegetes, the more the conviction grew that they expressed buried truths and lost secrets (Sauneron 1957: 123–7).

Thus, to the last priests of a civilization sinking into oblivion, hieroglyphs appeared as a perfect language.

(of Kircher and his attempts to decipher hieroglyphs before the Rosetta Stone):

The hieroglyphic configuration had become a sort of machine to the inducing of hallucinations which then could be interpreted in any possible way.

—UMBERTO ECO, *The Search for the Perfect Language*

THE THIRD TRANSLATION

1:   A MOORING POST

THIS MORNING I'M THINKING about the shape of a man's life, the chiseled arrangement, the pigments and textures. The way in the end it comes together to project a phantom in the mind of another, a smoky trail seen over the shoulder. The image of Alan Henry is stronger than any idea, and to this day I can still see him, bursting into our flat that night like a loosed rhino. The image of Mick Wheelhouse isn't quite so sharp, dim around the edges, like brittle papyrus.

I know that I remember them this way because of the part I played in their deaths. This was in London, the end of October 1997. I had a week left on my contract with the British Museum to solve the cryptographic riddle of the Stela of Paser. My daughter, whom I'd abandoned at a young age and whom I hadn't seen in three years, was due to arrive in London in a matter of days.

Alan Henry said we had to go out that night, that we had to meet this new friend of his. I was looking forward to a quiet night on the battered love seat with Gardiner's work on the Twelfth Dynasty Hymns of Sobek, but Alan Henry was not one to be obstructed by the passive pursuits of Egyptology. He wore a white T-shirt and a green fishing vest, and his boots looked like something from the circus, freakishly large and a gleaming, deep blue. My flatmate Mick was in his Y-fronts, frying a pan of sausages on our hot plate. He spat into the sink, fingered his thin hair into a ponytail and laid a staggering raft of Arabic curses on Alan and his family. But Mick put some pants on. I was trying to find my wallet in a stack of dirty laundry.

Mick Wheelhouse was my colleague at the British Museum, an Egyptologist and translator born and raised in England. Mick usually tagged along whenever Alan came by, complaining most of the time and fingering his prayer votives. Mick and Alan were both just young kids barely over twenty. I was forty-six years old then, still in the thick heart of my career as an Egyptologist and cryptographic translator.

Alan Henry had to duck his head slightly because of the way the ceiling sloped in our tiny flat. He was a giant man, over six and a half feet tall with hands like bunches of bananas. Alan Henry wore large, squared glasses with thick black frames, and he commonly referred to himself as "a scholar and a gentleman." He put his hand on my shoulder and regarded the scaled-up copies of the Stela of Paser I had on the wall. They covered one whole side of the apartment; the other walls were papered with copies of glosses of the Stela and my hand-drawn charts of the transliterations, as well as some of Champollion's tables.

Ah, yes! he said. Fascinating stuff. But let's move! He waved his massive arms at Mick, who was scowling into his pot at the stove and whispering into his small carved wooden-ear votive of Deir el-Bahri. He held it up to his mouth like a tiny secret telephone. Whatever he was saying, it wasn't complimentary.

Before we left the flat Mick had to pack away his stylus and clay tablets, wrapping each carefully in wax paper to keep them damp. The floor was always covered with shavings because Mick carved his own styluses, the reeds imported from Cairo. Mick's specialty and true interest lay in hieratic and demotic scripts, which are essentially the shorthand or cursive forms of hieroglyphics. He was an expert on troublesome translations, from just about any period, and Dr. Klein brought him here two years ago from Cambridge to tackle the Stela of Paser, but like the others before him he had come up with nothing. Now there was me.

Our excursions with Alan usually started this way; he was always discovering some fascinating or important figure we had to meet. Once, Alan's friend was an old New Zealand rugby legend, another time it was a German nuclear scientist who claimed to have his own personal satellite. He tried to show it to us from the vantage point of an alley in Mayfair.

See? he said, pointing into the vague, yellow-gray London night. That one there.

I saw a few specks of light, but nothing seemed to be moving.

That one? I pointed up in the general area of a few white dots.

No, not *zat* one, *zat one!*

I'm not one to find much fascination in eccentric behavior, though my ex-wife used to claim I did. Yet while it seemed that he was always bursting into our flat and dragging us out somewhere, I liked having Alan Henry for a friend. He was still just a kid and always fired up about something.

Alan Henry lived down the hall in our old Georgian row house one block from Tottenham Court Road, in Bloomsbury, London. Alan was a writer from North Dakota doing a book about a secret failed Canadian moon-shot mission in the late fifties. I still have no real idea why he was in London to do this. He did enjoy lurking in the new British Library, doing research, reading dusty hermetic religious texts, esoteric mysticism, and theoretical physics. That's where I first met him.

A minute later we were following Alan's booming feet as we stumbled down the seven flights of stairs to the street. Great Russell Street ended to the west into Tottenham Court Road and Oxford Street, the busiest intersection in all of London. The streets were thronged at this hour, teeming with tourists and locals all out for a night on the town. It was the kind of area that, much like Times Square in New York, attracts crowds who come to see the crowds. And then there is the whole left/right thing. An Englishman will want to walk to the left of course, but since a full half of the people on the streets are tourists who want to go right, what you are left with is a complete muddle of head fakes and dance steps as the opposing crowds attempt to sift through one another. Alan Henry just bulled his way through the milling bodies and stomped across Oxford Street with Mick and me in his wake, heading into Soho. The theatre crowds were just letting out, the Dominion Theatre on the corner was running *Les Miserables* and the tourists were thicker than desert flies. The night was cold with the kind of dampness that somehow, despite waterproofed and insulated footwear, manages to seep into your shoes and roost deep in the knuckles and sockets of your joints. It was the peculiar kind of English cold that never leaves you, the kind of cold that wakes you up in the pale hours of the morning, huddling under a rough tent of four blankets, to inspect your bluing toes with blind, numb fingers. The kind of itching, irritating cold that might drive you to conquer and colonize the far corners of the globe.

Along the way Alan told us that this guy he wanted us to meet was a favorite author of his, whom he happened to bump into in a bar. The next Salman Rushdie, he said. Believe it.

Alan Henry was always going on about some new writer. As we walked he was swigging from a huge flask he kept with him at all times in his vest pocket. He passed it to me and I took a slug. The gin warmed from his body sank into my chest like hot sand. The flask was engraved with a picture of a jaunty old British sailor and the words:

HMS *Valiant*. Mick sniffed it suspiciously as Alan waved it under his nose, then took a grimacing sip.

Oxford Street was especially crowded as a large semicircle of people had gathered around the entrance to the Virgin record superstore to catch a glimpse of some American professional wrestlers who were apparently shopping. Alan was a big fan of this particular sport.

It's the modern Roman arena, he said, swiveling his bristled, boxlike head, except we're more civilized. We've distanced ourselves from the violence, made it cartoonish and unreal. The cultural feed bag for the great unwashed masses. Just like Elizabethan theatre.

Gutter poetry, Mick muttered, flicking his cigarette ash.

That surprised me. I didn't think Mick gave a damn about anything, other than industrial-strength insecticides and his secretive translations and mutterings. But I was wrong about a lot of things then.

Crowds in that area of the West End aren't so unusual; various famous people occasionally shopped around the intersection of Tottenham Court Road and Oxford, the gateway to Soho, and they often drew huge crowds. We plowed through the craning throng and made our way down Frith Street. When we reached Soho Square, Alan took a couple of skipping steps and started doing slow, heavy cartwheels through the cigarette-butt grass of the tiny square, his bulky frame rotating like a wagon wheel. He did at least six in a row, spinning through the shadows of the pitiful, choked trees staked out with wires. Mick and I trotted after him to keep up. The dark places of Soho Square were filled at night with groups of paired men, pants around their ankles, embracing madly under the stunted elms and the dim light of London stars, and they clutched knees and shoulders in fright as Alan rolled through to the other side and into the street where he rounded off his last turn with a whoop and a deep bow. Alan burned like a torch in the night. He was excited for us to meet his new friend, and remembering him now, how I wish I could see him like that again.

I think that maybe I was their last hope, the last chance the museum and Dr. Klein had to get the Stela solved. I was perfectly happy out in Abu Roash, just outside Cairo, working on a dig with an Italian group who liked my work when Klein cabled me from London. In those days I was just wandering around to wherever a translator specializing in Egyptian cryptography and paleography was needed. I guess you could say I had little ambition, at least in terms of prestige or money. I was getting to the point in my life when I really should have been thinking of settling into something, something with some kind of security and retirement. But it never seemed like it would end.

I know Mick resented the fact that the board stuck me in his flat on Great Russell Street, three blocks from the museum. The Blooms-bury area of London is extremely expensive and open flats are rare, so the board had to scrimp a bit to make it work. I didn't mind the cramped living arrangements too much because the perks were huge: unlimited access to the British Museum, day or night, with the most extensive collection of Egyptian antiquities in the world, guaranteed publication and a bonus for solving the Stela of Paser, not to mention a chance to work independently on one of the last remaining crypto-graphic puzzles of the ancient world.

Though our flat was like a matchbox. Mick and I shared a bed-room, and when I sat up and swung my legs off the narrow bed, my knees touched the edge of Mick's mattress. You had to leave the bath-room door open to sit down on the toilet. The roof was steeply sloped because we were in an attic space, and to get to the one small window in the narrow rectangle that was our living room you had to get down on your hands and knees. It had been built for diminutive seventeenth-century Englishmen, not massive, sprawling Americans like Alan Henry or chubby types like myself. Mick was small enough, built like a reed quill, or the wandering-snake hieroglyph that curls over the moon. Still, I didn't mind. I've never been comfortable with even slightly extravagant lodgings. We never spent any time there anyway; we practically lived in our lab with the Stela.

The surviving fragment of the Stela of Paser is 112 centimeters by 85 centimeters, a large section of the original slablike limestone monument, the kind often set up in tombs or temples. It's essentially shaped like a gravestone, and our conception of the gravestone comes from this Egyptian form. It has a deeply incised frieze of deities along the top, with the rest of the tablet covered in a grid of incised lines, each square containing one hieroglyphic symbol, sixty-seven squares wide and eighty squares deep. We know this based on calculations, as a good portion of the bottom section is worn beyond recognition, the edges are shattered and incomplete, and a large fissure runs diagonally from bottom left to top right, rending the piece in two parts. Much like the Rosetta Stone, only about two-thirds of the text is available.

There is also a name or signature in the top corner, identifying the author as one "Paser, True-of-Voice." True-of-voice is an ancient Egyptian epithet referring to judgment after death, indicating the person as deceased. For the ancient Egyptians, only in death comes the power of truth; the ultimate power was the ability to cross back and forth over the two lands of life and death. With this title Paser was claiming the knowledge of the dead, an understanding of the other side of life as well as this one.

The top line of text that lies outside the grid reads like a title or set of instructions. It reads: *As for this writing, it is to be read three times. Its like has not been seen before, heard since the time of the God. It is set up in the temple of Mut, Lady of Isheru, for eternity like the sun, for all time.* That's the easy part. It's the "three times" that throws us off, because we can only read the text in two ways at this point, horizontally and vertically. The other obvious possibilities, like backward and diagonal, have been tried and proved unsuccessful. Mick spent three months trying to put together a gloss of the outer ring of the Stela and came up with nonsense. Most of it is a direct hymn to the goddess Mut, an obscure figure in the Egyptian pantheon, popular among ancient Egyptians but little studied in modern scholarship. She is mostly referred to as some sort of moon goddess, often contained in what Egyptologists call "crossword pieces" like the Stela of Paser, due to their physical resemblance to crossword puzzles, though in fact they look much more akin to a "word find" game.

The truth is I'd been working on the Stela for a few months and produced nothing. All the other translating work for the British Museum had been offloaded to Mick, to allow me to concentrate fully on this one project. Mick had been working almost exclusively on the cursive scripts since the board took him off the Stela. That was the easy work; anything past the Third Intermediate period was child's play to any Egyptologist worth his gypsum. But there were lots of cursive and funerary hieratic scripts laying about the museum, and Dr. Klein's desk was stacked with documents and requests from museums from Cairo to Berlin for translations.

Mick had a lot of these projects already laid out on our shared worktable in the lab in the basement of the British Museum, covering most of it with his guides and script keys. I didn't mind since I had most of my guides and grids pinned on the walls. I had large-scale reproductions taped everywhere, with colored sections marking certain aspects and grammar, plus my handwritten sheets on either side listing all the possible determinatives and other notes. In our lab the Stela itself was fixed to an iron stand, angled like a drafting desk, with a wire grid that I'd rigged up on the front surface. Each symbol was in its own box and marked with note tabs, numbered and outlining consonant shifts and bilaterals. I was better able to study the possible patterns this way. I preferred to work standing up and pacing, which drove Mick mad. He worked on one of the tall stools, perched like a water bird flipping his papers back and forth between his fingers as he tried to work out the ligatures. I'd never spent this long on a single piece before; most pieces of this size I could knock out in a month tops—give or take a few extra days for the poetic translations and possible transliterations, if they wanted them.

Our lab was bigger than our whole apartment, and we had it all to ourselves, just the two of us and the Stela.

That night in late October Alan Henry brought us to the Lupo Bar in Soho, West Central London, a tight, deeply cushioned place with a plaque hanging out front depicting Romulus and Remus suckling the she-wolf. We found Alan's writer sitting on a couch set in one of the back rooms. He had a young woman draped on his shoulder. It was the usual Soho crowd: young, carefully coifed, and clad in black. I was probably the only guy in London who habitually wore a pea-green corduroy jacket and slacks. Alan thumped off for the bar so I took it upon myself to do introductions.

I'm Walter Rothschild, I said. And this fellow, I said pointing at Mick, is Dr. Mick Wheelhouse.

We pumped hands and said English sorts of things like *cheers* and *right* and *brilliant* and then sat down. Alan brought over a rack of double gin and tonics with a plate of lime wedges. The writer was a rumpled Anglo-Pakistani named Hanif and his lady friend was called Erin. She had a round elfin head and spiky black hair with purple tips like a crown. Slight like a boy in her stretch pants, with a tight, long-sleeved black top that formed around each individual breast like a mold. A sharp nose and lips painted maroon. I'd seen lots of girls like her around in West Central London. She was a Soho queen to be sure.

I drank off most of my glass right away. I got nervous around new people, particularly friends of Alan Henry. It was never quite clear when the shouting would begin and I wanted to be adequately numbed. The gin tasted like clear electricity and popped blue lights in my eyes, deepening the music's pulse into a comforting, though rapidly increasing beat. I didn't have a particular attraction to booze, but sometimes it helped to stifle the process of translation and interpretation, which, after twenty years of training, almost perpetually occurs in my head. It can be a problem sometimes.

Hanif was a swarthy fellow with a wild head of curly jet black hair. I'm pretty sure he was already stinking drunk when we got there. I'd never heard of him, but then I don't know much about writers, or at least writers of this millennium. I could tell you all about the rich poetry of the twelfth-century B.C. scribe Tjaroy or the lyrical prose of Amennakht, son of Ipuy, but not much about anybody after the Arab conquest in A.D. 641. Alan said Hanif was supposed to be something special, a hot writer who was part of the new wave of Pakistani neo-post-colonialism that was sweeping Britain and the U.S.

Hanif said he met Erin last week "on holiday." She offered us some cigarettes in a silver case and I took one. I noticed she had three fresh packs of cigarettes stacked on the table as well. I'm about as ambivalent toward cigarettes as I am toward alcohol, but I did like the shifting shapes of smoke. Hanif began enthusiastically lecturing us on the merits of British women versus Pakistani, his eyes squared and his lips flecked with spittle.

The modern British woman, he slurred, is the perfect construction of decadent sensuality and imperialist fascism. She has no regrets or pretense of altruism. Decades of selective breeding have produced a singular race of such inept spiritual fortitude, braced only by the technology gap, which they use to hold sway over the developing world.

Alan seemed to hang on his every word, nodding his head and smacking the table with his palm to punctuate Hanif's points.

She wears ridiculous silk knickers to bed, Hanif continued, then immediately dives for the crotch, *insatiable*. Yet she insists that you take off your socks, even if it's bloody freezing in the flat!

Bollocks, I heard Mick mutter under his breath.

What is to be done? shrieked Hanif, sweeping his arm and clearing the table of drink glasses and ashtrays, sending them shattering across the floor.

I watched Mick eyeing the tight curve of Erin's folded legs. She was curled up against Hanif, her eyes almost closed as he rambled on at a frenetic pace. Erin nodded and smoked, and when Alan came back with more drinks, she sat up quickly and downed her glass, sucked on the lime wedge for a moment and went back to Hanif's shoulder with a contented look. She looked supremely relaxed. Her eyes blinked slowly, languidly. The liquid in our glasses shook with the thumping bass of the music, something eerie and intricately syncopated.

Then Alan explained what it was Mick and I did for a living, though I don't think Hanif was ever quite clear on it. But Erin started asking me questions about my work.

Normally I'd be scared to death of a woman like Erin. She was young and beautiful. But I was feeling the gin coursing through my arms and legs. So I slouched in the deep velvet cavity of my chair and started telling her about the Stela of Paser, but somehow ended up talking about my daughter, Zenobia, and her mother, Helen.

Zenobia's mother was a musician I met while I was at Berkeley. Helen was the first-chair cellist for the San Francisco Symphony for seven years. Now she gives private lessons and teaches at a boarding school. I can't say that our marriage, short as it was, or our falling in love, was accidental or tragic. But I didn't see it coming. I was just admiring the way a good cellist can stretch a note, so unlike the sharp concise quality of other instruments, like the piano. Helen played Bach's Cello Suite no. 1 for her thesis recital, and sitting in the front row of the auditorium I felt for the first and last time the truest stirrings of something like love, or as close as I could get to it.

It's true I should have known better. I work in lost time, in the lasting binds of history. I am surrounded by monuments and records of time and loyal remembrance. Three years after that recital I was away at a dig in Syria dusting off a bit of papyrus, looking for an inscription when I realized I didn't want to go back. I remember sitting in the desert at night and looking back at my home, the little white walk-up we had in North Beach with a small, common atrium space in back, lined with brick paths around roughly trimmed topiary, where Helen would practice afternoons and the group of elderly Italian ladies next door and across the way would clasp their hands together and shower her with gardenia petals. She would play little cuts of Verdi sometimes and the ladies cooed like swallows in the fading light. I remember standing with my daughter clutching my finger in her tiny baby fist like it was an anchor to this earth. The sour, earthy smell of her chubby body. And I knew I shouldn't have been there, it should have been someone else in my place.

I'd only seen my daughter twice in the last six years. I saw her briefly a few years ago in New York and she stopped by my Princeton apartment for a night in 1991, when she was on her way to New Hampshire for a Grateful Dead show. Zenobia was a junior at Mount Holyoke then, studying English literature. She had two guys with her, skinny fellows with long hair and smelling strongly of incense and body odor, and they smoked pot all night. I made spaghetti and bread with some Chianti I brought back from Italy. She treated me almost like a stranger, and I guess I deserved it. I sat there in a chair while they smoked and talked and tried not to look at her too much. The two guys seemed to think what I did was interesting, but Zenobia just rolled her eyes whenever I spoke. Several times she deliberately mocked me, making fun of my current life, being deliberately cruel to me. But I didn't say anything about it. I wanted to do the right thing.

I went to bed at about two in the morning, and I woke just about an hour later to the sound of my daughter screaming. I was halfway down the hall in my underwear before I realized it was the sounds of the three of them having sex. I went back to my room and standing there in the dark I concentrated on the hanging icicles outside my window. I felt dust collecting around my bare feet on the cold floor. I was beginning to understand the stillness of age and the slow slipping of time. I want to say that I wept all night, and that in the morning I begged for her forgiveness and we were reborn. But I didn't. For most of the night I looked at the faint city stars from my window and pieced together my own constellations, Horus, Ra, Seth, Amun, Helen, even my daughter. She had a place there, faint but still part of the order.

In the morning they were gone and a note was stuck to the fridge that said:

Thanks for the food and couch space.
Miss you.
Zenobia.

That's when I wept.

I sipped my drink and tried to explain to Erin how most people see Egyptian culture as a two-dimensional history, flat on the walls, cold and austere. Most people even think that the Egyptians were a race of tall, thin people, with immaculately manicured hair and clothes. Those are just ideal representations. They were just as fat, old, and balding as I am. I told her how most museums wanted the straight literal translations so they could print them on the little cards in six languages for any visitor to read. They weren't interested in the clues that poetic interpretation can bring, the way it might change how we view ancient cultures. The poetry and humor of the great scribes like Tjaroy, or the stately, restrained and ironic prose of the Nineteenth Dynasty scribe Qenherkhepshef, when given their full literary license in translation, produced texts that could match and surpass the Greeks or Babylonians. I tried to explain to her how the culture of pictographic symbology could be seen as the highest point in the history of creative writing in the known civilized world. Think of it: The words and pictures are all one, the visual representations melded with the written. Since the Early New Kingdom, around 1550 B.C., when hieratic and demotic scripts, which are essentially the cursive and everyday form of hieroglyphic writing, begin to take prominence, the entire history of language as we know it up till today centers on the controlling factors of speed and simplicity. Even in the creation. It took days to write a single page of full-color hieroglyphics in the Old Kingdom form. Stonework took lifetimes. The symbols were etched out delicately for scale, then deepened with slow, careful strokes. They were rimmed in black ink with reed quills then gilded with the brightest golds, reds, and greens they could conceive of, the plumages of river birds, the gaze of the unblinking eye, the flesh of the pointing hand. Theirs was a sacred task. They brought gods to life with every line.

Erin nodded and smoked as I went on. There was a broad stillness in her eyes, the blue seemed mottled and it faded out into white like the desert sky. I tried to tell her about the unknown beauty of pictograph writing; it isn't like what you see in a museum. The experience of a sealed tomb with untouched original color is something like a dream. Up close you can see the delicate tracings of hair and feather in the symbols, the carved coiling patterns of rope, textured strand by strand. I was the first one in the Eighteenth Dynasty tomb of Amosis at Coptos in 1984. The air was still ancient when I stepped in the first chamber, and taking a big lungful of it I could taste the oils and embalming materials, along with traces of rotted flower and meat. I could also taste the nitric gases that put me flat on my back after six steps. When I opened my eyes and repositioned my starlight goggles it looked like a horde of vermilion demons with golden eyes hovering above me, then emerging into the distinct symbols, the prayers of longing, hope, and the next world. When I fell the hired diggers ran out quickly as they feared the curses. I lay there on my back, my lungs burning with a thousand years of time, for a half hour. They started pumping oxygen into the chamber, and by the time the feeling came back to my legs, I had already solved the major cartouches and structural transliterations. I would've had the rest if they hadn't dragged me out of there. We used infrared to protect the paints but you could see the effect of fresh air on them a day after we opened it. Like when you catch a fish and drawing it into the boat the fish begins to die in your hands. You can see the living colors of blood and life fading right before your eyes.

Alan jostled me with one of his cucumber-size fingers, nearly pushing me out of my chair. Hanif was holding out his small gray palm. He had about a dozen extremely large blue-and-white capsules in his hand and was giving me a look like: Eh?

I waved my hand to decline, trying to smile. Everyone else started washing down pills with long pulls from their drinks. Erin slipped two on her pink sliver of a tongue, sipped her gin. Alan Henry had at least half a dozen in his meaty fist, and Mick examined a capsule before biting into it like a tiny sausage. Hanif was puffing on a cigarette with his eyes closed, still ranting out of the side of his mouth. I excused myself and went to the bathroom.

In the bathroom I stood in front of the mirror, swaying and watching the changing lines on my face until I almost got sick. There was only a single dim bulb in the ceiling and the walls and bathroom stalls were painted deep black. A struggling, scraping sound came from one of the stalls that loomed back in the darker reaches. I took some deep breaths. I wanted to keep myself straight. I tried to visualize the anchor trailing away from my ankle, holding me to the earth.

When I washed my hands and rinsed my face a narrow sleeve suddenly emerged from the darkness holding a small towel. I let out a short *Ha!* and jumped back. A shrunken man sat on a stool by the sink, dressed in a black tracksuit and nearly indistinguishable from the murky air. He didn't say anything but continued to hold the towel with a steady hand, gazing directly at me with one eye, the other covered with a patch. The grappling sound from the stalls had stopped, and now it was dead quiet in the bathroom except for the muted thump of the music and the slow ticking of water dripping somewhere. I apologized and wiped my face on the towel, which I then immediately regretted. It was damp and smelled like boiled meat. I watched the little man's gaze follow me in the mirror. He looked maybe ninety years old, of Middle Eastern descent, a narrow hooked nose, like a shriveled one-eyed Horus, years after Seth tore out his falcon eye, the wedjat, the eye of truth, the eye that later came to be the fearsome arm of revenge and destruction on earth for the gods. It was as if Horus finally quit the endless battle for superiority and resigned himself for eternity to this dank loo in Soho.

I suppose a lot of Egyptologists and translators get a bit too involved in their work. It was hard not to see the symbols or the gods in everything, even in your sleep. It's not as though I truly believe in the Egyptian gods, but I believe in their power over men on earth, the way they have affected us and the way we have thought and acted for thousands of years. My personal pantheon is a mix ranging from pre-Babylonian to Hittite to Ptolemaic period gods with a bit of Judaism thrown in, that from my parents, though they were never really practicing or even religious. A myriad of humanoid forms with animal features and overlapping powers and duties, the multitude of accompanying symbolic elements, figures, votives, glyphs, all of it, songs of praise, relief, and forgiveness brought to life by masters of the art. That's my religion, worshiping the artistry of the great scribes.

But now old Horus was watching me as I searched my pockets for a tip. I didn't have any change on me. The fumbling in the stall resumed, the soft scraping sound of cloth over skin and Horus's baleful eye flickered for a moment, away from my face.

Sorry, I blurted, and walked out.

Hanif was now at the bar, gesturing to me with both hands. I walked over a bit unsteadily. My legs felt like soft wax, and I had to negotiate a circuitous route through the low tables filled with clumps of smoking and drinking people. Hanif was standing with his arm around a blond woman in a tight dress. She bobbed with the music and sipped an enormous drink through a straw.

Hanif leaned over and shouted in my ear: *Give the slapper a few of these!* Then he jammed a bunch of pills into my front pocket.

This is Pam, he said, pulling her down the bar with his arm. Her drink sloshed a bit, dripping over her hand as she searched for the straw with her fat purple tongue.

Pam, he said, meet Dr. Rothschild. He works at the BM. I mean, the British Museum of course.

He grinned and Pam let go of the straw long enough to let out a sound that might normally issue from a diseased camel but in some circles would perhaps pass for laughing. I'd heard the joke many times before; the British are obsessed with the scatological. It is easy to understand why after eating English food for a few months.

I shook Pam's hand. Hanif scampered off back toward the table. We stood there, Pam stabbing her face with her drink straw, me just looking at the top of her dress that forced thick gouts of pale flesh into the black lights.

I'm so fucking *pissed*, she said.

Really? I said.

I can't find me friends, I think they might of left me. The fucking wankers.

As I looked her over a bit more I noticed that she was bulging out of the dress in several surprising places.

I'm so fucking *pissed*, she said again.

I realized she meant she was really drunk, not angry, but that wasn't exactly a great thing to hear, either. She swayed a bit and her pupils were so large and unfocused I wondered if she could see anything but bright, curved, wavelengths of light, warped colors like a fish-eye lens. I didn't know what else to say so I took out the pills Hanif gave me. I held them out to Pam.

Would you like one of these?

She bent down and scrutinized them for a bit.

Bollocks to that! What? You fink I'll take anyfing some focking bloke 'ands me? Fuck off!

Sorry, I said, never mind.

I jammed them back in my pockets and for a minute we both scanned the bar wearily. The music thumped.

Out wif 'em, she said tiredly, gimme free.

I sat on a nearby stool and watched my friends at the table while Pam washed down the pills with long pulls from her drink. Mick was whispering to a small piece of folded paper he held in both hands. Alan was sitting at a nearby table in a circle of angry-looking men wearing kilts, gesturing furiously. He had two candles in his giant hands and was moving them across the table at different speeds, trying to convince the men of something concerning the relation of their speeds. They weren't buying it. I'd seen it before: Alan was always trying to explain some principle of special relativity, something about the speed of light and the stopping of time. Hanif appeared to be napping, a peaceful smile on his lips. Erin was looking right at me, bathed in a cloud of her cigarette smoke. She had a slight, feline tilt to her head and her lips were parted showing a sliver of teeth. She looked at me like that for a long time.

I glanced back at Pam. She was sweating through her dress, dark crescents forming under her arms and bosom. Her teeth were chattering so loudly I could hear them over the booming music. She grinned crookedly and put her hand on my crotch and something flared in me as I felt the instant, uncomfortable tightness of folded flesh trying to straighten. She gave a little squeeze and in seconds I was like a board. I felt an odd sense of triumph. I watched her hand as she passed it back and forth in my lap, not wanting to look at that chattering face. I felt steely, and like the giant staff of Umenkepf, I thought it might burst out, blue and gold, and sprout hands and speak at any moment. She seemed to be appraising its size. Then I caught another glimpse of Pam's sweat-beaded face and the clacking yellow molars and I experienced a momentary softening, a depression. Looking away I saw Alan break from the Scotsmen and return to the table, jostling Hanif in his chair, who drowsily stretched out an arm and roughly cupped Erin's breast in his hand as if he were hefting a small melon. Mick had stopped muttering his curses into his votive and stared as Hanif's hand explored the elegant scoop of Erin's chest. Erin was still staring at me, without any reaction to Hanif's groping hand, eyes half lidded and her expression smooth. I excused myself and went back to the table.

I sat down and there were a few moments, or maybe an hour, of a sort of stunned silence, when everyone seemed to hold very still, just glancing back and forth. I didn't understand why Erin had those extra packs of Silk Cut cigarettes on the table when we arrived, but I did now. Everyone was powering through them, lighting one after another, including me, and now everyone's eyes began to widen and change shape, pupils elongating and stretching the color of the iris to either edge. The individual shapes of our exhalations became combined in one cumulous formation hovering over the table. As I watched my companions I began to translate the silhouettes, the suggestions, the outlines they created.

I took out a pen and started doodling some scripts on cocktail napkins. I don't think I was doing it to try and gain Erin's attention. Either way it worked. She slipped around the table and sat next to me, leaning into my arm. I could feel her warm breath on my neck as she bent in to look. She put her lips up to my ear and asked me to translate for her, to tell her what it said. I did some lines from Amennakht, son of Ipuy's poem on the city of Thebes: *What do they say in their hearts daily, those who are far from Thebes? They spend their days sorrowfully invoking her presence, they dream of her heart.* Erin seemed to like that so I did a few lines from the Ptolemaic caption to a scene from a wall of the temple of Horus at Edfu, praising the god of writing Thoth and the seven falcon-headed gods called the "utterances": *These mighty ones created writing in the beginning in order to establish heaven and earth in their monument, they are lords of the art of acting correctly, a mooring post for those who travel on mud . . .*

Erin put both arms around my waist and her tiny head onto my shoulder. I froze and watched Hanif and Alan for a reaction, but there was none. They didn't seem to be paying attention, just chatting to themselves and gesturing about the room. She nestled against my arm and I inhaled her strong smell of lilacs, cigarettes, and sweat. There was a warmth and softness to the sensation that I had almost forgotten.

Write something for *me*, she said.

I grabbed another stack of napkins and wrote out a line from the Instruction of Amennakht: *Let your heart become like a great dike, beside which the flood is mighty.* She smiled and fingered the napkin, tracing over the hieroglyphic for heart, a literal drawing of the human organ. I didn't tell her that this is how the Egyptians expressed love. It flowed about them, and you only had to position your heart to channel some of the waters, like cutting canals and watering fields from the Nile. A Twelfth Dynasty frieze from a tomb at Deir el-Bersha has a similar expression referring to love: *Washing the heart.* This is what you did when you lost it. You washed it in the waters like old laundry, and hung it up to dry.

It's beautiful, Erin said. Lovely.

Hieroglyphics hold four known separate characteristics. I would add to this the possibility of a fifth: a cryptographic or poetic interpretation. But that view is something that most other Egyptologists, including Mick, don't agree with or even recognize. The kind of interpretation I'm talking about requires a layering sort of translation, overlapping sheets of these qualities that yield meanings and actual spoken sounds. For example: The word for "hear" is *sdm*, written as an ear symbol above a squat desert-bird figure. The first sign is actually a cow's ear, and occurs as a logogram or determinative in the word for both human and animal ears. It could also be used for the semantically related word meaning "to be deaf." But it goes beyond that still.

The votive of the cow's ear or human ear was a prominent symbol through the writing and small sculpture of Early and Middle Kingdom dynasties. These are most often taken to mean "listen" or "I hear you" depending on the context. Large ear votives, in picture or sculpture form, were placed around prayer scripts in order to invoke the god to hear more loudly or clearly the prayer of the disciple. Some monuments and tombs have thirty to a hundred ear votives decorating the walls and ceiling, to present a sort of amplified message.

I had a carved wooden-ear votive from a site near Gebel Zeit, on the banks of the Red Sea. I think most Egyptologists have at least one; Mick had several that he kept with him at all times. I kept my votive in my pocket or when I was working I'd lay it on my desk, and in quiet moments late at night, when the symbols lay in twisted knots on the page and in my mind, the grids flapping like sheets in the wind, I'd use it. Or on those nights when the basement lab felt like a mountaintop and my heart was heavy with thoughts of my daughter, and sometimes even my ex-wife, I'd whisper into its delicate folds and channels. I didn't know what else to do. I'm listening, I'd say. I can hear you.

Up until the Third Intermediate period, or about 800 B.C., the Egyptians believed that words themselves were gods, that they had a power in their actual existence beyond this world. To give utterance to a word was to make it real. To put words down was to preserve them for all eternity. Priests would often pour water over certain inscribed symbols and prayers and then drink the water or drip it over their bodies. That way they could actually ingest or be covered in the protection of the words, the gods. Tiny papyrus or votives with invocations or spells inscribed on them were put into amulets or armbands and worn as protection. They believed the words had life, and by altering or changing a script you would affect the reality that was associated with it. This wasn't a game of simple translation.

Each word, each symbol is a spirit waiting to be released into the world, not just the world of its creation but every world after that. Every day, I see so much sadness here, everyone seems convinced that they will be alone in the next world, just as they walk alone in this one. Sometimes I never want to lift my face from the page.

We were packing up and heading out the door. Erin gripped my arm as we stood, grabbing her thin jacket and scarf without letting go. We shuffled out, weaving around the tables, past Pam, who was clutching the bar with both hands, head down between her heaving shoulder blades, vibrating.

Take me to see it, Erin said to me. I want to see the Stela.

Are you interested in ancient Near East history? I said.

You make it sound interesting.

It was such a bad idea. They don't get any worse. Sure, I had keys and my badge, but the British Museum had guard stations manned twenty-four hours a day. You can't just waltz in at two in the morning toting a wall-eyed young woman with perfect breasts and purple-tipped hair. But I enjoyed the way her fingers held the napkins, framing the symbols with delicate strands of skin and nail.

You know, she said, I've never been in the British Museum before. It's true! I'm a bit embarrassed to say so, but it's not exactly what I do. You know what I mean?

I didn't. What *did* she do? That's what I should have been thinking. Instead I slipped my hand into hers. She seemed startled by it, but pleasantly, and in that moment I felt the pull of something close to love, as close as I could understand it.

You should sit up straight, eyes wide, and listen sometimes. Take the route that seems clear and reasonable. But you don't. You have that last drink, stay the extra hour, the extra week, year, you take another chance on something you don't even understand. And then the cities and towns are spiraling away under your feet on cold bleary-eyed mornings spent rubbing your eyes in the baggage check. The signs, the symbols become vague reminders of where you've been, whom you've known there.

There is a vastness to age that compels one to gather things of this world about them, as if to make a larger piece, something that may be noticed. The ancient Egyptians were not only aware of this compulsion—they embraced it. People collect people too I suppose, some people have children for these reasons. You can see it in their faces, the slope of their shoulders as they stand in line for the cashier or in reception lines, the realization of it hitting them like a club across the back of the neck, a slumping, stunning sensation. There are worse things I guess. But building people and things around you only makes a speck into something a bit more than a speck, and a bit more preposterous. The ancients could never have envisioned the scale of the world as it is now, and I'm glad for it. The only way to make a place in it, to make sense of the magnitude of time and the space and span of humanity on earth is to grasp onto the one thing that gives you a clear look.

My wife Helen used to send me things for the first few years after our separation. Sometimes she'd include a picture of our daughter. It's an uneasy thing to see your child grow up in scattered pictures.

When Zenobia was nine I got a picture of her in her soccer uniform, and for the next two years, until Helen sent me another, I thought of her eternally in that uniform, sleeping in it, wearing it every day.

They both came to visit me in Cairo one summer when Zenobia was fourteen. Helen didn't give up on our relationship easily; I have to give her credit for that. I don't know why she even bothered, as I rarely answered her letters. She was very civil to me years after I'd been gone, right up until our last few days together.

It started when we were at the beach, which Helen and Zenobia always loved. They both had beautiful golden skin, like the baked brick of the pyramids, and liked to swim in the ocean. For three days we went to the beach, different beaches each time. The beaches in Egypt are truly vast, most of them almost completely unknown. So I picked out some nice places that were remote and clean. However, each day, at each site, we would place our chairs and towels on the sand with no one else within three hundred yards of us, and after about twenty minutes a man would come walking out of the dunes, a different man each day, and slowly make his way toward us. They looked just like other regular Egyptian men, middle-aged and decently dressed. They would stop about fifteen yards away, a respectful distance, sit down in the sand and looking furtively at my wife and daughter begin to masturbate vigorously.

On the third day Helen insisted we get a cop and tell him. It was easy enough because they usually followed us back through the dunes and into town, always remaining at a safe distance. I told the constable, a huge black fellow in a sharply pressed uniform, and pointed out the guy, still cowering behind us in the crowded street. Without a word the constable signaled two officers who grabbed the man, and taking out his nightstick the constable walked to where they held him on his knees in the street and proceeded to shatter the man's face with repeated blows. The streets were full of people and nobody looked or said anything.

Back at the hotel Helen held Zenobia on the edge of the bed, both of them weeping, and called me a bastard for the first time. Throughout all of it, she'd always said she believed in me and wouldn't give up. Maybe that was what I was relying on.

This is the only part, she said, rocking our daughter in her arms, the only part of this whole thing I can't understand. That you would choose this, that *this* is what is keeping you away from us. I can deal with the rest, Helen said, but not this.

I stood by the window with my hands in my pockets. It was dusk already and the markets were shutting down. Through the window I could hear the final calls of the merchants. Zenobia cried herself into exhaustion and slumped against her mother, eyes closed, her face streaked and swollen.

They were leaving on a flight the next morning, and it is this scene, the last time the three of us were together, it is this scene that I will carry with me every day for the rest of my life.

When we reached the corner the crowd still surged and eddied about the Virgin megastore on the corner of Oxford and Tottenham Court Road. People were massed in a giant semicircle outside the entrance, spilling way over into Oxford and onto the opposite sidewalk. Police barricades were set up and several police cars were parked down the street. People were standing on tiptoe, looking over the heads of others, a few up on shoulders, everyone craning their necks to see who or what was going to come out. Two long white stretch limos were parked in front of the entrance. Mick was gone. I remember the last time I saw him that night he was lingering behind on Frith Street, mumbling to himself and eyeing the women who stood under the spinning red lights of the taxi stands, idly shuffling their feet in the cold and smoking angrily.

Erin tugged on my elbow, both of us tripping across the curbs and kicking through the trash that lined the streets. She clutched my arm as we wound our way through the crowds, following Alan and Hanif. A ripple shivered through the crowd and people started yelling. Someone was coming out of the store entrance. Names were being shouted and people started surging toward the front, pressing their hands on the people in front of them, and the crowd became a shifting, moving anemone of heads and hands. Hanif and Alan stopped suddenly, and as if by some secret signal Hanif quickly clambered up on Alan's broad back to take a look. There was a series of extremely large men filing out of the store. Hanif let out a long, shrill, keening cry, something like the Muslim call to prayer.

What the hell is going on here? Erin said.

She looked up at me with those massive eyes.

Wrestlers, I said. American professional wrestlers.

They were easy to recognize, more like cartoon superheroes than real people. Alan Henry shouted their names with the crowd as they emerged from the store: a man in Lincoln green called the "Pied Piper," followed by "the Angel," "the Bartender," and an enormous bearded fellow simply called "Gigantica."

My people! Hanif started yelling. My people!

Alan bellowed a reply and the two of them started into the mob, Hanif clinging to Alan's back like a jockey. The police were having trouble holding back the surging crowd to begin with and when Alan hit the line it was like an exploding dam and everyone poured into the cleared semicircle. The wrestlers looked terrified as Alan with Hanif on his back led the charge of screaming people. Erin held on to me and I grabbed a lamppost to keep from getting pulled into the eddying swirl. It was as if a large drain had opened in the center of the street and everyone was getting sucked like bits of flotsam to the sink bottom. I wrapped both arms around the post and Erin locked her hands around my waist with surprising strength. It quickly became a full-fledged melee, the air full of police whistles, shattering glass, shuffling feet, thudding bodies and the screams of hundreds of people, led by Hanif's throaty roar.

The last time I saw Hanif he was being lifted high in the air by Gigantica and tossed overhead into the crowd. He twisted and fought like a cat. Alan was standing off to the side having an intense conversation with the Pied Piper. The Bartender had a small, thrashing man up in his patented move, "the cocktail shaker," and the Angel leaped from police car to police car with a woman slung over his shoulder like a sack of laundry.

I retreated a block away, toward Great Russell, with Erin still clinging to my arm. She was trembling and I looked at her wide unfocused eyes and she seemed to see the whole scene, the whole crowd, the riot, all of it, all at once. I thought that perhaps this was the kind of vision I would need to understand the Stela.

I want to see the Stela, Erin murmured in my ear. I want to see what it is, what you do.

There was the matter of the security guards, locks, and alarm systems. But I remembered how she traced her fingers over the symbols on the cocktail napkins, and I didn't want her warmth on my arm to go away. I looked at her dark eyes, swimming with iridescent circles of desire and something else. She held me with an urgency that I hadn't felt in years.

It was easier than I thought. We went around the building and into an entrance on the southeast corner, a small set of stairs that doubled as the education service entrance and a back way for those of us in the Ancient Near East section. Mick and I were the only ones who had a key to the exterior gate, to ensure that we could enter at any time. Then through another keyed door and past a security desk and through a passage to another stair that led directly to the first basement, where Mick and I had our lab, and then farther on to the first of the two primary Ancient Near East storage areas in the subbasement.

The security staff kept at least a half dozen men on duty through the night, most of them at the main security station in the north-wing basement. I knew that Simon would be working the desk tonight, one of the few guards that seemed to like me okay. I buzzed him on the internal intercom at the desk. I told him that Erin was an American Egyptology graduate student from Princeton who was leaving tomorrow and hadn't had a chance to see the Rosetta Stone yet. Simon just chuckled and flipped the switch to send us through. He knew it would be my ass if anything happened. I also asked him to cut the alarms for the whole Rosetta exhibit, as well as the Ancient Near East gallery number four, the upper chambers fifty-nine through sixty-five, where the funerary exhibits were, and the main basement corridor so we could get to the lab and the Stela. There are no closed-circuit cameras in the British Museum, to this day, for reasons unknown to me.

We walked under the Great Court, where the new reading room was under construction, and came up the west stairs into gallery four, which housed most of the Egyptian statuary and large antiquities.

Under the low half-light of the museum the various items in their cases glittered golden and blue. We moved quietly, just a slight shoe squeak, gliding through the rooms as if on a conveyor belt. I showed her the Rosetta Stone first, and she nodded gravely at the significance.

On the way to the Stela we passed the large wall paintings from the tomb chapel of Nebamen, a mural of Egyptian commerce, shaved men driving herds of cattle and birds to market under the watchful eyes of their lord. I translated a few lines for Erin as we passed: *Come on! Move off! Don't speak in front of this favored one, Nebamen. People who talk are his horror! He does what is true; he will not pass over any complaint. Pass on quietly, truly!*

We walked through the low-slung cases of funerary equipment, the mummified remains of men, women and children, twisted in rotted cloth and grinning. Through arched doorways you could see the rows of sealed glass boxes glowing with red light, holding the brittle remains of letters, orders, and prayers. The laser beams of the alarm system in the other rooms snaked their way between table legs and over cases at varying heights and formed a crosshatched pattern, designed to make it impossible to jump over or around them.

I showed her the Heart-Scarab of Iuy, a dung beetle carved from green feldspar, an amulet to be placed on a mummy at its heart. The green scarab was a symbol of regeneration for the ancient Egpytians, who felt the dung beetle and its tendency to roll spheres of dung across the desert to lay eggs in were a representation of the sun and moon being rolled across the heavens. In the afterlife the scarab would become the heart; it would bring the body back to life and continue the endless cycle into the next world. Inscribed on the scarab was a spell that particularly illuminates the cynical worldview of the ancient Egyptians: the spell was designed to prevent the heart from testifying against its owner at the final judgment.

When I opened the door to our lab I could see the Stela of Paser looming in the corner like the open mouth of a cave, the fissure that rent the lower half of the stone in two parts like a pale vein working its way upward into the black. It seemed to give the room a sudden feeling of weight. As usual it was freezing in the lab. Our breath hung in front of us like small banks of fog. Erin let go of my hand and held back a bit as we walked toward it, as if she was afraid. I flipped on the overhead spotlight, casting a smooth light over the stone.

This is it, I said.

And what's the problem again? Erin said.

I explained to her the "read three times/ways" issue. Most Egyptologists familiar with the Stela of Paser just assumed that the three times referred to the ritualistic practice of reading hymns and prayers aloud. In this case it just meant repeat it three times, out loud. But Klein wasn't convinced. There is something else to the piece, the way the instructions specifically state that *nothing like this has been done before*, the masterful, crosswordlike manner in which the glyphs are placed so that the hymn of the Stela could be read two ways, to the same effect—a feat that seems an impossibility and that has never been duplicated—that made Klein suspicious of something else. The text itself speaks of illuminating *the Two Lands* and *the way between*—the mythical "Third Land." The place where the chaos of life becomes as regular and predictable as the flooding of the Nile. That is what every ancient Egyptian seemed to desire. Then adding to the mystery is what we know about Paser, "True-of-Voice," the author of the Stela. Which is almost nothing. Then there's also the question of the goddess Mut, to whom the hymn is directed. So Klein went with his hunch and brought in Mick and me.

I put both hands on the grid and stared at the streams of symbols. The falcon over the urn and tomb, eye and two bars over a bowl, a peacock and ankh, the staff and open hand. *The everlasting power, Mut, she will illuminate the Two Lands.* I tried to set up the ordering grid in my mind, and began to count the consonants. But the symbols seemed to burrow deeper into the dark granite, each growing smaller and more indistinct. It bore into me like a fine light from the oldest tunnel in the world. I realized then that I had spent the majority of my life looking at such things. And for the first time, just for a moment, it seemed an incredibly foolish thing to do.

I don't know how much time passed, but Erin was gone when I turned around. I heard whispering in the hall, back toward the exhibit area, a sound like hushed chanting. It certainly didn't sound like Erin; it didn't sound like anybody. The basement corridor was empty. I felt the dampness under my arms and back as I squinted hard into the dark corners where artifacts and funerary monuments lay stacked with other debris. If she was hiding in here then someone else was out in the hall. If she strayed into other areas she could set off the alarms. I ran back up the stairs and then into gallery number four, between the rows of cases, checking behind the large sculptures, the colossal head of Ramses II, the row of Sekhmet she-lion statues, the vast dark hall echoing with my panting breath and slapping shoes.

When I reached the end of the hall I heard a faint clatter, coming from somewhere up the west stairs. My chest lurched and dropped, and for a second I thought my heart had assumed the shape of a pyramid, like it does several hours after death when the organs begin to shrivel and sink, collapsing in on themselves.

I took the stairs two at a time, both long flights. I heard another rustle through room fifty-nine, Early Mesopotamia, back into the upstairs Egyptian section and the main funerary halls, sixty-one to sixty-five. I saw a dark lump on the floor by the first row of sarcophagi. It was her clothes, puddled like they just dropped off her. I crouched by her clothes and felt them with my hands. They were still warm. I called her name in a loud whisper.

She was standing under the green glow of the way-out sign, in the doorway to the next chamber. The light cast a greenish cloak over her from behind, and dust motes swam in the air as if she were emanating a fragrance, a power. The arched doorway above her formed a perfect royal cartouche, the name symbols of royalty. There seemed to be a jade mantle about her shoulders, shot through with threads of gold and river blue. Her slim hips and wrists and elongated legs, indicative of honor and truth, were parted slightly. In her hands she held the crook and flail, arms crossed over her chest. Then she held out her hand to me, turning slightly, and I could see the long, thin scythelike curve of her beak and the avian eyes. The mask of Thoth.

Erin walked toward me, her bare feet noiseless on the floor and her arm still upraised. I couldn't move. I felt that if I moved, I might somehow cause damage to the antiquities she was wearing. She put her hand on my shoulder and tilted her head so that the long-beaked mask looked up into my eyes. The mask she wore had never been worn by a woman, ever, in its four thousand years of existence. It seemed to fit her perfectly. I fingered the ancient threads of the robe about her shoulders, running my hands over her breasts that hung naked under the mantle. I touched my lips to the rough wood of the mask and tasted the ancient paint. I felt her hands fumbling with my belt, and she pushed her thin body against me, moaning softly behind the mask of Thoth. I could feel the sudden vastness of the museum, the two of us like grappling insects while the rest of the hulking structure towered around us, ticking and echoing in the darkness. I gripped Erin's hips and put my face in her neck, warm and damp with sweat. She kept the mask on when I lowered her to the stone floor under the shadow of the massive sarcophagi of King Intef.

The ancient Egyptians believed that man was composed of separate spiritual elements that remain harmonious, in this life and the next one. These elements included life span, destiny, birth, shadow, and name, and together they gathered into personality in the form of the *ka*, or soul. After death the person who maintained the proper harmony became transfigured into *akh*, or enlightened spirit. Those who failed became *mut*, simply meaning "dead." When the *ka* reaches the underworld for the final judgments of the dead, jackal-head Anubis sits by the scales, weighing the heart against the feather of Maat. Thoth, the scribe of gods, stands nearby, broad shouldered, attentively recording the findings, logging the destiny of the newly dead. The markings of the scribe seal the fate of all who pass through the portals of the Third Land. I knew that Erin was on some kind of amphetamine and had just picked things off the walls and put them on for a kick. But the symbology of Egyptian clothing has its own complexity and I couldn't deny the fact that Erin had somehow managed to put together the suitable outfit for judgment after death. Just as in the underworld, in this life it inevitably comes down to the weight of the heart: the heavy volumes of love and joy, or the sheer density of sorrow and regret.

2: THE FLOOD IS MIGHTY

THERE WAS A FAINT rustling of air, a whisper of breath, her warm body against mine, her arm thrown across my chest. We were naked and the marble floor was cold. Through my eyelids I could see fluttering shapes, colors swimming overhead. I opened one eye slowly. A gray swath of sky drifted through the skylights. The exit lights at the end of the hall cast a faint green glow across the walls. I could see the outlines of large figures, which I knew were the shadows of the large statuary in the room, the sarcophagi and mummy cases. The darkness cleared and the shapes settled into definitive, recognizable things. A massive blocky shape rose up over us, the tomb stela and "false door" of Ptahshepses, a beautiful structure that still held good quantities of blood red and ochre color on its face. Egyptian false doors are small carved doorways, without any kind of real door and leading nowhere, covered in funerary texts and placed in the tomb. Egyptians believed it would allow the deceased to reenter the world of the living to collect their offerings of food, shabti, and other things they would need to live a good life in the underworld. This was where the soul spirit, or *ka*, could always find an open door between the two worlds.

I blinked in the darkness, watching the false door closely. I heard the faint sound of voices, the scraping of footsteps, echoing up the west stairs. I checked my watch: 8:00 A.M. I was wide awake.

I had a hard time making Erin understand the gravity of the situation. I was still reeling from the alcohol and having trouble trying to gingerly remove the mask and robe from her while she climbed on me like a koala bear. We were kneeling on the floor in a spiraling swirl of priceless Egyptian artifacts. Her eyes were huge.

Give a girl a kiss, she whispered, will you, Dr. Rothschild?

The museum would open in another hour. Any minute now the curators and museum-services staff would be moving through the exhibits and making sure all was set before the rush of tourists.

Please, I said, let me have these things. We have to go.

I almost dropped the mask as she tried to wrestle it back from me. The artifacts were liable to explode in a cloud of dust at any minute.

I don't think we should leave, Erin said, let's just stay here.

We can't. We have to get out of here right away.

I don't think I *can* leave. She clutched my arm and looked balefully around the room.

Of course you can, I said.

I tried to slide her tiny shirt over her slippery head. She tucked in her chin and stymied my efforts by twisting her neck.

The space to the door seems so far, Erin said.

I looked at the doorway to the next chamber. It looked just fine. Close even.

It's not, I said. We can do it. Please.

It's eternity! she shouted.

My head was ringing slightly.

I got her to her feet and tried to lead her toward her trousers that lay by the entrance to the funerary room. She leaned into me like a child.

Let's go get a drink, she said, suddenly brightening. Let's go back to the bar.

I don't think that they're open right now. It's too late or early for a drink.

She looked at me.

This is London, Dr. Rothschild. There's *always* a place to get a drink.

Please, put your clothes back on.

She clasped her arms around my head and kissed me hard. I could feel her shivering, and I was struck with a deep sense of guilty nostalgia. Helen used to kiss me in much the same way, pressing her lips firmly to mine in a smile, breathing deeply through her nose and squeezing her eyes tight. But it wasn't the odd sense of nostalgia that filled me with a feeling of completeness and belonging, despite my terror at being discovered, and I couldn't connect it directly with Helen. All those things seemed individual segments in a chain of re-verberative events, a spiraling helix into space, something like the glyph of Anubis in the afterlife; the icon of otherworldly justice, recognizable for its distinct shape and placement, yet its meaning never clear. It was the touch of Erin's quivering fingers, the press of her warm lips, the want in her shoulders and arms that made that spinning helix move, bending to touch me here and now, marking me for future judgment.

I got the artifacts together that Erin was wearing and started to arrange them in their cases, only after I made her promise not to touch anything or go anywhere. Even so she scampered about some of the other rooms, giggling and calling my name. The high windows in the funerary chamber began to turn from gray to violet-gold as the morning broke.

It took me about a half hour to arrange the pieces back in their appropriate positions, and even then I wasn't sure. It was likely that the hall curator would notice that the folds in the robe were completely different, and that the mask was missing a few chips of paint, but that couldn't be helped now. I got down on my knees and swept into a little pile the dust and paint slivers that had come off the materials, and licking my palm I gathered them up and rubbed them off in my jacket pocket.

The quickest way out was through the front, the main entrance. We hustled down the stairs and through the Egyptian statuary hall, through the coat-room hall toward the front court. Museum staff were already streaming in, coming in the front doors and separating off to their different destinations. I had Erin by the elbow, my head down, trying to appear as nonchalant as possible. I hurried her outside to the main courtyard, the morning air sharp in my lungs, the stone walls of the courtyard covered in a glistening sheen of dampness, trying to stifle the urge to run by holding my arm around her. She kept glancing at me and giggling like a little girl.

Once we were outside the gates and on the sidewalk and it was clear that nobody was following us, I relaxed our gait and began to smile myself. We walked along Great Russell toward Tottenham Court, heading into the murky sun, rising just over the tops of the buildings along Oxford Street, the sky like washed-out parchment. I was exhausted; I felt like I'd been stoned and flayed and slept on the floor of a cold tomb. Erin didn't seem like she was coming down anytime soon, but the sky and outside air seemed to occupy her to such an extent that she was rather calm, just rolling her head from side to side, resting it against my shoulder as she pointed that tiny chin into the air and grinned, her eye makeup smeared and darkened like a pharaoh's handmaiden. She sighed a lot, and held my arm tightly.

I didn't know where she was going, or even if I wanted her to go.

As we neared Tottenham Court I did some quick calculations: Where was Mick anyhow? Would he mind if I had Erin over for some tea and toast? Maybe we could spend the morning together?

While I was mulling this over Erin spied a black cab lurking outside the Palace Theatre and flinging off my arm in a grand sort of gesture she raced for it. She moved with startling speed and agility for someone wearing shoes with heels like ice picks.

Erin! I called, starting to trot after her. My joints ached, my knees particularly. She was already opening the door of the cab.

Erin! I called again, stumbling along the sidewalk.

She turned to me as she was stepping into the car.

Rothschild! she shouted, *The flood is mighty! It's bloody mighty!*

Then she was gone, and I was standing there at the now quiet intersection of Tottenham and Oxford, practically in the same spot where it all began last night. A few cars pulled through the intersection, seemingly enjoying the relative tranquility of that hour of the morning. The paper stands under the Dominion Theatre marquee began to set up their plywood booths and a small trickle of people began to disappear down the stairs to the tube station. I shivered and pulled my hands up in the sleeves of my corduroy jacket.

Despite this development I felt a glorious strain of self-contentment coming on, a juvenile pride I had forgotten. It was a cold day in London once again, and I was burning like a candle in my own personal storm glass. I fondled my wooden-ear votive in my pocket, feeling the delicate contours. I swaggered down Great Russell Street. I felt the dull ache of a coming hangover, but even that sensation seemed to lend itself to a feeling of accomplishment. Watching the faces of my fellow pedestrians I felt that delicious effect of a tremendous breakthrough. The impassive faces of the barristers and bankers hustling around the corner to High Holborn seemed ruddy and good natured, the bent woman in the plastic coat practically skipped across the crosswalk, and the newsagents seemed crowded with benevolent strangers waiting for their papers, cigarettes, and beverages with patience and anticipation for the new day. Each person seemed to be such a profound expression of uniqueness, fecundity, and goodwill. The pleasures of aesthetic and intellectual experiences always make the world for me seem suddenly filled with angels.

A fine morning for some breakfast, check the answering machine for any message from my daughter, and then the gut and brain work of Egyptian cryptography, a long day spent with the Stela. Life was good.

I was halfway to Eve's Cafe for coffee and a roll when I realized I didn't have Erin's last name, a phone number, I didn't have anything.

It didn't do any good to spend a massive amount of time just staring at the thing. Though it bears a strong resemblance, the Stela of Paser isn't really like a crossword puzzle or other types of mind games; you couldn't just keep looking at it and eventually it would come to you, like remembering the title to a song that you heard an hour ago. The Stela was different; there was no key; we were starting from scratch. There are a few other puzzles, such as Mayan hieroglyphics, Meriotic script, and Linear A that pose similar problems. We have somewhat deciphered the symbols and have a vague understanding of the alphabet and grammar, but we still can't figure out how to translate it entirely. But the Stela of Paser is unique in that it is actually written in a text that is completely decipherable, or so we thought. It was constructed around 1150 B.C., and found by Belazoni in the vicinity of the Great Temple of Amun at Karnak, who sent it to Dr. Thomas Young in England in 1890, the preeminent expert along with Jean-François Champollion of France. Thinking that it might be another sort of Rosetta Stone, Belazoni wrote that he hoped the piece might help Young in his work of deciphering the Egyptian alphabet, a rather ironic mistake considering it must have only complicated matters.

There is no written record of Young's reaction to the piece or if he made any serious attempts to translate it.

So much of the meaning depends upon the cultural, literal, and sculptural contexts and what we understand about the writers themselves. Hieroglyphic symbols are relatively easy to translate word for word, but this is inadequate in terms of the information conveyed by the text. Then again, these kinds of cryptographic puzzles could be labored over for fruitless centuries, then the solution comes in a momentary imaginative leap. In 1972 Davies reportedly did the coffin of Tanetaa of Thebes, a piece that had stymied Egyptologists for a hundred years, in six minutes after a few pints of bitter and a packet of prawn crisps. There was very little reason why I couldn't solve the Stela from a park bench in Russell Square. If I needed to I could scratch a few symbols in the thin dirt, or for that matter I could draw up the whole thing. I've never spent this long with a single piece before and I had every symbol in its appropriate place burned into my memory. I saw the Stela every time I closed my eyes.

When I got back to my building, I saw Alan Henry leaning against the outer door, his massive boots folded over one another and his face held up to the faint late-morning sun, his broad forehead looking burnished bronze. The sun was so rare in London that whenever the slightest glimpse of it put its colors on the walls and sidewalks, whole crowds of Londoners would stop and raise their faces to the sky, a momentary lull in the swirling chaos of downtown London. Alan's eyes were closed, as if he were napping. I was figuring I'd just let him stand there and try to slip in, when he spoke.

Think of it, Alan said, at this very moment *billions* of neutrinos, sub-quark particles, are pouring out of the sun and passing through our bodies and through the earth.

Well, I said, that's—

The light, Alan went on, the warmth, the sensation of the sun. The individual atoms of our bodies are as far apart to a neutrino as the stars of our galaxy would be to a spacecraft traveling between them. Depending on the speed of course.

Of course, I said, listen, I have to get—

Alan's eyes snapped open and in two strides he had my arm and was pulling me into the doorway.

We have a situation, Alan said. We have to go down to the police station right away.

I fumbled with my key and Alan swept me aside with a giant palm and tore the key from my hand, inserted it and opened the door in one fluid motion.

You have any money, Rothschild? he asked. How much you got? We're going to need it.

What? Why?

Alan rushed me up the stairs to my flat.

Hanif got pinched, Alan sighed. It was a bit of a lapse on my part. But I'm betting that slippery little minx had something to do with it.

Alan was pacing about our cramped living room as I searched for some money, or at least made the pretense of searching as I knew I didn't have any.

Who? You mean Erin?

He stopped and rotated toward me, his eyes flashing.

Have you seen her? Where is she?

No! I mean, I haven't since that thing . . . on Oxford Street. The wrestlers.

Well, I'll find her soon enough, Alan said. She has some explaining to do.

It turns out Alan's famous Pakistani writer was broke and couldn't make bail. Alan patted me down, going through my pockets, examining my ear votive for a moment as if to ascertain if it had any value, even ruffling my small swatch of hair. I explained that I didn't have a pound on me, and that I didn't have anything in the house. I didn't get paid for another six days, my final paycheck from the British Museum. My hangover now began to hit me with a burning fury. Alan danced before me, enraged. He seemed awfully protective of this writer Hanif, perhaps in a dangerous way. I thought of Seth, the feared and unpredictable defender of ancient Egypt, the dangerous god who cut Osiris into tiny pieces and threw him in the river. How Horus would avenge this act, bringing order back to the Two Lands.

Where's Mick, Alan said, where is that little bastard? He's got some cabbage on 'im.

I grabbed my twill crusher hat and my beige mackintosh from the closet. As we hustled down Great Russell toward the museum Alan Henry explained Hanif's financial problems.

He has a problem with young ladies, Alan said. I mean *young* ladies. Like that girl Erin last night.

My head filled with a white light and I almost walked into a mailbox.

What?

That's what I'm going to find out, Alan said. I don't think Hanif's really happy with the broad right now. She ditched us last night, right when the heat came down. Suspicious.

I staggered, then took a leaning tack to catch up with Alan as he surged ahead, talking all the while. My brain slipped inside my skull from one ear to the other with each step like an egg yolk, sloshing, lashing fire in my temples and behind my eyes.

Well, personally, Alan went on, I think Hanif's got enough problems to worry about. Probably just some remnant of that Pakistani Muslim paranoia. They all think the world's against them. He needs to cure this problem. With the little women. Some of these girls aren't quite restaurant quality, if you know what I mean. Can't get enough of them. That and the 'ludes. But the guy needs help. You just can't abandon one of the most important literary figures of modern Britain to rot in the tower. This is an essential situation. This is the way you refute the powerful forces of the proto-capitalistic hegemony. This is the kind of thing that saved Borges, the way Céline was sold up the river!

As I trotted alongside Alan Henry, trying to keep up with his heavy, loping strides, the rush hour was beginning and the streets began to fill with sluggish auto traffic and brisk sidewalk commuters and tourists along Great Russell Street.

If you see that slippery little minx, Alan said, you let me know. Hanif wants to put the screws to her. She knows something, he's sure of it.

Do you think so? I said. She's responsible for his trouble?

Alan actually slowed his pace for a moment and looked slightly pensive. Then he rotated his broad face to me, stonelike, impassive.

They *all* are, he said. Always. Every one of them.

And then with a spring he tore off down the sidewalk again. I hoped Mick was in the lab, and that he had some cash on him, because I was a bit afraid of what Alan might do otherwise.

Mick usually slept till noon, then came into the lab moaning and cursing the lousy coffee that Sue and Cindy, our interns, prepared for us in the morning. I used to drink a lot of coffee back when I was younger, but I doubted I could stomach the stuff that Sue and Cindy brewed up. They didn't seem to care much what Mick wanted; they rightfully pinned him early on as a nasty sort. I've heard the two of them mutter *wanker* or the like more than once after he sneered at their coffee and spat on the floor by their desks on his way out.

I remembered Mick the night before, the way he chomped down on that speed capsule, his sweating brow and racing eyes. He might be solving the Stela at this very moment. Alan had at least half a dozen of those pills as well, but nothing seemed to faze him much.

Thankfully Alan wasn't allowed down in the lab. I could've gone through one of the smaller side gates, but I purposely brought him in through the front gate, through the main entrance, already teeming with crowds of Japanese tourists, who always showed up right at opening time. To get to the lab through the front you had to go down the southeast stairwell, past a security checkpoint that had several guards there at all times. I recognized Colin and Rasheed, two security guys I'd seen coming through here before. I was glad to see them, because often the guards would be baffled by my special staff pass with the black diagonal stripe and no designation code under my name, so they would have to call it in and get some kind of confirmation from Dr. Klein. That was one of the reasons Mick and I had our own entrance at the corner of Montague Place and Great Russell, which led directly to the central basement corridor.

I left Alan Henry at the security checkpoint. Several of the security guards had already made a sort of loose extended defensive perimeter around Alan, eyeing him warily, hands on their utility belts, fingering their cans of pepper spray.

Shake him down, Alan said to me, his bronze forehead flashing. I'll be right here. Please refrain, Rothschild, from messing about with the various knickknacks you've got gathered about down there. Time is crucial.

He patted his watch-less wrist and sat on the edge of the security table, making it groan and tilt sharply, much to the surprise of security guards Colin and Rasheed who were sitting there on their break with a fresh cup of tea and reading the *Daily Mirror*.

Oi! What the . . . ? Colin got up and pulled out his nightstick as I ducked down the corridor to the basement.

I hurried down a flight of stairs to the set of coded doors that I could open with my staff pass, which led to the long central basement hallway that ran the entire length of the British Museum, sending out tributaries to other branches, the storage rooms, labs. The vaulted hall was carved out of rough white limestone and had low ceilings. The public parts of the museum are beautiful spaces, architectural delights with glorious ancient mosaics inlaid on the stairwells, luminous tapestries adorning the walls, finely carved balustrades, crown moldings and soaring painted ceilings fit for royalty. Down here in the basement it was dusty cement floors and bare fluorescent lighting; water pipes and wiring ran naked along the wall, puddles formed in subtle depressions when it rained, and it was always cold. It wasn't too surprising to find fragmented Roman busts or ancient Persian tapestries propped up against the wall or each other, waiting for a designated space in the storage rooms that often never came. At the end of the hall there was another coded door and then the hallway that led to our lab. There were other stairways that led farther down to subbasements and sub-subbasements under our lab, mostly for storage of various antiquities and overflow from the old British Library that still hadn't made the move to the new location and now sat moldering in even more remote obscurity. Or perhaps rooms where other odd pairs of men in the employ of Dr. Klein worked quietly in solitude, huddling in damp, dimly lit rooms, poring over other problem antiquities and curious artifacts. There was much I didn't know; the British Museum is nearly as vast, meandering, and secretive as the antiquities it holds.

At the main corridor junction Sue and Cindy were dutifully manning their desks and the coffee machine, wearing sweaters and mufflers against the wet chill of the basement. Their countenance brightened considerably when they saw me. They began straightening up their desks and pouring cups of coffee.

Sue and Cindy were two extremely earnest Egyptology graduate students from Oxford. A blonde and a brunette, both with short, bob-style haircuts, horn-rimmed glasses, and bad teeth. In my American teaching experience I found that you couldn't tell the fashion-merchandising majors from the geologists. But here it was different, perhaps still the way it is seen stereotypically, the way it used to be years ago: Intellectuals in Britain are for the most part homely and awkward, without a plan or chance for the ephemeral beauty the rest of the world enjoys.

Certainly Mick and I fit into this same category. Mick with his shaggy head of black straw and his ferret face. He had a set of teeth that all seemed pointed toward the center of his tongue, a concave structure that seemed more suited to cracking walnuts than to human speech. We both were part of the vast, muddling middle, the usual sort. All my life I've found that if I kept my mouth shut and head down, I could spend weeks without drawing any apparent notice of any kind.

As for the heated man in the temple, an ancient scribe wrote in *The Instruction of Amenemope, He is like a tree growing indoors; A moment lasts its growth of shoots, Its end comes about in the woodshed; It is floated far from its place, The flame is its burial shroud. The truly silent, who keeps apart, He is like a tree grown in a meadow. It greens, it doubles its yield, it stands in front of its lord. Its fruit is sweet, its shade delightful, Its end comes in the garden . . .*

Sue and Cindy were both ferociously dedicated to our work on the Stela of Paser. If we pulled off this bit they would both get recognition in the forthcoming publications of course, as well as vitae items that would ensure them placement in almost any museum, foundation, or university that they wanted. They lived together in a flat somewhere in Shepherd's Bush, though they seemed to be hovering outside the lab door twenty-four hours a day. They were determined individuals and I often wonder what happened to them.

I remember how remarkably well Sue and Cindy dealt with the rats in the museum; between midnight and about six in the morning you had to stand against the wall in the lower passages in order to let the river of rats go by, coming and going from their nocturnal foraging. Like a lot of the night staff, Sue and Cindy had a spare set of tall rubber boots that they would wear late at night; I'd come out of the lab to see both of them busily writing reports or typing memos or doing god knows what, with rats the size of small dogs thumping under their table, foraging on the pipes that ran along the wall. I often thought Sue and Cindy were determined to be available whenever Mick and I

45

were about, in the vain hope that they would be present when we cracked the code, as if one of us would come running out of the lab yelling *Eureka!* and the flashbulbs would start popping. It is more likely they were just hoping we would have something for them to do.

Yes, morning, Dr. Rothschild! they chirped as I approached.

Sue and Cindy both had that odd British habit of starting every statement with "yes."

Good morning, I said. Is Dr. Wheelhouse in the lab?

Their faces soured a bit at this query. Cindy tried to hand me a shaky cup of coffee.

Yes, he is, Sue ventured, I mean at least we think so.

Yes, said Cindy, we, um, heard someone in there, and since, well, you are here, then we figure it must be Dr. Wheelhouse.

Sue waved a clutch of papers at me.

Yes, he must have come even earlier. Would you like to read our progress reports? We've condensed and formatted the things you and Dr. Wheelhouse gave us last week.

Progress reports? I had no idea what they were talking about. I took the proffered cup of coffee, apologizing my way past them and keyed into the lab.

Mick *was* poring over the Stela, which was surprising since he hadn't looked at it or barely mentioned it since I'd gotten here. But then Mick never said much at all to me. At least not *directly* to me.

Mick was reading literature at Oxford when he was fourteen, specializing in Old English, Greek, and Latin, but his focus quickly shifted to ancient Egyptian texts. In his third year as an undergraduate Mick shocked the Egyptology department at Oxford when he produced a few stunning translations of the funerary monuments to the Fifteenth Dynasty pharaoh Shabakah. He could do a hundred lines of hieratic in a day, including the transliteration, gloss, and pronunciation, without consulting Van Metre's keys or the standard overlays. He was now only twenty-three and was one of the top pure translators of ancient scripts in the western world. It was too easy for him, I think. He tossed off translations of full-color funerary papyri without considering the poetic implications or even admiring their pictorial beauty. His translations were too cold and literal for me.

Dr. Klein was turning over new projects to Mick to allow me to be completely free to concentrate on the Stela. Klein seemed to be using him to eat the backlog, to clear up the untranslated inventory. It was a good idea, really, because Mick was fast, tearing off batches of papyri and entire funerary pieces in a matter of days. Mick was also employed doing a series of private projects for Klein, things for private collectors and other entities that came to Klein for help.

The Stela of Paser was mounted on a stand with a set of metal brackets that held it at a nice angle for viewing, about chest high. A floor-mounted spotlight stooped over the Stela, casting a clean circle of light around it. Often when working on the piece we would put our hands on either side of the stone, leaning into it like the wind. Mick stood like this now, a small stack of crumpled papers in his mouth. The place reeked of tobacco smoke and unwashed Englishman, and the cement floor was littered with cigarette butts. I could see his legs trembling. If you get on track, if you get on to something, some particular line or theory concerning the structural gloss of a thing like the Stela, you wouldn't want to be bothered until you ran the thread to the end.

I stood there by the door thinking about this until Sue came running down the hallway yelling something about my American friend tossing the lobby about. I closed the door and turned the bolt before she got to the doorway. Nobody had the key to this lab but me, Mick, and Klein.

Mick, I said, look, I'm sorry, but we have a situation.

Mick straightened up and swiveled his head around. His eyes were wide and heavily circled with crimson rings. Like me, he was still wearing the same clothes he'd had on last night, and his shirt had deep sweat rings under the arms. His frazzled hair framed his head like some kind of degenerate page boy and I could smell him from twenty feet. He took the papers out of his mouth.

'Ave to get s'more of those pills, Mick said. Knackered.

He looked at the papers he held in his hand. Then he looked at his other hand. A smoldering butt in his thin, blue fingers.

Fuckin' 'ell! Mick said. Did it again, didn't I?

He tossed the butt to the floor at my feet. There was just a half inch of white paper left, and since Mick always smoked Camel filters, that meant he must have smoked it the wrong way, lighting the fiber filter first and smoking through it, something he was prone to do when he was deep in concentration.

Someone started pounding on the door, and I could hear the combined voices of Sue and Cindy calling for me.

Look, I said, you have any money? I need to borrow some quick. Hanif is apparently in jail and Alan is tearing the place apart trying to raise some money to bail him out.

Mick hacked up something—*kaff! kaff!*—his body lurching like a puking cat, and spat wretchedly into a piece of paper that he then wadded up and tossed into the corner. He nodded slowly, and went over to the far corner of the lab, where there was a tall row of file cabinets that we had filled with random ostraca, papyri cases, journal articles, old newspapers, any amount of archeological flotsam. Mick shuffled around a pile of stacked pottery fragments and pulled out a small curved ox horn inlaid with some sort of hieratic script. He pulled out a wad of bills and walked over to me, counting off notes. Then he handed me the whole wad, a bunch of fifty-pound notes.

That's a thousand, he said.

I know Mick was actually still drawing student loans, working through an extended-study thing he had set up with Oxford. I'm not sure why he was doing this, as we made, at least theoretically, enough to live on, and Mick hadn't darkened an actual classroom in over five years. But more remarkable than the fact that Mick was squirreling away mysterious wads of cash in our lab was that this was the first time I had come to Mick with a request, and he promptly and without issue came to my aid. I was speechless.

By the way, mate, Mick said, *I'd be fucked* before I'd *sleep* in *this place*.

I hadn't considered the possibility that Mick might have returned to the museum rather than going back to the flat; for all I knew he could have been lurking in a dark corner in the lab when I brought Erin in, watching with his rodent eyes and fingering his votives, anticipating the opportunity for my exposure and humiliation.

Mick flicked his needlelike fingers around the room.

This whole fucking place is full of bodies, he said. Hundreds a' bodies and things taken from their tombs. Eh?

I'm aware of that, Mick.

And all these hymns and spells, ya? Designed to keep this very sort of thing from happening, couple a yobs like us, mucking around with their kit?

I know all this, Mick. What's your point?

He shrugged and lit another cigarette, stalking back to the Stela, so I figured I'd better get out while I was able. Sue and Cindy were still banging on the door to the lab, urging me to hurry up to the lobby, where I could hear the sounds of shouts and whistles and Alan's bellowing voice ringing dimly through the ceiling. All I really wanted to do was slip out our private entrance and get back to the flat and take a shower.

Then Alan was shuttling me out the front door of the museum, jamming my hat back on my head, and we were tripping down the steps, through the wrought-iron gates and onto the sidewalk, scattering flocks of pigeons gathered around the chestnut vendors stoking their coal fires at the front gates.

How much did you get? Alan held me up with a handful of my jacket, while his other hand began to paw around in the vicinity of my pockets.

I handed him the wad of money and leaned against a lamppost.

That weasel Wheelhouse, Alan said incredulously, actually coughed up some funds? I wouldn't have believed it. The guy has been known to surprise me, I'll tell you. I think you underestimate the man, Rothschild. He has a certain charm about him, you have to admit!

We pushed through the tourists on Great Russell Street, heading toward Tottenham Court, Alan laughing in the crisp morning air. The sky was clouding over again; it looked like rain. I had large purple spots hovering about a foot in front of my eyes, a small constellation of planets orbiting a hazy sun.

I'll tell you another thing, Rothschild, Alan muttered, if I ever get my hands on that lousy mick who kept clouting me on the back—what kind of incompetent cockneys do they have working at that blasted museum? You call that acceptable security measures?

Instead of going directly to Waterloo to bail out Hanif, Alan led me to a pub in Soho, a little place called the Spanish Bar, just off Oxford Street. He was still moving with such force and at such a pace that I assumed this was an important part of the process. It was only maybe ten in the morning but when Alan rapped on the door a tired, middle-aged woman opened it for us immediately, as if she'd been hiding there waiting for us. Alan led me to the bar in the cramped room, painted a deep scarlet with flashes of bronze and gold and crowded with a variety of Irish memorabilia. A faded Victorian molded mural was still visible on the ceiling, neoclassical scenes of cherubim and seraphim shot through with filaments of red. The woman stepped behind the bar and poured two pints of Guinness and set them before us, then walked back into the kitchen. Alan put the glass to his lips and drained half of it in two large gulps. The woman had put graceful Irish harps in the foam of the beer when she poured it, something you don't see too often. I really didn't feel like drinking so I just looked at Alan as he scrubbed his head with the flat of his hand.

What? I said. What are we doing here? What about Hanif?

Alan sighed and suddenly looked tired. Perhaps he was finally coming down from whatever it was he'd consumed last night.

He'll wait, Alan said.

I shrugged and took a sip of my pint. It tasted like cigarette butts and bile.

Listen, Alan said, still staring straight ahead, I'm sorry to get you involved in all this. But you must believe me when I say it is of the utmost importance.

I shrugged again. I didn't know what to believe.

Alan Henry frowned deeply.

I'm sorry, Alan mumbled, about that last tussle. Wasn't . . . part of the original plan.

What plan?

Hanif put a thumb in Gigantica's eye, Alan said. A complete accident of course. He was just getting into the spirit of the thing. Apparently these wrestlers have crack legal teams, because Hanif was thrown in the clink and civil charges were served in the English, American, and international courts before he could point his prayer rug to Mecca. If Gigantica wakes up this morning with his iris intact, Hanif will have a better shot at getting off. Besides, there was the whole riot situation, something we were *not* responsible for.

It was quite a crowd, I said.

Alan thunked his thick, sausage fingers against the side of his pint glass. On his middle finger he had a blocky signet ring inlaid with some kind of carving.

The normal status, Alan continued, of civil order was completely disrupted; the streets belonged to the hooligans. We got sucked into the dark star, the gravitational field. Like some kind of fucking black hole. What happened to you?

I managed to stay clear. On the periphery of the crowd.

Ah, Alan said, on the cusp of the event horizon. Very crafty of you, Rothschild. Let's see, the whole fracas lasted about five minutes? Assuming the center mass of that particular black hole was average size, let's say a million times the mass of our own sun, according to Schwarzchild's calculations you should be, ah, about ten years in the future now. How does it look? Maybe you could help me out, time traveler. I told Hanif I'd gather a legal team that could get him off. He told me to contact a buddy he had who lives on New Bloomsbury and has several legal degrees and ties to the courts of justice. Some sort of Hare Krishna, but in this country that doesn't carry the same sort of baggage as in the States. You know that Krishna restaurant in Soho, the vegetarian buffet for three pounds fifty? The place is a front. They run a legal office out of the back for the exclusive service of their brethren and other worthy individuals. Some seriously good curries there. Hope their barristers are as sharp.

Alan frowned again and gulped at his beer. I caught a glimpse of his signet ring. It was decorated with a rendering of a scarab beetle, a desert dung beetle, carved out of some kind of blood red stone. I had never noticed such a thing before, and I wondered why Alan would be wearing a scarab amulet, an Egyptian symbol of life and regeneration, and why it was a red stone as opposed to the traditional green. Alan had never expressed much interest in such things before.

Well, Alan said, we'll find out soon enough. As E. M. Forster said: *Our final experience, like our first, is conjectural. We move between the two darknesses.*

Then Alan Henry drained his glass and stalked out the door. I thanked the lady behind the bar, who now sat smoking on a stool, eyeing me coolly, and I hurried out. Alan was already a block away and moving with such purpose that it was clear my audience was over.

I turned and walked back to Great Russell Street to my flat to see if Zenobia had called. Mick's rattling answering machine thwarted me for a few minutes, unresponsive to my prodding. I didn't have much experience with this sort of technology; telephones and electronic communication were things that I avoided. I was hoping that Zenobia would leave a message with explicit instructions as to when and where we might meet.

No message on the machine. I lay in bed with a stack of glosses and transliterations of the Stela, going over Stewart's translation, my modifications, and my previous attempts at a comprehensive translation. I couldn't even keep the bilaterals separate from the trilaterals. Instead, through fogged, half-closed eyes, I saw Erin, the way she held a cigarette, the way her hips moved under the shendyt, the traditional pharaonic kilt, how her tiny hands cradled my jaw when I bent down to kiss the wooden lips of the mask of Thoth. When I drifted to sleep I dreamed of large-masted sailing ships, moving swiftly over foamy seas, with birds, large-winged birds in flocks following in their wake, all moving away and out over the ocean, moving over the horizon.

The next morning I went over some glosses, trying to get myself back on track with the Stela. I wanted to do a bit more background on Mut, go over that material again. I dug out Herman te Velde's work on Mut and looked for possibilities to work with, going over the German and Dutch versions as well as the English translations, looking for subtle nuances. Velde is really the expert on Mut, and the *only* one. Despite Mut's having been a rather popular goddess for a decent period of time, not much scholarship was done on her when compared to similar goddesses like Isis. Isis has all the good parts in the mythologies, the spells and magic—a much more glamorous choice.

It wasn't just a matter of working with this single entity, this particular goddess. Most Egyptian gods are interrelated, in that very often the same god or a god with the same characteristics and symbolic elements would go through several name changes as popularity, regional strength, and general fortunes and attitudes evolved throughout the Egyptian kingdom. Mut herself was just an extension of Sekhmet and Hathor, all being "divine mother" gods who also have the capacity for massive fits of rage and destruction. Mut was the principal Theban embodiment of divine fury, ravaging the land and its people when the gods were angry. Hathor, the daughter of Ra, was sent to destroy mankind in revenge for their disrespect. Bovine and leonine imagery is often used to express this duality—the cow representing the placid, soothing, motherly love and the lioness her fury when provoked. Sekhmet was widely worshiped and feared; one site near Thebes had over five hundred lion-headed female figures in standing and seated poses, ranged around the mortuary temple of the pharaoh Amenophis III. Apparently he was determined to placate her before he died, or it was an attempt to ward off plague and destruction. Plague years were often recorded as *The Year of Sekhmet*. Almost identical statues were also found at a Theban temple of Mut, further confusing any attempt to clearly distinguish between the goddesses.

As time went on I kept finding myself running over the phrases I'd sketched out for Erin, the way she looked at them, the way she held the damp swatches of paper, the swimming iridescence of her pupils in the black light and neon of the Lupo Bar. The way she clung to my arm in the midst of the melee with the wrestlers on Oxford Street, her pleading with me to see the Stela. *The flood is mighty*, she'd yelled to me as she stepped in the cab, from the Instruction of Amenakhat, the bit of it I'd written out on the napkin. The chilling sight of her dressed in funerary garments and the mask of Thoth, her small breasts pushing against the ancient fabric, the urgency of her hips and hands as we writhed on the museum floor, the sound of her breath panting lightly under the wooden mask that pressed against my cheek when I pushed myself inside her, the way she bucked and then went rigid, her muscles like iron, holding me inside.

A note came sliding under the lab door, presumably from Sue or Cindy. That is generally how they communicated with us since we never answered the door. Mick ignored it and kept whittling away on some of his styluses for a personal project he was working on. I wandered over and picked up the note. It had my name on it. It said Klein wanted to see me straightaway at the Truckles of Pied Bull Yard.

Truckles was a small, elegant wine bar in Bury Place off Great Russell Street with an excellent selection of handmade ales and choice wines that Klein liked. It was also home to the London Mensa society, of which Klein was an active member. Klein was proud of his membership, and he liked to have his personal conferences with us at Truckles to remind us of it. Nobody ever doubted Klein's intellectual prowess, least of all me. He was the first to solve the Stela of Senitef back in 1976, just one piece among his multitude of successful translations, and Klein supervised and cataloged all the digs in the Valley of the Queens in 1984. These days, as Keeper of Egyptian Antiquities for the British Museum, he wasn't much more than a bureaucrat, but he was a former working Egyptologist, one of the best in the world.

Klein had total control of the new acquisitions and display budgets, and this included dating and establishing context, as well as translation and interpretation. To the other curators and staff we had a sort of shadowy existence, two rumpled individuals who crept up and down from the basement at odd hours, with no real apparent work being done. They mostly regarded us with a wary nod and little eye contact.

Certainly Feynman and Witten, the head curators of the Egyptian collection, were aware of the Stela of Paser project, but none of the other dozen or so curators and the multitude of archeologists and staff at the museum knew anything about what we were doing. I'd met a few people here and there, and many of them were also aware of my previous work in Cairo and my Princeton publications, but other than that Klein kept them in the dark. I think it had something to do with the predisposition of many Egyptologists to dismiss the Stela as some kind of gimmick, and then there was the "three ways/ three times" issue. Because of the worn edges of the piece, the bifurcating crevice, and some missing sections, a certain amount of conjecture is needed—my specialty. Klein felt that if we could come up with a decent approximation of the missing sections, which I've done, then we could have a solid go at the "third way" and maybe open up the world of translation and cryptography, not to mention the psychology and philosophy of the ancient Near East, in a whole new way.

I found Klein at his usual table at Truckles, in a corner down in the brick-walled cellar bar with arched ceilings that recalled its former use as a wine-cask storage room. He was wearing a crisp linen suit of a sort of almond color, clean though very worn, an obvious holdover from his days in North Africa in the sixties. A few other Mensa types, older white guys who looked a lot like me, were sitting around the tiny tables drinking ale and wine out of metal flagons. Klein chain-smoked Lucky Strikes with an intensity that I've always admired. He motioned me over and I took a seat on one of those uncomfortable little wooden stools they have in places like that. He started to pour me a glass of wine from a steel decanter, and when I waved him off he shook his head and kept pouring.

We have a situation, Dr. Rothschild. A real problem.

Klein left Berlin in 1956, but somehow he retained German hitches to his English. I think it was because he knew six languages fluently and didn't have enough time or mental energy to devote to clearing up his accent in English. In this business, English was less important than French, Dutch, Arabic, and, with the emergence of the new Berlin Museum as an antiquities world power, German.

He stared at me as if he expected me to say something. I just looked at him and shrugged. Then it hit me: Alan Henry.

I'm awfully sorry about the behavior of that man in the lobby yesterday. I don't really know him. He's a sort of neighbor of mine . . . and I'm sorry about Rasheed's glasses—I already told him I'd get him a new pair . . .

Klein waved his hand and sighed, then lit another cigarette.

Not that. Another thing. You had a friend? Over to the museum? For a little midnight visit, no?

His eyes, blue and baleful, were creased with intricate crow's-feet from staring into the harsh North African sun for so many years. I picked up the full wineglass Klein had poured for me and tried to gulp it down. The first mouthful was awful and I struggled with it, putting the wineglass back on the table immediately. Rivulets of wine poured down my chin.

Do you want to know how I know this?

I finally swallowed and a fiery ball of red wine burned through my esophagus and into my stomach.

Security guard? I choked.

Klein shook his head.

Not until after the fact, that one. Yes, he tell us everything, but that is not how we know about your friend.

Klein sat back again and looked up at the ceiling, smoking.

We give you complete access, yes? Day or night. You come and go as you please, and nobody bothers you. You bring someone in . . .

He shrugged and frowned.

. . . who's to know or say anything. That is no real concern. However . . .

Klein sat forward and stubbed out his cigarette and put both hands flat on the table and looked directly at me.

... when your friend removes something ... takes it from the museum grounds ... something that is priceless, then we have a problem.

My head went light and airy. Klein sat in a sea of sparkling light. I went through the set of events in my mind. Could she have copped something when I was putting the artifacts back in the display?

Oh god. What was it?

From the funerary room. Parchment number 370.

Parchment 370?

What the hell was that? I quickly ran through my mental catalog of the rare papyruses.

Parchment 370, Klein said, is something we are calling the Song of Amun. From Karnak.

Amun at Karnak!

Karnak was the Stela of Paser site. Anything from this site was always immediately turned over to me to see if it had any possible connection, any clues for the Stela of Paser project. Why hadn't I heard of this before?

What sort of parchment was it? I babbled, why wasn't I told anything about this?

Klein rubbed his cheeks with both hands and sighed heavily.

We acquired it from a private collector a few weeks ago. When we sent Feynman over to Cairo? I ... I was looking it over myself for a bit as, well, you see you have only six more days on your contract and—

You're bailing on me already?

Bailing?

You have to let me see it. Surely you have copies.

Not complete. It ... it is an oversight.

I don't believe this.

But the point here is, Klein said, lighting another cigarette and jabbing it at my face, what we have to talk about now, is that it has been stolen. And your friend took it. Feynman was alerted to its absence yesterday, but assumed it was taken back into storage for cleaning. It was in the funerary-room closet. It was locked, the computer records indicate the locking timer was set correctly. But your friend drilled the lock. Destroyed it. Because you had them turned off, there was no alarm. And as you know, there is no closed-circuit television in the museum. So we have very little to work with.

Oh my god. I don't see how—

This young woman, Klein said, pretty thing I hear.

Klein smiled weakly. I wiped my damp forehead on my sleeve. I could feel the humiliation surging to my face.

Dr. Rothschild, Klein said, I must ask you: What exactly did you think a young woman like this was doing here, with you? Surely you don't believe that she had some kind of . . . romantic interest? I'm just curious, you know. I mean, it seems a bit obvious, doesn't it?

I am not a naive man, never have been. But it seemed, at the time, that Erin was something brought to my circle by the hands of fate. The kind of thing you didn't know you were looking for until you found it. I felt humiliated.

Just in case, Klein went on, there is a mistake, this morning we checked the registers and there is no record of the piece being removed. I immediately had Feynman and Witten, along with those two interns of yours, search the middle stocks, the cleaning rooms, the basement storage. This combined with the drilled lock leaves us with the only possibility: It is stolen.

Drilled the lock? Where the hell could she have possibly hidden a drill? How could I have not been aware of a power tool? How did she get those pieces she was wearing out of the cases to begin with? Weren't they all locked as well? Why hadn't I thought of all this before?

I thought of what Alan had said to me yesterday as we went to bail out Hanif, his cryptic apology. I would have to talk to him about this, about Hanif, something I didn't look forward to. I guess it was always clear that I feared Alan Henry. Not in the plain physical sense, though that was there too of course. I somehow feared his vitality, his life force, the brutish spirit of will that propelled him through the world, stumbling and clubbing his way to perfect self-completion, without doubts, without regrets. He was, I suppose, in that aspect a perfect writer.

I told Klein I would have it back. Soon. He nodded, sending bilious clouds of smoke toward the rafters.

It will be our secret, Klein said, this would not . . . be the sort of thing we want leaked.

Who knows right now? I asked.

The full story? Only you and me. The others know only that it is missing, perhaps stolen. Of course, most of the security team knows about your visitor as I doubt Simon was able to keep it to himself, *ya?*

What about the Song of Amun? I asked. What period? Literary hieratic?

Twentieth Dynasty. 1160 B.C. Full-form hieroglyphs.

This made it concurrent with the Stela of Paser. It could be a companion piece even.

Funerary text? Instructions? Invocations?

Not yet clear, Klein said, but it may be some sort of key. Dr. Wheelhouse was taking a look at it—

Mick! I shouted, he couldn't . . . the Stela is *my* project! You brought me here—

We will give you three days! Klein barked, then it is out of our hands. Your contract, obviously, will be terminated at that time. You will have your own legal and professional matters to worry about. Besides, Dr. Wheelhouse assured me that he would share his work on the Song of Amun with you as soon as he made progress. Speak with him.

I knew that if I couldn't recover the Amun papyrus I would be legally indebted to the museum for an incredible amount of money. Items in the British Museum are considered the Queen's personal collections, and the penalty for stealing from the Queen wasn't anything you would walk away from lightly. Especially being an American. It would effectively end my career as well; no museum or archive would trust me with their collections ever again.

I stood at the corner of Great Russell and Museum Street for a few moments, looking into the windows of the antiquary shops that lined the road, hawking so-called "authentic" ancient Egyptian, Roman, and Greek antiquities. Mostly coins and small pottery pieces, there was nothing of real value, most of it was no more than a few hundred years old. The possibilities were vague. Not much was known about Amun in relation to that period, except that his name was almost universally stricken from any representation during the reign of Akhenaten in the Eighteenth Dynasty, as part of some religious reforms, in favor of the sun-disk god Aten. The pharaoh, originally named Amenhotep, attempted to purge the sun god Amun, "the hidden one," and replace it with hymns and temples dedicated to Aten, the physical presence of the sun or "the solar sphere." He changed his name from Amenhotep, "Amun is content," to Akhenaten, "of service to the Aten," and moved the place of primary worship to Karnak, where he built a massive new temple in the desert plain. This revolution included the sometimes violent desecration and destruction of all references to Amun, a particularly serious deed to the ancient Egyptians who believed the inscribed words carried the soul of the things and persons depicted.

If you drew on a piece of papyrus a knife transfixing or cutting a person or an animal, as was occasionally done to the demon serpent Apopis, then it occurred to that entity in the afterlife for all eternity. You could also write the name in the "unlucky" color of red, and even put a spear through the determinative sign to disrupt the efficacy of the inscription. Revenge was simple in ancient Egypt; if you outlived your enemy, you could break into their tomb and destroy their destiny. A good example of this is from the Sixth Dynasty tomb of

Niankhpepy at Saqqara. In one scene the relief is destroyed around the head of the tomb owner and a crude text is incised nearby, an obvious later graffito: *You enchained me! You beat my father! Now I shall be satisfied, for what can you do to escape my hand? My father shall be satisfied!*

In this way the name of Amun was chiseled off stelae, hacked off temple walls, even destroyed at the tips of obelisks under the direction of Akhenaten. The style of depiction during this period shifts radically, in which the rays of Aten the solar sphere are shown bathing the pharaoh and his family in their warming light. More interesting was the change to the figures of the royal family, in which the king Akhenaten becomes a grotesque figure with exaggerated facial features, slight torsos, feminine hips, and lacking any sort of genitalia.

The androgynous nature of the king and its artistic purpose is a much debated and popular subject among Egyptologists as well as amateur scholars of ancient esoteric ephemera and mythology. Many Egyptologists feel it was an aesthetic decision, an attempt to perhaps show a mixture of male and female features, showing Akhenaten as both father and mother of Egypt. However, the body of a male member of the same family was recovered at Thebes with very intriguing skeletal features, including abnormally wide hips and a slender, femalelike torso. The images of the mummified body are incredibly disturbing to look at, and I am told that to view the body in person is even more bizarre.

So it was a tempestuous time, a strange time to write a song or prayer to a banished god. It was not an uncommon thing for the reigning monarch to reorder the hierarchy of the gods and to banish some altogether in favor of their own personal deity. The cult of Aten is rumored to have existed far into the Late Egyptian Period, long after Ramses reversed the changes of Akhenaten, perhaps well into the Ptolemaic. Mick said once that Aten cults stuck around long after the demise of the Coptic language, reaching western Europe only to vanish in the Dark Ages, when it was subsumed by that much later monotheistic religion, Christianity. But why would Erin want it? The Song of Amun was an extremely valuable item, but clearly she could have taken anything she wanted that night, and even the garments she wore had more value on the black market than an obscure hymn to Amun.

I looked at my reflection in the shop window, a shadow looming over the coins in their red velvet cases, each slipped into a notch like winking eyes. A weak chin with the hair to match, a light patch of brownish fur surrounding my bulbous cranium; small gray eyes behind steel-framed glasses sitting crookedly on my fat nose. A middle-aged man in a tattered corduroy jacket, wrinkled slacks, and scuffed loafers. My skin looked especially poor, spotted with a slight wisp of stubble on my neck. I thought of Erin. A woman in a green rain slicker carrying shopping bags brushed against my back, causing me to rock forward, butting my head lightly against the window. I held it there for a few moments and gazed at the coins in their neat cases. Worthless.

The sun was still shining a bit, now and then casting pale shadows on the sidewalks, and as the clouds drifted across the city, causing breaks in the haze and sending occasional pure shafts of light onto the cement and asphalt, the crowds on the sidewalks would pause, each pale face tipped toward the sun. Then as the clouds moved, returning them to the soft shade of midday they tucked their chins again and moved on. It was like a waltz, a broadly orchestrated scene of hundreds covering the streets of Bloomsbury, a pause, gazing upward as the light fell on them like the beneficence of Ra, then moving on again as darkness fell. It is a wonder that the ancient Celts and peoples of Britain didn't have a more central sun-god figure. Not in the same sense as those religions in the Middle East and Africa of course, where the sun is omnipresent and permeates every aspect of life, but perhaps a sly, trickster sort of god, one who tantalizes and teases with fleeting glimpses of the life-giving warmth that we all seek.

The flood is mighty, Erin had called out to me as she fluidly inserted herself into that black cab, remarkably adept for a woman who had been up all night taking amphetamines like breath mints, knocking down at least a fifth of vodka, shagging an oldster like myself on the cold midnight marble of the museum floor while dressed as a prominent figure in ancient mythology. Not to mention in the midst of this managing to drill the lock of a storage closet and make off with a priceless artifact. I had drawn a dozen different hieroglyphs on cocktail napkins throughout the night and translated lots of things for Erin in the museum. Why would she choose to remember that, and why would she call it out to me as she jumped in that cab? Did it have something to do with the Song of Amun papyrus? The sky paused again, the sun emerging, and I took out my ear votive, moist and warm from my pocket hand-holding, and held it in the light, up to my lips, but I had nothing to say. Instead I stood there like the rest of London and turned my mute face to the opening sky.

3: ZENOBIA

ALAN HENRY WASN'T HOME. We were probably the only two guys in London who didn't own a mobile phone, and considering his erratic schedule, meeting up with him would be difficult. I went to the front desk of our building and tried to convince the building-management guy, Eddie, to let me into his room.

Eddie wasn't cooperating. Eddie, like every building-management guy in London, was a swarthy balding fellow who wore white oxford shirts with black vests and sweated profusely. He zipped and un-zipped the huge nest of keys hanging from his belt as he spoke in his heavily clipped cockney.

What? You fink I just let any fockin' bloke inna another man's flat? You know wha' I mean?

Eddie, you know I'm his friend. You see me here all the time.

No fockin' chance, mate, yeah. If you'll excuse me I've got me cuppa coolin' 'ere.

He walked back into the little side room behind the desk where he had his telly and electric kettle. I assume there was a football game on. In England, there is always a football game on.

This is very important, I said. Alan would give me permission.

Bollocks, mate. No chance.

I figured I had to do something drastic. I headed back to my flat.

A few minutes later, when I figured Eddie would be having his tea, feet up on the desk watching the game in the back room, I was at Alan's door with a few of Mick's largest chisels and his hammer stuck in my coat. Mick used these for large inscriptions, stonework mostly, though I hadn't seen him do much of it in a while. There wasn't exactly a large market for customized hieroglyphics. But Mick was always willing to pick up a few quid wherever he could. For a moment I considered the ramifications of what I was about to do, but in this matter they weren't very clear.

The hallway was empty. There were only three other flats on this level and I'd never seen anyone come in or out of them. I put the largest chisel in the slight chink between the doorknob and the door and gave it a quick whack with the hammer. The doorknob popped off cleanly and dropped to the floor. Good old eighteenth-century English construction. I stuck the chisel in the hole and rattled it around a bit. The metal chunk of the mechanism fell into Alan's flat with a clunk. I pushed the door open.

I'd never actually been in Alan's room; he always made us wait in the hall while he rummaged around in there, cursing and banging things about. Alan's flat was smaller than mine and Mick's, by a long way. It consisted of one closetlike room, with a sink and mirror in the corner. The place was spare and incredibly immaculate. He had a folding cot against one wall next to the window, and an old card table and chair set up facing the door. That was the only furniture in the room.

Alan Henry didn't have a kitchen or a bathroom. That was another reason he was always barging into our flat. Mostly he would ask, in that special way that Alan asks (*Wheelhouse! I need a gallery to display my special gift for intestinal sculpture!),* but sometimes he would be in such a rush that he would burst in the door, already unbuckling his pants, belt loops snapping, red-faced and swearing, squeezing into our loo with great agility considering *I* barely fit in it, his clown boots sticking out the door and into the hallway. Then came the Alan Henry serenade, as he would shout and pound his way through his abhorrent movements, thumping the walls with his fists, once ripping our towel rack off the wall and dislodging quite a few bathroom tiles with his stomping feet, emerging after a good half hour, disheveled and exhausted, collapsing on our couch to doze as his fetid aroma quickly forced Mick and me out in the hallway.

There was Alan Henry's laptop computer on the card table, a few books, and a tall stack of paper. On a corner of the desk sat Alan's flask: HMS *Valiant.* The books were apparently physics texts: *Super-Strings: A Theory of Everything?, The Fabric of Reality, The Quark and the Jaguar, Foucault's Pendulum, The God Particle.* I resisted the urge to read some of Alan's Canadian moon-shot book. For a few seconds anyway.

If Greene's explanation of T.O.E. is correct, then the Super-String model would prove, as all strings are identical, that all matter is, in the end, composed of the same substance. This idea was presupposed by Edgar Allan Poe in the nineteenth century in his brilliant philosophical tract "Eureka," in which he developed his own Theory of Everything, forecasting not only string theory but Quantum Mechanics and nuclear fission. Current string theory asserts that the basest form of all matter is made up of singular, vibrating strings, their oscillations directly proportional to their energy and molecular weight. Average size for these strings, or Planck Length, is almost too small to contemplate; if a basic atom were the size of the entire known universe, then one of these strings would be about the size of a man. It is these vibrating strings that make up our known world.

The early pre-Copernican believers in the so-called music of the spheres, those crusty medieval scholars who believed in the cosmic grinding of the planets, the eternal song of praise for God's creation, were right all along, they were just thinking on the wrong type of scale. The music of the spheres is not the chiming of planets in their orchestrated revolutions around the earth; it is a cosmic symphony on the subatomic level, the smallest orchestra ever conceived, that sings our praise, that makes up everything that we are.

The chief scientist for the Canadian space mission, Dr. Jason Corner, holder of a Ph.D. in physics from Manitoba Tech and an M.A. in nineteenth-century American literature from James Madison University, was a devout disciple of Poe. It was his theories of magnetic-fission propulsion methods and vehicle trajectories based on the inherent dynamics of curved space that produced the successful manned mission, paving the way for Canadian theoretical physics and space travel

I had to stop at the end of the first page for fear of disturbing the arrangement of the stack, the pages of which seemed fitted at perfect angles like pyramid stones. The walls of Alan's flat were bare, white, and one small window opposite the door looked across the compact courtyard our buildings shared and into the wall of the building across the way. It must have been even cheaper to rent than our flat, but then again Alan didn't seem to have a job and I have no idea where he got the little money he had. I stood there in his cramped room, the compass of one man's life, and felt awkward and ashamed.

This wouldn't work. I was wasting time; I had to find Erin.

I closed the door and tried to replace the broken doorknob.

When I slipped out Eddie was eating a greasy newspaper full of chips and grunting at the telly.

Atta boy! Push, lads!

For a brief moment I thought I could enlist Mick to help me. He probably already knew about the theft since he had been working with the Amun papyrus. Maybe he could tell me more about the cult of Aten, if there were any remainders from that ancient religion running around Europe.

I froze once again on the sidewalk. *Everyone* would know! Even if Klein himself hadn't told anyone, they would know I had something to do with it. Feynman and Witten, the other curators, Sue and Cindy, they would all know. I stood on the corner of Great Russell and Museum Street, perched on the edge of the curb, out of the swell of foot traffic. Across the street men in suits streamed in and out of the Plough Pub, stepping out with a stretch and a wink of their bleary eyes. Sometimes it seemed I had spent my life working to protect myself from situations of discomfort and embarrassment. I was normally quite good at it.

Unlike Alan's place my flat was in its usual state of extreme disorder, my dirty clothes lying over the backs of the kitchen chairs and Mick's wood shavings littering the carpet. Mick must have been at the lab.

I took a shower and shaved and got out a fresh set of clothes. We had one of those bathrooms that have a shower nozzle sticking out of the wall and a drain on the floor; you just closed the door and everything got wet. The plumbing was entirely unpredictable, as most of the pipes were nineteenth-century patch jobs on the original, and much older, equipment. When you flipped the hot-water switch the heater would start a steady banging, thumping against the shower wall as if someone or something was trying to break through.

The thermostat in the flat was shot so we kept the heat cranked up and the window open. After all, the museum was paying for it. Mick wanted the windows closed, but I didn't like to simmer in the fetid, close air of two grown men living in a tiny space. Even with the minimal air that wafted through the window, which of course reeked of garbage, smoke, sweat, all the smells of London, our flat was like a concentrated box of halitosis, dead feet, intestinal gases, noxious cooking, and of course Mick's insecticides. We were on the sixth floor, the attic floor, and the back of the building was under some sort of curious construction. There was an extensive set of scaffolding all the way to our window and beyond, and various men were always climbing about out there and shouting to each other in comical accents. None of them ever wore a helmet and they had seemingly dangerous building practices. The most common shouted phrase I heard was either *Watch out!* or *Catch this!*, often followed by a loud impact of steel or wood on concrete and a vicious string of cockney curses that defied translation.

As I put on my fresh set of clothes in the bedroom a lean black man with long dreadlocks squatted on the scaffolding outside the window and puffed on what looked like a marijuana cigarette. He had on a yellow rain slicker and jeans with a few tools stuck into his back pockets. The sweet, acrid smoke wafted through the open window.

He grinned at me as I struggled with my thick woolen socks.

Good day to ya, sir!

I waved to him and put on my shirt and jacket and went back out to the living-room area. Next to our coin-operated phone the answering machine was blinking. I never used the phone myself, partly because the thing would suck down a pound in a matter of seconds and then you were frantically pumping pence into the slot and watching your credit countdown instead of talking to anyone. At least that's what happened to me. I pushed the button on the answering machine and heard Mick's thin, cracking voice with the clipped Oxford accent that he was able to assume when he wanted to:

You have reached the domicile of Dr. Mick Wheelhouse, special attaché to the British Museum's Egyptian Antiquities Collection. If this call concerns private translation and cryptography services, or my new book The Ashmolean Museum's ABCs of Hieroglyphics, *please call my answering service at 0171-253-8764. Otherwise, leave a message and I will try to get back to you as soon as I am able.*

The bastard hadn't even put my name on it.

Hello? This message is for Dr. Rothschild. This is his daughter, Zenobia. I wanted to tell him that I will be arriving in London tomorrow, Sunday, November second. I'll be staying at Clairbourne's, in Mayfair. If you could tell Dr. Rothschild that he could reach me there tomorrow afternoon, at 171-629-8860, I would appreciate it. Thank you.

The electronic distillation of vibrations transmuted onto fine paper cones, the sound waves translated into artificial replicas of the human voice. I can't see how everyone does not see this as a terrifying process. To me it is the most distant and unnatural form of communication there is, like a voice coming out of the false ether, a phony sunrise, the movements of toy planets.

The last time I spoke with Zenobia she seemed rougher and sarcastic, so unlike the sincere and professional voice on the machine now. I'm not sure what I was expecting. Perhaps unfettered rage. I deserved as such. I suppose I was experiencing what people call the conflicting aspects of destiny, when it seems the choices one is faced with have no reconciliation, there is no chance of defending oneself, as when Anubis weighs the heart against the tomes of your life.

But it often seems like these decisions present their possibilities in two very distinct ways; there are usually two paths to take, but no middle way. This is similar to what the ancient Egyptians called "living between the Two Lands." The metaphor was all around them; and like most things in Egyptian culture, it all begins with the Nile.

The land of ancient Egypt, as with most ancient cultures, was described in terms of its fertility, flooding, and available freshwater. The fertile floodplains of the Nile and the delta that begins at Giza and Cairo, where the Nile fans out into the Mediterranean, was called Kemet, meaning "the black land." The harsh landscape of the Sahara which surrounds the Nile valley was called Deshret, or "the red land."

The ancient kingdoms of Egypt were also divided in other ways, most notably by their respective elevations. The southern areas of Egypt, where the Nile runs out of the Sudanese highlands, gathering the runoff from the springs and streams in the vast mountain ranges of central Africa, was called the Upper Kingdom. From Memphis to the delta that spreads to Alexandria to the west and Tell el-Farama to the east, the Lower Kingdom. The kingdoms of Egypt were thought of in terms of these two distinct areas, the narrow valleys and hilly terrain of the Upper Kingdom and the fertile crescent of the Lower Kingdom.

In this way ancient Egypt often referred to itself as the "Two Lands," a reference to the difficult task of unifying upper and lower Egypt, something that was repeatedly attempted throughout the history of Egypt. And the idea of the separated kingdoms, or the division of the world in fact, never left the consciousness of the ancient Egyptians. It permeated their thoughts and ideas and philosophies. They always searched for a way to unite the two worlds, to live in the "Third Land," the third way.

I stepped out onto Great Russell Street, clamping my hat down with my hand against the fierce wind that rattled down the narrow street, pushing newspapers and trash down the sidewalks and gutters. I didn't like the idea of Mick's keeping such close company with the Stela while I was occupied, but what could I do? As I began to walk north, up Gower Street toward Euston and the British Library, a light rain began to fall from the darkening sky.

My daughter Zenobia had a theory of why I left them, my family. She told me about it three years ago. This was in 1994, when we had lunch together in New York. I was doing a series of lectures at NYU and I had a free weekend. She was twenty-one and working as an editor for some sort of magazine that seemed to be mostly occupied with the avant-garde art scene. The last few times we've gotten together it's ended badly. Ever since that last visit to Egypt, when Helen held her as she wept on the edge of the bed in that small dirty room in the western quarter of Alexandria, ever since then it seemed as if the spirit of Zenobia bore down upon me, a puzzling sensation that shifted from bemused tolerance to possible reconciliation to straight vengeance. The Old Kingdom scribe Sahure wrote in 2373 B.C.: *My daughter, born under a heart-shaped moon, and the sun a bloody sickle*, a reference to the seemingly contrasting motivations of one's children. There was always about Zenobia the tense, coiled energy of a bloodhound following the trail to the last squirrel burrow, or perhaps in my case, a swatch of greasy fish wrapped in newspaper. She was always looming up like the shadow of a massive obelisk in my dreams and waking life.

We'd exchanged a few letters after she left San Francisco, maybe two a year, just to keep in touch. I could never explain to her how she was a part of all my waking moments, how the ideogram for children, the simple rendering of a seated figure raising food to her lips, how this was always her, how in all the ideograms of ancient Egypt, in every image I would always see her. But that doesn't mean much to a girl when she is eight years old and her father spends all of his time in another hemisphere digging around in the dust.

It's a classic male problem, Zenobia said.

We were sitting at a tiny little table in a cafe in the East Village. I was struggling with an elaborate falafel. Zenobia just drank large cups of black coffee and smoked.

It's the flight syndrome, she continued. We've always been told that the male creature is so much stronger than the female. That it is men who seek out conflict and struggle. Yet women are so much stronger. When it comes to clashes of emotion, to conflicts of the heart, men run like dogs. It's true. Just look around, at some men. Look at their eyes. A woman's eyes are naturally open and frank, emotive and fragile. Men live their lives a few inches behind their eyes, hiding behind them, keeping themselves out of any real danger. They look at the world as if through a mask.

Okay, I said. What was I afraid of then? You seem to have this figured out so clearly, then maybe you could tell me what exactly it was that scared me away?

Zenobia stubbed out her cigarette.

Simple. Me. You could barely handle one woman in your life, Mom, and the idea that another one was quickly growing scared the fuck out of you.

That's a nice way to talk, I said. You learn how to talk like that here in New York?

Jesus, Dad.

It's interesting that you seem to know so much about men and women and relationships. Have you been married?

Forget it.

No. I'm interested. How did you learn so much?

Zenobia blazed in her chair. Her eyes searched my face. This was when I became afraid. We argued for another half hour before Zenobia had enough.

Remember, she said, how you told me about the execration lists, *Dad?* The lists of enemies the Egyptians put together so they could curse them in rituals? Remember the ones you drew for me that day, six years ago?

Zenobia flopped her long leg up on the table, knocking over my water glass and bunching up the tablecloth in the middle, the black sole of her thick sandals resting on my plate. The thin iron legs of the table creaked and swayed under the weight of her leg. On the sole of her shoe she had a crude incised rendering of a cartouche, or hieroglyphic name, with the determinative of a man.

It was *my* name, spelled phonetically. It was an execration cartouche. I remembered, years ago, telling her about how ancient Egyptians would inscribe figures of their enemies on the bottoms of their shoes, so that they could trample them with every step. She had drawn it, carefully, with a permanent marker on a scrap of plastic fastened to the bottom of her shoe.

I first did this when I was fifteen, she said. Now it's a habit. Perhaps a superstition. What do you think it does to a little girl, *Dad*, Zenobia said, to have your father walk out on you? For no other reason than digging around somewhere in the Middle East, hanging around in old museums? Hey? Or was it something else?

She lit another cigarette and her hands were shaking. The heel of her sandal was resting on the mashed remains of my falafel.

Fuck you, my daughter said. Fuck you.

Listen, I said, it wasn't—

No, fuck you. You don't say anything. You just take it. No running away. Not right now. You need to just take it.

4: THE CANADANAUT

I KNEW A FEW of Alan Henry's hangouts: the bookshops on Charing Cross Road, the British Library Rare Book Room, Johnson's Court, and of course the bars of Soho. There were too many little second-hand bookshops on Charing Cross to check them all, each with tiny back stairways that led to basement rooms and niches, usually containing the most esoteric or occult material in the shop, which is where Alan would most likely hang out. I didn't feel like poking around in that little corner of insanity, and I'd had enough of bars for a while, so that left the library. I headed up Southampton Row, north, toward St. Pancras.

I knew that Alan preferred to do his reading in the Rare Book Room at the British Library, where he would pore over old editions of medieval scholasticism and science texts. He had a particular interest in the electromagnetic spectrum, the physics of light and the early phases of space travel. Alan told me that this was part of his research on the top-secret Canadian moon-shot mission, done well before the American attempts. He was always raving about some satellite or some other aspect of lunar technology or physics, quarks, gluons, something called the "Lorentz Contraction."

No one else in the world seemed to corroborate Alan's belief that this thing really happened, that the Canadians put a man on the moon before anyone else. Alan said the reason it was hushed up was because this particular astronaut—or Canadanaut, as the Canadian Aeronautical Administration supposedly called him—never made it back.

They miscalculated on the trajectory and the fuel-to-weight ratio, Alan said. The Canadanaut, a wiry little Canuck trapper named Jacques, brought along some extra weight without telling the engineers. When they had their trajectory problems, and Jacques had to resort to manual control to guide the landing craft to the lunar surface, the booster rockets used up the return-flight fuel.

At this point Alan Henry got a little misty eyed. We were sitting at the bar in a curry house on Eversholt Street, behind Euston Station. He cleared his throat and looked up at the stained ceiling.

Sometimes I think of that little bugger, Alan said, leaving the module and trekking across a landscape unlike anything anyone had ever seen, yet oddly reminiscent of his homeland in northern Canada, vast expanses of wasteland and mountain ridges. The lunar surface is much like the upper reaches of Saskatchewan, at least until the sun comes around again and the surface heats up a thousand degrees. Their spacesuit technology wasn't so sharp either. Basically a glorified set of long johns. The poor bugger might have had it as soon as he blew the hatch bolts. Or, perhaps the suit held up, the oxygen system, a crude setup based on recycling bodily sweat to create carbon dioxide, maybe it all actually worked, and Jacques set out across the lunar plain. A perfect specimen in many ways, Jacques. The guy could barely speak English, but he was selected because of his remarkable physical characteristics. Five foot two and a hundred and twenty pounds, four percent body fat, incredible cardio fitness, and his g-shock testing was off the charts. He could also withstand tremendous amounts of radiation without any detectable effect. They radiated that poor bastard with about a million regs and the X rays showed nada. Their payload method involved a massive charge of some kind of liquid thermal propulsion run through a series of high-powered, super-cooled magnets. The bullet principle of propulsion—a single explosion of weak gauge bosons made fissionable by a neutrino accelerator that was six miles in diameter—rather than the conventional method of sustained burns. The launch explosion left a glowing crater half a mile wide. I've seen it. Melted forty feet of ice down to the Cambrian shelf. That rock hadn't seen the light of day in five hundred million years. Now there's a slight bluish hue to the crater, and the Geiger counters still blow up when you get within fifty kilometers. There wasn't any radiation shielding for this kind of thing, Jacques was just sitting in that tiny tin capsule in his underwear.

The team heard about Jacques from some other locals; a few years before he had been forced off his homestead by Canadian Space Administration officials to build their moon-shot complex. The stubborn bastard wouldn't go, and the officials had to eventually bulldoze his hut and take away all his possessions. The way the story goes, Jacques was standing there in the heart of the brutal Saskatchewan winter in his skivvies, nothing left but a few of his dogs that eluded capture and cowered at his feet. No tools, clothes, or even a speck of food, nothing. Everything had been carted away, just a near-naked man standing on an empty frozen plain. They expected he would freeze or give up. As the officials watched from the heated cabs of their Sno-Cats, Jacques stared at them for a moment, then squatted in the snow and defecated grimly. He picked up his excrement and molded it into the shape of a knife. It froze in a matter of seconds and taking hold of one of the dogs at his feet Jacques cut its throat in a quick motion, pooling the steaming blood in a small bowl of ice. He butchered the dog, skinning it, stripping out the meat and organs. Using the cleaned bones and tendons he fashioned a makeshift sled, using strips of hide as ropes he hitched up his remaining two dogs, and slung the remaining skin over his shoulders. He packed up the frozen

blood and strips of meat. Then as the officials watched in pure amaze-
ment, Jacques mushed the dogs and sped off over the frozen tundra,
heading into the whiteness. When the scientists heard about this,
they knew they had found their man. You could drop him off on a gla-
cier with a handful of salt and the guy would survive for weeks. Not
exactly a scientist though, and it isn't real clear if he had any idea of
just what he was doing.

It was at moments like this, when Alan was ruminating about the
Canadian moon-shot mission, that I began to understand a bit of why
he was working on this project, this book of his. He wanted to tell the
story of this man, this French Canadian who may not have ever existed. Alan maintains that he had a phone interview with the last surviving scientist on that top-secret Canadian team, some guy who was
now living in Florida. The rest of the team was supposedly dropped
in a bottomless ice crevasse somewhere near the polar cap or something. But if it was real or not didn't change things for me. It seemed
like an awfully noble thing, and many times I listened to these stories
about the Canadian crew and began to dream these characters to life,
and to me they existed as much as anything else I'd ever been told or
read, much like the figures and stories in my work.

You know what he took with him, Alan said, you know what it
was that threw the whole weight thing off? It was his bear trap. The
poor bastard thought he might do some trapping in that wilderness up
there. A six-pound iron bear trap.

He sighed again and I swear I saw his eyes tear up. Then he
slapped the table and pushed his thick face with those square glasses
and that blunt nose right up against mine and said: You know what I
can't wait for? For that unlucky bastard who walks somewhere in the
area of forty-six degrees latitude and twenty-eight point four degrees
longitude, somewhere on the eastern rim of the Sea of Tranquility,
and steps into that bear trap. Wham! Won't that blow the stack of the
American scientific establishment? Imagine the world reacting to

such news! It would change the entire way we establish the international hierarchies of space!

I watched his working face. He was almost weeping with exasperation and wonder.

Think of it Rothschild, Alan Henry said, think of the ramifications! The combat for truth is eternal and omnipresent; surely *you* understand this. The greatest sin is to be unconscious—Jung said that. Our dreams are but a fragment of the real, the world we inhabit. We must not let them overtake us. We do not strive to realize our dreams, but to realize the *real!* You know why? Because eventually we all have to *wake up again!*

Then Alan Henry had clutched his curry bowl with his thickly knuckled hands and stared into the ranged bottles of liquor on the shelves behind the bar as if they might hold the secret to something; maybe if he looked hard enough, wanted it enough, the symbols would begin to rearrange themselves, create some sense of order. Sometimes I think that Alan and I are more alike than I would like to admit.

Alan used the same desk in the Rare Book Room all the time, number thirty-six, which was his favorite number and something he was very serious about, something to do with the Rosicrucians, Masons, and Knights Templars.

But when I found it, desk number thirty-six was occupied by a tall African gentleman who appeared to be studying a very old edition of *The Anatomy of Melancholy*. He had a cart next to him stacked with six more thick volumes with old strap buckles. The room was mostly full, so I wandered about the lines of desks, trying to look nonchalant, looking for Alan's bulky shape.

The British Museum was too crowded to hold both the museum

materials and the entire collection of the King's Library along with every other book and manuscript ever published in England and most of the world, so a few years ago they began the process of moving the books and manuscripts to a new location. This was supposed to free up a lot of space for more antiquities, but the museum storage rooms didn't seem to look a bit different, still stuffed to the rafters.

The new library was an impressive structure though; the King's Library—a collection of the rarest books, including the Magna Carta and an original Gutenberg—was sealed in a fireproof, bulletproof glass tower that was set through the middle of the building like a titan's elevator shaft. The rest of the collections were divided into a half dozen smaller reading rooms, sorted by discipline.

In the Rare Book Room you passed through lines of low, caramel-colored desks, each with a number and a green-shaded reading lamp. The room branched to the right, creating an L-shaped space, where the computer-catalog terminals squatted, glowing blue and red. The request desk was along the wall of the long side of the room, a polished wooden counter where the numerous denizens of the library staff, a mixture of blasted older types creaking about in tweeds and wool and twenty-somethings with colored hair and thrift-store clothing, scuttled about pushing wheeled carts with stacks of rare volumes arranged like gilt-edged cityscapes.

I'd spent some time in the British Library myself in my first few weeks in London, mostly in the Rare Book Room, looking over old Egyptology texts, including a first edition of Champollion, Kitchen, Gardiner, and Stewart's original 1971 translation and text on the Stela of Paser, and some nice copies of Thomas Young's early efforts. There was also a modest library at the Institute of Archeology on Gordon Square, but in terms of original ancient Egyptian texts, most remained in the museum basement. The rare-book acquisition staff at the library would have a stroke if they saw the priceless volumes we had in the storerooms, stacked on top of old filing cases, sometimes on the floor, spread out over various stelae or sarcophagi, or jumbled in with boxes of other ancient detritus that tends to gather in massive museums. The organization at the new library was so intense that it was somewhat disconcerting to me, accustomed as I was to field sites and cluttered museums, but at other times I found it a refreshing break from our gloomy lab and Mick's constant mumbling and spitting.

I first met Alan Henry at the new British Library. I had only been in London a few weeks when one day at closing we both left at the same time and Alan noticed that I was taking the same route back to Great Russell Street. When I followed him up the stairs in our building he challenged me in the hallway, poking a sausage finger in my chest and asking me what my business was. After I explained myself and he nosed around my flat, peering into the kitchen cupboards, inspecting our bedroom, and patting down a scowling Mick who was just returning from the corner kebab shop with a paper cone of doner and chips, Alan seemed satisfied that we were legitimate. After that we walked home together from the library a lot, Alan often pulling me into little Balti house takeaways for a quick curry or masala dosa on the way, or wedging ourselves into a table at a pub along Euston for jacket potatoes and pints of bitter.

I miss those days; it was nice to pack up my things after a solemn nod from Alan, his desk stacked high with hermetic manuals and occult biographies, the two of us usually the last to leave. Nice to follow his bulky form into the darkness of the brick courtyard. Every time was a small adventure and I was just a passenger along for the ride. After I'd exhausted the translation stocks at the library I stopped going, spending all my time at the lab with the Stela instead. But I knew he still came here; if I waited around long enough he'd show up.

A young woman behind the collection counter caught my attention. She was removing little slips of paper from a towering stack of books on a cart and placing them in pigeonholes that ran along the wall. It was the way her waist stretched when she reached to the top of the stack, and the quick flickering motions of the hands, a dynamic sort of energy. She had short, spiky hair, tipped with purple like a Nile lily.

It seemed unlikely, yet oddly appropriate. She finished stacking the books and walked through an open door in the back. I could see some sort of conveyor-belt system with books on it back there, and other staff walking around and pushing carts full of books or documents. She was speaking with an older man, explaining something with her hands. Her tight pants revealed the supple rise of a boyish behind and muscular legs.

It couldn't be *that* easy.

Then she was gone, into the intestines of the library. I walked over to the banks of computer terminals and entered my identification number and desk number. At the prompt for key words I entered: "Egypt Past Present." I clicked on the first book on the list.

Thompson, Joseph P. *Egypt, Past and Present.*
Jewett: Boston, 1854. 1st ed.

I clicked the request button and went back to my desk. I sat there watching the open door waiting for Erin, if it was her, to reemerge. After about ten minutes the light came on at my desk and I went to the counter to pick up my book, joining the short queue. No sign of Erin.

When it came to be my turn another young woman at the desk took my ID card and went to retrieve my book. It was a woman I'd seen before, someone who had even helped me find a particular volume that I couldn't locate on the computer. Like Erin, she was slim and wearing tight clothing, but she had her dark hair piled up on top of her head in a way that seemed vaguely Victorian. The young Victorian returned with my book, a small, gray volume. An identification badge hung on a cord around her neck. "Penelope Otter."

Excuse me, I said, Ms. Otter?

Her eyes had already drifted on to the next customer and now she looked back to me startled, but pleasant.

Hi. My name is Walter Rothschild. I think we've met before.

Blank look.

You helped me find some things a while back? Anyway, I was wondering if you had anyone who worked here named *Erin*. A young woman. Short hair?

She pursed her lips and looked upward.

Hmmmm. I must tell you, sir, that there are more than a hundred people here on staff, so I think it's likely there are several Erins in fact.

But one that works right here, like you do? I just saw her a second ago.

She shook her head.

Can't say I do. But I haven't been here all that long.

She leaned a little closer across the desk, the edge biting into her stomach and making a small fold. She had a slight overbite and dark, thick eyebrows. I caught the slightest scent of something earthy on her breath, like carrots.

To be honest, she whispered, I don't know the names of any of these people here with me right now.

I could feel the queue shuffling behind me, anxious. I turned around and looked directly into the knobby throat of the tall African man I had seen earlier at Alan's desk. He stared down at me with a placid expression on his face. Because this was Europe, where personal space doesn't exist, his nose was less than six inches from my forehead and his cheekbones were so wide that they filled my entire range of vision. I looked away from his face, my eyes trailing down and off his body to some indeterminate space to the side. That's when I noticed the bulge in the side of his suit jacket and what looked like the peeking edge of a revolver handle nudging against the crease of his lapel. I looked up again quickly. His face shifted as if he was going to say something to me, so I quickly turned back to Penelope and thanked her for her time, and went briskly for the door, trying to keep a controlled gait. Halfway across the room I glanced back and saw the man with the gun watching me with an amused smile on his face, still standing in the queue. I walked briskly out the door and through the lobby, out onto Euston Street and headed south toward Great Russell. Nobody seemed to be following me.

It was the early part of the afternoon, and the Indian restaurants that line Gray's Inn Road were empty, the tables decked out in white tablecloths, the smell of curries steaming out the doorways where the waiters stood in ankle-length smocks of various muted colors, awaiting the afternoon rush. Delightfully oblivious of my panic, they smiled at me placidly and agreeably as I jogged past their stoops. I stopped into a Pret A Manger to gather my breath. Why was I afraid of that man? Did I think he was after me? He could have just wanted to ask me the time.

I bought an egg-and-watercress sandwich for ninety p and sat on a stool by the window, watching the north end of the street. That's when I realized that I had inadvertently walked out with the Thompson book, *Egypt, Past and Present*. I had it in my jacket pocket.

5:   CRYPTOGRAPHY

I WENT BACK TO the library and waited until closing time to see if I could catch Erin coming out, but it seemed like the employees must have used a different exit as all I saw was an unending stream of bleary, rumpled scholars. The only other option seemed to be to go back to the Lupo Bar in Soho and see if anyone there knew Erin or Hanif or where they might be.

It didn't matter what night it was; the streets of Soho were jammed from Oxford to Leicester Square as soon as the sunlight dimmed to that respectable level that denotes the eventide, the call to prayer, the klaxon horn of release, the soundless song that welcomes the coming excesses of drink in the West End. Pedestrians crowded around the entrances of popular places, mushrooming outside pub doors, across the sidewalk and into the streets. Empty pint glasses were lined like pigeons along window ledges all down the block. It took me a few turns around the central part of Soho, Compton Street across to Greek Street and back over Wardour, before I was able to locate the Lupo Bar, the distinctive hanging sign of a sow and a suckling Romulus and Remus, the inky dark windows, the pulsing rhythm thrumming like a heartbeat.

It seemed a completely different place: the lighting a bit brighter and the mood relaxed with groups of people chatting at the bar. A few couples crouched at the low tables of the main room, squinting at each other. I wandered around trying to find the back room where we met Erin and Hanif but couldn't seem to locate it. None of it looked familiar. Was it possible that they changed the setup of the room? Did the arrangement vary from night to night?

I stepped up to the bar, the approximate spot where I had my interaction with Pam, and asked the smiling bartender if he knew Hanif or Erin or Alan Henry. He grinned and shook his head gamely, as if I had asked for a drink that didn't exist. When I asked about the room arrangement, he just shrugged. The vacant look suggested he wasn't listening at all, his hearing being precisely tuned to catch only the significant phrases above the din, things like: *gin and tonic, pint of lager, 'ow much?* Did Alan choose this place on purpose? Could Hanif have set up the whole operation? I thought of Pam, she of the clacking molars and nimble fingers, what part did she play? Was that an important element of distraction? From what? I should have known *that* was a ruse. I thought of the *Dream Book*, a manual for interpreting dreams by Nineteenth Dynasty scribe Qenherkhepshef: *If a man sees himself in a dream: seeing his penis erect: BAD: this means victory for his enemies.*

I stood on the sidewalk and reviewed my options. The only way to stave off the very possible cataclysmic ending I was spiraling toward was to consider the matter in a very deliberate and rational manner. I wanted to run screaming to Heathrow and get the hell out of London, Europe altogether. But my daughter was here now, somewhere. And the Stela was still waiting.

I decided to approach it as I would a particularly difficult piece of cryptography.

It seemed plausible that Erin or Hanif or even Alan Henry might be about in Soho somewhere, especially on a Saturday night. Soho proper wasn't much more than eight square blocks altogether, laid out roughly like a grid, and I could approach it systematically, moving through the grid in a pattern, block by block, checking each establishment as I went along. I would take careful note of the places I visited as well as the multiple configurations of people, ethnic groupings, dress, personality, and overall ambience. I figured that the various types of places in each area would help me triangulate the most probable position for someone like Alan or Erin, allowing me to use the grid to strengthen my probability. I'd start at the northern end and move south, from Oxford, working down Wardour, Dean, Frith, and Greek Street, all the way to Shaftesbury and Chinatown.

The first problem with this tactic was that each establishment had its own particular sort of entrance procedure, which often included a cover charge. It was apparent after moving halfway down Wardour that I was quickly moving through my available money and would have to readjust my strategy. Compounding this was the fact that I felt a bit guilty about coming into a place and just wandering around looking for people so I usually ended up buying a drink. At pubs I naturally had a pint, bitters were the cheapest and the easiest to drink, a bargain I suppose at two pounds twenty pence. I left these unfinished on the bar. At cafes like Mezzo or Bar Italia, to avoid alcohol I would have something that came in a teacup.

The variety of decor, ambience, and furniture was astounding from place to place; from spider-thin metal furniture to woolly bean-bag chairs, circular platforms with patrons piled about like laundry on low cushions siphoning flavored tobacco products through the sinuous strands of large glass hookahs, to the more spartan and elegantly minimalist sort, smooth plastic-slab tables and functional stools, a bar that looked very much like the deck of a spaceship. In every sort of place the customers seemed equally louche, self-possessed, and bored, smoking derisively and sorting through whoever walked through the door with hooded eyes. In every doorway, for just a moment, I had a flash of panic when faces turned to me and bodies shifted to attention at my presence. Despite the cold weather the fetid air of the bars soon had me sweating through my corduroy jacket.

The one other consistent element you could count on in Soho was the insistent drubbing of deafening electronic techno music. It seems completely incongruous to me that in London this sort of music is played in nineteenth-century Victorian-style pubs, Indian restaurants, even sunny vegetarian deli-cafes. I suppose patrons find the beat of the music to be synonymous with good times. The incessant thumping incites them to match the rhythms with the clink of glasses, the consumption of booze and the ringing of coins as more beverages are purchased and another song, as relentless as the last, begins, everyone working to keep up with what could be called the overture of Soho.

Soon it was just after midnight and I had only covered a few blocks. I had maybe four pounds left in my pocket. My original grid was in disarray and I wasn't sure exactly where I started from. I'd consumed a lot of drinks by this time, and I felt an insistent hammering at the back of my skull. It seemed like I was under the influence of a growing, lurching panic. I was clutching at handrails and chair backs, cursing under my breath as I kept my face low, under the glare of the lights.

The next place in my grid was a grungy little bar, tucked between two much more directly marketed establishments. "Garlic & Metal." The area just inside the door was set up like a cafe, a half dozen empty black tables and the bar area in the back similarly deserted save a bored-looking girl in torn black pants and a black T-shirt that read "Garlic & Metal" with a blood red skull emblazoned below. She was leaning on the empty bar and must have had at least a dozen metal implements in her face—bars, studs, rods—emerging from all angles. Her hair was a shocking-pink color, plastered almost straight up, but to the side, as if she had been driving in a car with the window down all day. It looked like a very promising place to locate Erin or Alan Henry.

While I stood there in the doorway and looked at her she gave an almost imperceptible nod of her head toward a dark slot in the floor to her right, a sort of trapdoor with a set of stairs leading down. As I moved toward the hole I discerned a mighty din of screaming, clanging, guitar-driven music.

Despite the fact that I was married to a professional musician for several years, I know very little about music. I listened to the usual things in passing while growing up, the stuff you can't escape, whatever was on the radio, and Helen's music when she played something on the record player, mostly classical or her collection of popular rock-and-roll albums. It just wasn't something that I could ever seem to approach in a clear consistent manner. It never seemed to open itself up to me, the way an Old Kingdom manuscript would unfold like a flower in front of me as I went through the transliterations, each element flowing naturally from one glyph to the next, until the entire shape and fabric of the message presented itself. I suppose that Helen would say that is the problem: that I can't expect music or anything else to behave in the way that ancient texts do.

It never dawned on me that I had spent my life, the vast bulk of it, living in a world without music. I had no device for playing music in my flat; I never have. I didn't own any records, tapes, or compact discs and I'd never wanted them. Helen used to say that everyone has a personal sound track playing in their heads, that we all live in a world filled with music, if only our own. I said I couldn't hear any music, and she would sigh and say, Aww, Walter, you're just not *listening*. I didn't get it; it seemed to me awfully quiet in my head, a long stream of stillness and silence, and that's the way I liked it.

The stairs wound in a clockwise fashion, ending in a room suffused with deep red light and deafening music. I squeezed into a spot at the bar and let my eyes adjust. The low ceiling was hewn unfinished rock, producing a cavelike effect. The walls had niches that held smoldering candles in pools of hardened wax. The patrons were all uniformly dressed in variations of deep black, laced with the steely glints of metal studs and hoops, the occasional splash of color in the hair, most often standing at odd angles from the head. I didn't know that here, in 1997, after all this time, they were still around: Punks, underground, in Soho, Mohawks, leather, metal studs, giant safety pins through the nose; it was like some kind of minor archeological find, a shallow sort of discovery.

I caught the bartender's eye, another young woman done up in the same fashion as the bored girl upstairs, and she handed me a drink menu. Apparently the only thing you could get at this bar were shots that came in thin glasses in an array of muted colors, all containing garlic. I ordered a "Metal Martini" shot and tried to circulate through the room. This place was cheek to jowl with flesh, leather, and metal. I worked my way toward a low archway opening, apparently into another room. Everyone was exceedingly polite.

I ducked under the archway and found that it opened into a single, low room, a narrow vault, barrel shaped, with one long table in the middle and benches along the wall. The walls were covered in graffiti, pen, marker, paint, nail polish and lipstick, words and slogans and expletives in at least twenty languages. Candles were lined down the middle of the table, wax spilling in multicolored pools on the smooth, glasslike surface. There seemed to be something under the table, a form of some kind, a smoky outline under the candles and the dozens of empty shot glasses.

It was a body, a human body, stretched out prone, faceup, arms crossed: a desiccated corpse under glass. This wasn't a table, it was a coffin, a wooden sarcophagus topped with Plexiglas. The people seated around the coffin seemed to take little notice of me as they continued to shout at each other over the crashing guitars and drums, everyone smoking at least one kind of cigarette, tattoos arching across their faces and hands in smoky footprints. I sat on the end of one of the benches to take a closer look at the body.

It was obviously only a few hundred years old, maybe seventeenth century, judging from the clothing and condition of the body. It was preserved in the usual western fashion, involving various solvents pumped into the corpse, keeping it full of liquid as opposed to drying it out like the Egyptians. It was a man, dressed in some rather regal robes, with a long sword held in clasped hands encased in heavy gauntlets, a helmet with nose bar and chain mail, toes pointed in metal slippers. An elbow jostled me from my contemplation of the dead man.

That, my friend, is Sir Toby Belch. Eh? You like?

A leering, grinning fellow, with black hair gelled in a symphony of spikes, his accent heavily Germanic. He had a large metal knob protruding from his bottom lip that seemed to interfere with his speech. He rapped on the top of the coffin.

Wakey, wakey, eh? Sir Toby! Wakey, we need your help!

He collapsed against me, laughing hysterically. He smelled like a long-haired pack animal left out in the rain.

My name is Anton, he said, proffering his hand. You are American, yes?

Yes, my name's Walter. Nice to meet you.

This, Anton said, slapping the arm of the man sitting next to him, is Gunnar.

Gunnar turned to me, his face flushed and eyes watery pink. He grinned broadly.

Ay! How you doing?

Gunnar had his head completely shaved with a series of rather intricate swirls and symbols tattooed across his clean dome; mostly Celtic, perhaps with some old Norse or Germanic things thrown in.

He was wearing headphones attached to a small tape player on the coffin table. Anton jabbed me with another elbow to the ribs.

What you doing? Eh? Why are you here, Mr. American?

I'm actually looking for someone. A certain woman, actually, maybe—

You come to London, Anton said incredulously, to find *a woman?*

Ah, no, I thought you meant—

Anton slapped his comrade on his leather-clad arm and rattled off a stream of Dutch. It was easy enough to understand what he said; rooted in the Germanic, like English, modern Dutch closely resembles the language of eighth-century Britain. It is our English past speaking from under the centuries of morphological change and semantic generalization, amelioration, and abstraction. Vowel shifts and lexical loss and gain. The precise science of linguistics quickly renders all Germanic-based languages back to the mother tongue.

Both men laughed hard, toothy, hacking laughs. Anton handed me a hand-rolled cigarette, twisted into a large cone shape.

Very cool, he said. Very cool. But *not* a good place for that, no?

Anton and Gunnar stared at me with expectant grins, their pupils deep and wide as the eddying pools of the Nile. I thought of Seth emerging from the marsh reeds, his long snout quivering expectantly, an offering in his outstretched hand: a lotus flower, Lily of the Nile, its upturned face open to the sun, the rigid stamen, the delicate folds of color. The scent of mud and heaven.

I took a drag off the cigarette. I may be an oldster, a classic square, a budgy anorak, but I've spent a lot of time in North Africa—I know hashish when I smell it or taste it. I handed it back to him.

We are from Holland, Anton said. Here to play music. Would you like to hear our band? Yes?

Sure, I said.

Anton handed me the hash cigarette again and I took a polite puff. The hash was strong but the smoke felt good in my lungs. It also struck me that this was the first real interaction I'd had with anyone all night. In London, if you appear like you want to be left alone, as I always do, then you will be. Londoners are always perfectly willing to mind their own business.

Anton took the headphones off Gunnar and put them on my head. He rewound the tape a bit, then hit Play. I was slammed with a cascade of guitar and drum, a wall of sound. It was quite impressive, at least in terms of the volume of sound they were able to produce. Both men watched my face expectantly, smiling, bobbing their heads to the time of the music that was so loud I'm sure they could hear it as well. I nodded and smiled. Really I had no idea what it was, how to begin to describe it.

Then I was smoking the hash again and more songs were passing through the headphones, separated by punctuated gasps of relative silence and I found myself leaning back against the wall and looking at the rounded walls and ceiling of the low crypt, reading the inscriptions written in a multitude of languages that covered nearly every inch of concrete. My French was weak, my Spanish even weaker, though I felt confident with my German, Latin, ancient and modern Greek, Arabic, Farsi, Urdu, and a half dozen Northern African dialects. The graffiti ranged broadly from anarchy slogans: *Fuck the system! Corporate dogs will die! Don't make me put my foot in your ass! X Ignorantiat ad sapientium.* To the more moderate calls for action: *Peace in Palestine. Destroy your television. Legalize it! Hatten ar dor!* To the rather sweet: *My heart cries for you. Raphael loves Martine? I'm lost here.* To the downright cryptic: *Free-range Chickens! Glasnost + Reagan + Absinthe = Good Love. Utom Hammar Bys Fam. God Is Busy.* There were several ancient languages represented, including an inscription in Aramaic, a language that hasn't been spoken in a thousand years, the ancient Middle Eastern language of Jesus. Even some scratching on the edge of the archway that looked suspiciously like cuneiform, possibly Akkadian, though that would be highly unlikely considering maybe three dozen people in the world could compose sentences in that ancient tongue.

A lot of the writing was in the form of a pictograph, the idea presented with some kind of artistic rendering without words; band names, anarchy/peace symbols, brand-name logos, actual representations of people or objects, including a few crude portraits, and a couple odd things that I couldn't place in an existing symbolic record. Certainly there were things that might have been just personal symbols, a sign between friends, something that a drunk scrawled on the wall in a spurt of creativity, or the particular shape that we find ourselves doodling again and again in the margins of our boredom. But even most of these can be interpreted, and cryptography is the study of just these sorts of scripts.

There is a sense of play involved in the creation of a script; ancient scribes used old signs with new values, adjusted or created new signs, and combined others into semantic or poetic devices like puns. Or syllabic orthography, when words of foreign origin, like northwestern semiotic, would be recast into something new. It required a vast knowledge of the existing or known sign patterns, and then the imagination to construct the other possibilities, to see them arranged in possible visual patterns and using all the tools at your disposal, all the instruments of history, to come up with meaning.

Anton was putting the headphones back on my head.

Try this, he said, you like poetry, yes?

A man in a thick Irish brogue began to recite rolling, rambling poetry:

> *Gaze no more into the bitter glass*
> *The demons, with their subtle guile,*
> *Lift up before us when they pass,*
> *Or only gaze a little while;*
> *For there a fatal image grows,*
> *With broken boughs, and blackened leaves,*
> *And roots half hidden under snows*
> *Driven by a storm that ever grieves.*

For all things turn to barrenness
In the dim glass the demons hold,
The glass of outer weariness,
Made when God slept in times of old.

I shut out the poem, I heard it without listening. I closed it off into another compartment. I had a rough arrangement forming; I could see them unfolding, hear them in my head, moving like ancient gears, pulling the shapes into place.

Considering that this bar was obviously frequented by a certain segment of society, a certain sort of disaffected youth with leanings toward a specific style of music and code of dress, and along with that particular basic political leanings, personality structures, codes of ethics, morals, social outlook and psychology, even a preference for certain kinds of art, certain sorts of symbology that reflect these values, and an attraction to the very venue itself, the low-vaulted crypt containing a rotting corpse, darkness, candlelight, deafening metal music, and garlic-laced shots. All these components played a role in the development of the symbols. Then there were other clues, the style of writing, the relative boldness or faintness of the print, the type of marker or pen used, the placement of the symbol on the surface, the slant it takes, upside down or straight, the particular spelling and punctuation of any adjoining text, and the surrounding text and symbols. Considering that many of these scrawlings were answers or responses or challenges to preceding symbols—or were they grouped together with like symbols, in philosophy or in the actual rendering of particular representations? There is no such thing as arbitrary expression; the illusion of randomness is nature's joke, the humor of the gods who hide the framework in our own shallow, chaotic urges. To think otherwise suggests an unwillingness to confront the code of our purposes.

I began to arrange the grid in my mind to sort the pictographs, to set up groupings.

What could have made her peaceful with a mind that nobleness made simple as a fire, with beauty like a tightened bow . . . a kind that is not natural in an age like this . . . being high and solitary and most stern? Why, what could she have done being what she is?

The city of her Father . . . she protects him with her body . . . there is no form that escapes her flame . . . she gives sunlight, the great one of the sun disk, which shines down upon her likeness, her beauty and power . . . she is the heart of all people being glad as she ascends to her house, her temple . . . she has appeared and has shone like a woman of gold, priceless, the goddess mother . . . yet so much sorrow, so much regret, and the Two Lands weep for her.

When I looked around again Anton and Gunnar were slumped over on the bench, sleeping, the crypt empty.

This wasn't exactly a surprise; it was common for time to compress when I was translating texts. When I finally raised my head, neck aching and eyes sore from the strain, shaking off the reverie of translation, I would often find that the day was gone and night had fallen, my circumstances and surroundings altered.

But something was different; the text I was deciphering was a version of the Stela of Paser text, a variation of Stewart's translation with some adjustments I hadn't seen before. It was from the upper third section, covering the walls and ceiling of the crypt.

I looked away quickly, resting my eyes on the bloated, festering form of Sir Toby Belch in his plastic case. The music still raged in the main room though my headphones were quiet. I leaned over and took a good look at the tattoos that arched across Gunnar's cranium. They weren't Celtic or Norse symbols as I had originally thought, rather a series of elaborate depictions of the lotus flower, done in the distinct Egyptian style.

I couldn't believe I could have made such a mistake. I was obviously stoned and hallucinating. I stared hard, shook it off, and I looked again: It was the Nile lily, an almost perfect ancient Middle Kingdom representation, stretched like a map on his scalp.

I slipped out of the crypt while the Dutchmen slept.

Then I was weaving through the after-midnight crowd that seemed to convene at Oxford and Tottenham Court Road. In an attempt to sober up I slipped into Dionysus and got a paper cone of chips, doused them with malt vinegar and salt and then made my way through the crowd, stabbing chips with a small wooden fork, trying to avoid the loads of reeling, swearing, sweaty, track-suited lager lads, their collars turned up like fins, strutting that peculiar quick-hipped London strut: *Wha the fuck you lookin' at?*, hounding the dark-eyed nubile Middle Eastern girls fresh from the clubs. A stray cross-dresser in platform shoes, wig askew, leaked out of the Pink Pounder and strode confidently down Oxford, towering over the crowd. The singular, leather-jacketed African men murmured *Minicab?* or *Hashish?* to every passerby while blinking Chinese girls stepped off the 24 bus at Tottenham and Oxford with full backpacks and guidebooks in hand, shrinking from the drunken, sallow-faced thirty-something men in dark suits fresh from some hip Soho dive pissing nonchalantly in any available niche that didn't already contain a body.

At that time of night on the corner of Oxford Street and Tottenham Court Road there is also every kind of lunatic to consider: the shouters, dribbling saliva and snot, gesticulating in the streets, looking to accost someone for something, to explain some horrible wrong, some great injustice that had been done to them; the most incorrigible sort of beggars and addicts, who, perhaps figuring their chances at a few quid were about to dwindle with the coming morning, went into high gear, their blanket or sleeping bag uniformly slung over one shoulder, tugging on sleeves, giving speeches about epilepsy and hepatitis and freezing babies and bus fare and girlfriends bleeding in the park, always looking you directly in the eye, as this is the route to universal sympathy.

No one seems to know where we are going, everyone wandering blind, confused. There is a fresh pile of vomit on every corner, quiet weeping at every bus stop, drunken shouting outside every pub. It is an odyssey of madness.

As I waited for the light to cross Tottenham Court Road with my cone of chips, a frail-looking girl in a stained and torn fur-collared coat appeared at my side. Her face was streaked with smeared makeup, long black tracks down her cheeks, the skin on her neck and hands covered with sores.

Please, she said, I don't want any money. I just want something to eat.

We both stood there on the edge of the curb, along with a line of other people, waiting for traffic. I had a forkful of chips halfway to my mouth.

May I *please* just have some of your chips? she said. *Please.*

Here, take it, I said, and handed her the whole greasy mess. She took it and bounded down the sidewalk and across the street, through oncoming traffic, disappearing around the corner toward New Bloomsbury Street. The light changed and everyone began to walk. The young woman next to me, an American college girl by the look of her, began to cry when we reached the other side.

Oh, god, she said. So awful, it's so awful.

Sobbing into her hands she wandered off to her hostel, or wherever she was staying, and I turned onto Great Russell Street, toward my flat, feeling the distance that separates all of us, of the individual worlds we all inhabit. The West End will do that. In West Central London, every night, everybody's lost.

6: SETH

I WENT DIRECTLY TO Alan's room. I found the doorknob lying in the hall in several pieces and the door slightly ajar. Nothing seemed to be disturbed, so I decided I'd better stick around. I'd be honest with him and clear it all up. I sat on his narrow cot and watched the door, my stomach churning its contents with a vicious severity.

As the night wore on, I settled onto Alan's cot and began to read the Thompson book that I was still carrying in my pocket. It was a typical nineteenth-century English account of Egypt. Thompson was apparently a wealthy older gentleman taking an extended holiday with the expressed intention of recording his observations of the fantastic oriental splendor along with sketches and engravings. His boat party entered at Alexandria, and the first chapter spent most of its time discussing the harbor, the curious habits of the natives, as well as Pompey's Pillar and Cleopatra's Needle, now located in Paris. After a while I laid my head on the pillow and closed my eyes. I took my ear votive out of my pocket, and held it in both hands at my lips, still thinking of Alexandria.

My ex-wife Helen loved the various types of tea shops around the harbor, where you could squat on a low cushion and share a bowl of strong tea for a nickel and watch the waterfront activity. The last summer she came to visit we spent a lot of time at the harbor front, Helen wearing long, pale cotton dresses and woven sandals. She went bareheaded, her dark hair shining deeply in the hard African sun. After a few days her skin was brown and she had fine white lines around her eyes. I wore my straw Panama and sunglasses whenever I was in Egypt, but Helen insisted on going bareheaded and without protection. In a sense we looked and acted like any other set of tourists, at least for the few days I was free from my duties at the Alexandria Cultural Center or at one of the periphery digs I was supervising. We probed the markets, haggling for trinkets, took walks along the Mediterranean; we even took a short camel caravan ride into the Sahara for a week-long camping trip.

I was terrified of the animals myself, so large and often unruly, but Helen took to it right away and after an hour she was riding like a Bedouin. We left in the early morning, the two of us, a Japanese couple and a few Australian teenagers, plus our four guides who also set up camp and cooked our meals. I remember the sharp smell of peppers and curries, the thick black stews cooked in rude clay pots, the way the Japanese couple smoked incessantly, promptly running out of cigarettes on the first night. They expressed complete dismay when the camel drivers were unable to magically produce more for them, having only their rough Turkish tobacco and leaf wrappers to offer. For the rest of the trip the Japanese couple kept their hats pulled low over their eyes, muttered their modern pictographs, and glowered at the unending rows of sand dunes.

The heat was incredible and our thirst insatiable. One of the camels carried a dozen large water cans and we went through our per-

sonal ration before each nightfall. But I had made a point of bringing
our own reserve stock, and each evening after dinner Helen and I pri-
vately sipped at a pint of cool minty Assam tea. At night the temperature plummeted at least forty degrees and Helen and I wound
ourselves tightly together in rough wool blankets, gritty with sand.
Our tent rippled with desert winds, the canvas snapping and popping
fiercely. The slight rustle and jingle of the harnessed camels, shifting
in their sleep, and the low humming of the drivers who smoked
around the campfire late into the night before rolling themselves into
blankets and sleeping piled together around the fire like old dogs. I
remember the smell of our bodies twisted together, cooling with
sweat, the scent of sage and sandalwood in Helen's hair, the soft
downy hair of her forearms and legs. Helen would nuzzle into my
neck and kiss me lightly and I returned her kisses to her forehead and
then she'd giggle and then we'd do it over again.

One night I disentangled myself from our blankets, Helen
sleeping soundly, naked and warm, and stepped outside the tent to
urinate. At first the darkness in the desert seems vast and complete,
like an underground cavern, and in the first few moments there is a bit
of panic at the infinite nature of it. But then after some seconds the
earth and sky make themselves clear, their division proper, an important observation that didn't escape the notice of the ancient Egyptians. Close to my feet, large black dung beetles, their heavily
segmented bodies moving clumsily across the small wind ripples in
the sand, rolled their small circular burdens of camel dung back to
their lairs. There were thousands of them, teeming across the sands,
spreading over the next dune, a mass shifting movement at low speed,
a rather unsettling sight at first, when the scale of their numbers is revealed. Until you realize that they have no interest in you. They have
their own burdens to care for.

It seems like you can see farther at night in the desert. You
glance upward and the sky begins to assert itself, cloudless, moonless,

as most nights in the desert seem to be, the stars emerging from brief smudges into burning pricks of light, whole multitudes, rivers of white light, the fine grains of sand in the wind making meandering ribbons of pale green and pink across the sky. I stood shivering, the wind sprinkling in gusts against my naked calves, holding my warm genitals in my hand, writing my name across the sands.

Then I was dreaming of Alan Henry, in his tiny little room. He was growing like a plant, his head sprouting out of the windows and door; his long meaty arms falling out and down onto Great Russell Street. His cask-shaped head began to shift and change and two large ridged horns curled out of his skull, his face taking on an almost dog-like shape, like an anteater, the aspect of the Seth animal, Seth, the ancient protector of Egypt and god of chaos, his skin turning white and hairy, the body more angular, larger, until his bulbous eyes poked out of the skylights on the roof, the brick straining against his expanding bulk, the entire building bowing outward.

I woke up when a crushing weight dropped on me like a sack of meal, making the cot squeal and forcing all the air out of me with a groan. A massive elbow drove solidly into my ear. It was a body, a large one. A human one. I could tell by the immediate warmth, the softness of flesh. The combination of the smell of spicy curries and chutneys and the shape of the bulk told me that this man was Alan Henry.

He sprang back out of the bed like a cat, and though my eyes were cloudy and throbbing from lack of air, I could see him assume some sort of shadowy judolike pose in the darkness of the room, the profile oddly pronounced, hands raised, palms forward.

You're going to regret this, Alan growled, and moved toward me as I writhed on the bed. My ribs felt crushed to splinters, and I could only manage a thin wheeze through my throat as I struggled for breath. He put one giant paw around my neck, then bringing his other hand over his head he began to piston his fist with even, arced blows into the side of my face.

The first punch closed my eyes, and the second seemed to restore my oxygen.

Alan . . . Wait . . . Alan . . . , I squeaked between punches.

7: THE MINDS OF INSECTS

WHEN I WOKE UP again Eddie was holding a slab of raw bacon on my face. The left side of my head was throbbing and was swollen taut. My ear was crusted with dried blood. I was curled in a fetal position.

There ya are, Eddie said. Back again amongst the living, yeah? Caught a couple of tough shots from that big bastard.

There was some vague light that looked something like daylight coming in from the window. I glanced around and saw that the room was empty; I was lying on the dusty floor of Alan's flat, with Eddie kneeling beside me. It was morning. The place was empty; all of Alan's things had been removed.

Where'd he go? I asked.

Dunno. Eddie shrugged. Left the key under me door this morning. He was paid up thro' the next two months as well, yeah? Strange, know wha' I mean?

I took the bacon out of Eddie's hand and looked at it.

I thought you were supposed to put raw *steak* on a wound like this, I said.

Eddie snatched the bacon from my hands.

Do I look like a fockin' butcher to ya?

He stormed out and I was alone in Alan's little room. I got up and felt for any other injuries but nothing else seemed serious. I searched my pockets: My wallet and keys were still with me, though the Thompson book I'd stolen from the library was gone, and that wasn't all. Alan Henry had also taken my ear votive, one of the few objects that held some real value to me.

I went back to my flat to wash the layer of bacon grease from my face and see how bad it looked. A swollen purple-and-red welt about the shape of Africa curved from my forehead around my left eye and down across my cheek. I could feel my heart thumping in it like some internal machine, and I stroked it with my fingers like a cushioned creature that had attached itself to my face. My earlobe was split and throbbing, but the blood had clotted and the lower half of my ear was encased in it like a dark, crusty jewel.

Mick was laying down another layer of insecticides in the kitchen. He walked backward through the living room with a can in each hand, spraying with a wide side-to-side motion, like a man parking planes at the airport. Mick goes through about four cans a week, not to mention the rest of the pest-control devices he uses.

West Nile virus, Mick said. They found a crow in Finsbury that tested positive.

Mick, I said, I was wondering if we could talk about something.

Mick's eyes flitted across me momentarily. The wound on my face was now burning in the arid atmosphere of the kitchen, like someone was holding a blowtorch to it. Mick stopped spraying and set down the cans.

Yeah? What's that? There's something wrong with yer face, mate.

It's about the Song of Amun. I mean I know that you've seen it and—

Just a sec, Mick said, bending to the stove, let me get me kidneys out o' the oven.

He opened the oven door and using a napkin grabbed a small kidney pie off the baking rack. He set it on the counter and began rummaging for a fork. I still had my hands over my mouth and my eyes watered from the cloud formations of chemicals that drifted through the kitchen. Mick began forking the hot pie into his little ferret mouth.

The Song of Amun, I said, from Karnak? Klein told me about it, and that you'd seen it.

Mick was scraping at the pie tin; his face bent to it like a penitent.

I was wondering if you could tell me something about it, seeing as it is concurrent with the Stela and site specific.

Why don't you just look at it yourself? Mick said.

Well, I said, it's . . . it's unavailable right now. You did read it, right?

Mick wrinkled his brow. His skin was nearly translucent and fine blue veins worked their way across his forehead.

Nothing to say about it, mate. Trust me. Lot of sentimental rot, that mess. Nothing to it.

A few moments later Mick chucked his pie pan into the trash and picked up his insecticide cans and started spraying again, covering the kitchen floor in long even strokes. He glanced at me as he sprayed. He wasn't going to even mention the Song of Amun to me, much less share his translations. I didn't need this; I didn't have time to muck about with him when my career was poised to implode.

Somebody thrash ya last night, old man? Your face looks like fockin' 'ell, yeah?

For a moment or two I debated grabbing his skinny neck with both hands and twisting till his eyes popped out of his little rodent skull. I outweighed him by at least forty pounds and had a few inches on him. I knew that I could pummel him to within an inch of his life, if I wanted to. I'm not the violent sort, never have been, but the mild animosity I normally felt toward Mick was certainly peaking. Maybe I was just looking to wreak some kind of misdirected revenge. I had the urge to seize him and tear his puny body into little pieces and chuck him into the Thames, the way Seth tore Osiris apart and cast him into the Nile. Of course his mother, Isis, put him back together again and it just made Osiris all the more powerful in the end; he became the final judge in the afterworld. Nevertheless, I still wanted to thrash him.

You sure? I said. Nothing?

Mick shook his head. He was crouched under the sink, squeezing thin tubes of poisonous paste along the baseboards.

Where'd that money come from, Mick? I said. All the money you gave Alan?

Uni loans, mate. The checks arrive every four months.

You haven't been a student for years.

No matter. I register for a class every once in a while, yeah? I'm technically working on a degree.

Really? In what?

Ancient civilizations? Or cultural anthropology? I forget. I just send them some of the work I'm doing here and it seems to satisfy them all right.

How much are you in debt?

What, ah, I'd say at least sixty thousand quid.

I was afraid to ask just what the hell he was spending all this money on, other than insecticides. He dressed like a career rough sleeper, rarely engaged in much hygiene of any kind, owned almost nothing but a few changes of clothes and a moldy toothbrush, and seemed to exist almost purely on sausages, kidney pies, tinned meats, curry, takeaway from the corner chip shop, and occasional forays into the depths of the steamy Asian kitchens of Soho.

Mick busied himself with the traps next. The regular roach stations, as well as cricket and ant baits and specially designed hormone-emitting capsules that emanated a type of radiation that got into insects' DNA structure. You could tell it was working when you saw roaches crawling out to die with only three legs, or a second head coming out the side of their abdomens. Mick crawled about the kitchen, placing the various traps at intervals of about a foot. The fresh baits made my wounded face throb so I backed into the hallway and shouted to him.

When do you plan on paying all that off? Doesn't that worry you?

I don't plan on paying it at all.

Mick rolled on the living-room floor, attaching baits to the underside of the couch and coffee table.

Haven't got a living relative to speak of, except for me mum. She's nearly seventy now. If I die with no heirs, it's no problem, yeah?

You mean you'll just leave the debt? Just die with it?

He looked at me in utter astonishment.

Of course.

Who'll pay it?

Who gives a bloody fuck'all about that? I'll be dead, yeah?

He laughed through his ferret teeth, his eyes filled with something like mirth.

Mick always preferred the Ptolemaic view of Egypt, a world at odds with its own destiny, the tumultuous years. His was a mythology that I couldn't quite decipher. Despite his apparent disdain for things spiritual, Mick kept lumps of wet clay piled on a box down in the lab and was inscribing sets of tablets with passages in Demotic, Coptic, and some other cuneiform-type scripts I didn't recognize.

Often in the long hours of the morning or afternoon, while I was poring over the Stela, Mick would murmur things to himself while perched on his stool, mostly fragments of ancient Egyptian and Arabic as far as I could tell, as he pressed the damp clay with his hand-carved reed stylus, inscribing something that applied only to his personal twisted sense of theology and order. There was some kind of internal search occurring under that constructed shell of indifference; Mick had some passion for craft beyond the monetary, whatever it was. But he would never own up to it, and he took that secret with him to the other side. To this day I think of his whispered intonations as a kind of background music to those days in the British Museum.

Aye, Rothschild, Mick said, pie didn't quite do the trick. What say we get ourselves a bite to eat?

It was true that I hadn't had anything to eat in the last twenty-four hours other than half a soggy cone of chips.

Okay, I said, it'd be nice to get out and let these chemicals settle. But I get to choose. No Indonesian this time.

Mick grumbled, but assented. Mick's favorite restaurant, which he frequented at least once a week, was a gritty Indonesian place in the lower end of Soho. I was tired of it; not of the food, which was agreeable enough, but with Mick's whole ritual. Mick's favorite dish was some kind of bone-in fish lying prostrate athwart a chipped pale blue plate, swimming in a murky brown sauce that was thick with small insect pod-looking peppers and flakes of powdery red and black leaves. It was his custom to order it hot—*the true stuff, mind you, none of this tourist shite*, he would say to the bowing waiter, smirking in his rumpled knee-length smock.

When the food arrived the kitchen staff would come out and stand along the wall, a motley crew of Asians, crossing their thin, hairless tattooed arms across their splattered white tank tops and sunken chests, ebony cigarettes dangling from their wet lips, watching Mick with obvious amusement and anticipation. They waited as Mick sawed a forkful of the fish, weighing it carefully, allowing the sauce to drip cleanly onto the smeared oilcloth-covered table. Mick placed the tender white flesh into his little ferret mouth and, eyes closed, began to masticate furiously, the translucent skin of his cheeks rippling with the fine striations of muscles that swept like spiderwebs across his face and bulbous cranium. He swallowed and opened his eyes, always looking at me in the same way, a savory expression, as if to say he was sorry that I couldn't experience such a pleasure, that all of this was so far beyond me and my abilities that he was left feeling nothing for me but true pity.

Which I never quite understood, as I had ordered precisely the same dish and was quickly and unceremoniously working my way through the spicy fish with my own particular set of eating mechanics, wrestling bits of the tender flesh from the splintery plastic of the bones, dabbing it in the sauce, and washing it down with a small glass of lemon pop.

After a few minutes Mick's face would begin to go white, his self-serving, condescending grimace would begin to falter, and then his face would begin to turn the most alarming shade of yellow, as if his liver had exploded and the bile had run flush to his face. His Adam's apple began working furiously, eyes tearing, and it was always then, when the first tear began to run down his face, his gaze still locked on mine, that we would hear the stifled laughter from the kitchen lads, a snort and then the sound of lips pressed against the backs of hands to no avail, the halfhearted attempt at suppression, breaking into a keening wail of snorts and wheezes. Then they would all go bounding back into the kitchen, howling with that particular sort of laughter that defies a specific cultural or linguistic subset or structure—shrieks of pleasure brought on by the discomfort and misery of another. So universal that sound, the same all over the world. Mick then would sputter and begin to help himself to my water glass. He had already poured his own down the front of his shirt.

The slab of fish was a bit hot, true, but nothing that I hadn't seen bettered in the taverns of North Africa or various port towns along the Turkish coast. I tried to finish my meal grimly, with some sort of sympathy for Mick, feigning a struggle with the fish, nodding in agreement as he shook and spat into his napkin, cramming slices of bread into his chapped maw, draining glass after glass of water that the tearful hostess poured for him, by now running a fire line of ice water from the kitchen to our table, passing glasses hand over hand to Mick's trembling fingers. He wouldn't speak to me for the rest of the night, spitting in the gutters as we walked home along Charing Cross, muttering into his ear votives, as if it were all my doing, as if I were to blame.

Later at the flat I would be subjected to Mick's further intestinal anguish as he thrashed about in the bathroom. One particular evening after such a meal I went to use the toilet sometime late in the night. When I flipped on the light I found Mick trembling and naked, his wiry arms outstretched with a hand planted on each wall, hovering over the bowl, suspended in a seated position like some kind of freakish gymnast, his eyes blazing and bubbles of spittle on his white lips. I went back to the bedroom and huddled under the sheets, my need to urinate suddenly absent, and spent the next few hours trying not to listen to Mick's muffled moaning cries: *It burns . . . oh god it burns, it burns!*

Instead this time I led Mick to a place just off Endell Street, nestled deep in the circuitous windings of Covent Garden, a small, delightfully strange vegetarian restaurant called Cranky's, where you can get a bowl of warm organic barley topped with cilantro, carrot shavings and pine nuts, and wash it all down with a cool glass of celery-beet juice, watery green and thick with chunks of murky purple sediment. There were a series of restaurants like this in the Covent Garden area where you could get such organic-type vegetarian fare, many of them run by the powerful English Krishna organization that called London home. I figured I'd gut down something organic and perhaps maybe catch a glimpse of Alan Henry, as he frequented these places, haunting the small inner courtyards and plazas of Covent Garden. I'd often seen him there conversing with Krishnas or other men wearing robed dress.

I didn't actually care much for the food, but sometimes after a few weeks of fish and chips and Yorkshire pudding a man feels like he needs to detox the system. Flush it out with something that hadn't been shitting and fornicating on a mossy hill in Cumbria a short time before. Considering his diet I thought this was something Mick might appreciate.

We walked the half dozen blocks in a mild downpour, Mick spitting and smoking furiously along the way. And then in the recess of Cranky's, a dank, cold place despite the walls being painted brilliant saffron, we took a table and Mick sat grumbling over mixed organic greens, warily eyeing the olive foccacia bread with sun-dried tomato spread, fingering the bowl of rough hummus with his spidery digits, keeping an eye on the doorway.

Is something the matter? I asked him.

Let me ask you something, Mick said, fixing his eyes squarely on me, something he rarely did.

Sure.

Have you ever noticed the most common form that the figures of, oh, let's say, aliens, take in western culture? How about the devil?

I shrugged.

Insect. Easily the most popular. Why? Insects are by far the most alien-looking and -acting things we have on this planet, yeah? Do I need to remind you that they have an exoskeleton? A hard outer shell that contains a mix of fluids? I'm sure you've noticed that you can drop a spider or a roach off a ten-story building and the fucking thing will scuttle off to its den, like it just stepped off a fucking bus?

So?

I'm sure you've heard about the theory of collective consciousness? The massed collective working for a single goal, yeah? Absent of any individual thought or aspiration? We know that different sorts of bees are born into a caste system which designates their particular function in the hive. They are genetically predisposed to carry out these functions. We also know that the workers can somehow communicate complex sets of instructions to the rest of the hive, including navigational elements, that allow the other bees to then seek out the food source.

They communicate with movement, I said. A little dance.

Forget the dance, Mick said. Not complex enough. That's like saying you could write Old Kingdom funerary instructions in Coptic.

So?

The metaphor of the hive is literal. Each is merely an appendage of the larger body. Do you know how each bee is given its designated position at birth? Besides the queen they are all genetically identical. It depends on the amount of food, essentially sugar water, that each pupa is given by the worker bees. That determines their function. The more sugar, the larger, more powerful their position. All this decided without any thought. Pure instinct. Every action determined by some kind of hardwired instinct.

You've got some serious problems, Mick. Some kind of phobia.

Fuck that. Some minute impulse that travels down the threadlike spinal cord from that small lump that serves as a brain. Reactions. Light, temperature, movement, pure reaction to the external world, yeah? Flying blind in a sense. Know how a moth, or a butterfly, will sometimes fly blindly into you? Because they do not recognize you as a living being? You are just a fucking object, another set of intake parameters that is filtered through their microscopic nervous system and engendering a predetermined set of actions! Now, I ask you . . .

He jabbed a finger into my chest, his ferretlike teeth gnashing. I tried to draw away from his ray-gun halitosis as best I could in the narrow booth.

. . . what is more terrifying than that? What? Than action without thought, no rationalization, no intellect, no emotion, no process of any kind? Ruled by instinct metered by a collective consciousness, an actual fucking physical memory! There is no feeling of loss, of sorrow, of pain even. All secondary to survival. You would think that it would make them ultimately predictable, but on the contrary it makes them the most unpredictable living creatures in the world, at least in our in-

teractions with them. Why? Because there is no *reason!* Their consciousness is so completely unlike our own, that they *might as well be
fucking aliens.*

It was the longest conversation we ever had.

Right after that Mick determined that he couldn't possibly con-
sume *any of this shite,* and proceeded to light up a fag even though
there were no-smoking signs everywhere. We were promptly ushered
back up the stairs and out into the rainy street by a pair of tall, reedy
dreadlocked youths, apparently working security for the Krishnas. I
was still chewing my garlic tabouli with tomatoes as we hit the street.

Krishna wankers! Mick said. Christ! Fucking poncey shite.

Any idea where I might find Alan? I said.

Nah, mate.

Hanif?

No fucking clue.

Heading up St. Martin's back toward Bloomsbury we passed a
dark little pub called the Four Bells. The windows were glazed with
condensation and grease.

Couple a Scotch eggs, Mick mumbled, and wheeled off into the
pub, leaving me there in the street.

I don't know why I even bothered. I walked home alone in the
rain, holding my broken face up to catch the cool drops. Wincing in
the rain, I cursed Mick's very soul, his dark, twisted little soul.

8: MUSIC

BACK AT THE FLAT I pumped some coins into our phone and called Zenobia's hotel. She had left a message for me to meet her there that evening at seven for dinner.

I tried to wash my face without touching the purpling bruise, then sat for a few minutes on the couch with a sock full of ice held against my face. The construction crews had called it off early, and the empty scaffolding outside the window swayed slightly in the wind that tunneled down Great Russell Street. I wanted to crawl into bed but I had to do something quick. I had a few hours so I decided to head back to the British Library and look for Erin. Maybe I could quietly return and avoid being accosted for unknown reasons by a man with a gun in his pocket. I couldn't be detained; I didn't have the time. But despite the fact that I had stolen a book that was subsequently stolen from me by Alan Henry, I had to risk it.

Desk number thirty-six in the Rare Book Room was occupied by the same tall African gentleman. His long body was hooked over a thick tome braced with silver buckles, his suit dangling off him like a coat hanger. His features were distinctly Nigerian. He looked up at me as I came in and smiled, a broad, toothy grin. He sort of nodded, as if we shared some kind of secret. I pretended I didn't notice and continued on to the circulation counter.

I didn't see Erin, but I was relieved to see Penelope Otter shuffling about with a stack of cards in her teeth and scribbling on a clipboard. I stood in the queue with a half dozen other scholarly types waiting to pick up their selections, my head down, trying to shrink into myself. When it was my turn a wizened old man beckoned for me to approach the desk. It took some time to explain to him that I just wanted to talk to Penelope.

Penelope had a puzzled expression on her face when the old man brought her out to the desk, leading her by the arm. When she saw me her lower lip puckered. I tried to smile warmly, though, as my ex-wife pointed out many times, this is not something I'm normally able to do.

I'm Dr. Rothschild. I spoke to you yesterday? I'm in here every once in a while? One time we looked for that text on Nubian kings? A few months ago?

Hello, she said. Yes. I remember you.

She folded her hands on the counter.

On the whole the British may be one of the most unattractive races of people in the world. In all my travels I have never seen such a myriad of physical unfortunates, at least to our late-twentieth-century codes of aesthetics. But Penelope had that delicious overbite that, when paired with a decent bit of dentistry and orthodontics, produces some of the more attractive specimens on this island. Her skin was a bit ghastly, ruddy and spotted about the chin and cheeks, shining slightly. Her glasses were small, square horn-rimmed affairs and her eyes overflowed the frames.

The little wizened man remained at her side, her elbow still held firmly in his bony fist. His eyes flitted back and forth between us as we spoke.

You were looking for someone yesterday, Penelope said.

Yes. A young lady named Erin. Perhaps your age, a little shorter, spiky-type hair.

Yes, that's right, she said. Are you all right? What happened to your face?

You know her?

No, Penelope said, at least I don't think so. Phillip?

She turned to the old man at her side, who was still gazing at me as if he were trying to recollect me from some dusty dream of prior acquaintance.

Phillip, Penelope said. Do you know a young woman who works here, in this room, by the name of Erin?

A few more moments of abject staring. I fought a surge of panic, thinking he was perhaps remembering me as the man who'd stolen a rare book from this room just yesterday. But it became clear he was examining my facial injury.

Phillip? Penelope said, louder.

Shaken from his reverie, Phillip pursed his lips and frowned. He kept his eyes on me, his hand on Penelope's elbow.

What's that? he wheezed.

Erin, Penelope said, slowly. A young woman named Erin who works here? Spiky hair?

Now, Phillip said, there's a lass by that name, sir. Has the spiky bit with the hair. Never about when she's scheduled.

Oh, Penelope smiled. *That* Erin. Though she isn't quite in her early twenties.

Erin had looked like a twenty-year-old to me. But then what did I know about the relative ages of women? My experience was limited.

Phillip left us to check the roll and see if Erin was indeed on the staff today. Penelope fiddled with a stack of colored slips of paper.

Why are you looking for her? she said.

She has something that I need back. It's a matter of extreme urgency.

Does this have anything to do with what happened to your face?

Penelope was wearing a loose cotton blouse with small pointed collars. Her shirt gapped at the front and I found myself drawn to examining the pale triangle of flesh exposed there. It was the pallor of a born Englishwoman, devoid of any hint of cleavage, and it drew me like a moth. She had her hair piled on top of her head in the same Victorian manner as she had yesterday.

No, I said. I don't think so.

Phillip returned to the desk and drew himself erect.

A young woman, Phillip said, by the name of Erin did in fact work here. At least, sir, she did until yesterday. She was removed from the schedule at that time.

Did she quit? Or was she fired?

I'm afraid, sir, that is information I cannot give you.

With that Phillip stepped back in deference, though remaining in a place where he could continue to observe our obviously outlandish behavior.

Penelope was doing a little pout thing with her lips.

I'm sorry, Dr. Rochester.

Rothschild. Walter.

Walter.

Yes. See, Penelope, I'm actually in a sort of a bind. I wonder . . . if you might help me out. Some information.

More Nubian kings?

No, no. It's this Erin person.

I tried to lower my voice and leaned toward her over the counter, motioning with my hand for her to lean in, to get closer. She only wrinkled her forehead and leaned farther back, so I sort of had to whisper loudly. I could feel the queue stirring at my back.

I don't suppose, I whispered, you know where she lives? Could get me an address or something for her?

Her mouth fell open, slightly.

You takin' the piss?

No, no. I mean, it's nothing . . . not like that. I just need to find out where she is.

Why?

I can't really say right now. But, it's real important. A matter . . . a matter of . . . national security. I work for the British Museum, Ancient Near East Division. Look, here's my badge.

Penelope crossed her arms and chuckled. But I could tell she was curious. I don't think I normally come off as downright mad; people usually assume that I'm a sane person, and my requests are taken seriously and honored.

The people in line were beginning to stamp and shuffle. The woman directly behind me began letting out a series of long, plaintive sighs.

Bollocks! Penelope laughed. You trying to get into the slapper's trousers? What, you some kind of agent? You takin' the piss, are you?

By now the other counter personnel had stopped helping people and were watching and trying to listen in. The various patrons who were lined up to receive books began milling around in confusion like animals at the feed trough. Idle conversation at the book desk was a blatant insult to the serious scholarship being done here. I understood this of course; these were my people. All of a sudden *I* was the outsider, the interloper in the placid and orderly realm of contemplative research that was normally my domain.

Please, I said, you must help me. It's nothing . . . bad. Not like that.

The whole scene was creating a strange eddy in the flow of people and books, confusing some scholars who bumped into each other, their book carts piled high with leather-bound volumes, dropping sheets of paper that they held pinioned in their armpits and the pens that dangled out of their mouths.

A sweaty young man in line suddenly fumbled a heavy, antiquated volume that thumped awkwardly to the floor. The whole operation came to a standstill in a moment of quiet panic. The young boy knelt over the fallen book while the others stood about him in horror. Phillip stole forward from behind the desk, bent down to inspect the injured volume, and with a sharp cry seized the tome. With alarming speed and dexterity for such a decrepit-looking individual, he dashed off into the bowels of the library, the distraught young scholar at his heels.

I figured they would have some sort of photo record of her at the employment office, something I could see to verify that the woman I met and slept with on the floor of the Egyptian Statuary Room was in fact named Erin, hopefully with a last name as well. An address would also be helpful. Everyone who went into the reading rooms of the British Library was photographed and their data entered into the computer, and around their necks the employees all wore ID badges with pictures.

Please, I said. I don't want to get you in trouble.

Penelope seemed unconcerned about the scene we were making. I could tell by the way she held her head that she was sympathetic to my plight.

A rather odd girl, she was, Penelope said. Hasn't been here long. She did have a pint with me and some of the other girls a few weeks back.

Did she say *why* she was working here? Any reason?

Ho-ho, Penelope said, holding up a pale palm, I can't really say I remember anything like that.

Anything would be helpful.

Mmmm. I'll think about it. Listen, I really need to get back to work here.

Could I speak with you again about it? After work? Tonight?

Mmmm . . . I have a . . . plans.

It's really serious, I said. Life-and-death-type situation.

You could be some kind of nutter.

No, actually I'm nothing like that. Really.

Penelope finally agreed to meet me after her shift in a couple of hours, at the Bricklayer's Arms, a pub a few blocks north across Oxford Street. She was due to meet another friend there, but she said I could talk with her for a bit if I wanted. I made my way out of the library quickly, avoiding all contact. I didn't direct a single molecule of my presence anywhere near the tall African man at Alan's desk, though I felt his baleful eyes burning on my swollen face as I crossed the room.

I spent the next two hours down in the lab, staring at that implacable piece of black limestone, the Stela, gripping its worn edges with my hand. My face throbbed with every beat of my heart, and I couldn't help but touch it lightly with my fingers. Mick was crouched at the worktable inscribing a series of tablets with some kind of early Assyrian cuneiform script, pausing to murmur occasionally into an ear votive that he pressed to his lips. His whispers echoed about the stone floor and walls, driving me to distraction. My face ached and just thinking about the pain and my predicament—the stolen papyrus, the stolen book, my daughter, my inability to focus on the Stela in my last few days—almost brought tears to my eyes.

I laid out Stewart's translations again, next to my own version and the rest of my notes, scattered them out on the floor around the Stela. My current attempts hinged on the three clearly incised strokes at the top edge of the upper register, as noted first by Glanville and Burch. They misread the three marks, placing them with the sign above as part of the "raying sun" symbol. But it was the moon symbol, not the sun. I tried to sort through some of the basic horizontals I'd come up with:

Line 16: . . . *She is the great one(?)* . . . *She is his noble wedjat eye, the great one who is before him and who under the king as if the very throne that supports him* . . . *She who gives to him the sun* . . . *when he sails across the sky eternally* . . . *She who gives everything* . . .

I couldn't set up the ordering grid in my mind. I switched to more thematic possibilities: the pervasive elements in the present translation that might present some kind of subject-matter key to the third way. The central figure being Mut of course, a rarely used goddess when compared to Isis, for example, whose few references and subtle allusions generally placed her in the role of a "divine daughter" of some larger god figures. The iconography and epithets stick to a few key ideas: Mut as the bearer of the double crown, the unifier of a divided Egypt, a sort of "Mistress of Heaven," and perhaps most troubling, the "eye" and "daughter of Ra," or the all-powerful über god. Several references are made to how she "becomes the uraeus resting upon his brow," a sort of sprouting-forth metaphor similar to that of Athena: the daughter who springs forth from the forehead of the father. And finally, there are the references to what could be described as the fiery, tempestuous nature of her personality. I was trying to construct a loose template of these themes as another way to read the text, a way that might suggest a shape to the overall narrative.

I touched my face with one hand and cursed under my breath, waiting in the small glow of the spot lamp. I couldn't shut it out: Mick's whispering, the odd murmur in the hallway or a creak through the ceiling, the scratching of the rats moving into the basement corridors en masse, the sounds of electric pumps switching on somewhere deep in the bowels of the building, power, weight, energy shifting through the walls, and that other sound. Waiting, and watching the surface of the stone for movement.

Years ago my wife Helen would often heft one of my books, a scrap of ostracon, or perhaps hold a bit of papyrus gingerly in her hands, sitting in the study of our North Beach home or in the kitchen of our apartment in Jersey, and smile and shrug as if it was all something beyond her. Yet it seemed beautiful to her all the same. Helen was able to attach the significance that I desired, that this material existed in terms that went beyond our ordinary ability to understand them as simply written texts or historical documents. She understood what beast was driven before the flail. Even so, she held on the best she could.

When Helen came to visit me in Alexandria back in 1988, we would often go to see performances of traditional Egyptian music, something she was interested in. To me the music of Egypt sounded quite discordant and unsophisticated, based upon a musical system that was as foreign to general western conceptions as the hieroglyph itself. But Helen thought otherwise, and she tried to explain to me the differences and the similarities.

It's still all based upon a metered system, a set of regular beats, she'd say as we sat in some smoky, battered auditorium in the old quarter, at a table with fresh linen tablecloths and two bottles of still water, sweating in the heat. Ceiling fans stirred up the hot air into swirling vortexes that you could see forming in the fog of cigarette, cigar, and pipe smoke. The musicians on the stage sat on thick cushions in various poses and plunked and picked at a variety of oddly shaped instruments, from classical sitars to angled guitars that sounded roughly like banjos, as well as types of percussion instruments, some made of animal skins and others consisting of bells and wooden chimes.

We were the only westerners present, and multiple waiters hovered nearby, bringing a succession of water-beaded multicolored bottles that we had to refuse over and over. The rest of the spare crowd seemed vaguely annoyed that we were there. Many of them stared at us, this white couple, me dressed in my usual linen suit, Helen wearing a vague cotton dress and sandals, until I ordered our drinks in Alexandrian dialect, a very distinct patois that nobody but locals spoke anymore.

To me the concert sounded mostly like the band was still warming up, throughout the entire performance. But Helen was enraptured by it.

There is still a repeated theme, she said, a motif. It presents itself in far more subtle ways than western music. But it's still there. You have to listen a bit more closely.

Like jazz? I asked.

No, Helen said. Not like that at all. There is a far more structured element happening here. The complexity of the arrangement is fascinating.

I listened some more, trying to distinguish the individual notes played by each instrument, and trying to discern their relation.

It's as if each section has a signal, a certain harmonious chord that dictates the rest of the preceding piece, Helen said.

Like a hieroglyphic determinative, I said. In that it helps determine the meaning of the preceding phrase or statement.

She kept looking at the stage, her head nodding slightly with the swing and beat of the percussion. I know she resented the fact that I tried to apply everything to Egyptology and my work. It was my template, all I had to work with. I knew that I would never come to understand music in the way she did, and that these kinds of comparisons were just my attempts to enter that world.

The musicians wound up their set with a particularly chaotic clatter of strings and chimes, and the audience began to get up to leave. Helen was the only one who started clapping, and she stopped after a few moments.

Helen took a sip of her drink and then looked at me.

You know, she said, you could just say that you understood, for once. You could just agree and go on with it.

She picked up her bag and I followed her as we walked out into the night, the warm streets empty and bright with moonlight.

Penelope was waiting in the Bricklayer's Arms when I arrived, drinking a pint of cider and smoking a cigarette. She was wearing a different pair of glasses, thin, black ones that cut across the top of her round face like a Gothic bridge. There was a guy next to her on a stool, wearing one of those fashionable black turtlenecks and black jeans. You could spot him as a Swede from a mile away.

This is Magnus Magnusson, Penelope said. Magnus, this is Dr. Rothschild. He's the American nutter I told you about. Magnus met Erin before, didn't you?

Magnus grinned, displaying perfect, Swedish teeth. He was a very small man for such a grand name.

Ah yes, he said. Erin with the fine drugs and beautiful body.

Magnus is a computer programmer, Penelope said. He's developing his own interactive dating site, where you can pick out people you like and animate their pictures to see what they would look like doing certain things. You can even take off their clothes and see their virtual naked body, put them in poses, run them through a series of everyday activities. To see what they'd look like, yeah?

Yes, Magnus said. New site. Fully interactive.

It's a bit barmy, actually, Penelope said. You can even do a complete virtual date online. The Web site will factor in all the personal information provided and suggest a series of locations, all replicated digitally on-screen, and the whole thing will play itself out in real time. You don't even really have to do the date at all.

Yes, Magnus said. Real time. Video streaming.

That's really interesting, I said.

I spoke, Penelope said, with a few of the others at work. This girl Angie went around a bit with Erin. Said she liked some strange things, mysticism, Rosicrucians and such.

Sounds right, I said.

And, Penelope said, *and* that she was apparently using her time at the library to research Egyptian myths.

I took a large gulp of my pint of bitter. It tasted awful, as usual. Penelope watched me sideways from her stool. She seemed proud of herself. I'm not sure what sort of reaction she was expecting to this news. I reminded myself that I didn't know anything about this woman. I'd just been fleeced in much the same manner, and I wanted to be suspicious but the fact was I didn't have anything else to go on. She really didn't seem the type anyway.

We smiled into our drinks. The bartender was playing a string of 1970s radio hits, Electric Light Orchestra, Steely Dan, Super-tramp, songs I remembered from the radio and Helen's music collection. Penelope pulled a folded piece of paper from a microscopic black purse.

Here, she said. And you bloody well better not tell anybody where you got this.

It was a copy of some kind of basic employment record. In one corner there was a photo, a grainy, digitized snapshot, black and white, but it was Erin all right. "Full name: Erin Kaluza." The address cited was in Cambridge. I had been to Cambridge once before to give a talk on hieroglyphic poetics, but that was more than fifteen years ago. Penelope offered that it was a university address. Queens College.

Her age: thirty-eight. Stunning.

I got Ms. Intyre to run that off for me, Penelope said. She didn't even ask me what I wanted it for.

Does . . . would Erin remember you? I asked.

I suppose, Penelope said, she might recognize me. We talked a few times. She asked me to help her find a manuscript. An Egpytian translation of something or other, now that I think about it. Hey, it's all coming together now, Dr. Rothschild, innit?

Penelope gave me a leer and quaffed her cider.

Yes, I said, it seems it is.

I referred her, Penelope said, to the British Museum and UCL Institute of Archeology. I remember something about spells in the otherworld or afterworld. Written on little figurines. So what happened to your face?

I touched my swollen eye and forehead.

An accident, I said. Someone mistook me for someone else.

It didn't seem to fit. Most of the texts involved with mummification or the death ceremonies were made up of spells or oaths, often designed to protect the deceased in the afterworld. Many were written directly on the sarcophagus, and others were inscribed on the shabti, the little mummiform figurines that were placed in the tombs. Was that the "little figurines" that Penelope mentioned? The shabti were designed to carry out the physical burdens of the deceased in the afterlife, to act as a sort of slave labor. The Amun papyrus, based on what we knew about the Temple of Amun at Karnak and the Stela of Paser itself, was much more likely concerned with warnings, protection spells, and various proclamations to Amun and Mut. Not shabti.

All this time Magnus smoked and grinned at me like I was some sort of juggling lunatic. It was beginning to bug me.

When did you see Erin last, Magnus? Penelope said.

Ah, few weeks ago. She was at a party of my friends. She drank all my vodka. I lick her neck and she give me some good pills. I was up three days.

Well, I said, do you have any idea where she might be right now?

My friend, Magnus said, maybe I can tell you.

Magnus looked at Penelope. She shrugged.

Come to my flat, he said. Tonight. We are having a party.

He took out a business card and wrote an address on the back of it, then handed it to me. It said: "Magnus Magnusson. Interactive Web Page Design. VirtualDate.Com—the Latest in Interactive Matchmaking Technology."

I knew I had to meet Zenobia at her hotel in Mayfair for dinner; I would have to wait till after that. I wondered if Zenobia would possibly like to come along to the Swede's party.

You come at, say, midnight? Magnus said. Maybe Erin be there tonight? I think I invite her last time. Bring vodka.

9:   WASH THIS HEART

SOMEHOW MY DAUGHTER ZENOBIA had become a giant. She has always had a presence, a certain intimidating power, and she uses it well, standing as close to you as possible, leaning in, eyes fixed clearly on yours. I suppose it served her well in her business. Things had changed since our last meeting in New York when she was running that tiny women's magazine. Zenobia started that magazine with a few friends of hers from Mount Holyoke and apparently a few months after our lunch a massive New York publisher bought the thing and installed Zenobia as the principal vice president in charge of design and layout. She was only twenty-four years old.

Zenobia was coming to London for a meeting with the London publishing office of her new magazine corporation. Her hotel, Clairbourne's, was one of those hotels in London that are so exclusive and expensive they don't even have a sign or distinguishing mark on the building to let you know it's a hotel. I suppose if you don't know, you can't afford it. I waited in the small, hushed lobby, done up in the popular minimalist style, dark colors and bare walls. I was sitting on a delicate black couch that perched like a spider on a thin bamboo mat. A small, neat fire flickered in the fireplace. A thin man in a dark suit stood in an alcove, frowning at me through his green-tinted glasses.

An elevator door opened at the back and Zenobia came striding into the room, followed by another woman. I'm only about five-ten and my wife Helen is no more than five-four, but our daughter Zenobia is a towering figure, six feet tall, a huge mane of dirty-blond hair, wide shoulders and hips, large feet with wide, flat toes that draped over the edge of rough leather sandals, fastened to her feet by a system of thick straps that wound up her knotted calves. She was wearing a tight olive skirt and a matching well-tailored blazer. She had her hair long and uncombed, no makeup or distinctive jewelry of any kind. The room seemed to shrink before her.

Zenobia was dictating something to the woman at her elbow who was scribbling furiously on some kind of electronic organizer. When she saw me standing there she finished up what she was saying. Then she turned to me.

Hello, Dr. Rothschild.

I walked over to her. The woman at her elbow, who was wearing thin glasses that were tinted yellow, stopped scribbling.

Hello, Zenobia, I said.

I reached out with one hand. She just stood there, with her arms at her sides, and I ended up just sort of lightly tugging on the sleeve of her jacket.

It's good to see you, I said. You look great.

You too, Dr. Rothschild. The picture of health.

Zenobia turned to her assistant.

Is the car ready?

The assistant took a mobile from her jacket pocket and flipped it open.

Mort? This is Jean-Louise. Is the car around? Good. We're coming out.

Let's go, Zenobia said. I'm starving.

We walked outside and got into a long, dark Mercedes that idled at the curb. Jean-Louise walked us out and closed the door, then bending down to the open window she said: When you are through with this we need to meet with Gillian and Ariel about the corporate-sponsorship package. I've programmed the address and numbers.

Jean-Louise handed Zenobia a mobile phone through the window.

If you need anything, she said, ring me.

Jean-Louise looked directly at me and her eyes narrowed, yellow.

Nice meeting *you*, Dr. Rothschild.

I gave the driver instructions to the restaurant, which turned out to be only about ten blocks away. I tried to keep the bruised side of my face, the enormous purple welt that now covered a full third of it, turned away from her.

I figured we'd just walk, I said, but since you have this car and all . . .

Zenobia just nodded and continued looking out the window at the gaudy display windows of Harrods and the other high-end department stores and boutiques of Mayfair as we passed through toward the Strand. She made a small motion with her hand, as if to say, *whatever.*

I took her to my favorite Indian place in London, the India Club, in the Hotel Strand Continental. The restaurant is on the third floor, up a dingy flight of stairs, a narrow, cramped place with cheap wooden tables and chairs, bathroom tile floors, bare walls, even cheaper food, and curries that were the closest thing in London to what you might find on the streets of India. We went up the tottering stairs, past the faded and smoky men's lounge on the second floor filled with elderly Indian men in white T-shirts and linen trousers, sitting on the tattered furniture, frowning at the television. Zenobia was completely serene, unflappable. I opened the unmarked door to the simple dining room, feeling proud and a bit mystified by how my genetic material had produced such a being.

I ordered a variety of curries and chutneys for us along with rice and nan. I offered to run down to the newsagent to pick up a few bottles of Cobra beer, quite good with a hot curry, but Zenobia politely declined, saying she'd rather just have water. The place was full of English businessmen, many of them actual ex-colonials, sitting about tables filled with small silver dishes of food and empty bottles of Cobra, older, portly, silver-haired gentlemen of the kind who still wore three-piece suits with pocket watches, and who seemed rather lighthearted and pleasant, perhaps due to the surroundings that may have reminded them of the easy days of British colonialism. Zenobia looked positively regal as she stared my eyes into the table. The waiters hustled to bring her fresh water after she drained her glass.

I loved her in those moments more than ever.

I was not some kind of automaton; I had felt the twisting burn of love before. And not just paternal love; besides Helen and Zenobia, the largest loves in my life, there were others as well. I was not invulnerable to the charms of desirable women. The situation I was in made that abundantly clear. There was a linear progression stemming from my failing in this department. If only the solution were a matter of backtracking or adjusting course, making a tacking maneuver into the winds of the future, or destiny.

The science of translation, much like mathematics, is so obvious in the same manner, or at least it appears to be. There is no confusing the right or wrong answer. But the science only goes so far. The ancient Egyptians had a sense of poetry and subtle inflections of metaphor the same as we do. This is made even more puzzling and frustrating for the cryptographer by up to four thousand years of cultural perspective and historical interpretation. An ancient Egyptian cryptographer feels for the words in the dark with his hands lopped off, digging in the sand with his stumps to find answers.

Zenobia had her mother's stubbornness, to be sure. She still seemed to desire to flail away at the possibility of a relationship. Our last meeting in New York did not go well by any means. Zenobia stormed out of the cafe, and I ended up staying in a cheap hotel in Brooklyn for my last few days, wandering around the borough and along the East River, trying to consider the possibility that it was all over, once again.

At the moment she was powering through the curries like a harvesting combine, taking large dollops of chutneys, wiping up the excess with broad leaves of nan, and knocking back whole glasses of water at a time.

We talked about her new job, the magazine and related matters. The large media company that bought her fledgling magazine was so impressed with her work that they basically jacked the budget up tenfold, with a massive injection of marketing. The distribution was set to go through the roof, as there was no real magazine of its kind on the market. Zenobia had almost complete authority on all content matters as well as design. A women's magazine without the usual lead stories on sex and dieting, a magazine for the real modern woman, as Zenobia put it, none of this eye-candy garbage that put a generation of girls into eating-disorder clinics. She was still chewing and spooning chutneys into her mouth as she talked.

While I was doing my master's at Columbia, she said, I discovered that most women's studies and humanities departments were engaged in a form of hypocritical liberal fascism, victimization, and debilitating group-think strategies that eventually were swamped in a morass of ambiguity and academic jargon that prohibited the real ideas present to make a dent in anything beyond the theoretical models. This magazine is intended to change all that.

I didn't know she had gone to Columbia and gotten a master's degree. I suppose there were lots of details that I didn't know about her life. To be honest I had no idea what she was talking about.

It seems like an awfully large task, I said.

She wiped her mouth daintily with her napkin, one cheek bulging with curry.

Ambitious, I said. Sounds great.

The influence, she said, of magazines and glossy print media in general is unprecedented among women.

Zenobia looked at me, staring hard, as if she was expecting me to contest this idea. I shrugged and watched the oily paths of chicken madras ripple across my plate.

How's your mother doing? I said.

Zenobia laid down her fork and spoon for the first time in almost an hour. She chewed for a moment, her eyes on her plate, then swallowed audibly.

She's doing well, she said.

What's wrong? Is she still playing?

Yes, yes, she said. That's all fine.

Zenobia put her chin in her hand and leaned on the table, looking around at the tables of businessmen surrounding us, silver-haired, vested gents clinking their beer glasses together in solemn toasts, their faces flushed with booze, curries, and age.

I don't really know, Zenobia said. She's still playing. And giving lessons. But she doesn't always seem happy. You understand?

No, I said, I don't. Not really.

That's just what I don't get, she said. Don't you ever experience emotional turmoil in any way? Are you ever unhappy for no particular reason?

Yes, I said. I do. I am.

Helen's last trip to Egpyt was the end of it. The first day we were standing on the shores of the Red Sea. The crystalline waters, blue and edged like stone, stretched out before us in the gentle bow of the horizon. This was in 1989, two years after the last time Helen and

Zenobia came to visit me in Cairo. Zenobia was now sixteen, and going to a private boarding school in New Hampshire. I was grateful that Helen came, that she agreed to make another trip after what happened last time. I was trying to be gracious and accommodating, but it wasn't working out.

We were walking along the shore, watching the sunlight play off the water and a small group of Muslim women in full black burkas, covered head to toe, windsurfing in the light chop. I have no idea where they came from as there was no one else on the beach or in the water. The women ripped through the low waves, executing sharp cuts back across the grain of the wind, their burkas popping in the wind, flashing by one another in wordless displays of athletic ferocity. Occasionally one would waver and topple, only to emerge a moment later, the flat sail springing to life and the massy, dripping form of the dark veil would rise upright, whisking along the blue water. It made Helen smile, and she cheered them on.

It must work like a wet suit, Helen said, laughing.

I was feeling grand, resplendent. I swept a hand in front of us, over the horizon.

The compass of our simple firmament, I said, it's so clear to see from here.

I was trying to be humorous. Helen often liked my pedantic style of oration and what she called my "intellectual phrasing." But she scowled at this.

That's stupid, she said. Don't you know that is an optical illusion? You can't actually see the curve of the earth like that.

I watched the waves touch the sky as I stood in the water up to my ankles. It lapped warmly around my calves and feet in surges, thick and salty like blood. I watched the burka windsurfers rip along the water, their clothing snapping behind them like flags. It's my fault, I know it. I never could unfold the image of a woman. I clutter it up. Like using the wrong gloss on an unknown transliteration.

We stood there for a few more minutes, watching the windsurfing burkas disappear in a line somewhere over the bend of the horizon.

It just got worse from there. We spent most of the rest of her trip at the American hospital in Cairo. Even though I told her not to, she sat on the beach one day in just her bathing suit, without a blanket under her, and parasites that live in the sand corkscrewed themselves into the soft flesh of her buttocks. They had to burn them out with a laser. She was on her stomach for five days, and I sat by her bed the entire time. We didn't hold hands and barely spoke. I tried to give her a check to help with Zenobia's private-school tuition, but she tore it up. In the evening she would cry silently, wordlessly, until she fell asleep. I sat there and watched her breathing relax and turn even, and through the window the night rose up like a cloak of stars over Cairo, turning the ancient sandstone of the old quarter a pale green in the starlight, and bathing my wife, my beautiful wife, in its warm glow.

So I laid the whole thing out to Zenobia, my current dilemma, my eminent dismissal from the world of Egyptology. I left out certain parts of course.

That'd be a bitch, Zenobia said.

That's one way of putting it.

Is this item worth a lot of money?

Not really sure, I said. I mean, I haven't actually seen it yet. It is very likely priceless.

Who would buy it?

Certain collectors of antiquities. There's always a market.

Zenobia used her last wedges of nan to wipe her plate clean.

So you don't mind? I said. If I take off for Cambridge tomorrow?

Did they knock you out first? What'd they hit you with? A shovel?

Not quite sure, I said. Well, I know it was a man's fist. But that is a whole different thing. I mean it's not connected. Probably.

Go ahead, she said. Save your career. Doesn't bother me.

Something else, I said. Could I borrow some money?

Jesus.

She looked even more disappointed, if that was possible.

For what? A new jacket? You were wearing that same one when I last saw you, like, five years ago. You look like hell.

For the tickets to Cambridge, I said. And it was three years ago. I like this jacket. I'll pay you back next week. How long are you staying? I'll be back tomorrow night.

She leaned back in her chair and looked at me, genuinely sad, or at least considering something that seemed awful and tragic. I'm not sure what she wanted me to say. She took out her leather organizer and tossed a few crisp pound notes on the table.

You can check for me at the hotel, she said. I don't know how long these meetings will take. Maybe all week, maybe a few days. Besides, I'm supposed to meet up with someone else for a brief holiday at some point. So maybe.

Who? A man? A boyfriend?

She scowled.

You are ridiculous, she said. Do you know how ridiculous you are?

What?

She just looked at me for a few moments. I had my hands up in the air, my shoulders shrugged. I really wanted her to tell me just what was so ridiculous. I thought about *The Instruction of Any*, a New Kingdom instructional text: *When as a youth you take a wife, and you are settled in your house, pay attention to your offspring, bring them up as did your mother. Do not give her cause to blame you, lest she raise her hands to god, and he hears her cries.* After a while I put my hands down and pawed at the remaining traces of curry on my plate. Finally she sighed heavily and dropped her head, covering her face with her hands.

What?

Dad, you should know something, she said through her hands. She raised her head and looked me straight in the eye.

Mom isn't alone anymore, she said. There is someone else now.

The waiter walked up with our check on a small silver tray. Zenobia grabbed it before it hit the table, drew out her organizer again, like a pistol, threw some more bills on the table and stood up. I had a scrap of nan in my hand that I was playing with, drawing little designs in the remaining sauce on my plate. I was suddenly aware of this, and I looked down to my plate with a strange sense of wonder. I didn't even understand what she was saying.

Well, sure, I said. I figured there was.

Well, it's more than that. She's not just *with* someone.

I concentrated on the glyphs forming on my plate. A cluster of three signs: the horned asp, a flowering reed, a loaf of bread—crudely positioned and rendered with some difficulty as the sauce thinned. I debated pouring more sauce on the plate. *Her father.*

She remarried, Zenobia said. She got married last year. She didn't know how to tell you.

The sauces on my plate began to thin and run together like watercolors. My bruised face ached and began beating audibly in my ears and I could feel the blood pumping through the smashed vessels and trickling around the tender nerve endings. I put one hand to my cheek, the other still tracing faint symbols.

The seated offering, the actions of the eye, the asp over the hand, the broken bowl.

I instinctively felt my pockets for my ear votive. Gone. I felt it again, coursing through my face, a radiating wave of something, beating with a separate heart.

Zenobia turned and walked out of the restaurant. I collected the empty plates and lined them up in front of me, wiping them clean. I took all the remaining metal bowls of curries and chutneys and arranged them by color and using my scrap of nan, now soggy between my fingers, dipped it into the bowls and drew out the rest of the hieroglyphs.

My daughter, born under the heart-shaped sun and the sickle moon.
Her mother, my wife.
Where is the river that will wash this heart?

I walked along the Strand and back up St. Martin's Lane toward Bloomsbury and my flat. It was near eleven o'clock and the streets were running high with stragglers, various people whom the night hadn't yet coughed up onto their beds, exhausted and wondering. Mostly couples and clusters of blokes just out from the pubs, staggering and laughing and jesting with one another in that distinctly English way, a grip on the shoulder and a handful of charcoal suits and black mufflers, the women swaying under the unsteady arm of a man, holding the glowing nub of a cigarette, their eyes on the sidewalk, a faraway smile on their lips.

They streamed out of the pubs in long lines of cursing and laughter, small tributaries feeding into the river that moved along the sidewalks, emerging from Garrick Street and Long Acre, feeding off into the cabs that swooped along the curbsides like ravens, all the while chatting, screaming, expressions and sayings archaic and often unintelligible to my American ears. Other couples stripped off the main branch and fled into the dark corners and alleyways to grapple among the cigarette butts, urine stains, and fluttering trash, leaning against stone doorways, half-shadowed from the streetlight and noise, pressing their black-clad bodies together, pasty faces mashing with eyes closed in that characteristic European fashion of unabashed romantic physical contact.

At night the dark alcoves of the streets of London were always crammed, nook and cranny, with groping couples, each trying hard to solve some inscrutable mystery that lay in the face of their partner, on their tongue, their lips, their neck, feeling with their hands for the next possible secret, working with exhausted limbs, feverish, shuffling feet.

Certainly this fervor was mostly temporary. In the morning they would wake up, hungover, out of cigarettes and late for the train, each trying to piece together the evening, hastily applying makeup, tying a double Windsor, and hoping all the while to remember what it was about this pallid side of flesh snoring in the sheets that had brought them to this bleak shore of morning. No, the affairs of the heart are simple, fragile, and as unpredictable as the movement of leaves, the minds of insects. Only the physics of order, the planetary concerns of history held any real balance, any weight, any lasting power. Normally this sort of observation would allow me to pull my collar up around my ears and hunch down into the jacket of my personal diffidence and sense of superiority. But tonight, as I made my way past the theatres and dimly lit pubs, I found myself wishing for something brief and tenuous, of momentary significance, something to push myself up against in the dark doorways and alleys for a few frantic moments in the late hours of this world.

10: SWEDISH PORN

I GOT A BOTTLE of vodka from the corner store and flagged down a cab, all paid for with Zenobia's generous loan. The address Magnus had given me was way up in Kensington, past Notting Hill Gate, off Ladbroke Grove. The cabbie had to circle the block a few times to find the place, apparently located above a shop on a narrow alley of Arab butchers and kebab shops. To get to Magnus's flat I had to walk through a butcher shop specializing in halal meats and other Middle Eastern meat products.

The man behind the counter didn't even glance at me when I walked in. He was tall and severe-looking, with a short, curved dagger, something I recognized as a jambiya, the traditional weapon of men from the country of Yemen, stuck in the belt of his futah skirt. The scabbard was inlaid with all sorts of stones and tracings of gold. One half of the meat case was filled with glorious slabs of marbled meats, glistening on wax paper like jewels, and the other half of the case was filled with tender bunches of qat, the green leafy narcotic that Yemenis chew as a routine part of their day. There was no one else in the place. The shopkeeper's right cheek bulged with a wad of qat that he chewed in a gentle circular motion.

At the other end of the room there was a door that led up a short flight of stairs to another door. I could hear the sounds of music and voices coming down the stairs like water. The music was steady and thumping, and because I was alive and somewhat conscious in the 1970s, it took only a few seconds to recognize the beat and tune: ABBA.

I opened the door holding my vodka in front of me like a talisman. It was dark and hot inside the flat and cigarette smoke was issuing forth into the hall in tunneling channels. Immediately I tripped on an enormous pile of shoes, and pitching forward I clumsily tossed my bottle of vodka into the arms of a man standing by the door before I hit the ground. It was so dim in the hall that I couldn't make out his face, but he helped me to my feet and explained, shouting over the music in a thick Swedish accent, that it was traditional at Swedish parties to take off one's shoes at the door and walk about in your socks or bare feet. I was rather embarrassed by the state of my socks, which I'm sure didn't match, but the hall was so dark I couldn't see my feet anyway. I retrieved my vodka and added my sad loafers to the sprawling pile.

It became immediately clear that this party was populated by a race of enormously tall, fleshy, grinning, towheaded beings who smoked and chatted in clucking tones over my head as I walked this dim gauntlet. I knew I had some Scandinavian stock in my blood from my mother's side, Danish merchants who cornered the cod market in the nineteenth century, but at this moment I felt most deeply my father's Hebrew roots, dark and swarthy, like a gnarled Shylock crawling from under a bridge.

As is natural in most desperate situations, I headed toward the only clear light source, which turned out to be the kitchen. Here giants relaxed in various poses, sitting upon the counter and squatting on the bowed kitchen table, their enormous feet tucked under them, all holding bottles or glasses of ice and alcohol, mostly vodka, all smoking and talking in several languages at a furious rate. There was a slight smudge to the crowd that turned out to be Penelope, a squat mushroom among the stalks of Swedes, leaning on the sink, talking with Magnus Magnusson, who also looked positively tiny next to the towering blond female who bent near him. As I made my way toward them, vaulting over outstretched legs and hurdling an array of long, stockinged feet, I began to realize that most of the people in this room, especially the blondes of extraordinary stature, were female. Most of the men were built much more like Magnus, a bit shorter than medium height, wiry, with hair the color of dirty dishwater.

Penelope looked bored, staring at some indeterminate space between Magnus and his amazon companion. Magnus was gesturing with his hands in such a way that made it perfectly clear he was discussing either some technical aspect of his computer exploits or a particular sexual escapade. The tall blonde seemed most concerned with polishing off her glass of vodka without ruining her lipstick. I stared at Penelope, just long enough for her to feel it, and she looked up, smiled broadly at first, then seemed to be aware of it and frowned to compensate. She waved me over.

Magnus clamped his cigarette between his teeth and stuck out his hand.

Ah, Dr. Rothschild! Here is someone I want you to meet: Dr. Rothschild, this is Siegrund.

Siegrund swallowed my hand with hers, a puzzled look on her forehead.

Beautiful, yes? Magnus shouted.

I nodded to both of them and smiled.

Any sign of Erin? I asked Penelope.

She shook her head. Magnus took the bottle from my hand and refreshed everyone's drinks. He reached into a cabinet without turning around and fished out a tall glass. He grabbed some ice from a bag in the sink, poured the glass full of vodka and handed it to me.

Cheers! Siegrund is beautiful, yes?

I took a sip of the burning liquid. Penelope grabbed my elbow.

So. Dr. Rothschild. What are you *doing* chasing this girl around anyway? Are you going to explain all this or what?

Siegrund looked at me expectantly. It was clear that she didn't know English and wasn't understanding any of this, her brows gathered between her eyes and her head cocked like a spaniel's.

Magnus, have you seen Erin? The woman I told you I was looking for?

But Magnus was busy ripping off a stream of Swedish to Siegrund, shouting into her neck. The smoke in the kitchen was overwhelming. I sipped my drink, and thinking of that first night at the Lupo Bar I was struck with panic. What was I doing here? For a moment I thought I might vomit.

I don't think she's here, Penelope said.

I'm going to take a look around, I said.

I'll come with you, she said.

We navigated a circuitous route through the party, traveling between various small rooms all jammed with Swedes smoking and drinking furiously. The flat was surprisingly large for London, though most every room seemed to have bedding and other personal effects. It was quickly clear that Erin wasn't there. But, as Penelope shouted in my ear, that bloody well doesn't mean she won't show up later. After all, it was barely past midnight.

As we emerged from one room, Magnus cornered us in a small passageway, again with another tall blonde on his arm.

A beautiful blonde, no?

Yes, very nice.

I tried to nod politely at the woman. I gave Penelope a look that she seemed to pick up right away.

Magnus, she said, why the fuck you so bloody interested in what Dr. Rothschild thinks of Swedish women?

It's all right, I said. Really. I don't mind.

Magnus just grinned and kept nodding his head toward his companion. Penelope glared at him.

Step outside for a sec? Penelope said. I need to get out of this fucking smoke.

We walked down the stairs and into the Muslim deli. Penelope went up to the counter and spoke a few brief phrases in Arabic and was rewarded with two cups of steaming dark coffee and a handful of damp qat wrapped in newspaper.

Outside I asked if she was fluent in Arabic.

Nah, Penelope said, but I was born and raised in the East End. Bayswater, yeah?

The night was cold and damp, and the streets were empty. The halal meat store was the only place open. To the east we could hear the distant sounds of traffic in West Central London. We sat on the steps outside and Penelope stuffed a wad of the leafy greens into her cheek and then handed me the paper. I took what I thought was a respectable pinch and starting chewing. It tasted roughly like raw spinach leaves. The stimulating narcotic effect of the plant combined with the cup of strong Turkish coffee had us both on our feet in a few minutes, jabbering at each other like magpies.

I know it has something to do with blondes, Penelope said, and the strange fascination men, particularly American men, have with them.

I was doing a little heel-and-toe shuffle on the sidewalk.

Hmmmm, I said.

You know, the whole bit with pornography. "Swedish Porn" and "blond Swedish girls," Penelope said, making little quote motions with her fingers.

Why do you think that is? I said. I mean, why would a culture that is perhaps more well known for its frigid pragmatism and an ancient legacy of violent expansion now become the byword for pornography?

Exactly.

We should ask Magnus, I said.

Penelope shifted the qat in her mouth and spoke around the juicy wad with some difficulty.

It must be, she said, the unconscious rejection of that same history, the blond connection. Blondes are dumb and like sex, therefore Swedish girls, who are mostly blondes, must be dumb and like sex.

A whole nation of sexpots.

Brilliant, Penelope said. And how they embrace it.

Always practical, I said. Willing to capitalize on the prevailing winds.

Like Leif Eriksson.

Wanna dance? I asked.

The Scandinavian races, she said, are so *bloody* curious.

Same stock here as well.

It's just men, ya know? The Swedish fantasy? Some kind of subconscious projection. You know, how when men do the cross-dressing bit? How they always turn into the girls that men want: the oversexed tart, basically a whore with wit and wisecracks?

I'll take your word for it.

Women, on the other hand, when they assume a male dress and persona, they most often turn into the kind of man they *hate*. The nasty sort. Lager lout, cat's-bottom type of bloke, obnoxious and all that. The very kind that's nasty to women.

Maybe women just don't like . . . women?

You're a bloody genius, Professor.

Thanks.

Then some guys will put on a dress and become a quiet little mouse, a little sweetheart? I think that's *so* sweet. Maybe that's what we should do to figure out what kind of guy a bloke is? Get him to put on a bit of dress and eye paint, see what he turns into? Know what I mean?

You seem to have thought a lot about this.

Problem is, even with this information we'd probably *still* go with the real pricks.

I felt a bit anxious. I removed my qat, a dripping, soggy mess, and tossed it in the alley. Penelope did the same, and to this day I've never seen a woman remove something so large, soft, and terribly disgusting from her mouth so unselfconsciously and gracefully. It was a beautiful thing. She slugged back the rest of her coffee and looked at me. Her eyes were like moons.

Did you say something about dancing?

So there I was, dancing with Penelope, or at least what might pass for dancing, in the midst of a gaggle of whirling Swedes, a strict disco-only policy in effect. Penelope mostly jumped straight up and down, her eyes closed. I made a point of trying to hold on to her hands, mostly because the thrashing crowd threatened to bear either one of us off at any moment. Penelope's forehead was crimped with delicate lines as she bounced in time to the beat of Chic's "Good Times," her head flopping from side to side. She wiped the sweat from her face and grinned at me and I was struck by her pale dumpling face, the dark brown eyes that sparkled in the dim light of the Swede's apartment. Then Penelope executed a quick spinning maneuver and after a few rotations her momentum sent her staggering into an end table, knocking a couple of glasses and an overstuffed ashtray to the floor. When she attempted to recover, her big toe hooked an electrical cord and sent a small floor lamp airborne, angling like a knobby javelin into the dancing crowd. A cloud of Swedish curses erupted.

I need a break, she shouted in my ear.

The kitchen, I shouted back.

At around three o'clock Magnus came by to bring us cans of a stimulant drink called Red Bull and bade us mix it with our vodka. He called it a "Smartie." Very sweet, and slightly mediciney tasting, but the energy jolt was almost immediate, and disguised well the enormous amounts of vodka. This on top of the slight buzz from the qat and Turkish coffee produced an effect that I can only describe as infinitely possible. I also felt taller, maybe a bit Swedish. Then someone put on a song, a Supertramp song, the same song we'd heard in the pub earlier.

Hey, I said, it's that song!

Penelope looked puzzled.

What are you talking about?

We heard it in the pub earlier today. Supertramp.

More frowzy brow wrinkling from Penelope. It was so cute, really.

I just like the song, I said.

Then it was over and the next song blared forth and suddenly in the large room a dozen or so people were dancing frantically to the Bee Gees. Soon Magnus, Siegrund, and most everyone else was stomping their way through "You Should Be Dancing," adding another layer of bass to the music, and bringing most of the pictures off the walls in sporadic shatterings of wood and glass. I was grateful that Penelope wanted to stay in the kitchen and talk, which was mostly cleared out except for a couple of Swedes smoking a cone-shaped joint that was as wide as a beer can at the large end. The smoke generated was incredible, and the Swedes fell into severe fits of convulsive laughter, broken by occasional singsong replies in their language that would send them into more paroxysms of howling. Penelope and I sequestered ourselves on the kitchen counter, looking at each other, red eyed and dripping with sweat. I wasn't even thinking about what I was there for, how this all began, the trouble I was in. I would soon see my daughter again; I would have another chance. Even the Stela was a dim shadow, lying somewhere over the horizon. This was current time, this moment, the present, now.

So, have you actually been to Egypt? she asked.

Many times, I said. I was just there last year.

The sphinx, the pyramids, all that?

Of course.

Is it true, Penelope asked, about Napoleon's soldiers defacing the sphinx? Shooting the nose off or some rot like that?

Well, I said, it seems that they did pass through there and there are written accounts of soldiers using the sphinx for target practice, but in terms of the actual damage, they didn't do much. The deterioration of the sphinx has much more to do with the fact that it was carved out of a shelf of living rock, the limestone plateau of Giza. Old Kingdom. Fourth Dynasty. When they were quarrying for the great pyramids they decided to go ahead and carve something out of the resulting hole, so to speak.

What do you mean, *living* rock?

Well, I mean living in terms of geology, I said. There are three separate stratifications of rock in the sphinx. It's still moving, shifting. It's evolving. One of the layers is as soft as talc—you can scratch it with your finger.

Surely it won't last another thousand years?

Might, depending on preservation efforts, I said. However, with something so fragile and shifting like it is, I doubt it.

Does that bother you?

I'd rather it stayed put.

And that's pretty much what you do, isn't it? Try to keep things like the sphinx up and intact, eh?

I suppose, I said. Though I mostly deal with ancient texts. I'm technically a cryptographer, a translator, not an archeologist or geologist or anthropologist. Though those fields often intersect.

So where did you come from? she said. How did you get here?

I work at the British Museum, I told you.

I mean before that.

I watched the dancers in the other room. Magnus was being tossed like a beach ball between a pair of giant female Swedes, a mad grin on his face as he hooted with delight. Penelope lit a cigarette, blowing a plume of smoke from her jutting lower lip, and rearranged herself on the counter, sitting in a lotus position so that she faced me.

Okay, she said. Let's hear it. Dr. Rothschild's story. How you came to be who you are.

I wasn't sure if I'd ever even considered it before. So I started at the beginning.

11:   THE ENGINEER

MY FATHER WAS A careful man. He was also a self-made millionaire, two things that don't often seem to go together. My father was the son of a bootlegger and small-time crook in rural Virginia. As a boy he spent his free time taking apart the tractor and building crude radio crystal sets in the woodshed. He was the only one of his eight brothers and sisters to leave the county and go to college. After his B.A. at Virginia Tech, he won a scholarship at Syracuse to continue his engineering studies at the newly formed School for Applied Civic Engineering. It was a radical new system of pedagogy, based on the certainty of scientific and mechanistic innocence, a thing to be developed correctly and brought to the world for its own benefit. The study ranged from Christopher Wren to Frank Lloyd Wright to Tycho Brahe to Oppenheimer to the great dam builders of Mesopotamia. A new class of engineer walked out of the halls into the hazy New York sunshine, pale, stooped, blinking, with great visions of spinning turbines and gleaming spans, new polymer plastics, untested shapes that clung to the briefest hint of theoretical physics, of changing not just the shape but the very fabric of the landscape.

It was only a few years later that he was one of the chief engineers for the Saint Lawrence dam project, overseeing two hundred million dollars worth of federal funds and hundreds of laborers, architects, engineers, hydrodynamics scientists, everybody. He was successful as a civic engineer because he was both visionary and cautious. He took the safety and logistics of his projects very seriously, and I suppose this carried over into his private life. My father carefully chose a wife, my mother, and carefully had a single child, me.

I grew up in the double-wide trailers and prefab on-site office spaces of massive civic-engineering projects. My parents basically left it up to me and I chose to live the first sixteen years of my life in such places as Fishkill, Arkansas, and Sewanee, Tennessee, where my father was building massive dams and soaring bridges. Would any young boy choose differently? Each project seemed to take just about a year, and in between we'd head back to Syracuse, where we had a comfortable upper-middle-class home, and where my mother lived, baking loads of sweet confections and often changing the decorating scheme of the house. Every time we came home we never knew what to expect; she would gut the place as soon as we left and replace everything with some other style of decor. We went through French Country, Willow, Timber and Mahogany, Arts & Crafts, and a long stint with variations on Art Deco. I guess it was the loneliness that did it; she had to fill the time doing something. But when we came home it was all smiles and hugs, she was so proud of us and glad to see us again, and did we like the new furniture? Would we like to see the new flowers in the garden? How about some fresh ginger snaps and herbal tea?

My mother grew up in Buffalo, the single daughter of a wealthy chemical-company executive. She met my father when some of her sorority sisters from Buffalo State College took a trip to Syracuse to attend the annual Cherry Blossom Festival. My father helped her park the enormous Buick she was driving and lit her cigarette. After she had me she started suffering from several clinical emotional disorders that required her to take massive doses of high-grade lithium for the rest of her adult life, focusing her manic energy on pleasant and orderly sorts of tasks. Our backyard garden was legendary in the neighborhood. I never witnessed a single gesture of affection between my father and mother as long as they were alive.

I was in school for only about half of the time I was living at home. As most of the project sites were way out in the sticks, far from any decent school, most of my education was done at home, or I should say, "self-taught." My father let me order any book I wanted out of whatever catalogs I could scare up, including whole sets of encyclopedias and mini-libraries of classics and world history. I suppose you could say that my education was reading books. My father never really checked up on me, never really tried to direct my reading or help my education along in any real way other than by supplying me with reading material.

So I spent most of my early days lying on a cot in my father's on-site trailer, reading for hours at a time while just outside the door my father dug, scraped, hammered, and poured vast monuments to the miracles of modern industry. Certainly I did lots of exploring of the various sites, climbing around the structures and squeezing into dangerous spots like any other kid would feel compelled to do. But I was quickly accustomed to the kinds of massive structures my father built; I looked into the cavernous yawn of canyons freshly dammed, watched a million gallons of cement poured into the steel frames, plummeting hundreds of feet into the darkness, watched the curious spiderlike piecemeal work of bridge building, where slabs of steel and concrete were placed like so many toothpicks by bored titans. Enormous machines that crawled, crammed, and hoisted the materials across chasms, vehicles with tracked treads, wheels that weighed thousands of pounds, vehicles that could pass over the trailer where I lay without so much as scraping their bellies, vehicles that thundered with deafening tones, belching smoke and noise, vehicles that created and destroyed with the wrench of a rusted lever. The earth literally exploded beneath my feet; mountains moved, seas were redirected, all the various forces of nature were brought to bear under the power of machinery and science. This feature, the destruction and creation of lands and rivers, is the figurative marker, the determinative of my youth.

I was twelve years old when my father was picked as a consultant for the Aswan High Dam project in August 1962. I spent the next eight months in Aswan, just above the first cataract of the Nile, the traditional southern boundary of Egypt. When the U.S. and other European powers bailed on funding the project, the Soviets jumped at the chance. Egyptian president Nasser had nationalized the Suez Canal, and the Soviets saw this as their chance to get in on the ground floor. The Soviets had bit off a bit more than they could chew, though, and they surreptitiously recruited a few select international engineers and designers, mostly from a Boston firm that my father was loosely associated with, to serve as consultants. There was also the matter of the relocation of the local Nubian inhabitants and several large ancient structures like the Great Temple of Abu Simbel to higher ground. It wasn't seen as a patriotic thing to do necessarily, working with the Russians, but my father could never resist the next great challenge. He was always seeking out larger and larger projects, always wanting his constructions to be greater in size and scale. He only took on jobs that seemed to be a profound expression of man's ability to exert control over the massive forces of nature, anything that was beyond scope, beyond what had been done before.

My father was technically working with the Egyptian government as an international overseer, but he was doing more than that. He spent most of his hours in the company of Soviet architects and engineers, sweaty men in dungarees and broad hats, talking in his pidgin Russian in an excited manner, waving his hands over topographical maps and stacks of wrinkled blueprints. The Russians chain-smoked cigarettes and did a lot of nodding and smiling whenever my father spoke.

While my father drafted plans in the rows of dusty Quonset huts that the engineers used as offices, or scouted the valley with a team of engineers and architects, I wandered about the streets of Aswan, along the river and on the low bluffs above the city, roaming among the ruined temples and crumbling walls of the ancient quarter, occasionally venturing out into the eastern desert on excursions with my companion Hakor, a local Nubian boy a few years older than me whom my father hired to serve as my guide, and guardian. Hakor also became my first friend.

We were supposed to be there for fourteen months but it didn't work out that way. My father made a mistake and the Soviets sent us home early. The choice he made had been the right one, something I realized even as a young boy.

When I was sixteen my father announced one day that it was time for me to go to college. At this time we were in Montana, where he was building a series of hydroelectric dams on the Big Hole River that would eventually power half the state. My father had contacts with all the major universities in the Northeast, so his secretaries prepared all the forms and applications, I took a few tests, signed my name, and the next thing I knew I was at Princeton.

When I reached Princeton, that frigid, dark, and precipitous place, I discovered the vast treasure troves of the university library and the powers of interlibrary loan. I was sixteen years old and had never had a proscriptive educational experience of any kind, or much of what you might call a social education either. I didn't know anyone and I didn't have the first idea how to go about meeting or knowing anyone. Eventually I was able to meet some people and develop what you might term friendships, though mostly they were academically based, people with whom I shared a common interest. Such relationships only ever happened for me when another person essentially tripped over me in the dark, or when my father hired them to look after me, like Hakor, or when like Alan Henry, just took a liking to me and dragged me out places with him for some unaccountable reason. Helen was the first person I ever met who wasn't thrust upon me in some way.

Obviously, at first I was quite a mess socially; it took some time getting used to the amount of interaction I was supposed to have with my peers. I was quickly drawn to the Ancient History Department, where I was surprised to learn that many of my fellow students hadn't read most of the principal historical texts, and if they had they didn't seem to retain much. My instructors weren't much better. By my second year I was taking mostly independent-study classes, mostly with the director at that time, a Dr. Nichols, a specialist in ancient civilizations. He directed my further reading, giving me lists of books and documents to study.

My apartment was a nice place, third floor, a narrow studio with western-facing windows and a nice view of a stand of elm trees, a kitchenette I never used, a futon bed, an old dresser my mother shipped to me, a desk, and a few folding chairs. It was a stone's throw from the largest of the many vast gorges that dotted the craggy hillsides of Princeton, just a few blocks from Carl Sagan's nest that perched on the edge of such an abyss. I often thought that Sagan would have only to look out his study window, rather than to the skies, down into the windswept chasm that lay under him, the darkly veined basaltic rock pitted and stricken with crevasses, howling, channeling winds that funneled out into the air, the bleakness of it, to see the full extent of the cosmos that he sought.

The rent I paid was a waste of money because I was never there. I spent all my time in the library, huddled in my reserved carrel on the fourth floor, bundled up against the cold, eating apples or takeout, poring over the classical works of Young, Champollion, Belzoni, the great pretenders and misguided translators like Gustavus Seyffarth,

Carl Richard Lepsius, Hinck's work on Assyrian grammar, James Burton, John Wilkinson, De Rouge, the great Samuel Birch's *Dictionary*, including the painstaking handwritten copy by Wallis Budge, then the "Berlin School" of Stern, Erman, and Sethe.

Then I moved on to the modern greats, Griffith, Gunn, and Sir Alan Gardiner, whose *Egyptian Grammar* never left my satchel for the next six years. I taught myself the rudiments of hieratic, demotic, and full-form hieroglyphs, Old and Middle Egyptian cursive and pictograph forms, as well as ancient Akkadian, Assyrian, Nubian, including Meriotic script, the elements of cuneiform, as well as more modern scripts like Coptic, Greek, Latin, and Arabic, practicing late at night on the huge blackboards in the lecture halls of the history department, writing out reams of script, diagramming the translation, working out the ligatures, transcribing the great epics.

I moved from there to the science of cryptography, from the mathematical number-theory magic of Alan Turing and the German *Enigma* codes, to ancient secrets like meriotic scripts, Mayan, and Linear B. I spent three months trying to come to terms with Roger Bacon's thirteenth-century cipher, one of the great mysteries of cryptography. I carried with me at all times a copy of the Voynich manuscript with Newbold's notes. I still don't accept his theory of the microscopic "shorthand" characters, but it was all thrilling work.

It was disconcerting at first, the quiet of the library, the absence of the struggle of machine and man against the earth, but I got in the habit of wearing ear plugs, which essentially filled my head with the sound of my own beating heart. It was strangely very similar to the pile drivers and pneumatic pumps that my father often used to plant structures deep into the ground. I found that if I brought a large thermos of coffee along I could read and take notes well into the night without much discomfort. I got used to sleeping on the floor under my desk, my leather satchel for a pillow, listening to the echoing groans of the old building settling in the night. It was a comforting sound then and still is; I have always felt most at home in such places: empty libraries at night, the dusty back rooms of ancient buildings, the dark basements of museums. Lying on my back under the desk I intoned the phonetic transliterations to myself into the early hours of the morning, the struggling approximations of sounds that hadn't been uttered in three thousand years echoing down the empty corridors.

I took to wearing wool sweaters that I could layer shirts under, thick corduroy pants and leather boots two sizes too big to accommodate my extra-thick woolen socks. I had a blue watch cap that kept my ears warm and fit neatly right to the top edge of my glasses. I found insulated shooting gloves in a surplus store, the cropped trigger fingers perfect for turning pages and handling pencils, and I wore them always. Still, my hands and feet were always cold, obviously some sort of circulation problem. In the winter I would boil a pan of water to soak my blue feet in.

Occasionally I would take breaks to stretch, pacing the dusty halls of the stacks, or out onto the front steps to get a breath of fresh air. I remember I would often find it remarkable that so many students would be out there, many rushing back and forth, others talking in groups, living out lives of such furious activity. It inevitably made me long for the calm and placid life of the written records of ancient Egypt. I spent the vast landscape of my late teenage years, that bright, shining time just before adulthood when the world spools out in front of you playful and endless, the way it appears to you on television shows, the way other people remember it and talk about it, I spent that time living in another era, a world not endless but bound by a definite sense of time, place, and history. And I loved it. Did I have any idea what was going on outside, in the present world? A lot of things were happening. I knew about them, but I heard them like you hear faint music rolling down a long hallway in an empty building, the sound of someone else's home, a private conversation through a motel wall, the crash of dishes in the kitchen at midnight. It wasn't anything that I was paying attention to or anything that seemed like it needed attention. I had a place to sleep and food when I wanted it and almost unlimited access to all the books I could ever want to read. The world seemed complete for me as it was.

I suppose many people like the idea of walking on the ground that others walked, thousands of years ago, to enter the buildings that once housed the ancients, where men and women lived and died. Almost everyone has a general attraction to these things; that's why the British Museum is packed with people from all over the world every day. It is a way of assuring ourselves that we are not alone in this moment, this blip of time, that the story of the human race is a long and glorious one. The fascination with history, the artifacts, and particularly the mummies in the Egyptian exhibits, is that here you could gaze on the remains of another man or woman who once walked the earth much like us, so long ago. I suppose it makes us feel like we are not alone; not in the today-and-now sense, but in the long view, the big story, earth, the whole of it.

But that feeling fades the closer you get to it, the more scrupulously and intensely you study. Eventually you come to a plateau where it becomes clear that nobody would ever know the ancients, who they were, the way they lived, what they ate, how they died, what they wanted, even with these little traces they left behind—a scrap of pottery, a cornerstone, the rude inscription on a piece of woven paper, a massive stone monument buried in the desert.

The odd factors of chance, conditions, environment; why this piece and not another? Why this man and not another? Is there any logic to the way history is transferred from the gray areas of past eras to this one? You could work on that problem alone for a lifetime and never get to the end of it. What we really wanted to know was the interior aspect of this history, what they felt inside, how they envisioned their place in the world. Then they would be alive again, and I felt this would be a great gift to receive and to give to others.

This particular sort of life didn't last of course. I stayed in Princeton for six years. Then I was prodded from the library by Dr. Nichols and a few others and nudged out into the world with a stack

of degrees that I didn't really remember getting. But they didn't abandon me there. Dr. Nichols had some friends at Berkeley, including the
great Egyptologist Miriam Lichtheim, an expert in Middle and New
Kingdom translations, and they offered me a lecture position that had
almost no teaching load and would leave me free to work on my independent translation projects. I moved out to San Francisco and within
a month I found myself in California, a breezy afternoon standing outside a concert hall waiting for Helen, my future wife, to emerge. A
small peninsula of the present day emerged into the ocean of history,
a place I nosed up against in the foggy hours of the morning; before I
knew it I was beached there. The ocean was too big, too blue, and the
beach too warm and inviting. Even this rude metaphor I'm wielding is
drawn from ancient texts. But inevitably they all are. There's no way
to escape it.

Zenobia was born the next year. I was twenty-two years old.

Penelope shook her head, her thin lips curved into a smirk, a lopsided
drinking vessel, the glyph for "mouth."

You're a strange bird, you know that, Dr. Rothschild? It's a mira-
cle you turned out.

Sorry, I said. It's a boring story.

She laughed.

No, no, Walter, not like that. I didn't mean it like that.

My jaws throbbed, and suddenly I ached to move.

Dance?

Penelope lifted her head and smiled, her prominent front teeth
spanning the fine expanse of her lips and the corners of her mouth
spread out and back. It was a beautiful smile.

We bumped and bounced about the room for more songs, many
more than I expected to. We danced to Rose Royce, Evelyn Champagne King, the Trammps, and Van McCoy & the Soul City Sym-

phony, disco songs I remembered vaguely from car radios driving through Berkeley or San Francisco.

I spun Penelope around into an awkward dip and she squealed with delight. I don't know many things about women, that's for sure. But I *do* know that all women want to dance, as often as they can, and *every* woman wants to be *dipped*.

As I brought her back up I found myself looking directly into an enormous midsection struggling against a belt with a giant buckle the size of a dinner plate and the shape of Texas. I looked up to see the shaggy melon-size head of Gigantica, the wrestler from that riot on Oxford Street, squinting in the smoke and dim light with one eye, the other covered with a gauze bandage, bobbing his head in time with the music. Gigantica rotated slowly, bouncing expertly on his enormous bare feet that looked like twin dancing badgers. His partner was an equally large Swedish lass whipping her blond mane about in a circular pattern. Gigantica looked down at me as he twisted around, nodded slightly and winked with his free eye, as if we were old friends. He couldn't have recognized me, as I never came into contact with the wrestlers that night, but regardless I felt a cool spike down my neck and I suddenly lost what little coordination I had. My legs went wooden and my back hurt. I shouted in Penelope's ear that I had to get home, and we threaded our way back to the kitchen to find Magnus so I could thank him and say good-bye. I didn't get the chance; he had apparently locked himself in the bathroom sometime earlier and refused to come out even when Penelope pounded on the door.

I walked Penelope to her Austin Mini down the block. The sky was lightening to the color of milky tea, and the streets were slick with a short rain that had fallen sometime in the night. The halal meats store was still lit and apparently open, but everything else on the street was dark. A man in a turban on the corner was busy opening up his paper wagon, wrestling the stacks of papers into the small plywood stand and singing softly to himself. I was wearing the wrong shoes, that was for certain. One was a loafer that was somewhat similar to mine, but the other was a positively titanic sandal-type shoe that flopped about as we walked.

Have you ever been to Cambridge, Penelope?

Did my first degree there. Peterhouse.

Familiar at all with the Fitzwilliam Museum?

Sure, she said. Good collection of Constable paintings, some ancient Egyptian materials. Nice museum. I had a roommate who was reading history.

What are you doing tomorrow? I asked. Come with me to Cambridge. I need a guide.

I stood on the sidewalk as she sat in the driver's seat of the Mini and put her hands on the wheel. She fired up the engine and the radio was tuned to one of the innumerable techno-music stations they have in London, broadcasting a steady thumping beat with a series of shrieking sirens wailing in the background. She sat there and stared through the windshield.

I'll pay for everything, I said. Have you back right away.

Penelope looked up at me and raised an eyebrow. I was shivering in the cold morning air, my clothes still damp from sweat. My bruised face felt numb.

She smiled and reached in her purse and took out a pen.

Some paper?

I searched my pockets and found Magnus's card. She wrote her number on the back and handed it to me.

Call me in the morning. I'm not working so I'll be home. I need to sleep on it. Can't really make a decision like that now, can we?

In the cab on the way back to my flat I put my head back and gratefully closed my eyes. In the front of my eyelids a warm, reddish glow spread over my mind, carrying the traces of symbols, the slight representational images of language. My bruised face was numb and seemed to hang on my skull like a sack of meal. I opened my eyes as we passed Bond Street and on to the upper reaches of Oxford Street, the low walls of the buildings ablaze with neon signs for stereo equipment, electronics, housewares, the cab sliding down the dark seam of road, unhindered. I wanted to go back down to the office under the British Museum and sit with the Stela for a bit. Forget the rest of it, just feel the cold, smooth limestone, my fingers in the incisions of the symbols and then trailing across to the rough-hewn edges of the slab. The heft, the secure massiveness of the dark stone. I tried to focus on this bit of consistency.

But instead I thought of Helen as I was used to imagining her over the years. I imagined her with her cello, plying her bow with an ardent grace as if she were kneading the shoulders of an unruly child, the half sneer on her lips, eyes puckered with effort, holding the tawny cello between her legs with a tenderness, a loving nestling between her womanly thighs, her creamy, dimpled knees bobbing ever so slightly, a foot padding on the dusty hardwood floor of our old San Francisco town house, the afternoon light coming through the window. The sound of it, the resonant tone of the taut strings, the brutal dragging of hair, the tension, and the ragged sobs it drew from that mysterious instrument. But it wasn't our house in San Francisco. I never saw her there like that. I mean, I wasn't looking at her like that then. I only did that now, so many years later. I was making up the image of it, changing around the details, making it seem so much more glorious, beautiful, meaningful than the reality of a practicing professional musician. But what was there to do? It doesn't make it any less true. In fact that image is what makes it real for me. That is how I choose to remember it, and that is always how it will be.

When I got home I dialed Penelope's number.

She laughed, that bright musical laugh.

You know what fucking time it is? she said. Are you fucking nutters?

And then she said yes.

From *The Instruction of Papyrus Insinger: One does not ever discover the heart of a woman any more than one knows the sky.*

12: DETERMINATIVES

I WOKE AT TWO-THIRTY in the afternoon, just enough time to shower and get out the door to meet Penelope at the Holborn station at three o'clock. I threw on some fresh clothes and strapped my stainless-steel vacuum-sealed papyrus case on my shoulders. The case was extremely light, with a rechargeable battery pack that powered the digital thermostatic climate controls. I had the presets locked in to a variety of environments, so at the touch of a button I could alter the air inside the case to mimic the dry, oxygen-rich atmosphere of Egypt in the year 2000 B.C. or the more moist, tepid air of first-century Britain. It looked like an enormous thermos or a steel arrow quiver hanging crossways over my back. It was a gift from my colleagues in Cairo when I left there in 1989. What else do you pack when you are traveling to recover a priceless Egyptian antiquity from a ring of speed-popping thieves?

Mick was nowhere to be seen. His answering machine was full again, various requests and replies about his side jobs. There was no doubt I hoped that this would keep him away from the Stela. I knew that I would burn with envy and shame for the rest of my life if Mick solved the Stela behind my back. He was just the guy to do it.

I had reservations out of King's Cross for Cambridge that afternoon, with an open return. I told Sue and Cindy that I wanted to look at some manuscripts at the Fitzwilliam Museum and consult with Dr. Hardy about some possible transliterations for the Stela, if anyone were to ask. Which of course no one would. Dr. Hardy used to be one of England's foremost experts on paleography. He was part of the bastion of dusty old Englishmen in this profession, guys who seemed to have existed since the nineteenth century, complete with pipes, tweeds, righto-chap and all that rot.

It was now Monday, November third. My contract was up on Friday. After that I would be broke, jobless, and my career finished, and lucky if I managed to escape jail time unless I was able to return the Song of Amun to the museum. Or perhaps solve the Stela. Hopefully both. And then there was Zenobia.

I did briefly consider the thought of hightailing it out of the country, doing a runner and forgetting the whole thing. I knew a few remote corners of the world that I could rely on to conceal me. In most of these areas, particularly in the outer limits of Northern Africa, not many people would *want* to come looking for you. But I also knew if anyone could find me, it would be Klein.

If it came to it I figured I'd work on the Stela in prison. I had it in my head anyway, the entire grid. I could do it in the dark. I just needed a slight crack to wedge into, a small opening that would free up the possible transliterations and glosses.

I gave Dr. Hardy a call before I left my flat and told him we were going directly to the Fitzwilliam, and that we would be in later tonight. Dr. Hardy agreed to put us up at his house in Grantchester, just down the road. He had a guest cottage in the back, and he said he'd leave it open for us, so we could get in whenever. I wasn't planning on staying there overnight—I'd promised Penelope I'd try to have her back the same day, but you never know.

I'm interested to hear, Hardy had chirped in our phone conversation, how the work is progressing on the Stela of Paser. Dr. Klein told me a few months ago that you were the man to break it. Have you read my recent paper on paleographic mysteries of the Middle Kingdom? Published last summer in *Egyptology Quarterly*? Some ideas that might be useful.

I didn't tell Hardy that his "ideas" were thirty years old, and essentially worthless. The old guard of Egyptologists had a habit of rehashing the same ideas over and over, mostly an updating of the findings of Champollion, Young, and Gardiner, as if nothing had happened in the last four decades. And in many ways nothing had happened; Gardiner's tables were still the industry standard, but we had moved far beyond that now in terms of the figurative hieroglyphs and cryptographic translations that Mick and I worked on. Guys like Hardy put out papers like that every few years, and they invariably got published, mostly because of their seniority and prestige in the field. I didn't look forward to listening to him babble on about his "ideas," but I only had about twenty pounds left after buying the train tickets and we might need a place to stay.

I look forward to reading it, I said.

Yes, perhaps we can compare some notes? The Stela of Paser, quite a piece. Confounding. Brilliant, really.

Well, I said, I'll see you tomorrow.

I've been working, Hardy continued, on some theories of synecretism, using New Kingdom funerary texts. Tutankhaten and Tutankhamun, that sort. Perhaps we could go over some notes and sketches?

Sounds good. We'll talk about it when I get there.

Right, then. Superb. Till tomorrow! Cheers!

❧

Penelope was late, running across High Holborn Street with a back-pack on her slim shoulders, smiling openly in the crowd. The station was thronged with the early after-work rush, so she held my arm as we slipped into the station along with the rest. We grinned at each other as we went down the escalators and through the tunnels, touching our hands together lightly from time to time to keep contact.

The train jolted out of the city and into the countryside, the light already waning, the coach infused with a baleful glow.

Penelope was pursuing her doctorate in comparative literature at the Sorbonne, with a particular focus on the Bloomsbury group of Virginia Woolf and Pre-Raphaelite painters like Rossetti and Burne-Jones. She took the gig at the library while she was working on her dissertation because it would give her unlimited access to her research, and she said she needed a break from France. She was planning on returning to Paris in the summer to present and defend the document.

I'm at about eighty pages, she said, with half of the writing yet to go. But I've got the research bit wrapped up at this point. Just arranging it all now.

That seems like quite an undertaking, I said. What do you plan to do afterward?

She shrugged. I dunno. Drink wine? Walk the streets of Paris? Get a job?

I don't know much about the Bloomsbury group, I said, but I think I've seen that one painting, from Shakespeare, Ophelia? Lying in the river holding flowers? What's that called again?

Look, Penelope said, still looking out the window, are you going to tell me what this is all about? And I'm not sleeping with you.

Believe me, I said, I have nothing like that in mind. Not that . . . well, I'd like to get back as soon as possible, tonight. My daughter is in London and I'd like to spend some time with her.

Really? Your daughter?

Penelope propped her chin on her hand on the window ledge, tilting her head to look at me.

Married?

No, not anymore.

So the daughter is coming for a visit?

Zenobia is the editor of a new women's magazine, I said. She's here on business.

Really? That's brilliant! Zenobia, what sort of name is that?

Zenobia was the queen of a neighboring province called Palmyra. She invaded Egypt in A.D. 268. Caused some serious havoc for the Roman rulers at the time.

You named your daughter after some obscure Egyptian queen?

Not Egyptian really. From Palmyra.

Whatever.

There's more to it than that.

I guess you're lucky, she said, that I have no real life, otherwise I wouldn't be doing this. My life is *extremely* dull. Too much time in little rooms reading old books, looking at old paintings, know what I mean?

Believe me, I said, I know what you mean.

She grinned. Such un-British-like teeth. Her father must have been an orthodontist.

Well, Penelope said, you look like you need some help. What's with the metal tube?

I had the document case between my knees, as it was a bit too long and valuable to trust to the luggage rack. I suppose it looked a bit odd.

It's for documents, I said. Valuable documents. That's what we are doing.

Trying to find a document? In Cambridge? The Fitzwilliam Museum?

Her eyes brightened.

Like an A. S. Byatt novel?

A. S. Byatt? I shrugged.

So I told Penelope all about it. I didn't exactly say that I'd slept with Erin, but she probably figured it out. It was all a bit embarrassing. When I finished she sat quietly, gazing at the document tube that rocked gently between my knees. Maybe she was reconsidering her gesture of help. I felt the train pick up speed and my stomach began to churn, driving more pumping blood into my face. I'd had more hangovers in the last few days than I'd had in the last ten years together.

I leaned back and closed my eyes and thought of the Stela, the Amun papyrus, and of prison. I thought of myself in prison, and then I thought of being in prison with my eyes closed and thinking about the Stela. Then the prison became vast slabs of obsidian limestone, a field of hieroglyphs broken into grids, lasting far into the horizon, fading into confusion.

That was just the problem, the damaged edges of the Stela threw everything off. We can conjecture as to what was there, what was said, from the parts we can translate, that is vertically and horizontally. Another part of the problem lies in the curious nature of the determinatives, the signs that follow other hieroglyphs and define the category of meaning. Because vowels were not written, determinatives were necessary in order to distinguish between words with identical consonants.

The problem with the Stela is that because of the crossword-puzzle nature of the piece, determinatives have to act in different ways for the vertical or horizontal lines of expression. The same sign that acted as a determinative in the horizontal could also act as a logogram, or sound-meaning sign, for a vertical line, denoting a particular sound used in the pronunciation of the word expressed. Trying to distinguish the nature of this sign, in a *third* direction, was the frustrating aspect. It was mathematical in scope; the possibilities seemed endless. But of course they weren't.

I often thought the third way sat like a bowling ball on the membrane of the grid, creating a depression around which flowed the determinatives, taking the path of least resistance, moving into the curve created by the overall metaphor like orbiting planets. It was just a matter, as mathematicians say, of placing yourself within the context of the problem, understanding the rules of the numbered system, and walking out the most reasonable door that presented itself. Simple.

I must have dropped off a bit, for suddenly Penelope was talking and handing me a cup of tea. The train was rattling through some indeterminate section of English countryside.

I've always felt, Penelope said, that historians and archeologists suffered from a dangerous preoccupation with immortality. Of course this is something they share, in part, with artists and writers.

I was stretching my legs as well as I could in the cramped seat.

We are certainly interested, I said, in the lasting monuments of history. But I think my preoccupation lies more in an attempt to discover or understand the minds and attitudes of ancient peoples. Trying to understand their thought process.

She shook her head.

That is a smaller aspect of the larger preoccupation I'm talking about. All those things fit under the rubric of obsession with immortality. You want to understand those who came before you so that *you* may more likely be understood, forever.

Perhaps.

Look, Penelope said, let's say that you were going to die. How would you like to have your body disposed of? Hypothetically, you know? You are somehow able to spare no expense or trouble, the most extravagant, fantastical thing you could imagine. How would you do it?

I thought about it for a few moments.

Well, I suppose I would like to be mummified, in the New Kingdom style, with my bodily organs placed in earthen canopic jars at my feet. Brain corkscrewed out through my nose and disposed of. My body cavity filled with spices and flowers, entombed in some hidden nook in the Valley of the Kings perhaps. A modest tomb. Not much in terms of materials to take into the next world or anything like that. The standard things, beer and bread, a few shabti servants perhaps. Some nice lines on my behalf, written in hieroglyphs, demotic, Greek, and English. Something like that.

Penelope looked puzzled.

Whup. You are farther gone than I thought. It's all about what you leave behind, yeah? I like it though. Anybody else in there? Family? A wife perhaps?

I'm not sure, I said, that my ex-wife would desire such a thing. She would more likely want to be interred somewhere in the States. Perhaps with her parents in Kentucky. Though she is . . . has recently remarried. My daughter? No way. I have no idea what she would want. My father is in a small plot in Virginia. My mother: cremated. In a jar at her sister's house up in New York.

Penelope was scribbling in her notebook, a rough sketch of a few mummies sitting around a table, apparently playing cards. The train was going through a stretch of fenced farmland dotted with muddy clumps of sheep.

Clearly, she said, still doodling, this aspiration is a very thinly veiled desire to live on into the future as long as possible. You chose mummification in part because of the way that this peculiar process allows bodies to remain in a generally recognizable state for thousands of years.

That's not necessarily true; the mummification process—

Hang on a minute, Dr. Rothschild. The reason you want to be

mummified is not based upon a belief that this process, complete with the appropriate ceremony, et cetera, is going to put you through to some sort of Egyptian heaven, correct?

I suppose not. However—

So no hope for the afterlife, eh? Exactly. That is why you want to preserve this bit of you that you have on earth, your earthly existence, for as long as possible. The hope is that many moons from now some-one will unearth you again. Much as we unearth these mummies now. Then you will become alive once again, living on in the minds and memories of a new generation of people.

Really, I said. Why don't you tell me what your funeral would be like then?

Penelope leaned her head back against the headrest and closed her eyes. Her teeth showed slightly over the smooth crescent of her bottom lip.

The northeastern coast, she said, of Greenland, the Lincoln Sea, perhaps the Queen Elizabeth Islands, up past Baffin Bay to be sure. A forty-foot reconstructed Viking longboat. Something like the Sutton Hoo ship. June, just when the ice sheets begin to break up. Fully rigged out, sails, pennants, arms, the whole deal. Build a massive fu-neral pyre of stacked cordwood cut from the short hills of Cape Sheri-dan. Sometime in the evening, just before sunset, rig the sails up, douse that fucker with reindeer fat and set it alight, and I float off into the Arctic Ocean toward the North Pole, into the sunset.

I suppose there are mourners weeping on the banks? I said.

And just maybe, Penelope said, I slip between the massive ice-bergs that clog the polar seas, through a small crack in the giant Arctic ice plate, and find myself circling the North Pole. Maybe even *under* the ice, that would be something. Into the big drain, as Edgar Allan Poe speculated, through the center of the earth and out again at the South Pole. You know that in the nineteenth century a lake high in the mountains of Portugal was said to contain the wrecks of ships lost at sea, sometimes on the other side of the world? Every few months, another wreck would come bubbling to the surface. Chinese junks, man-o'-wars, Nantucket whalers, Peruvian canoes, you name it. The passengers and sailors missing of course. Perhaps in the course of their travels through the channels of the earth they reached their personal Valhalla. I'd be drinking mead at the great table, getting pissed on the Elysian plain.

This isn't a funeral wish, I said, it's a scene from some sort of Norse myth.

She shrugged.

Yes, I said, but if there is no one to see it happen, to record it—

See! You just can't consider doing something that is not somehow recorded or logged for posterity. This is what separates the artist from the scientist.

But they want the same thing, right?

Yes and no. One seeks the immortality of the heart, a story to be sung in the great hymns around the fire. The other seeks the quantifiable preservation.

I suppose I'm the scientist?

It's actually less selfish, she said. You hope to leave something to instruct the future. That's why you study the dead, to respect this passing of information and make use of it.

This sounded reasonable to me, but then where was the Song of Penelope, and who would write it? Penelope yawned, touching her palms to the overhead rack.

So what's our plan anyway?

First, I said, I need you to help me find a particular address, in Queen's College. And an address in Grantchester. And help me positively identify Erin.

What? You mean you can't recognize her yourself?

Well, I only met her briefly. I'm not sure. She might have changed her hair. And I was drunk.

Penelope raised her eyebrows and put her hand to her lips in mock surprise.

What about Grantchester?

Dr. Hardy. A . . . colleague of mine lives there. That's where we are staying tonight—I mean only if we need to.

She looked out the window, but I could see the reflection of her smile on the glass.

And what if we don't find her?

I shrugged.

What if she doesn't have it?

I don't exactly have a plan for that either.

What if she doesn't want to give it to us?

I haven't exactly had time to think that kind of thing out yet.

A tall black man wearing a long dashiki-type garment of a strong mustard color entered our compartment and started walking down the aisle. It was the African gentleman from the British Library, the one sitting at Alan's desk and reading *The Anatomy of Melancholy,* the one with the gun in his coat. When he caught me looking at him he lowered his eyes and folded his tall body into a seat a few rows ahead of us. I wondered if he was going to Cambridge. I made a mental note to keep track of where and when he got off. A few minutes later I fell asleep again.

We arrived in Cambridge just after five o'clock. I awoke with my throbbing face pressed against the smeared seat back. My head rang with pain. The tall African man was gone. Penelope seemed sleepy and I was a bit hungry, so I bought us some tea and rolls from a stand in the station. I figured we'd head directly to Queen's College and Erin's address. Penelope said she was familiar with Queen's College, as well as Grantchester, where Dr. Hardy lived. She spent her fourth year in Grantchester, while she was finishing up at Peterhouse. She was renting a flat from one of the Victorian dons, a rather fat man who had the bad habit of showing up in the tearoom at night while Penelope was watching the telly, wearing nothing but his Y-fronts and socks.

Lonely old bugger, he was, Penelope said, almost wistfully. But the chap knew a few things about Victorian novelists and painters. That's the way it always is, eh?

The way what is?

Forget it.

We took the King's Parade across to the college backs, the backsides of the old colleges where they butted against the Cam River. It was the best way to navigate the colleges, Penelope said. I hadn't been out of London since I arrived in England for this job, and I had almost forgotten that it was fall, the season of the brilliant lament of dying foliage. The college backs were exquisitely manicured, with freshly clipped grass and bordering box hedges. Even the buildings, the austere, monstrous hulks of stone and brick—Saint John's, Trinity, Clare, King's, and Queen's Colleges—even the ivy on the buildings was trimmed into clean lines and squared corners. The fine, pale gravel of the paths that snaked across the back lawns down to the narrow green ribbon of the Cam were smoothly raked and lined with freshly weeded flower beds that bore the stumps of autumn. As school was still in session, the backs were lightly populated with small groups of people walking about the lawns, standing in clusters, or couples leaning into one another, gazing into the waters of the river. It was a deeply reminiscent experience, reminding me of my days at Princeton when all the present world was the ordered spaces of a college campus, the weedless, sorrowless days of intellectual youth and vitality.

We crossed the backs until we came to Union Street, where an arched stone bridge carried foot traffic into the heart of Cambridge. The streets were half filled with an evening crowd of meandering tourists and students earnestly toting backpacks along the cobblestones, hurrying along home in the remaining hours of daylight. The wind swept awkwardly along the narrow streets, and a light rain began

to fall into our faces as we turned up Downing Street, off Saint An-
drew's, on our way to Queen's Lane, the gate to Queen's College.

A bored guard stood in a small phone-booth-size box by the gate,
but Penelope grabbed my hand and whisked us through without a
glance. The inner yard of Queen's College was nearly empty, clean-
swept paths of pale gravel circling the squared yard of brick and ivy.
We circumvented the central lobby and headed directly for a wing of
the building, then tramped up a dim, dusty, and narrow stairway.
What would I say to her? Would she even remember me? Penelope
was reading out the door numbers as we climbed the stairs and came
to an abrupt halt before a door on the third landing.

Here we go.

She stood aside with a flourish and a slight bow, gesturing to the
door. Music was throbbing faintly from behind the door, something
bouncy and jangly.

I cleared my throat and shuffled a bit.

Know what you're doing?

I think so, I said.

I'll just stand here then.

Penelope stepped dramatically to the side and clasped her hands
behind her back. She was enjoying this. I had a flicker of suspicion:
Where exactly were we? Who was behind that door? I had let this
woman lead me here without really ever questioning why she was
helping me or anything. But what else was there to do?

I knocked, and after a moment we could hear the sound of footsteps coming across the room toward the door. They got right to the
door, paused, and went quickly back. Penelope looked at me. I
shrugged. In a moment the footsteps returned, quietly, surely. The
door jerked open with a wrenching sound. A small figure stood in the
shadowy room, lit from behind by flickering candles. The music was
definitely something like country and western as they call it in the
States. A strong smell of incense wafted into the hall. It was a woman,
short like Erin, and with short hair like Erin's. But it wasn't Erin.

Yes? the woman said in a thin voice.

Hello, I said. We are looking for Erin? Erin Kaluza?

I could see her shoulders relax and her face turn upward, her eyes bright and blue. Her torso protruded strangely and her bare feet on the dusty wooden floor were puffy like a child's hands.

Oh! she said. Oh! Of course. You must be the Egyptian people?

Yes, I said, I am. We are.

Yes. Hmmm.

She looked around the room for a bit, distracted. Her accent—she was an American.

Yes. Um. Come in. Come in and I'll be with you in a second.

She turned and scampered off into the darkness. We heard pounding feet and a door open and slam quickly.

Definitely *not* Erin, Penelope said.

We stepped inside. On the floor against one wall a crowd of candles of various colors and sizes blazed like a small bonfire. That was the only light in the room. A low futon couch lay in front of the candles, a small tea table with several burning sticks of incense, surrounded by floor cushions. A standard English-university flat: the dull wooden floors, dusty corners, paneled walls yellowing with age, a small kitchen area toward the back, with a couple narrow bedrooms and a bath off to either side, the entire living-room space not more than twelve feet across. The girl was rustling around in a bedroom for a few more moments before she flung the door open again.

Voilà! she said. *C'est tout!*

She was carrying a small, carved wooden box in her hands, held out in front of her like it was a special meal she had prepared. She was a remarkably shaped little woman. Her head and facial features were large and sensuous, her torso roundly robust and her enormous breasts jutting and magnificent. She wore little jean shorts and her fleshy legs quickly tapered down to diminutive, round feet topped with impossibly tiny ankles. Her hair was white-blond and cut short like a boy's.

She put her hands on her hips and looked at us with her head slightly cocked.

Thought you'd be bigger, she said. In real life I mean.

Is Erin here? I asked.

Her huge smile turned up a bit more. She shook her head.

Of course not.

Is she coming back soon? Penelope asked.

She waved a finger at us and sat on the couch. She opened the box and revealed a gleaming set of stainless-steel hypodermic needles and some vials of fluid.

Fuckin' 'ell! Penelope said, taking a step back.

Ah, the girl with the magnificent breasts said, her eyes going soft. I'm sorry.

She looked into her lap, sitting in a lotus position on the couch. Her shoulders began to quiver.

I like the music, I said.

Really? She sniffed, looking through enormous eyes that held water like crystal goblets. This girl was just a young kid who was obviously mistaking us for someone else. This was all a big mistake.

It's Emmylou Harris, she said. I just *love* her. You know?

We all stood there for a moment, listening to Emmylou's throaty, warbling cry.

Isn't this what you wanted? The girl gestured at the box of syringes.

Not exactly, Penelope said.

The girl jumped to her tiny feet and wavered there, pausing as if to give her breasts a few moments to settle their own equilibrium.

Oh, god! she said. I'm such an idiot! Aren't you the ones here to pick up the stuff for Oldcastle? That creepy old Egyptian guy?

Penelope made a quick movement in the periphery of my vision and I felt her steely fingers shoot under the back of my ribs like an arrow.

Of course, Penelope said. Oldcastle. We just weren't expecting, it, like that, I suppose.

Penelope slapped me on my back as I coughed, holding the stitch in my ribs from her jabbing fingers. The girl with the enormous breasts scurried around the coffee table.

Are you okay?

She seemed genuinely worried, and I smiled at her gratefully. Penelope settled us both onto the couch, crossed her legs, and languidly linked her fingers together like she planned on staying awhile.

You're an American? I coughed.

Canadian actually, she said.

Sorry.

Don't worry; I get that all the time.

So, Penelope said, what have you got for us? *Besides* that I mean. She waved at the hypodermic rig.

The girl clapped her hands and pranced back to the small box lying on the table and opened it up.

Let's see . . . we seem to have a variety of other things here today.

Penelope and I exchanged glances on the couch. I tried to pantomime to her *Why the hell did you dig me in the ribs like that? Do you think I'm that stupid?*, and she pantomimed back *Yes, you are that fucking stupid.*

The girl rummaged through the box, flipping through a series of little plastic baggies that held various powders and other materials.

I felt silly just sitting there like that. I held out my hand.

By the way, I said, my name's Walter Rothschild, and—

Penelope crushed my toes with the heel of her shoe. I shut my eyes and concentrated on staying upright.

And my name is . . . *Delilah*, Penelope said.

The girl jumped up and danced around the coffee table.

Ah! So polite! Usually nobody actually introduces themselves; I think it's so stupid. But it is so nice to meet you! I'm Joannie.

Joannie pumped my hand with a miniaturized iron grip.

So nice to meet you both, Walter and Delilah.

We arranged ourselves on the couch. Joannie pulled out a few baggies containing various hunks of dark substances and vials of yellowish powder.

Here's some other things that Mr. Oldcastle requested, Joannie said, her voice taking on an even, professional tone:

First, we have some high-grade Turkish hashish laced with synthetic mescaline and just a trace of upper to keep the high clean and fast. And then here we have a classic one-ounce nugget of Harlem indigo, hydroponically grown and sprayed with PCP and a touch of windowpane for extra color. Then we get into the stronger stuff, like this Hungarian—

That's fine, Penelope said. We'll just go with the hash. If that's okay.

Of course, Joannie chirped. The usual amount?

You got it, Penelope said.

Joannie jumped up and scampered off into the darkness beyond the candles.

What are you doing? I hissed.

Look, that other stuff there is heroin, Penelope whispered. I'm not getting into that. Plus I hate PCP. You always end up shirtless and brawling. Besides, I'm a little curious about the synthetic mescaline—

Curious?

Jesus, Walter, Penelope said, don't you know anything? We have to hang around to see if we can figure out where Erin is, right?

Yeah.

She might even show up here. This is her place, right? Maybe we can get more information out of Joannie. Besides, we can't just take some stuff like this without trying it. Too suspicious. It's against the code.

Code? What code? And what is it with all the hash around here? Doesn't anyone smoke plain marijuana anymore? And how are we going to pay for it?

You *are* an oldster, aren't you? We'll worry about the money later. What is she going to do, *make* us pay?

Why don't we just *ask* her where Erin is, right now?

Then do it! Penelope hissed.

Joannie came scuttling out of the darkness toting an enormous globed green-and-blue glass hookah the size of a beach ball, the kind they had in Moroccan coffee shops. Three tubes tipped with ivory mouthpieces dangled from the sides. I really didn't want any part of this. She placed it in a wire stand that sat on the coffee table and then took up a crouching position across the table from us.

Okay, all set? she asked. The hash it is then.

She set about with a tiny pair of scissors cutting off chunks of the brown material in the plastic baggie and placing it in the large, saucer-shaped bowl at the top of the hookah.

Say, Joannie, I wonder if you know where Erin is, right now I mean?

Hmmmm, she frowned. I thought she was with you guys at the estate.

Well, yes, I said, she *was*. But we haven't seen her lately.

Joannie shrugged and picked up a lighter.

I can't really say, she said. She could be back here any minute. But I figured she'd be, like, waiting for you two over at Oldcastle's. I mean, like, the normal thing is Erin or a couple of the Americans come round to pick it up. Often it's the extremely large fellows. I never know which, really. Makes for a bit of confusion sometimes.

Yes, of course, I said.

But she might show up here any time, right? Penelope said.

Yup, Joannie said. So, you ready?

Joannie held a lighter poised over the bowl holding a few hunks of the fragrant hash, a small mound of dried mud. Penelope already had a tube clenched between her grinning teeth.

This seemed like an absurd method for solving any of my problems. I thought of the Stela back in London, Mick's hunched form hovering over it in the dark. My daughter striding down the Strand, flagging down a taxi, her face set with lines of disappointment.

I took up a mouthpiece.

The smoke was surprisingly light and fruity, with a hint of cinnamon or nutmeg to it. After a moment Joannie closed up the valve to her mouthpiece and motioned for the two of us to continue. I could feel the draw of Penelope's breath pulling at the back of my lungs as we competed for the limited air inside the chamber. Then I relaxed and closed my eyes and felt her insistent sips of air tugging at my chest, drawing the air from my lungs. My face stopped throbbing. I opened one eye as we continued to draw from the chamber. Penelope was eyeing me closely, like she was studying my reaction, her cheeks quivering lightly with effort, a slight grin spreading across her pursed lips. I opened the other eye and the powers of stereo vision, the depth perception it allows, was an astounding development. Penelope was closer to me than I thought. I felt like she was pulling me inside out.

Joannie exhaled noisily, then giggled. As I watched, Penelope's face bloomed like a flower, unfolding itself, white and open, the purest Nile lily, then blue and golden with smiling eyes. It was beautiful.

Jesus, Joannie said. Walter, what the *fuck* happened to your *face?*

13: THE BLUE MAN

RAIN WAS FALLING STEADILY when we staggered out of the Queen's College courtyard. It was pitch dark and I had no idea how much time had passed since we arrived, though it was most definitely night. I know that Penelope gave an impassioned hour-long primer on the Bloomsbury group and the paintings of Edward Burne-Jones. I did some recitations from *The Book of the Dead*. Joannie particularly liked Chapter 77, the spell for transformation into a falcon:

Formula for appearing as a falcon of gold. I am a great falcon who is come from his egg, I fly, I alight as a falcon of four cubits, my wings are of greenstone. I have come from the cabin of the nightbark, and my heart was brought me from the eastern mountain. . . .

Then there was some kind of ruse where we pretended we didn't know our way back to Oldcastle's estate and had Joannie draw us a map, which quickly turned into some kind of elaborate fractal pattern involving trees and sound waves, covering several sheets of paper. I was also pretty sure that Joannie, after performing an elaborate set of interpretive dances to two different Emmylou Harris albums, was curled up in a ball on the floor when we left.

I found it odd how the hash seemed to collapse time; it was condensed and expanded depending on the recollection, almost like when I was in the throes of decipherment. I kept checking my watch, thinking hours had passed, only to find that it was just a few minutes later. Then I'd check it a few minutes later and an hour had passed. But it wasn't like the night at Garlic & Metal with the Dutchmen; I didn't spin off into some vertiginous zone of overzealous symbolic interpretation, at least not entirely, not yet. I think it had something to do with Penelope. It was such a wonder to watch her talk so expressively and earnestly. She was like the mule in the bullpen, a calming influence, a source of security perhaps.

As we walked onto the lawn I took my twill crusher hat out of my pocket and stuffed it on my skull.

Let's go, I said. Let's find the little minx.

Nice hat, Penelope said. She caressed the hat like she was petting an animal.

My Rex Harrison hat, Helen used to call it.

Who's Helen?

That's my ex-wife.

Oh. Yeah. *My Fair Lady.*

Helen loved musicals and Audrey Hepburn, and I have to admit that I always envied the elocution and accent of Henry Higgins. I'd had the hat for almost twenty years now. It gave my head a warm feeling, as if it were being closely held, encircled in someone's arms hovering somewhere about my head.

We took off on a listing, gamboling stroll across the lawn, stepping through the rows of immaculate azalea bushes and peony flowers that lined the walk. It was like walking on the moon, or what I think walking on the moon would be like. We were definitely *swimming on the sixth sea* as Alan Henry used to say when he was exceptionally gassed after what seemed at least a dozen pints. I was doing that blotto-high-step, lifting my feet excessively high with each stride, like I was stepping over an invisible foot-high threshold. The grass was slick and soft like a bog from the rain, and Penelope took off her shoes. She held the short-heeled shoes by their back straps and walked with her chin held up high and her eyes seemingly closed. Her hair hung across her cheeks in a few thick wet strands, and her lips moved as she sang softly to herself. The sound of her voice, a soft melody running over the constant steady drumming of the rain, seemed to me then a vehicle of some delicious transport. I stopped listening to the words, trying to visualize the music itself, the motes of sound, to pick them out in the air, and to arrange them in some kind of shape that I could read. But the sky was a swirling mass of fog and mist; the rain came out of the sky in spiraling patterns, like pale funnels of water.

Sorry 'bout the blows to ya tum, Penelope said softly.

She put an arm up around my shoulder and traced light circles with her palm. It felt like the touch of the morning sun.

I'll try, she said, to keep my hands off you from now on.

She took her hand away and started singing again.

I reached out and took Penelope's hand; a slight hitch in her tune, then it continued on as before. The falling rain seemed to slow down, so that I could see each drop in flight, each drop carrying a thin atom of sound. The sound itself became fluid, and I could see the patterns in the repeating waves of water droplets as they fell from the clouds.

Then I could see her seated in a dusty room, Helen, bathed in a dry halo of light, her cello cradled between her thighs. She bowed the strings furiously. A man sat in a chair facing her, leaning forward, elbows on his knees. The face was distorted, shimmering, like it was still beginning to form out of the air, vaguely translucent, changing. The sound of the cello was distant, a humming from down the hall, growing faint. The man shifted in his seat, the face wavering, then burning with a pinprick of light. He was bright blue and little waves danced in rows along his body, a small corpulent man, much like the representations of the Nile in pictographs. In his hand he held a palm rib, the sign for "year," in reference to the yearly flood of the Nile, and he wore the fabled Blue Crown, the unified crown of upper and lower Egypt. On his breast he wore a scarab amulet, blood red. Helen and her cello faded as if over a horizon, the wooden floors of the dusty room stretching on and turning to black stone, bending over the curve of the earth.

Penelope squeezed my hand, and the present roared back like a train into a tube station. I boarded the reality of my situation: staggering through the rain, being led by the hand by a relative stranger.

The sound of the rain. A form of percussion. Most often aligned with what? Weeping, it seems. Strange. I felt elated. Could the sound of weeping bring someone great joy? I remembered something that Alan told me once, sitting in the British Library lobby one afternoon, something about an early form of the novel, *The Booke of Margery Kempe*, twelfth century, I think, some sort of early English memoir by a woman who traveled about seeing visions and hearing the voices of God.

A lot of crying going on, Alan said. All through the book, the blasted woman is wretched and wailing something or other about the piety and goodness of God. She felt very guilty about a variety of things.

Alan Henry flexed himself in his chair like an overgrown panther, rolling his pillowed shoulders, his vertebrae cracking audibly in a series of alarming pops.

Just an overcompensating lunatic, Alan Henry continued. Anyway, each attack she had, the fits she went into, were always accompanied by a sort of song, some kind of heavenly melody that she was always trying to describe. It's true that melody is the traditional accompaniment to mystical experience, but I think this gal was just plain barking mad.

Melody and mystical experience. Was this a mystical experience? It sure seemed like it. But what was imparted? Wasn't a mystical experience supposed to lead to some kind of revelation?

Suddenly Penelope wrenched her hand from my grasp and then quickly struck me across the chest with a thumping blow.

Hsst! Did you see that?

I was bent over at the waist, rubbing the spot where her bony little fist connected with my breastbone. Little arcs of light spread through the thick parts of my chest.

What? What?

I didn't see anything. Then I realized I had my eyes closed. Apparently I was watching the sparks of light that skittered about under my eyelids.

There!

I opened my eyes. We were on Trumpington Street, just outside the gates of the college.

There! Penelope hissed again, her skinny arm swinging, angling through the night.

I tried to peer through the rain and darkness. Things began to materialize. Streetlamps that glowed like some kind of iridescent ruby, the gnarled edifices of gray stone buildings, thick fog swirling about. The mist seemed to move in bunched, curling shapes about the lampposts, moving concentrically around the poles and down across the street and about my legs. But Penelope was stamping and pointing and so I went back to the street, the sidewalk, something moving down the sidewalk, a shape, legs, a person, walking quickly toward us! No, away!

It's her! Penelope hissed again, dragging me forward with her.

Something pushed aside the fog for a moment like an ice scraper, revealing a thin stripe of clarity, and I saw a small woman turning the corner, walking a bit too quickly, it seemed, as if she were moving in an old silent-film reel where the madness of the slapstick comedy was accentuated by the speeding up of the film, the odd aspect of things and people moving quickly with fluid movements.

She saw us! Penelope murmured. She was coming back home, the silly *bitch!*

Penelope increased her grip on my upper arm and we began a shuffling trot toward the corner where the woman disappeared. I couldn't keep my feet moving in a straight line or at regular intervals. We staggered down the sidewalk, listing from side to side, my document case dangling about the front of my neck and my jacket flapping around my knees. By pure force of will Penelope got me to the corner. We turned the next block and a slash of movement on the other side of the street caught our eye. We saw her, hurrying along the shop windows, heading toward the backs. She looked back over her shoulder and for a moment I thought I caught a glimpse of her furtive, gray eyes burning through the rain and fog. It *was* Erin. Her speed was amazing. She ducked down an alley to her left in one smooth movement like she was on rails.

Come on!

Penelope pushed me forward with both hands, forcing me into a stumbling jog. I slipped on the cobblestones of the street and did a quick forward-back recovery, something that seemed at the time incredibly agile.

She has to cross the river, Penelope said. I know a shortcut to the bridge.

We jogged down the road a few blocks, then took a quick left into a narrow lane between a pub and some kind of haberdashery. Penelope held the end of my jacket sleeve and dragged me along the alley. I thrashed through a stack of grimy trash cans, sending them rebounding against the walls of the alley, a shower of sparks coming off the edges as they scraped the wall and cobblestones, creating what seemed to me an incredibly cacophonous, night-splitting din, and all the while Penelope dragged me on. I was going purely on some sort of created instinct, something I designed and set up for the moment, which mostly consisted of putting all my energy and coordination into keeping my feet under me.

We seemed to run for whole nights, alternately sprinting and jogging, cutting through alleys and even college quads on occasion. I began to wonder how Penelope came to be in such great shape. When I caught glimpses of her face in my spasms of running and leaping, she seemed serene and her lips were set tightly together. How could she be breathing out of her nose like that? How many miles had we run?

Then suddenly the alleys opened up and we were on a wide green lawn, running in the steady rain through flower beds and leaping small hedgerows. I saw the thin, gray ribbon of the river ahead. We were sprinting across the backs, our feet skimming the tufts of grass and the peonies that bowed under the weight of the falling rain. The moon shone dully on the river, smoking through the ebbing of the tides of clouds and fog. We started running in a gradual arc to the left along the river, cutting toward a set of buildings that were set right up against the water. We reached a cement walkway and jogged in the narrow space between the massive brick building and the river. The bridge was strange, a geometric construction with multiple support spars of thick wooden beams that were woven together like a rattan backing to a chair. It was Newton's Mathematical Bridge, the bridge that had no bolts or fasteners—it was all held up by the basic principles of geometry and physics. At least it used to be; Cambridge scholars in the nineteenth century took it apart to try and figure out its secret, and were unable to put it back together again. Now it was nailed together just like any other bridge. I remember Alan Henry telling me about it; he was somehow relating this botched job to the incompatibility of the Newtonian theory of gravity to Einstein's Special Relativity, how it all served as a sort of metaphor for the paradox of modern physics. I don't understand this particular comparison, but I did realize that what this meant was that we were back at Queen's College, the side facing the river. We'd only traveled a few blocks.

Penelope was crouching at the foot of the bridge, peering under it upstream toward town. She still held her shoes in her hand. I squatted next to her and looked up the river. Arcing trees hung over the water and dropped their branches to the opposite bank. From this vantage point under the bridge the Cam looked like some sort of underground river, a fissure burrowing into the skin of the earth's crust.

There! Penelope hissed, her narrow arm pointed upriver into the dark, I knew it, I just knew it.

My glasses were beaded with water and I tried to wipe them off on my shirt collar, but only succeeded in blurring them further. I watched the point off the end of Penelope's finger and soon I saw a shape coming out of the darkness, something flat on the river with a thin figure moving rapidly on top. A vibrating piece of string. A bobbing bird on a board. An oil derrick on a box. A punt. Erin was punting down the river. She was coming fast, plying the pole like a professional. Penelope grabbed me and we scuttled up the riverbank behind the bridge abutment. Pause, silence, then the rhythmic plash of a punt pole being plied with great dexterity. We stiffened and Penelope clapped a hand over my teeth which were clacking like castanets.

Splash, pause, *whoosh,* and then the punt was shooting out from under the bridge, Erin crouched like a panther at the rear, one leg planted straight back, the other bent with her foot resting solidly on the push board, the long pole almost at the end of the push, the farthest extension of the stroke. Her hair was lavender in the moonlight, sprouting like a row of tulips in the dark. She passed no more than ten feet from us. She wore a tight black top and pants, and in her effort to recover the pole her teeth were set in a fierce grimace, her eyes glinting lightly, her forehead set with lines, and I could see the striated musculature of her arms, the powerful, pumping, pistonlike thighs, and that glorious arse set high in the air like a prancing mare as she gathered the long pole for another stroke. She still seemed to be moving at a terrific rate, an extremely animated sort of speed, something out of place with the way the earth around her moved in languid poses, or even my own jerking hysteria. There was something different about her severe dynamism, the intensity. I was terrified.

I squatted there, rigid, clutching Penelope's shoulders with both hands, and as Erin gathered herself for another stroke there was a slight *poof* sound, the sound coming from Erin's thinly parted lips. It was the sound of effort. I suddenly remembered why I was here and who she was and what she had done to me. I was on my feet and moving along the river behind her.

She was just a few yards ahead, gathering for another stroke. The river was only about twelve feet wide here, and the bank was a good three feet above the river. A few quick steps and a leap and I could be on her back and bring her crashing down onto the boat. I could have her. My nerves and muscles suddenly went alert and I picked up my feet in high, long steps, drawing my breath in fat, silent inhalations. I had no doubt in my ability to spring like a jungle cat onto her unsuspecting backside. I felt tight and coiled, and I found myself dreaming of that moment of sweet impact when I brought her down. Lying on top of her, her lithe, squirming body under me, both of us panting in the bottom of the punt.

I took a few quick steps and planted my foot to launch myself onto Erin's back when suddenly my legs were constricted and tangled together and I fell heavily, facedown into the wet grass. *Ooof!* My nose stabbed into the damp turf with a crunch. Penelope was on top of me, pushing my face farther into the grass with her elbow and hissing in my ear:

You stupid fuck. What are you going to do? Eh?

I stopped squirming. I felt the cold muddy soil seeping through my shirtfront. Penelope lay on me like a wrestler, her legs wrapped inside my knees, pinioning my legs apart, her hands locked on my wrists. I could feel her small belly pushing against the small of my back. She was breathing heavily.

We want the document, she whispered into my ear. She doesn't know we are following her.

Erin was fading into the darkness, still poling at a terrific rate of speed.

She will lead us to it. Don't move.

She was right, of course.

I think you broke my nose, I said. And maybe a rib. Again.

Don't be such a ponce, Penelope said.

14: SHABTI

WE STALKED ERIN AS she poled down the backs, slipping along the banks from shadow to shadow, throwing ourselves into hedgerows and under thick canopies of vines, winding our way through the gardens and walkways that lined the river. Erin kept up a fantastic rate of speed, her pole stretching, righting, and stabbing into the water with tremendous precision. We had to jog almost continuously to keep up with her. My lungs burned and my head felt like it was swelling to easily three times its normally large size, but I seemed to have an endless fount of mechanical energy; my legs churned underneath me like a steamboat wheel. Penelope led the way at first, dipping behind trees and scooting around bridges like a commando, but soon I took the lead and was pushing through boxwood hedges and sprinting across flower beds as we wound our way through the backs.

Soon we were in a stretch of serious woods. Deep, full, English countryside woods, heavy with oak and chestnut and the ground full of low brambles, mounds of sticks and leaves and heavy, clutching roots. The Cam had gone back to its prehistoric form, no longer the elegantly manicured stream that wound through the grounds of the colleges of Cambridge. Now the water looked steely gray in the filmy moonlight that filtered through the trees, and the banks grew wild and overgrown as the stream meandered severely in looping turns into the darkness of the forest. The current picked up speed and Erin had to work harder to go upstream, fending herself off the banks and steering around stumps and other snags that clogged the river. The sound of rushing water covered our rustling and crunching as Penelope and I moved through the shadows, flitting behind trees.

Sometime later the trees thinned out and the ground opened up and began to spread away from the stream. Penelope and I crouched behind a large cedar and watched as Erin steered to a small, makeshift dock that was sunk into the steeply sloping bank. Another punt of the same type was tied up there, as well as an ancient-looking rowboat. The banks were covered with beds of wilting blue lotus flowers, lily of the Nile, drooping in the cold. I figured I was hallucinating; you couldn't grow lotus flowers in this kind of environment. I didn't mention this to Penelope.

Erin tied up quickly, scrambled up the bank and started up a gravel path, passing through a wooden fence gate a hundred yards up the trail, leading into a long pasture of closely cropped grass that ascended to the top of a knobby hill ringed by massive oak trees and a series of gardens. On top of the hill stood an enormous mansion made of silver-pink stone, with colonnades in the front and outlying wings that stretched to either side. A series of statues led up the path to the massive front steps, and the lintel above the door bore an elaborate frieze of Egyptian motifs and hieroglyphs. The gardens were dotted with a variety of statuary. I noticed immediately a large obelisk that dominated the eastern edge of the garden, at least forty feet tall, certainly a copy.

We let her move ahead around the first bend toward the house before we stood up. Penelope's hair had come loose from her customary bun and fell in heavy wet strings, much longer than I expected, falling to her shoulders. Her glasses were smudged and sat crookedly on her face. Her clothes were streaked with mud and torn in several places. She was smiling. I took off my hat and felt my hair, soaked through with sweat.

Do you know where we are? I asked.

She shook her head and chuckled. She tried to pull her hair back into her bun for a moment, then gave up and let it hang down her back.

I have no idea. Somewhere roughly east?

She tried to clean her glasses on her sweater but ended up only making them more muddy and streaked. I took them from her, and I could feel her hands trembling, blue with cold. Because I was wearing a mackintosh and a blazer, my undershirts were relatively dry and clean. I wiped her glasses and gave them back to her, then wiped my own. I checked the dials on my document case, still dangling from my neck, and it seemed to be working properly.

Oldcastle, Penelope said. Mean anything to you?

Not a thing.

For the first time the stars shone clearly in the muddied sky, the clouds clearing a vast space in the heavens for them to shine, at least for a moment. Oldcastle's mansion was momentarily bathed in their clean, hard light. I wasn't afraid. Not yet. But the thought still ran through my mind:

Walter, how did you come to be in this situation? And just what are you going to do now?

The next moment the clouds shifted back and the deep night returned. We started up the hill.

The obelisk wasn't a copy. Judging from the hieroglyphs, worn faint, almost smooth by the damp climate of south-central England, the obelisk was an Old Kingdom structure, probably from somewhere in the region of Helwan, just up the river from Cairo. Standing along the outer ridge of the gardens, just inside the rusting gates, the obelisk canted over a few degrees, sinking in the soft soil. It was at

least ten meters high. In this condition, still readable and intact, it was
a priceless item; even the British Museum had only about a half
dozen of this size. Penelope watched the darkened windows of the
mansion as I ran my hands over the stone.

Well, she said, is it the real deal?

I've never seen or heard, I said, of a piece this size in a private
collection. The Bankes obelisk at Kingston Lacy, Dorset, is the
biggest one I know of, but that one's only seven meters. This is huge.

Curtains, Penelope said.

What?

The house, she said. Curtains. Look closely, you can see light
coming from the cracks. Someone's home. C'mon.

We continued toward the house. The rest of the garden was dotted with various Egyptian artifacts, a few funerary stelae, some totems
and statuary, mostly from the Old Kingdom period. There were a lot
of representations of lotus flowers, which is the traditional ancient
Egyptian depiction of some kind of narcotic ecstasy or enlighten-
ment, as well as the metaphoric qualities of eternal life, wisdom. We
can't quite figure out the narcotic properties of modern lotus flowers,
at least there doesn't seem to be any, but the way they are represented
in ancient Egyptian drawings appears to indicate that the flower had
some kind of kick to it. It could be purely metaphorical of course, but
it's certainly interesting that the vast majority of depictions have the
lotus thrust in the face of the god or human character, obviously taking a big whiff. Sure, they smelled nice, but lots of flowers smelled
nice; there was something in the very character or chemical composi-
tion of the lily that appealed to them.

The vegetation in Oldcastle's garden was in poor shape, with
withered, stunted elms and weed-choked flower beds. Rotting vines
drooped from splintered trestles. There was another pair of large statuary at the base of the wide set of marble stairs, human forms with
enormous, misshapen heads, standing pose, about six feet high. The
figure on the left didn't really have a head at all; the head was replaced

with a large tortoise. The one on the right had the head of a ram. Over the door the lintel was embossed with a huge sun disk, the symbol of the sun god Aten.

Guy with a tortoise for a head, Penelope said, what's that mean?

A shabti. Servant or protector. Pretty common, but only a lot, lot smaller.

I put my hands on the stone and ran my fingers in and through the symbols that covered the shendyt that the figure wore. Prayers to Amun and Mut, the obscure moon goddess referenced on the Stela. My document case dangling around my neck suddenly felt especially leaden.

How much smaller?

Much smaller. Like eight inches. Shabti are the tiny ritualistic figures they put in sarcophagi to protect and serve the body in the afterlife.

Tiny personal servants? Bloody creepy.

Each with specific duties, I said. With the appropriate spell, the figures would come to life. Just like hieroglyphs, the symbol makes the reality.

Penelope sniffled.

So what does the tortoise-head guy do?

This is a form of guardian demon. A protector. Sent from Amun, *the hidden one*.

What about the other?

That *is* Amun. At least the ram head is his emblematic symbol or animal totem.

But are they real?

Definitely. Somewhere in the Early Dynastic period.

Penelope shrugged and walked up the stairs. I followed. I wasn't sure what we were about to do. Should we just walk in through the front door? Knock first? Either way I wasn't too worried; the lingering traces of the drugs I ingested hours earlier put everything in a fine, high key. The moment felt bursting with portent. Penelope was obviously feeling the same way, as she was striding purposefully toward the front door.

What about this big sun thing, she said, over the door?

Aten, a sun god. Which is odd, the pairing of Aten and Amun here, they—

The front door swung open suddenly to reveal an enormous and extremely hairy stomach. Gigantica stood there smiling, wearing only a pair of tight biking shorts and a silky white eye patch. His hair-covered torso made him look like a grinning one-eyed yeti. Other figures moved behind him in the hall. Gigantica extended one massive paw out the door and wrapped it around my neck. I felt his fingertips touch around the back, and I instinctively clawed at his sausage fingers. I was drawn inside, my legs dragging over the doorstep, into the dim, warm light of the hallway. I tried to say something but only gurgled weakly. Gigantica looked at me closely with his one eye, as if he was remembering something in my face. Using his other hand he slipped my document case from around my neck and up his own arm and over his shoulder. Penelope started screaming.

Get your bloody fockin 'ands off!

I looked into Gigantica's deep brown eyes, his furrowed, shaggy brow. I could hear the scraping, scuttling sounds of a struggle behind me. Penelope started screaming.

Get stuffed you bloody poofters! Take your fuckin' 'ands off!

Gigantica released his hold on my neck and we both turned around. Just behind me the Pied Piper, head to foot in Lincoln green, and the Bartender, wearing a bow tie and a purple vest, each held a leg and arm of a thrashing Penelope. Gigantica laughed, a bark like a walrus call.

Oi! Another female voice shouted, *easy with the lass, will ya!*

Then Erin Kaluza was standing next to me, her face red and shining. She was shouting at Gigantica and the others.

What t'fuck is wrong with you, yeah?

The wrestlers holding Penelope, and Penelope herself, immedi-

ately froze in the pose of their struggle, the Pied Piper holding two ankles and the Bartender a wrist, Penelope bent in midair like a sprinter
at the blocks, her other hand buried in a knot of the Bartender's hair.
Erin's accent was decidedly rougher than that first night.

What d'ya fink ya doin'?

She nodded toward Gigantica, who now had his hand around my
shoulder in what seemed a strangely fraternal gesture. He patted my
back reassuringly. The Bartender and Pied Piper righted Penelope
and released her.

They were . . . resisting, Gigantica said.

That's a fuckin' lie! Penelope screamed.

We followed you here, I blurted. You stole something from the
museum.

Erin turned and eyed me coolly, her neck looking slender and
elegant. Though she looked tired, a bit worn out; her hair was flattened at an odd angle as if she had just been woken from a nap. Or
like she'd been speedily punting through the night in a downpour.

No shit, Walter, Erin said.

I just want the papyrus back, I said.

Right, Erin said, we'll get to that in a moment. Why don't you
boys take them to the sitting room and I'll notify Arthur that they're
here, yeah? Dr. Rothschild looks like 'ell already. And she don't look
so good either.

Fuck off, *slag*, Penelope said.

15: WHAT TO LISTEN FOR

PENELOPE AND I FOLLOWED Gigantica down a long marble hallway. The walls were covered with ancient murals, most depicting various pharaohs and notables offering lotus flowers to others, to themselves, and in their outstretched hands to the burning disk in the sky, the sun god Aten.

The sitting room wasn't much. A square table sat in the center with a few rickety high-backed chairs around. Shelving covered the walls, filled with books and stacks of papers. The floor had a thin layer of sawdust covering cracked and damply mildewed blue tile. It stank of earth and mold, and in one corner there was a large puddle of murky water. A small side room contained a lavatory, and one alcove held a rusted kitchenette. A tremendous clawed bathtub stood solidly in the center of the bathroom, but that was about it. I eyed myself for a moment in the mirror and immediately regretted it.

I began to examine the books on the shelves; most seemed to be a variety of Egyptian texts and translation manuals. The papers were covered in some kind of script, a modern amalgamation of various

types of languages, along with some unrecognizable symbols. I took a
few down and spread them on the table. Penelope leaned against the
wall.

Walter, she said, you think you could give it a break?

What?

Leave it alone. Gets on my tits, really. Just don't do anything for
a bit, right?

The Bartender, like a grotesquely overdeveloped butler in his
bow tie and vest with no shirt and dress pants, came in with a small
tray of tea and some cakes. He smiled uncomfortably as he set the tray
down, then left the room. I stood by the door to see if I could hear
anything in the hallway. My knees ached badly.

This was a mistake, I said. I shouldn't have asked you to come.

Penelope boosted herself up on the table and sat cross-legged,
holding a cup of tea.

You didn't *drag* anyone, Penelope said. Bloody hell, I practically
begged to come along. Can't say I was expecting this, though. Fucking absurd.

Why did you want to come anyway?

Penelope sighed. Her lower lip looked swollen and she had mud
smeared across her forehead.

The same reason, she said, that people do most things I guess. I
was bored.

You don't seem very upset.

I suppose I'm not.

She shifted and dangled her legs over the edge of the table,
clicking her boots together lightly.

I took the silver tray of cookies and offered it to her.

Biscuit?

Don't you think it's quite mad, Penelope said, this bit here with
the wrestlers? Doesn't that seem a bit silly to you? I think all these
people are completely fucking daft.

I suppose.

I'm not *really* worried, Penelope said. I mean, is this thing worth *killing* someone?

I really didn't know how to answer that one. On one hand this document wasn't worth much at all; to most it was just an old piece of paper with some curious writing on it. The interested percentage would be tiny. There were some very ambitious collectors out there, some who passed beyond fanaticism. But this wasn't like robbing a pyramid in the nineteenth century. You didn't concoct an elaborate scheme like this to steal this sort of item just for money. Which made it a bit more curious and perhaps terrifying.

Of course, Penelope said, I'm also still quite high from that hash. Excellent stuff.

I'll be missed, I said. Dr. Klein, Mick, Dr. Hardy. People know I'm here. At least in Cambridge. We'll be missed.

Zenobia?

Someone will wonder where we are, I said. They'll look for us.

Yeah, Penelope said, but they won't be coming for us anytime soon. At least I know nobody's coming for me. Nobody knows *I'm here.* I'm just worried about my cats. Another day and they'll start eating each other.

I didn't know you had cats.

Didn't you know that every single girl over twenty-three has a cat? Yeah, Basil, Harry, and Lewis. My boys. They've got a cat door though, so they're probably just out killing rabbits, nicking baby birds out of the nest and such. Little garden in the back of my flat. Lots of little animals about.

Those are very . . . human sorts of names. I never had a pet.

Named them after my ex-boyfriends, she said. You've never had a pet? Even as a lad?

We moved around too much, I said. At least my father and I. Then Helen and I got married. Then we had Zenobia . . . and it just never came up.

Didn't the Egyptians worship cats or something?

Not really, I said. Sort of. They liked certain things about them. Written records and pictographs give dogs actual names. Dogs and horses. Cats are just called "cat."

Penelope looked surprised. She blew a bit of wet hair from her face.

What about all those little statues you see of cats?

Well, there are plenty of representations of cats. They used them occasionally to personify certain deities, like the sun god Re in the form of a cat vanquishing the serpent of night, Apophis. Which makes perfect sense, as cats were definitely valuable for their ability to control rodent and snake populations. Grain was the principal crop in Egypt, and they had to store a lot of it for the flood season. Which meant loads of mice and snakes. There was a whole festival devoted to Bastet, a regional, cat-headed god from the Late period, most often represented playing a curious rattlelike instrument. Herodotus said that seven hundred thousand people would travel down the river to Bubastis, the center of the Bastet cult, to participate in the festival. Lots of music and dancing, more wine was consumed than during the entire rest of the year. All the women shaking the rattle-castanets things, a massive racket.

Odd, Penelope said, cats hate that sort of thing you know. Noise.

I hadn't thought of that, I said. Anyway, it has a lot to do with the ancient Egyptians' particular sort of animism. The way they used the animals of their environment to express the physical manifestations of deities, to express their characteristics, temperament, their place or duties in the world.

What did this Bastet do then? Lie around in the sun and play with shoelaces? The god of careful grooming?

The puzzling bit, I said, is that X rays of mummified cats, like the hundreds buried at the town of Bubastis, suggest that they were ritually strangled. There were so many of them around that farmers in the Middle Ages used them as fertilizer.

Hmmm. I almost strangle Basil every day. His favorite trick is to shred the bloody toilet paper whenever I leave.

But, I said, when a cat died of natural causes, Herodotus said that all the people in the house would shave their eyebrows as a sign of mourning.

I know a guy, Penelope said, who shaves his eyebrows, but he isn't mourning a cat.

We sat there quietly for some time then, listening to a set of thumping noises occurring somewhere in the deep recesses of the house. I was shivering in my wet clothes. Water dripped slowly down the wall in the corner and dribbled into the spreading puddle at our feet. Penelope was right: This was absurd, so ridiculous that you wouldn't really believe it if someone told you. I wasn't sure if I believed it myself, and I was there, it was happening to me.

I thought about Penelope's cats, waiting for her to return, and my flat back in London. Empty, unless Mick was slinking about. The next place I lived would be empty for sure, particularly if it was to be a prison cell. I thought of the solitary reaches of the museum basement, my lab, preparations being made all along for this ultimate end. Zenobia striding through Mayfair with fury burning in her breast. Helen remarried. How barren the land of my heart when engaged in careful study, turning the combinations. I never felt alone before, not before this. I still had the Stela, if only for a few more days. It would be there, waiting for me to return.

There isn't a single known visual representation of an ancient Egyptian wedding. And there is very little reference to any sort of religious ceremony involved with matrimony. Still, the term for marriage means literally "to set up a house," and monogamous pairing seems to have been a central part of Egyptian culture. Only royalty were likely to be married to more than one spouse, most often because they had married the daughters of neighboring rulers as a way to develop relationships and ensure peace. There is no apparent concept of illegitimacy in ancient Egypt.

I met Helen in 1973 in a secondhand bookstore called The Back of the Rack, just on the south end of Chinatown, in San Francisco. I was looking for a used copy of Dernier's seminal work on statuary and visual forms. Helen was smoking a cigarette by the front desk and paging through a dog-eared copy of Lionel Trilling's *Beyond Culture*. She wore dark cat-eye glasses, no makeup, lots of sweaters. One of those girls. Because of her comfortable stance and demeanor, I thought she worked there, and I asked her if she could direct me to the Ancient Egyptian section. She smirked and closed her book, eyeing me for a few moments. Her brown hair was long and straight and pulled back with a gold hair-band. Then she led me around a corner into a small room and to the history section. We couldn't find the Dernier—I knew it was a long shot anyway, but I liked to buy my books used, I always have. In fact it seemed remarkable to me that any historian would choose to read a new book when a used copy, a copy already with some sort of intrinsic history, is readily available. Often you could find underlinings, exclamations, curious symbols, cryptic messages and notes written in the front and margins, things to decipher and use to construct images of the previous readers and their lives. Helen smiled when I told her this.

I never thought of it like that, she said. But I guess I feel the same way. Look here.

She leaned toward me and showed me the section in the Trilling book she was reading. There were little penciled markings in the margins and sections underlined and circled. As I leaned toward Helen her hair swung against my shoulder. She smelled earthy, subterranean.

Are those your markings? I asked.

Helen covered her mouth and snorted.

Yes, she said. Don't tell. It's a habit. Pencil though; I can always erase them later.

Don't, I said. You shouldn't. Leave them.

I thanked her for her help and she told me that she didn't work there, that she was just reading something for a class assignment. Her narrow shoulders almost poked out of her sweater, loose around the neck, exposing her thin neck and that captivating slot or niche at the base of the throat, where the bones meet and the neck begins, the place that moved as if of its own accord whenever she spoke or moved her head, deepening or spreading, the texture and shading adjusting in constant motion, rippling like a sail in the wind. You know that place.

She said she was broke, and the guy at the counter, Perry, let her come in and read whatever she needed without buying.

She was reading an essay in the Trilling book for one of her humanities courses—a section called "The Fate of Pleasure."

It's nice to meet you, Walter, she said, sliding her book back on the shelf.

To be near her at that moment, to have her talk to me was like wandering out onto the plain of the future from some dismal cave of obscurity, to discover aesthetic beauty in the midst of the cold logic of mathematics. It was a feeling I have always sought.

I have to get back to the studio now, she said, walking down Norman Street to the bus station, I have to practice. If you want to hear what I do, then come to my recital next week.

She wrote the address and date on my hand with a felt-tip pen.

She waved to me from the bus window, shaking her head and smiling slightly. I took a cab across the bridge to Berkeley, back to my flat on Cheshire Street. I walked in the door and immediately wrote the date and address of Helen's recital on the wall in the bathroom with a permanent marker so that I would see it when I brushed my teeth.

I remember standing there that night in the midst of my cluttered apartment completely disoriented by my surroundings, like I was standing in another world. I didn't have any furniture except for a mattress and a torn leather armchair that I found on the curb. I had all my books and papers spread out on an old warped Ping-Pong table. The only thing on the wall was a large-scale copy of the Rosetta Stone. I had a stack of books covering the fireplace opening. I hadn't turned on the stove or any appliances since I moved in; I lived almost exclusively on shrimp lo-mein from the Hunan King down the street. Paper takeout boxes and Styrofoam coffee cups were stacked on the counter ten deep along with piles of faculty memos and teaching notes. The bathroom was a horror of grit and hair, the shower textured with ancient scales of soap scum. In my bedroom wooden packing boxes from Cairo and Alexandria burst from the closet. On the floor I had rolls of papyrus recently excavated from a site at Meidum (granary records—nothing vital), brittle as autumn leaves, spilling their tightly coiled innards like confetti. In the closet I had my one suit hanging there in an empty nest of wire hangers. The rest of my clothes I kept in two garbage bags: one clean, the other dirty. I had an excellent coffee machine and my mother's old rotary phone nailed to the wall. It was a good life—but things were going to change. I could feel it.

I went to The Back of the Rack bookstore every day that week, but Helen didn't show up. Perry, an emaciated fellow with a sparse goatee who chain-smoked thin clove cigarettes, said that he hadn't seen her. He didn't know if she was seeing anyone. He told me that he knew Helen because she used to come see his band play at house parties. He told me she played the cello and that she was getting her M.F.A. at Berkeley. Music. One thing I knew nothing about. Or perhaps another thing. Either way.

I arrived early for Helen's recital and sat in the front row of the small auditorium. The place never filled up, in fact there were barely more than a few dozen or so people there. Helen said later that there were so many recitals going on, for so many different musicians, that none of them was very well attended. I was surprised that you could come hear live music played for free; I suppose like many people unfamiliar with the actual realities of the musician's life, I always figured that live performances didn't happen without large crowds.

She came out in a loose, simple wine-colored dress that dropped to her ankles. As she walked across the stage I watched her body form and re-form under the thin cotton, momentary glimpses of her shape and then something amorphous and strange. The auditorium grew quiet and the lights dimmed. Helen sat down at the lone chair on the stage and spread her legs, taking the cello into the large folds of her dress, as if she were drawing it into the center of her body, like childbirth in reverse. The way a hieroglyph can assimilate another symbol to create a third, complete with a fresh, complex meaning. She held her head down for a few moments, gazing at some indeterminate spot on the stage floor, as if she were trying to remember something or make some kind of connection between the day and night. I watched her neck stretch and turn and I wanted to be close to her again, to have her sweet-smelling hair swinging against my face, to have her direct that funnel of attention toward me again so that I might bask in its radiance like the light of Aten. Then Helen put the bow to the strings, her face still and serene, her eyes flat and gray like a Renaissance portrait, and struck the first notes of Bach's Cello Suite No. 1.

I waited for her outside the auditorium. It was late afternoon, May, and a strong wind blew in from the bay. The air was sweet and thick with jasmine and honeysuckle, laid over the briny essence of the sea.

She shouted when she saw me. Her face was bright and sweating. She left the friends she was walking with and ran over to where I stood under a dogwood tree. She paused for a moment, then gave me a brief hug, resting her head for just a moment on my shoulder.

Walter. I'm glad you came.

Later at her apartment I tried to tell her that her music had moved something in me. I tried to say that I didn't know much about classical music or music at all for that matter, but that I thought it was beautiful. I said I thought she was beautiful, up there on the stage, the way she looked when she played. I said all kinds of things that I didn't really understand, but at that moment I meant them more than anything I had ever said in my life. I told her this too.

She laughed and blushed and gave me her battered copy of Aaron Copeland's *What to Listen For in Music.*

Maybe this will help you out, she said. You are going to need to understand music better if you want to hang out some more.

Of course, I said, I'll read it tonight.

But what I read wasn't Copeland's rambling discourse on the properties and foundations of music, rather I concentrated on the curious script that lined the margins, a cipherlike shorthand of lines, dashes, exclamation points, and the occasional phrase, like *chromatic scale* and *overt tone color* and *only Mahler would try this!* I spent the entire night poring over these notes, examining her cuneiform scratchings, and by morning I had constructed a base-line key of sorts, a way to translate the basic elements of her scribblings. I got so I could read her shorthand notes like my own. From this I formulated many things, about her life, about her art, about the way she read the world. I could see that she was a kind and loving person, the kind of person who would always remember everyone's birthday, and that she felt most alone reading in her bed late at night. I could also tell that I was desperate to be closer to her.

The next day I told her this too, while we were walking across the campus. She was on her way to a studio session. She laughed again, then she stopped and looked at me funny.

Your glasses are filthy, Helen said.

I guess I didn't notice, I said.

She reached up and took my glasses off my face. She untucked a corner of her shirt and began wiping my glasses off. Because we were standing close, her face was still clear and sharp, and I could see the world beyond her settling into the swirling chaos of diffused light and shadow.

Thanks, I said.

It may seem silly now, but I felt then the glinting pinprick of light in my head, that airy, swimming feeling, the kind of thing I feel when I've made a major breakthrough, when I've cracked the cipher and made sense of it. The world of the possible rose up before me.

You are, I said, the most beautiful person I've ever met.

And then she kissed me.

Fuckin' 'ell!

Penelope jumped off the table and started riffling through her jacket pockets.

I've got my mobile and here we sit!

She pulled out her phone and opened it. I stood up and looked at it with her, even though I had no idea what I was looking for, some sort of mysterious signal from the gray-green depths of the tiny electronic screen I suppose.

Well, she said, we have a signal. Maybe we should call the police?

Really? I said. What do you think they'd do? Do we even know where we are?

No idea, Penelope said. What about . . . I mean, if the police came, then you'd be in trouble as well, yeah?

Yes, I said. Most likely.

We stood there for a few moments, looking at the blinking cell phone.

I have to tell you, Penelope said, this is all terribly exciting. Just like some kind of story or something. You know?

Like A. S. Byatt?

She grinned at me with her mud-smeared face.

The doorknob rasped and twisted and Erin stood in the doorway. She had changed her clothes, and now she wore a short black dress that clung to her slight body. She looked like she had just taken a shower or refreshed herself in some singular way.

Dr. Rothschild! Erin said brightly, like I was an old relation come to visit.

Her skin was clear and her eyes bright, her accent back to the lilting Oxbridge from our first night together, and I have to say that I was once again stupefied by the seemingly unbelievable fact that I had had carnal relations with this woman.

Look, Erin said, you have to understand things are a bit tight around here right now. Sorry about that bit at the front.

She walked up to Penelope, still smiling.

The lady who brought Dr. Rothschild to us. Thank you so much.

Sod off, Penelope muttered. You know who I fucking am.

We were just about to sit down to tea, Erin said. I'm sure you both could use a hot cuppa'? How's our friend Magnus by the way? I heard you had a fine time at his party, Walter. Sorry I missed that one myself.

Smashing, Penelope said. You should have been there.

Simply brilliant work by the way, Erin said as we walked down the hall, getting someone at the library to help you out.

Erin glanced back and raised an eyebrow in the direction of my face.

A tough night of it? How'd that happen?

We stopped before a door. Erin reached out and took off my hat and smoothed my hair back. She straightened the collar of my shirt and tugged on my jacket lapels. My scalp tingled. She smiled and touched my face lightly. I thought of her fingers tracing over the crudely rendered glyphs, the twisting light of a late-night club, a wrinkled napkin, a beating heart.

What kind of lunatics, Penelope said, have fucking *tea* at four in the fucking *morning?*

16: EVENT HORIZON

ERIN OPENED THE DOOR and led us through. An old man in a suit was standing before a massive desk with his shirt pulled out of his trousers and held up with one hand, exposing a smooth, round, hairless belly. In the other hand he held an enormous hypodermic needle that must have been a foot long and as thick as a pencil, the business end buried deep inside his navel. He looked up, his mouth compressed in an uncomfortable grimace.

Do please excuse me, Oldcastle said. This won't take but a minute.

Oldcastle then proceeded to depress the plunger with a shaky hand. His face was composed and serene. Nobody moved. Oldcastle closed his eyes with a deep sigh.

Ah, he said. I'll be with you shortly. Just let me. Now then. Right.

A small trickle of blood ran from his navel, which he stanched with a piece of gauze. Then Oldcastle turned his back to us and tucked his shirt in. Gigantica stood to one side, eating something that looked vaguely like tandoori chicken out of a bowl with his hands. A man in a pale orange gown wearing long strings of beads stood discreetly in a corner. His head was shaved with the exception of a small topknot of thin graying hair. Penelope left us standing there on the deep rug in the middle of the room and sat on an ornate Roman-style reclining couch. The room smelled strongly of some kind of sweet incense and curry. A small hookah, a miniature version of the one at Joannie's, smoked faintly on the corner of the desk.

Oldcastle walked to a mirror beside the desk to straighten his shirt and tie. I noticed that he wore elegant, heeled boots that must have added four inches to his height. His legs curled into a sloping back that came around in the shape of a question mark, his head bobbing slowly from the top end, shoulders narrow and bunched around his thin neck.

Please, Oldcastle said, sir, madam, my apologies.

Walter, Erin said, this is Sir Arthur Oldcastle.

His suit was obviously tailored and fit his twisted trunk like snakeskin. He wore a cherry red four-in-hand and a bob and watch chain dangled from his vest pocket.

So, he said, putting his fingers together in a pale knobby steeple of bone and polished fingernails.

Look, Penelope said, can we skip this part? We've all seen this movie before. You play out the evil doctor thing, go on injecting whatever you want and play with your statues. *That* cunt stole something, and we want it back.

Pardon? Oldcastle said.

Good *lord*, Penelope said. If you like we can just ring up the police and settle it that way.

She pulled out her cell phone and held it up in front of her. I was thinking that Penelope might be acting out her role in this adventure a little too enthusiastically. The man in the saffron robes bowed his elegantly shaved dome and muttered something to Oldcastle in a kind of Nubian Arabic dialect, an odd thing for a Hindu Krishna to speak. He had a soothing voice and a comfortable, familiar face. Oldcastle frowned to himself for a moment, then walked unsteadily to his desk and opened a drawer and took out my document case. He balanced it in his hands like a sword or billiard cue.

A fine instrument, Dr. Rothschild, Oldcastle said. Perhaps later you would like to take a look at our walk-in hyperbaric chamber in the east wing? I think you'll find it quite interesting. It is the largest controlled environment of its kind in the world, at least in terms of five-thousand-year-old environments. But I'm afraid we can't let the document go.

No, Penelope said, that's not okay.

We feel, Oldcastle said, that it may be of some value to my investigations into certain matters. We feel that this might be quite a valuable piece of writing.

Have you read it? I asked.

Oldcastle smiled broadly, showing a crooked maw of discolored Chiclets. You could tell that at one time, many years ago, he had been a very, very unattractive young man.

My dear man, he said, that is why *you* are here.

You mean, I said, you can't?

Oldcastle's brow darkened momentarily. I noticed his face was getting more and more flushed, and one eye seemed to bulge slightly. He walked around the desk, gripping the edges with his wiry fingertips.

I will admit, Oldcastle said, making a brief, shallow, almost imperceptible bow in my direction, that in this instance I shall require your particular expertise. There are some patterns here, some bilateral and trilateral signs that don't fit the normal template. Figurative hieroglyphs, a bit of syllabic orthography. You were recommended to me by the highest of authorities.

Who recommended me? I thought to myself. Klein? Mick?

Fine, I sputtered. I'll do it.

Christ! Penelope shouted, why the fuck didn't you just *ask* him to do it? Doesn't this all seem a bit overly elaborate?

We didn't exactly plan it like this, Erin said. You two followed me here, remember? We were going to send for you, Walter, when we were ready. Some other elements . . . need to be cleared up. We need the original document. It may have a vital . . . connection to our project.

And what if we notify the police? Penelope said.

I seriously doubt, Erin said, that Dr. Rothschild would wish to mar his name or his reputation. He would never work in the field again.

Maybe I'll just retire, I said.

Please, Erin snorted. That won't happen. Besides, there is also the possibility of prison. And then there is your daughter too, yeah?

What do you mean? I said. What does she have to do with it?

Just do the translation, Erin said. You can do it right now. I know that you want to read it yourself. I know you've been wondering if it's a possible companion piece to the Stela of Paser.

Oldcastle took a step toward us and staggered a bit, causing Erin and Gigantica to move toward him protectively. Oldcastle appeared to settle himself, carefully placing his feet under his body, seeming to measure the distance between them. His snug suit revealed his curiously shaped body, narrow shoulders with a slender waist and broad, feminine hips. I could see his legs trembling. I swear as his jacket gapped at the front when he bent I could see a slight rounded swelling on his chest, like budding breasts. He held out the document case, and Erin slipped over to him and took it out of his hands. Then with an unsteady hand he took an envelope out of his jacket pocket. Erin brought them both over to me.

Of course we will compensate you for your trouble and expertise, Dr. Rothschild. As well as for your discretion in this matter.

See, Erin said, it all works out right, doesn't it?

I took the case and the envelope in my hands but kept looking at Erin, who stared me right in the eye.

My daughter, I said, is in London . . . I'm supposed to be with her right now. This whole thing . . . it's screwing it up. Why would you do this? Why to *me?*

Erin kept smiling, her tiny nose turned up and slightly to the side, the delicious arch of her eyebrows.

No, that is something else entirely. That is of your own doing, isn't it, Walter?

I handed the envelope to Penelope, who just shrugged and sat on the sofa, still holding her mobile phone for protection. Gigantica took me by the arm and led me through a door at the far end of the room into a small workroom.

The workroom was dominated by a large table stacked with more sheets of newsprint covered with that curious scrawl that was on Oldcastle's desk. The walls also had various scribblings tacked up, some that appeared to be Coptic or Cyrillic scripts and some other cuneiform-type scripts. There was also a series of charts and diagrams of what appeared to be planetary orbits as well as more abstract schematic drawings of curved grids and spheres arcing trajectories around cone-shaped objects. A blackboard on one wall was covered with mathematical equations. As Gigantica cleared away the table for me I picked up one of the newsprint sheets, covered with a crabbed script, but this one in modern English.

The universe is bound in tiny looped subdimensions,
each passing through every point in time simultaneously.
This can be conceived of in visual terms as a piece of rope
stretched across a canyon and which viewed from afar
appears as a line, existing only in a single dimension. Of
course, when the rope is viewed up close, it clearly has a
thickness that constitutes further dimensions. Perhaps our
present world, the way we see it, is like that rope stretched

across the canyon; if we were only able to get close enough, perhaps in this sense to examine the world at its most microscopic components, then we might be able to see these further dimensions. Imagine an insect crawling along that rope; if it is not aware of the thickness, the cylinder aspect of the rope, then it will think that it can only travel along the rope in one direction. We are that insect, traveling in the only direction that we are able to believe possible.

The nature of the hieroglyph contains this conception, this view of looped space, the past and present existing simultaneously, explicit in the ancient understanding of the hieroglyph as a symbol that is at once the life, the spirit, knowledge, love, the *ka* existing in all time for all time, as well as in the basic topography of the hiero, in their full relief form being independent objects, symbols, direct representations, phonetic keys, individual phonemes, while existing in the three apparent dimensions that we can visually experience. We can enter this realm as if emerging from the Necropolis through a false door, the passage of the *ka*, into the Place of Coming into Being, the land of Amun-Re and the spiritual throne of Aten. This is the place where curved space bends back through eternity to us, the place where time stops and goes on forever: The Event Horizon.

Automatic writing, Gigantica whispered out of the side of his mouth. You know, he said, she goes into a trance and just starts scribbling this stuff. A whole new language, planets and universes. The old guy likes the automatic writing.

I looked into his one eye. He was placidly chewing like a cow. He shrugged.

She's the one, Gigantica said, nodding his head toward the study. He winked at me conspiratorially with his one eye.

Got a link to the *other side*. Know what I mean?

I just looked at him.

You know, Gigantica said, Amun, Aten, that whole thing.

Right. How's the eye?

It's doing okay. Hey, thanks. Real nice of you to ask, Dr. Rothschild.

I'm sure he didn't mean it, I said. Hanif, I mean. Sticking his thumb in your eye. He's in jail, you know.

Who?

Never mind.

Oh, Gigantica said, hurry up.

He closed the door and left me alone.

Hanging on one wall was a large felt banner with the image of a rising sun in gold thread. Along the bottom it said: *Order of the Golden Dawn*. And then some Latin text talking about gnomes, fairies, elves and spirits in the trees or something like that. I dialed down the atmosphere monitor on my document case to lessen the shock of taking the papyrus from the twelfth century B.C. into the present. I pulled out the rolled papyrus and laid it on the table, trying to handle it as gingerly as possible, spreading out the corners, and began to sort out the upper register and the lists of determinatives.

Upstream ship, closed fist, cluster of reeds, offering table, owl, horned asp, river, sun disk, open eye . . .

17: DUNG BEETLES

THE CITY OF ASWAN lies on the east side of the Nile, with the long stretch of markets running along the Corniche past the Ferial Gardens to the south. In the mornings, when my father was going over the previous day's progress reports with the Russian engineers before breakfast, I'd quickly wash with the cloth and bowl of water that Hakor, my minder, brought every morning to the side of my cot before daybreak. When the call to morning prayer came squawking out over the loudspeakers from the muezzins perched high in the minarets of the mosque and the cooks and servants bent to their mats, Hakor and I would grab extra hard rolls out of the basket and sprint down the hill, past the work trailers and Quonset huts toward the river. Munching on the fragrant, crusty rolls lightly seasoned with cardamom, we'd walk past the still darkened bazaar as the shopkeepers were preparing their displays, rolling out carts of stunted vegetables, curious little fruits, and sacks of grains and spices. I liked to walk farther along the river, toward the old-city cemetery, filled with clusters of tombs and cupolas from the Fatimid period. Downriver the massive pylons of the construction site stretched across the river, fretted with a lace of scaffolding, illuminated with floodlights and thousands of bulbs strung across the wooden frame and forming an illuminated skeleton of the dam. In the early morning the air was relatively quiet, just the humming of the generators on the dam, the sounds of the market and the Aswan locals beginning their day. In another hour, when the sun came into its full sphere over the eastern mountain peaks that ringed the Gulf of Suez there would be streams of fellahs, the golden Egyptians and darker Nubians, a smattering of Russians and other internationals heading to the work site. The big engines would fire up, the large machinery, the shouting and talking in multiple languages, the thump of the pile drivers and the general cacophony of grinding gears and banging pistons. The noise would echo across the water, bouncing off the lumped, gray cliffs of Elephantine Island, and the entire Aswan area seemed to ring with the promise of success, and the majesty of progress. Everyone seemed to believe in the dam and what it would do.

Just to the east of the old Aswan cemetery there is an ancient granite quarry that hasn't been used in over a thousand years. In those days, when I was a kid in Egypt, before the Egyptian government realized the full potential and importance of their artifacts, or before they had the capacity to deal with them, it wasn't all that uncommon to come across ancient statuary propping open a shop door, or an Old Kingdom Stela bricked into the wall of a shop building. Hakor seemed to have a knack for stumbling across them. The quarry was to the lee side of an old granary that was still in use at that time. A jumbled fence ran around the edge of the quarry, which was rather small by today's standards, maybe fifty yards across. On the other side a group of bony cattle the color of butter stood chewing at the rough tufts of desert straw that grew between the ledges of granite.

An ancient flight of steps was hewn into the side of the pit. In the early morning before the sun filled the rough pit with heat and light, the soft glow of the lights from the dam made it just light enough to see a series of large shapes in the bottom. Amid the rubble at the bottom of the quarry lay several large pieces of granite, obviously quarried many years ago. At the center lay a particularly enormous piece, a long rectangle, at least eight feet thick and over eighty feet in length. A few large rocks piled against the base allowed Hakor to boost me up on top of the surface of the rock. I began to walk its length, and as the sun crawled across the mountains in the river valley, I could see a large fissure running through the rock, a crack about four inches wide at points, that traveled almost the entire length of the stone. I lay on my stomach to explore the fissure, prying my fingers into the crack, trying to determine how deep it went. It was deep enough.

I found out much later that this was an unfinished obelisk, hewn from the quarry more than two thousand years ago by Nubian craftsmen. It was most likely intended as a companion piece to the Lateran Obelisk from Karnak. But it was much larger than the Lateran; the unfinished obelisk would have weighed over 2.3 million pounds, making it the largest piece of stone statuary ever. The long crack running through the piece developed late in the process, and the task had to be abandoned. Now the site has tourist bathrooms and gates. I didn't know any of this on that day back in 1962, when as a boy I sprawled spread-eagle on the stone and pried my fingers into the crack that was the obelisk's doom. At least I didn't know the specifics. But it was as if you could feel it coming through the rock, in waves, like heat, the sensation of antiquity, that long fissure in the rock like a river through stone. That was my first handling, my first close-up experience with an Egyptian artifact, and I'll never forget that feeling.

I was free to spend the morning hours as I wished until the whistle blew for lunch at noon. My father would expect to see me around that time in the large tent on the bluff overlooking the river and the dam site where he ate his lunch with the Russians. They would tousle my hair, these young, gray-faced men, all of them smoking through their meal, holding a cigarette in one hand and a forkful of couscous in the other. We sat on low, flat cushions and a servant brought the food out in large wooden bowls, setting a stack of fried flatbread on a low table in the middle of our circle. I sat beside my father, sometimes going through the dusty pockets of his canvas jacket to search for licorice gum. I remember the thick knuckles of his hands lined with grime. He smelled like oiled leather and onions. He had me run to zip up the insect netting in the doorway when a late arrival neglected it.

Eventually I persuaded Hakor to arrange for a planked sailboat, or "sandal," to take us to the middle of the river, to Elephantine Island. The island dominates the river from the Cataract Hotels to the north to the Al-Matar road. On the west side of Elephantine Island lies Kitchener's Island, and to the South, Amun Island. We think that Elephantine Island was given that name because of the distinctive large white boulders that lie exposed in the river near the island, their rounded shape suggesting elephants to the later Ptolemaic kingdom who named it such. Earlier it was called Kom, after the principal god of the island, Khnum. This is where I first saw the English archeological concern working on the island, men in pressed khaki who boarded the small fleet of sailing ships each morning for the short jaunt to the island, laden with large satchels of tools and framing equipment for making charcoal rubbings. In the evening they would come back, their boats brimming with hunks of stone and broken statuary along with stacks of paper copies of stelae and other writings.

The English seemed rushed and intent on retrieving as much of the work as possible, an idea that the Soviets did not share. But the principal concern of the archeologists was farther up the river, at the first cataract, the Great Temple of Abu Simbel.

The Great Temple of Abu Simbel was built in dedication to the pharaoh Ramses II, though the temple is officially in honor of a triad of gods: Amun-Ra, Ptah, and Ra-Harakhte. The front of the building is dominated by four colossi of the pharaoh, each twenty meters high, and the overall facade is more than thirty-five meters wide and thirty meters high. An ancient earthquake damaged the statues, demolishing one from the waist up. Graffiti from Greek mercenaries in the

sixth century B.C. who passed through on their way to Elephantine
mark the lower reaches of the temple, around the knees of the seated
figures. The relatively remote spot was once the location of an older
shrine to the god Horus, and it is thought that Ramses had this in
mind when he built his temple. The king's family accompanies him in
statuary form, appearing in a much smaller size between his legs. The
top of the facade is crowned by a row of baboons, the totem animal of
Thoth, the god of scribes, writing, and knowledge.

The most significant part of the temple, at least in terms of engineering and structure, is that it is oriented in such a way that twice
every year, on the twenty-second of February and the twenty-second
of October, the rays of the early-morning sun shine through the front
opening onto the back wall of the innermost chamber. The sparkling
yellow shafts fell directly on the statues of four gods seated there:
Amun-Ra, Ptah, Ra-Harakhte, and Ramses II.

Not everything was able to be moved; not everything escaped
the flood of water that the dam brought down on the valley. The Soviets seemed completely ambivalent about saving much of the historical sites and antiquities, the Egyptians only a little less so. The money
wasn't there for it. Most of the pressure to preserve or move monuments and artifacts came from the European quarter, observers from
the British Museum and the Louvre, as well as a generous stable of
British gentlemen-archeologists. But it was just a gaggle of historians
and scholars squawking at meetings and gatherings about the neces-
sity of preserving the roots of this great civilization. They didn't have
any manpower or money or machinery, no way to actually get the
work done. They knew that much would be lost if they didn't do
something fast, before it was all covered in eighty feet of water. The
more fragile items, such as papyrus and ostracon, would be obliterated
immediately when the waters foamed in. The larger structures and
stone tablets would quickly deteriorate and decay as the various forms
of life that inhabit freshwater took root and spread over their dry,

porous surfaces. The Great Temple of Abu Simbel was the largest such structure and one of the best preserved Egyptian temples left standing.

It just wasn't on the radar for the Soviets. They had larger things to worry about, such as how they were going to relocate ninety thousand Nubians from the valley. The lake that would form when the Aswan High Dam was complete, to be named Lake Nasser after the former president of Egypt, would cover the land of the Nubians in 169 billion cubic meters of water. In order for anything to be done the archeological concerns would have to get the Soviets to agree, and more important, the Soviets would need to use their heavy equipment to save anything from the flood of water. The Soviets or my father.

My father and the Soviets often chuckled over the studious activity of the English, their intensity on this seemingly meaningless task. After all, when the dam went up, most of the stuff would be underwater and forgotten. What was the point, anyway? I had a pretty good idea what my father thought of Aswan and of Egypt in general: essentially a third-world frontier town, full of primitive treacheries, strange foods, a cultural trail mix, a cacophony of languages, of mystical arts, ancient religions, nefarious practices, and essentially otherworldly ideas and conceptions. It was a dangerous backwater, a knot in the tree of progress.

But at the same time he did seem to think it perfectly acceptable to let me roam free among the denizens of Aswan: the austere dens full of severe Muslim clerics who clucked disapprovingly, shaking their beards and clapping their hands at me, tea-sipping turbaned Hindus, laughing through their scant, marbled teeth, chanting holy men of the most ancient and unnamed religions dipping their palms in ochre and singing from dusk till dawn, ascetic pilgrims and seers gathering at holy sites long since gone and only existing in the memory of their garbled recitations, a small alley between butcher shops, a dusty street corner, a lonely oasis visited once every ten years; their

fervor and dedication to the unknown, unsung, celebrating an inti-
mately personal ancient connection with their god or gods. Their
commitment was matched only by the esoteric nature of their religion. This is what impressed me as a boy, this passion and dedication.
I never saw it as a third-world wasteland, the way my father saw
Egypt.

In Aswan it seemed all the mongrels of North Africa swarmed,
gathering in the markets to preach, pray, sell, buy, beg, or steal. Even
the smirking, smoking Soviets, slouched under cafe awnings in dirty
workshirts with the sleeves rolled up, laughing at the linen-suited Englishmen trundling crates of artifacts out of the desert, scattering the
ever present packs of roaming feral dogs, even the Soviets seemed a
part of this supernatural mélange of humanity. As a boy I certainly
never questioned its safety or security; it couldn't be worse than
climbing out after your father on the scaffolding that latticed a three-
hundred-ton hydroelectric dam in Lander, Wyoming, two hundred
feet above the water, at night, in the middle of a lightning storm, to
watch the bolts repeatedly strike the dam's conducting coils, sending
boiling balls of fire bouncing across the static wires and exploding into
the water with roaring white fury. As a young boy I wasn't afraid of
anything. Only as a man in his middle years have I become terrified of
this life.

Hakor, a Nubian, had extended family in the region that was to
be flooded. He's the one who told me of the massive semiforced relocation, the villages abandoned and the residents herded into prefabri-
cated Soviet-style dwellings on the outskirts of Quban and Beit
el-Wali. It was also Hakor who showed me the dung beetles and explained their curious behavior and place in Egyptian mythology.
Standing at the edge of the eastern desert, just a few miles from
Aswan, the undulating sand dunes began that stretch out to infinity.
No man can cross this desert alone, Hakor would say, *never*.

It only took Hakor a few minutes to locate one of the solitary,
trundling insects, working its way up a dune that must have seemed

like a mountain. More often than not, the dung beetle would be engaged in its life's work, constructing then pushing a ball of neatly tamped dung back to its lair. When making its ball, the dung beetle gathers the material in its legs, pressing it together while spinning the ball underneath it, making it perfectly round. The scarab always pushes the ball with its back legs, going backward, head down, driving with its forelegs. Often another scarab will appear to "help" the beetle as it rolls its ball of dung to its burrow. Once there the visiting scarab will wait, almost feigning death, until the beetle has disappeared into the newly dug burrow. Then it attempts to abscond with the ball. If discovered, it will appear to "apologize" and act docile again, until the next opportunity. *Always there is the thief,* Hakor would say, *waiting to steal the life that is yours.* Inside the burrow the scarab consumes part of the ball and then makes a pear-shaped "nest" of dung to house its egg. When the young beetle comes into the world it is surrounded in a cocoon of food, and by the time it eats its way out, it is strong and ready to repeat the cycle. Such devotion and diligence was rewarded in the next life. The silent and earnest daily struggle of the scarab fit the ancient Egyptian concept of success in this life.

In the times of the gods, Hakor would say, *the world was hard.*

Every day you pray that the next day is like this one, that you may be able to roll your burden up the hill and to your home. Supreme diligence is required to keep the order intact, and this is best retained through quiet contemplation and earnest study, not passion or emotional outcry. The ancient Egyptian sense of this is relentlessly recorded in so-called Instructional Texts, a distillation of the right way to live as recorded by various scribes over the centuries. They all have this root in common, that the truly silent inherit the earth. The Instruction of Amenemope, a Middle Kingdom scribe, makes this poetically clear: *The truly silent, who keeps apart/ He is like a tree grown in a meadow. It greens, it doubles its yield,/ It stands in front of its lord./ Its fruit is sweet, its shade delightful,/ Its end comes in the garden.*

The other way, the unknown, the way of the empty desert, that would mean death, emptiness: *As for the heated man in the temple,/ He is like a tree growing indoors;/ A moment lasts its growth of shoots,/ Its end comes about in the woodshed;/ It is floated far from its place,/ The flame is its burial shroud.* In adult life I have honored this decree. Yet I do not feel my end will come in the garden, wherever it is.

The sun makes its journey through the realm of darkness always to appear at the place of coming into being. Yet in the dark time the mind wanders over the vacant desert, wandering like the winds, looking for the warm firelight to see its face. Sometimes it is all darkness and cold in the horizon, sometimes the sun takes so long, an eternity, sometimes it never seems to come. It is as if the line of all human life spins silently in the dark. Here by the dying embers of the fire watching that place of coming into being, where the scarab brings the sphere back over the sand, the journeys of the gods who control our lives and destinies, and still yet as I watch dutifully I know in my heart I am only waiting for your face to appear.

18: ETERNITY

I WAS SITTING ON the desk closing up my document case when Erin opened the door.

Done? she asked. Did you get it?

She stood there with her hands on her hips, one leg canted to the side, so youthful and sure.

I knew it, she said. I told them.

What time is it?

You've been in here for about two hours.

She walked over to the table and put her hands on my shoulders.

God, Walter, your face . . . it looks terrible. You should get this looked at, yeah?

Yeah.

We knew you would be good, Erin said, but I could tell . . . after that night, that you had something else about you. It's hard to explain, but we needed someone who could approach this work in a more . . . spiritual manner. Several things came together to make you the best candidate, our only hope. You need to understand that.

Who else were you considering?

That's not important now. And you must know I really enjoyed myself. That night in the museum. All of it. So sweet.

If I would have known, I said, what you were really doing—

What? she said. What would you have done?

The fact is I didn't know. I still don't. But I said the first thing that came to mind.

I regret it, I said. It was a mistake. I wish I could take it back.

Erin just smiled even more.

Like you told me yourself, she said, this isn't a game of simple translation. Sometimes the river will not wash the heart clean. You would do the same thing again.

My mind was backtracking, trying to get over the misty hump of the last few days, back to that night, the bar, Hanif, the riot. Did I say that to her?

Let's have it, Erin said, holding out a pretty heart-shaped palm.

I held up the sheet of newsprint I had used to trace out the transliterations and a basic rendering of the text.

It's here, I said. I hope the Order of the Golden Dawn doesn't mind that I used the back of one of your automatic writings, as you call them.

Erin blushed beautifully, like the rosy-fingered dawn.

Walter, do you even know what the Order of the Golden Dawn is? I never made fun of your Egyptology work. This is what *I* do. I have a gift for it, just like you.

What are you talking about? I said. You stole from me, from the museum. I tried to tell you something important . . . you think that because you put together this nonsense when you're on drugs, that we have something in common? Don't compare this with what I do.

She looked at me sideways, her smile doing strange things.

Maybe it's something even you can't decipher, eh, Dr. Roth-schild?

She laughed, taking the paper from me and holding it up to the light.

There *is* a difference, Erin said, between us. What *I* do comes from inside, the internal connection, true and straight. There is no alphabet, no key for this language. The transcendent is the only true link to other worlds, including the world of the past.

But it's not a language, I said, pointing at the symbols on the newsprint.

Look, this here appears to be a logogram for the following set of markings, a prenomen of sorts, but with this sort of squiggle thing here—you can't just scribble whatever you want, call that a language. And what's Oldcastle think he's doing? All this Amun, Aten stuff. He's crazy. Is he trying to execrate Amun? To alter or destroy the depictions to damn him for eternity? It won't work like that. Akhenaten was a lunatic, his campaign against Amun was more about megalomania than anything else.

Erin's pupils were enormous and flexing like insect wings in the weak light.

I have to leave, I said. I have to get back to London.

Arthur's waiting for us, she said. Then you can go.

That crazy old man, I said, thinks *he's* Akhenaten. The feminine body shape. Did Oldcastle do that to himself? Is that what the injections are for? Some kind of hormone treatment? The whole thing with Amun-Aten, the rough transformation from polytheism to monotheism, what's that got to do with him, or you? What's the point?

You know, Walter, Erin said. The same as you.

And what's that? I said.

Oh, come on, Erin said. Something else . . . beyond the translation, you told me yourself. Here we are making the real leap, testing the actual limits of the transference of time, the way history moves. What you dream of doing. I thought you might understand, that you might want to go with us.

For this *leap* it's essential to steal stuff, get in costumes and do a bunch of drugs? You stole from the museum, from me!

I never needed those things, Walter, she said, drawing her face closer to mine, I didn't need that at all. Let's go, you'll see what I mean.

When we came back into Oldcastle's study the Arabic Krishna was missing. Gigantica busily gnawed on the bones of a fresh bowl of chicken tandoori. Penelope looked bored, sitting cross-legged on the couch, her chin in her hand, the other hand holding a teacup, seemingly tired of our little adventure. Oldcastle was still measuring the distance between his feet on the floor. He looked up when Erin closed the door behind us. Oldcastle's eyes were brimming with tears and his face was a deep hue of red, almost purple. I held out the piece of newsprint. Oldcastle made a motion with his finger and Gigantica put down his bowl and began to walk toward me.

Wait, I said, backing up, you have to promise something. I have to take the papyrus with me.

Why, Oldcastle mumbled, would you want that?

I translated it, I said, and I'll give that to you. But we keep the original. It belongs to the British Museum! It isn't mine!

Gigantica took two quick steps and once more had me by the throat. I tried to hold the newsprint away from him, waving it at arm's length. Gigantica snatched it away, then gave my throat a little squeeze that almost crushed my Adam's apple and brought tears to my eyes. He slipped the document case from around my neck and around his burly head, then handed the newsprint to Oldcastle, who pulled a pair of reading glasses from out of his vest pocket and held the paper under the desk lamp with a rattling hand. Gigantica relaxed his grip and patted me on the back, nodding reassuringly.

After a moment Oldcastle cleared his throat.

If I'm reading this correctly, Dr. Rothschild, you are saying that this really . . . isn't a Song of Amun at all. Or at least *to* Amun. Is that right?

I nodded.

That this, Oldcastle said, is in fact something else entirely. He put his hand to his temple and massaged it lightly.

And what about the, er, figurative hieroglyphs used?

Nothing too unusual, I said.

Oldcastle's face was now moving toward magenta. He put the paper down on the desk.

This, he said, is unpleasant news.

Wait! Penelope blurted, standing quickly. What if we trade?

She grabbed my sleeve and pulled me toward her.

Trade? the old man said, his head bobbing forward, what on earth, my dear girl, could you possibly have to *trade* with?

Something you want, Penelope said. Something we got from Joannie? In Cambridge?

Gigantica stopped eating. Oldcastle turned his entire body and looked at him. Gigantica shrugged meekly and smiled.

Oops, he said, his mouth full of tandoori.

Oldcastle turned back to us. He looked at Penelope. His eyes were bulging in his skull.

You silly little cunt, he intoned evenly.

Get fucked, Penelope said. Let us keep the document and I'll tell you where it is.

Oldcastle stood stock-still, staring at Penelope, his eyes straining in their sockets. Everybody was quiet for a few moments. Then he relaxed, his palsied hands still fluttering at his sides.

Never mind, Oldcastle said. It is no great loss.

He turned to Erin, who was gazing at Penelope with a sort of murderous desire.

We will miss out, Oldcastle said, on tonight's session, my dear, and in the morning you will have to run into town and secure another package. The spirits will wait.

Which spirits? I said. You mean Aten? Or perhaps Amun?

Oldcastle's face shook with fury. He took another step toward us, then suddenly staggered, his knees buckling, collapsing like an old folding chair in three sections, knees, waist, shoulders, clattering in a heap on the carpet. Erin let out a cry and rushed to him, lifting his head off the floor with her hands. Penelope began backing toward the door, and I followed her lead. Gigantica lifted his shaggy brow in my direction and shook his head.

Don't leave, Erin said, cradling Oldcastle's head in her arms. Don't leave, Walter.

Oldcastle waved a hand weakly, speaking to the ceiling.

No . . . it doesn't matter, he said. He cannot leave. This is eternity. This room. *Every* room, every confined space, is eternity.

He rolled his head to look at me. His pupils filled his eyes, making them black and shining.

You, of all people, Oldcastle said, you, Dr. Rothschild, should know that. That should be abundantly clear to *you*.

We continued to edge toward the door.

A simple principle, Oldcastle said, a matter of relativity. Reversing the proportions. A halving of worlds. Half the distance to the door. Take half of the distance left. Half of that. And again. And so on. You'll never get there. What you are left with is the bound nutshell of infinity. The world of time and space, the illusion of freedom. Eternity is everywhere. You can never leave. It is with us every moment.

Penelope opened the door behind me. Erin was looking at me with genuine sadness, what seemed a plea for help. I didn't believe her, or any of it. But something held me there, in that room. I was frozen, just a few steps from the door. I couldn't help it. I was halving the distance, over and over; I was halving the distance to the other side of the door, the distance to London, back to my life. The dis-

tance spread like the broad sands of the western desert, like the endless quests of the ancient kings, the royal lineage that spent eternity
trying to unite the two kingdoms, how broad and vast that must have
seemed. How could there be so much space, so much time that divided everything? I didn't see how I could make it. But then a hand
reached out, small and white, took a fistful of my jacket lapel, and
pulled me through.

19: THE WEDJAT

THE SUN WAS UP and the sky clearing as Penelope and I walked back through Oldcastle's gardens, a damp, glistening mist clinging to the hedgerows and the canted obelisk. Halfway through the gardens we heard the grating sound of a window opening. Oldcastle, his face swollen and distorted, was leaning out a second-floor window above the large sun disk of Aten. Strands of saliva ran down his chin and swung out into the wind.

I say, he shouted in a thick voice, *say hello to Mick Wheelhouse for me! That wee fucker! He's next! I'll do him straightaway!*

Then hands appeared behind Oldcastle, holding his shoulders and waist, and pulled him from the window, his bony claws clinging to the sill. We turned and kept walking.

On the grassy hillside below where the path ran down to the woods and the river, a cluster of men moved about slowly in the fog. A few wore the long pale robes and Krishna topknot. The others were large men, the American professional wrestlers. The Bartender, the Pied Piper, and the Angel, wearing a white bodysuit with a diminutive pair of silken wings sprouting from his broad back. They were all holding some kind of club in their hands. A round table stood to one side draped in a white tablecloth and covered with a full tea service, silver decanters and cups and a stack of delicate finger sandwiches and cakes. The men didn't seem to notice us; instead they appeared to be studying the ground intently.

They were apparently engaged in a game of croquet. The Bartender was lining up a ball with his foot about to send someone out; the Krishnas leaned on their mallets with concerned looks. Penelope just continued straight ahead through the middle of the group toward the break in the woods where the path to the river lay. We wound our way through the small metal hoops in the wet grass, and as we passed, the wrestlers and Krishnas looked up from their game, no real alarm or surprise in their faces. Then the Bartender drew back his club, stretching it far over his head, and whacked his ball with a grunt, sending a blue ball skipping across the field and down a short slope and into a ditch about fifty yards away. The others turned their gaze from us to watch the ball go. One of the Krishnas threw up his hands.

Fockin' 'ell, he said, what the fuck y'do that for?

We passed through them and followed the path down to the woods. They disappeared behind us into the fog, and all the way to the river we could hear their muttering followed by the clacking of mallet on ball. Penelope climbed down the dock and into the punt, and pulled a blanket that lay in the bow around her shoulders. I stepped into the punt and stood unsteadily, crouching, holding the sides with my hands.

Are you all right? I asked her.

She nodded, and I took up the pole from the bottom of the boat. We let the current carry us, slowly and silently, back down the river. I used the pole to fend us off the banks. Penelope's shoulders shook.

I'm sorry, Walter, she said. I'm so sorry.

It's okay, I said, it'll be okay.

I kept looking back as the river unfurled behind us like a narrow snake in the woods. I was afraid something was still bearing down on us.

After a few minutes, when we were well out of sight of Oldcastle's dock, I put down the pole and sat in the bottom of the boat. I reached under my shirt and took out the Amun papyrus that I had stuffed into the waistband of my pants. It was barely holding together, with long rents in the fabric of the paper and a few pieces hanging on by threads. The whole lower half was wet with my perspiration, but the ink, already sealed by three millenniums of arid climate, was still intact and readable. Penelope was still sitting in the bow, wrapped in the blanket, as the boat began to yaw and spin around in the lazy current. A light wind shook the bare trees that hung overhead, sending droplets of rain cascading down onto the river. I held out the papyrus in my palms.

Penelope, I said. Look. *Look.*

She unwrapped herself and turned around on the bench seat. Her lips were blue and she had large purple crescents under her eyes. She was coming down, hard. I too felt incredibly, painfully sober. She cocked her head at the torn and wet piece of papyrus that I held in my hands, puzzling over it for a moment or two. Then a broad smile spread across her face.

You surprise me, Walter, she said.

Well, I said, it was the least I could do. You saved me back there. You saved us.

Penelope gestured to the papyrus in my hands.

Is it still . . . readable?

Yes. Mostly.

So what's it say?

Well, I said, I'm still not really sure. It's not really the Song of Amun, at least not directly. It's . . . a letter of some kind.

So you told Oldcastle the truth?

Not really. Just a different sort of truth. It seems like some kind of paean to Amun, but disguised with an orthographic device intended to fool someone. Maybe the carriers of the letter, priests perhaps. Anyway, it's a fake; it looks like a traditional hymn or song of praise but really it's a personal letter. Or perhaps it's both at the same time. That's the trouble with this kind of interpretation. But that's the thing, that's what makes it even more rare. Very few personal letters survived—mostly because papyrus is so fragile. Ninety-five percent of the stuff on stone is religious in content, connected with funerary rites or worship. And we're pretty sure that only about one percent of the population was literate. But we know that letters were sent and some may still be out there. This one is quite amazing in that regard. I don't know if the museum even knows it.

The punt was bumping along the muddy banks. The sun was up and began to burn the mist off the river, though I was still damp and shivering in my coat. Penelope was facing me with the blanket wound around her waist.

Yeah, so what's it *say?* What's the *story?*

I watched her face as I told her about a merchant in Aswan, a seemingly noble and prosperous man who one day found himself many miles from home. How this man had sent this letter back to his family in Aswan by caravan across the vast emptiness of the western desert, from the tiny oasis of Kurkur where he was trading with Nubian tribesmen, trading spices and silver at a lonely outpost on the fringe of the empire, on the edge of nothingness, eternity. I told Penelope how this man was trying to express, through the seemingly stilted structure of formal hieroglyphics, something that would have brought joy and surprise and honor to his home, that he had taken the time and focus to construct such elegant language, the only modern analogy being if you sent your family a series of detailed pictures that you had painted in order to tell the story of how much you missed them, how much you loved them. I told her about how he described the desert region where he was trying to conduct his business, a business that he initially undertook in order to do what he thought was most important. I described how he was so surprised at finding himself like this, so far from home. And that he didn't know how he came to be there, or what to do to make it back again. He would make it home again, but he would never have that time back, never regain or relive the time apart, and how this made his heart heavy with sadness.

It was more complicated than that, it always is, and yet as I said all this I looked at Penelope and I thought of that spiraling helix that cast itself into space, the chain of reverberative events, the things that connected all the emotional moments of our lives, the most simple things, and I felt it kiss the ground, sweetly, once again. I found myself hoping that we could drift down this narrow river, this muddy creek, cold and shivering, alone, that we could ride this river all the way to the end.

Then it won't help you with the Stela, will it?

I don't know, I said, I mean it is obliquely about Amun, but in a way I haven't figured out yet. Something to do with the determinative, the category of meaning. The figurative aspect of the symbol for Amun, whom the letter seems to be addressed to, is a bit tricky. I've never seen anything like it. Or I've never seen anything in *this way*. It's hard to explain.

We looked at each other as the punt bumped along, coming to rest on a muddy bank.

Well, Penelope said, we do have this wad of money Oldcastle gave us. Must be like ten thousand quid in here.

You keep it, I said.

Don't be absurd. He was paying for your time, not mine. I was just along for the ride.

Just hold on to it for now at least.

Think they'll come after us?

I don't know. Maybe.

After a moment Penelope stood, stretched her thin body like a cat for a moment in the sun, then picked up the pole.

I suppose I'd better get us going, she said. Try to keep it together till we get back.

I crouched on my seat, holding the document at a shaky arm's length. Penelope fended us off the bank and began to push us into the current that carried us downstream, the water gurgling darkly at my feet.

We drifted back into Cambridge sometime in the late morning. At the Silver Street bridge we brought the punt in and tied it up to the others, ignoring the bewildered stares of the students who were in the midst of contracting with various tourists to take them on tours of the Cam. We were both sodden with water and flecked with mud, and I was still holding the remnants of the Amun papyrus in my outstretched hands, like some kind of disheveled Frankenstein's monster reading the morning paper.

It was Tuesday, November fourth. The streets were streaming with students and local merchants making preparations for the next day's Guy Fawkes Day celebration, and the pubs were lively with those who'd started celebrating early. We drifted through town like sleeping strangers to this world. After a few minutes of walking along the King's Parade, both of us staggering from lack of sleep and squinting into the brilliant daylight, we decided to head to Dr. Hardy's place in Grantchester to avoid being followed back into London, though more likely this decision was driven by fatigue or bewilderment or something else.

Penelope stood swaying slightly, watching the clouds over the graying tower ramparts of St. Catherine's College while I put a foot in the street and flagged down a minicab. I kept staring at her; I was drawn to her sweetly scrunched face, the earnestness it described. She was so generous and kind, and for what? In the cab Penelope immediately closed her eyes and leaned against the window as I riffled through my pockets to find Hardy's address.

As we wound through the low hillocks and pastures of the countryside outside Cambridge, Penelope dozed peacefully, her head rocking against the cab's window. I shifted on the plastic seat and felt the deep, clammy chill of my damp clothes. I could see half of my face in the rearview mirror, the half that wasn't bruised, but it didn't look so good either. We were traveling up a narrow lane bound tightly on both sides by tall hedges, stopping several times and backing up to a hidden drive to let Range Rovers manned by sporting chaps and ladies wearing houndstooth and argyle to pass by. Our driver seemed to have little consideration for the tight, blind corners that the hedges offered and sped along the gravel path, pushing the small engine into whining registers and lurching movements that roused Penelope from sleep repeatedly. She kept her head against the window, her eyes half lidded, her fair face still lightly marked with streaks of mud. I had the Amun papyrus laid out on my lap.

Hardy's place was tucked into a deep arbor that lay beyond a sunny clearing of pale gravel with an old Rambler parked at a low fence. The day was already fading into a hazy afternoon as we pushed through the gate and started up the flagstone walk. The cottage lay under a canopy of elms that spread over the entire thatched roof and the wide yard that was bordered by a narrow fence of stacked stone. Nobody came to the door when we knocked, but I could hear music playing inside, so we walked around the side of the house. The back opened up into a wide garden, rimmed by the stone fence and then clearing into a field that rose up a gentle hill to another stand of woods. At the edge of the woods stood another small cottage made of timber, plaster, and thatch. The country fell off on both sides of the garden beyond the fence; the smudge of Cambridge on the hills rolling into the foggy, indeterminate distance.

We found Hardy in a furrowed garden kneeling between a row of withered plants. He appeared to be digging about them with a trowel, though this was November and there wasn't a living thing in the garden, much less weeds. He had on an old beige mackintosh and a battered pith helmet, left over from the days when he was the one probing about the cracks of history in North Africa, instead of what he was now: an old windbag weeding his ruined garden in a tattered hamlet outside Cambridge, muttering over the same ideas and translations, producing dusty papers that no one bothered to read anymore. It was me, I supposed, in another twenty years. If I was lucky.

Hardy stood up and brushed his hands briskly on his trousers and removed his hat.

Ah! Dr. Rothschild! Hello! And this must be your friend? Ms. Otter? Penelope? Yes! Delightful! Good lord—you're both filthy!

He shook our hands firmly, warmly. He looked grimly healthy, a flush in his cheeks and his skin ruddy with cold. Hardy proffered his elbow to Penelope and she took it and leaned into him as we turned to go inside.

I'll have some tea up in a moment, Hardy said, you look like you could use some refreshment. So, did you have a pleasant time in Cambridge? Find what you were looking for?

I held up the soggy papyrus laying flat on my outstretched palms.

I *say*, Hardy said, what do we have here, Dr. Rothschild? A bit of something for the Stela of Paser, I'll bet. A secondary piece? How on earth did you get so dirty? Were you in an altercation of some kind?

We walked up to the back door of his cottage, a wide path of scattered flagstones in the lush grass.

Obviously, Hardy said, transporting the papyrus in this manner doesn't seem to be in the best interest of maintaining the integrity of the artifact. And good Lord, man, what happened to your face?

Penelope rolled back her head and laughed at the mackerel sky as Hardy led us into the back of the house and into the living room, where we were met by the smell of wood smoke, cinnamon, and pipe tobacco. Hardy put a fresh record on his phonograph, a string serenade of sorts, then bustled back into the kitchen and served us a batch of fresh scones with clotted cream and some cups of steaming black tea with milk and sugar. Penelope and I fell upon this refreshment like wolves as Hardy put the Song of Amun in a plastic sleeve and spread it on the kitchen table and chattered away about the obvious determinatives and brought out some reference manuals and began pointing out various points of significance and the like. I was concentrating on putting the warm, crusty, sweet bread and cups of hot tea down my gullet. Penelope seemed to be of the same mind, though she was at least politely listening. He directed several questions to me that I largely ignored, just shaking my head and helping myself to another scone and pouring more tea. Penelope was spreading cream with a broad butter knife, sculpting chiaroscuro mounds on the warm scone. Hardy eventually seemed to get the point and let us just eat for a bit. He was watching Penelope handle the knife and stroking his chin. He gestured toward the Song of Amun.

You know, Penelope, Hardy said, at the time of this writing, you wouldn't have been allowed to use that knife.

She paused mid-stroke.

Well, Hardy said, his crinkly old eyes twinkling with the pleasure of dropping this anecdotal nugget, you know, women in ancient Egypt weren't allowed to use cutlery of any kind. Too dangerous, I suppose.

Penelope stared at him. Too dangerous for who? she said.

Aha! Hardy laughed, good point, my dear, excellent point! But lest you think the ancient Egyptians were a race of chauvinists, I must tell you that it was quite the opposite. Women were not allowed to do the washing either! No laundry for them, no!

Crocodiles, I gurgled with a mouthful of dry scone.

Well, quite so, Dr. Rothschild, he blurted. There was the danger of crocodiles on the Nile, where of course the washing would be done, but still, um, it was quite an egalitarian society. Why, the earliest records of—

Then how come, Penelope said, women didn't do any writing?

Yes, well, Hardy choked, there was that, but . . .

I couldn't help but laugh a bit as Hardy stammered.

I know what you mean, Dr. Hardy, Penelope quickly said, patting his hand. I'm just having you on. I'm sure ancient Egyptian men were just as charming and gentlemanly as you are.

Hardy recovered and beamed at her and soon was prattling on, going to his bookshelf and flipping through another one of his dusty tomes. I tuned him out again and gazed out the back window that overlooked the garden. The sun was lowering over the small ridge of woods on the hill that lay just beyond the cottage. I had Penelope dial the number to Zenobia's hotel on her cell phone and I stepped outside to make the call. Zenobia wasn't in of course, but I left a message, explaining that I'd run into some problems and I'd be back in London early tomorrow.

When I came back inside, Hardy had the Song of Amun laid out in front of him on the table again and appeared to be translating it phonetically for Penelope.

I hope you don't mind, he said, blushing, I figured that—

I asked him to, Penelope said. I wanted to know what it sounded like.

She smirked at me, flashing her eyes, before returning to the papyrus to follow Hardy's finger as he intoned the basic transliterations.

I was going to mention that we really have very little idea how it sounded, how the ancient Egyptians pronounced it. We had the very barest of estimations. The vagaries of phonetic and linguistic adaptation and evolution are difficult to estimate back a few hundred years, much less four thousand, as any linguist will tell you. But Penelope seemed to be enjoying Hardy's overly elaborate, clumsy intonations.

The music stopped, the record finished, and Hardy paused in his speech and got up to put on another. In the quick silence the sound of the evening birds swelled in the darkening yard and the golden light played across the kitchen table, across the papyrus and Hardy's various papers. Penelope was looking at me strangely. I think I was falling asleep, perhaps even nodding off while I sat there; things were getting fuzzy and remote. Hardy put on another record, something light and tuneful played on the piano.

I was wondering, Hardy said, what you make of the particularly curious hieroglyphic grouping used for "Amun." It's most unusual.

Yes, I said. I noticed that.

Well, he said, drawing a breath, if I were to venture a guess, it appears to be a figurative combination.

Yes. And?

Right, Hardy said, and it seems that it is working with a basic syllabic representation, at least at first, but then there is this bit with the raying sun, some odd strokes, and this low hill, which I take to be the horizon, the place of coming into being, perhaps.

I stepped to the table and examined the ligatures. True, there was an interesting focus on the symbolic representation of the horizon. *The place of coming into being.* The raying sun done in the style of the instructional frieze on the Stela of Paser. The connotation of what is unseen in the text, that part of the cryptography is clear. Could it be that it was implying some kind of figurative "place" where the meaning would become clear? Or something would appear? I thought of Alan Henry's event horizon, the edge of time-space where time travel happens.

What were you thinking? I asked Hardy.

He held his chin in his spotted hand. His forehead drooped, creating thick, convoluted folds.

I was thinking, he said, about Amun itself. The word "Amun." "The unseen" or "he who is not seen." That would mean some rather interesting things for the apparent, um, *secular* aspect of the actual hymn.

Yes, I said. It seems to be a personal letter.

Extraordinary. Right, so then why use Amun this way? To produce this metaphor of the unseen? Or just to disguise the true content of the letter?

That's a good question, I said.

The old guy was sharper than I gave him credit for.

Well, Hardy smiled, I guess this is your specialty, Dr. Rothschild! That's why they have you at the BM, eh?

I guess so.

Then there's the paleography, a rather interesting hand, this piece. I think we can determine several things about the author.

Yes, I said, merchant class, obviously at some point educated as a scribe, highly intelligent.

And, Hardy said, obviously had exposure to other . . . figurative poetic texts as well? He's read the classics, shall we say, *The Tale of Sinuhe, The Tale of King Cheops' Court*, perhaps the *Instructions of Any*?

Possibly.

And such a delicate hand. Look here, how he manages to work in the musculature in the leg of an ox, the slight stipple of feathers on the ibis and owl. Remarkable for a papyrus piece. Simply *brilliant* work. Which makes the . . . content and apparent manner of its construction so odd. Don't you think?

Yes, I do.

Any relation then, Penelope said, to the Stela of Paser?

Yes, Hardy said, that *is* the question. Certainly on its own this is a remarkable piece of work. This sort of personal communication, and on papyrus to boot, is remarkably rare. Now there is a man, the curator of papyrology, Dr. Obbink at the Ashmolean in Oxford, he might have some other ideas—

No, I said. That's okay, thanks.

Well, Dr. Obbink has this thing with a computer database that—

I got it, I said. Don't worry about it. Don't contact anyone, please. In fact I'd appreciate if you didn't tell anyone that we were here. At all. Okay?

Hardy's fleshy jowls wobbled and he looked about the room like he was lost for a moment, as if he had forgotten where he was.

Right, he said.

Penelope smiled weakly at him and took one of his knotty hands in hers.

Of course, Hardy said. Right. Of course.

We sat for a few moments in awkward silence. The fire popped a discordant harmony with the soft tones of the piano on the record player. I asked Hardy if it would be okay if we stayed with him to-night.

Why absolutely, he cried, of course! I insist. You both look posi-tively knackered. It's still early but I like to turn in myself. You look like you might stand for some dry clothes as well.

Well, Penelope said, we wouldn't want to—

Nonsense! Hardy said. I insist. Mrs. Hardy has a full closet of things, all fresh and clean, though of course they will be a bit large for you, my dear, Mrs. Hardy being a bit more, shall we say, *stout*, than you are! Regardless, let me show you what we have and you can pick some things out. The guest cottage there, on the hill, has a working shower and fresh linens on the bed and everything else you might need. I keep the woodstove full of dry logs just for situations like this.

Really, Penelope said, for situations like this? You normally have guests showing up a day late, completely filthy and half asleep? You must lead an interesting life, Dr. Hardy.

Ah, quite so, quite so.

Is Mrs. Hardy around? Penelope asked. Perhaps she could help me out.

Hardy shuffled his papers about and cleared his throat, smiling weakly.

I'm afraid, he said, Mrs. Hardy is no longer with us.

He waved his hand at Penelope's falling expression.

No, my dear, no matter, he said. She passed several years ago, it's quite all right.

He looked at the papers in his hand, seeming to search for something to say. For a few moments we all just opted for the excellent English tendency of just saying nothing. The music on the record player played low and sweetly.

Sometimes, Hardy said finally, sometimes I forget myself. He gestured toward the bedroom. I still keep her things. Not sure why, really, but it's all there. Yes, it's been eight years now. I was at Giza at the time. For a new exhibit at the Great Pyramid of Khufu, you remember the one, Dr. Rothschild? Yes, I received a phone call my last night there. We had just wrapped up the final ceremonies. A wonderful event, really, so beautiful, the lights playing on the pyramids, a great gathering of scholars from around the world. Mrs. Hardy had a . . . an attack, right out there in the back garden. She was working on her peonies. By the time I got home, she was already gone. As Dr. Rothschild knows, without prior scheduling it is nearly impossible to get out of Africa and back to Europe in less than twenty-four hours. I . . . I never should have gone. She was . . . we were both getting on and . . .

We sat quietly for a few moments, all of us just looking at the light falling over the trees and onto the garden.

Hardy took a deep breath and stood up.

Right, he said, let's see about some dry clothes for you two. Dr. Rothschild, I believe I might have a suitable carrying device for that papyrus. Something to get it back to the museum with you at least.

I'm sorry that we didn't call, Penelope said, and that we didn't show up last night.

Quite all right, Hardy said. Come, let's get something dry for you, Ms. Otter. You *must* be tired. I'll show you where everything is in the cottage and get the fire started for you.

Even though I had drunk at least two quarts of tea, I was feeling the persistent tug of sleep, so much so that I thought I was going to fall over, the sort of sleepiness that suddenly makes anything or anyplace, the floor, the flower bed, the sidewalk, the dustbin, seem like a perfectly acceptable and even desirable resting place.

Wait, Penelope said, slapping my arm, I'd like to stay up and talk with you, Dr. Hardy. I'd like to hear more about the role of women in ancient Egypt. I have a lot of interest in such matters.

Ah, my dear, Hardy said, so very kind of you, but I must admit that I was planning on turning in shortly myself. You see, I have another compulsion that is even stronger than my interest in ancient cultures. I am quite the amateur *angler*, and I plan on visiting a certain stream tomorrow very early to see if I can land a few late-season trout. It is my greatest pleasure these days, to spend the early hours of the morning by the stream that runs through the back of the property here. Simply my favorite spot in the world. Superb. Drains into the Cam, incidentally. Years ago when the water was high enough I would often row down to Trinity Hall to give my lectures.

That's simply brilliant, Penelope said.

It's true! Not anymore, of course. Since I retired I spend my mornings angling, my days in the garden, and in the evenings I read the work of such brilliant scholars as Dr. Rothschild here. Yes! Quite a life. Really though, I must turn in to get an early wake, thanks. Simply have to get a decent night's kip at my age or I might not ever get out of bed again! Come now; let's find you something to wear for the night. You can hang your wet things by the woodstove to dry for the morning. I should be back around seven, and hopefully we'll have a bit of fresh brown trout to go with our egg and tomatoes, eh? Wish me luck for that. Right, off we go.

And with that we trundled into the bedroom where Hardy threw open his modest closet for us to choose from, anything we liked. Penelope and I stood there, shifting our feet like embarrassed children in front of the closet, our eyes on the floor, and allowed Hardy to thrust things at us. Hardy insisted that we take an extra set of clothes to wear back to London.

Just send them along whenever you can, he said. No hurry.

Then we walked out into the cold evening, to the cottage.

The cottage was essentially a large studio, with a set of French doors that opened onto the yard, and a small porch in the back that looked out into the woods. A large bed with a simple wooden frame that stood in one corner, a chest of drawers, a small writing desk, and the woodstove made up all the furniture. The floor was made of dusty planks of oak; the raw, dark wood of the large beams striped the ceiling, and the walls were bare stucco with a few hanging Egyptian prints. The woodstove roared to life quickly and Hardy filled the wood pail from a stack on the back porch. The room warmed up almost immediately, and the open stove door cast a flickering light over the simple arrangement.

I hope that the, er, bed . . . is satisfactory . . . The only other bed in the house is in my bedroom, and I'm afraid that's also rather small, Hardy said.

No problem, Penelope said, laughing, Walter will keep to his side, I can promise you.

I don't care, I said. I could sleep anywhere at this point.

When Hardy left, Penelope sat on the bed beside her stack of clothing. She looked at me sharply as if she expected me to say something.

What?

Look, she said, I don't see why you are acting this way. He really is such a sweet man.

What way? I said.

You've been basically ignoring him all evening.

Well, you know I've had a rather difficult few days; I'm not exactly feeling real friendly.

Do you ever?

What?

Feel friendly?

Sure. What do you mean?

Forget it.

It just seems sort of pathetic, you know? Rambling on like that . . . and the thing about—

Christ, Walter! He's a nice old man!

You don't understand. He's one of these guys who—

Don't give me this shite about scholarship or Egyptology or whatever! I'm tired of it! Do you even realize what a complete snob you are? Christ!

She gathered her things and went into the bathroom and closed the door. I stood there in the center of the room.

It's not that, I said, speaking loudly to no one. But then I didn't know what it was. I lay on the coverlet, perched on the very edge of the bed, and dozed while Penelope showered, and when I awoke I was shivering in my damp clothes and it was already dark. Penelope was burrowed under the covers on her side, curled up away from me, her hands clenched with cold. I staggered up and put fresh logs on the dying fire. I carried a set of Hardy's pajamas into the bathroom and stood under the shower for an indeterminate amount of time, finishing only when the hot water ran out.

When I came back out into the bedroom the fire was raging and the room warm. Penelope had flipped to her back and cast the covers off the top part of her body. She had on one of Mrs. Hardy's old nightshirts, a billowing, frilly cotton affair that tied at the neck. The firelight played over her open throat and sharp chin, and she breathed slowly and evenly through thinly separated lips.

Hardy had a large wedjat emblem, the falcon eye of Horus, done in shaky oil paints on a wood board, hanging over the bed. The eye of wisdom, stolen from Horus by Seth, the defender of Egypt and lord of the wild lands, the brother of Osiris. It was a symbol for the constant struggle to be made whole, to control the destinies of Egypt, of oneself. The world was a constant battle between the forces of chaos, being understood as the will and pride of man, and truth, society, and civilization, represented by the daughter of the creator god. She was the one who could bring stability, who could bring order. The wedjat was the emissary here on earth, sent to observe, to make sure we remained steadfast and truthful. I stood by the stove, sweating lightly in a set of Hardy's old flannel pajamas, and watched the eye of Horus looking over Penelope, looking over both of us.

Then I crept onto the bed, staying on top of the covers, and turned away from Penelope's gentle breath and open expression. When I slept I dreamed of Hathor, the daughter of the sun god Ra, the most popular female goddess in temples across Egypt, the destroyer, the avenger of the gods who paid the human race in kind for their disrespect. I dreamed of vast lakes of beer, colored to look like blood. This was the only way you could dissuade Hathor from the slaughter; she would become intoxicated and sweetly loving, a representation of both aspects of the female character: violent scorn and tender affection. I was on a punt crossing one of these lakes, a lake of blood, heading toward a woman who stood on the other side. The sky was black and hung low, so low I felt like I could reach up and through the fabric of the world. In my hands I held a scrap of papyrus that I knew was the Song of Amun, but as I raised it to my eyes in the dim light, the glyphs shattered and re-formed, turning into something from the P. London/Leiden "Magical Papyrus," a series of spells written in late demotic and Old Coptic script. Column 5 was illuminated—a spell for "A TESTED god's arrival," meaning to conjure up a vision in a dream.

If you put frankincense up in front of the lamp and look at the lamp, you see the god near the lamp; you sleep on a reed mat without having spoken to anyone on earth, and he tells you the answer in a dream. HERE IS ITS INVOCATION: FORMULAE: Here are the writings which you should write on the wick of the lamp: Bakhukhsikhukh.

I found myself repeating the invocation, murmuring to myself as I bobbed in the punt, *Bakhukhsikhukh, Bakhukhsikhukh, Soul of Darkness, Son of Darkness, Soul of Darkness, Son of Darkness . . .*

When I glanced up, still repeating the invocation, the woman on the bank began to shift and change, and soon I was watching a large-eyed cow, attending to a spindly calf that nursed around her ankles. She watched me with sharp, blue, intelligent eyes as she straddled the calf, holding it tightly between her hind legs. Just as I decided to continue onto the bank she changed once again, this time into a lioness, seated sphinxlike now with a young cub between her arms. Her gaze turned fiery, malevolent, and I tried to avoid her eyes but was too late. I saw her make a protective movement toward her cub, and begin to rise. I tried to turn the punt around, but I struggled with the slippery pole, making no real headway through the thick, viscous fluid. The lake seemed to stretch on forever before me; there was no demarcation, no horizon, no stretched point where it met space. I heard a roaring sound at my back and I began to pole faster, but the pole turned soft and slithered out of my hands like a snake, disappearing into the bloody murk. The roar was almost deafening and I felt a terrific heat at my back and I lay down in the boat and put my hands over my head.

20: ANGLING

I OPENED ONE EYE to see Penelope standing over the bed, dressed in one of Mrs. Hardy's beige pantsuits and a wooly jumper, holding a cup of tea in one hand and saying my name. The sun was coming in low through the large French doors and fell across the bed. The fire was crackling in the stove and I was sweating in Hardy's flannels.

Wakey wakey, Walter! she was saying in a singsong voice.

I sat up. I'd slept for more than ten hours and I still felt weak. I was also very hungry.

Where's Hardy? I said. Did I miss breakfast?

She handed me the cup of tea.

Haven't seen him, she said. It's nearly nine. I let myself in and made a pot. I suppose he's still angling. Couldn't find the bloody sugar. But I found some honey. At least I think it was honey. Maybe he's having loads of luck?

I sat up and sipped some of the hot tea. Penelope opened the doors and a cool draft swept into the room with the refreshing scent of lilac and rosewood.

Well, I said, we should be getting back to London.

Don't you think we should speak to him first? Penelope said. You know you've only got one eye open?

What about work? I said. I mean for you? The library?

Penelope looked out the doors toward the house and sipped her tea.

Fuck it, she said. I'm sacked.

Well, I said, I certainly need to get back. I have to get the Song of Amun back to Klein. And then there's my—

Christ, Walter, are you always this oblivious?

I'm not . . . what do you mean?

The things you say sometimes . . . do you ever listen to yourself?

She went over to the writing desk and sat on the corner, drawing up her legs underneath her. She had her hair pinned up on top of her head, like the first time I met her. In Mrs. Hardy's clothes she looked something like an older, frumpier version of herself.

I'm not leaving, she said, until we say good-bye to Dr. Hardy.

I need to get back, I said. We can't wait around.

Then get dressed and we'll go find him.

It was a fine morning for November in England. The air was cool and dew damp, but the sun was already bright and warming on the skin. I was wearing a pair of old chinos, a cotton button-down shirt, a gray lamb's-wool sweater and one of Hardy's old houndstooth jackets. My shoes were still damp and muddy and my legs ached in various places but my face was feeling much better. I tried to keep the injured side of my face tilted toward the sun as we walked over the short rise behind the guest cottage and down the path that wound into the shaded wood. I followed Penelope as she picked her way down the rutted path littered with exposed roots and gullies gouged out of the earth by rain drainage. We crossed over a small clearing and as we reentered the wood we could hear the sounds of running water.

About thirty yards into the wood we found the stream. It ran perpendicular to the path that drew up alongside it and then continued on a parallel course. A smaller, narrower track cut off and went the opposite direction. We stopped at the divergence and watched the clear water run thinly over a bed of smooth oval stones. The stream wasn't more than about ten yards wide and maybe three feet deep in parts, the water a soft golden color, and I could see numerous tiny fish darting about in the swift current.

I'll go this way, Penelope motioned. You take the road less traveled.

She jerked her thumb down the smaller path.

The old fellow couldn't have gone too far, she said. Let's meet back here in about fifteen minutes or so.

My path was merely a thin section of trod weeds and undergrowth that almost disappeared in sections. It ran just a few feet from the wandering stream though, stretching wider at some of the bends where the water cut into the banks, undercutting the twisted roots of the thickly set trees and developing small sections of rocky beach on the opposite side. I was picking my way through the bushes, watching my footing, touching my throbbing face lightly, and thinking of Zenobia. I was hoping that she was still in London, and would agree to see me again. I didn't know what I wanted to say to her, or what I hoped to accomplish, but I knew that something needed to be said, besides the explanation for all this. But I didn't know what that was. How did I come to be involved in this seemingly complex conspiracy? I didn't even know if it was real; it could just be a couple of eccentrics with a penchant for esoteric cryptography, strapping American athletes, and ascetic cults. It struck me then that I was hoping this was the case. What was frightening to consider was the possibility that it was something else.

And what the hell were Erin and Oldcastle doing, anyway? The Aten bit was puzzling. We know that the cult of Aten was brought to power by Amenhotep/Akhenaten in the Eighteenth Dynasty. It was the first real recorded instance of monotheism in the world, and it replaced the cult of Amun until it was restored by Tutankhaten, who changed his name to Tutankhamun in honor of Amun. Ramses further corrected the blip in the system, asserting the rightful order of the gods, by putting Amun at the head. Later it would be melded with Ra, a form of the syncretism that Hardy was talking about, by Ramses III to form Amun-Ra. But before that, Amun was known as the god of "the hidden," what was unknown. The creator of all things as universal and unseen, and perhaps you could see this connotation as the early seeds of the sort of recognizable monotheism that would rise to prominence in the modern era. This made references to Amun a bit tricky; there was always the connotation of what was "unseen" and not clearly represented. Ancient practitioners of figurative hieroglyphs or cryptographic writing could have a field day with this simple pun alone.

Personal letters in ancient Egypt were always rendered in the most simple kinds of writing, scratchy hieratic or demotic scripts. Full-form hieroglyphics were normally only wielded in their ultimate form, and by the elite members of the society, royalty and the clergy, and almost exclusively for funerary purposes. Which made the Song of Amun a bit peculiar in itself, as what was a rather common merchant doing with this sort of knowledge? If he had the piece contracted out to a royal scribe, which was most likely, why would he spend so much money and time, as it may have cost him more than he made all year, to produce a mere letter to his family? And what did Oldcastle hope to do with it? What did this have to do with the Krishnas or the Order of the Golden Dawn?

I stopped by a tree encrusted with thick vines and watched the moving water. There was something else to it. The fact that this letter was done in the Eighteenth Dynasty, during the reign of Akhenaten and the purges of all things Amun was curious. It would be a great risk to compose such a hymn to Amun, even if it was a fake. The penalty for praising, writing, or even mentioning the forbidden god would be severe. Why would a merchant take this risk? Did Oldcastle want to control or destroy the mentions of Amun from this period to somehow further the designs of his cult of Aten?

I brought up the Stela of Paser grid in my mind and began to sort the possible combinations. The broad determinative of the Song of Amun papyrus, was it just some kind of paean to remembered love? How was the story of this merchant and his family related to the concept of "the hidden" or perhaps the rise of Aten and the purges of Amun? Could I use this interpretation to find a similar hidden element in the song to the goddess Mut on the Stela? In my mind the stone was shining, ringing with light as I overlaid the possible Song of Amun determinatives on various aspects of the Stela, trying to match up the syllabic orthography. Suddenly the whole image jerked, and I became more conscious of the present world, the air filled with moisture and the moving trees, the sounds of the stream gurgling and spitting over the rocks.

Then I heard it, the sound of Penelope, shouting my name, screaming, echoing through the woods and over the water, traveling down the streambed like a tunnel. I froze and listened. It came again, rolling over the water, a fearful sound, the desperate cry of one's name, a cry for help, the direct appeal for some kind of unknown action. I waited for it a third time, the ringing sound of my name over the water, then I turned and began to run back down the path.

Penelope was crouching on a slice of rocky beach in a sharp bend of the stream, her head bent over something. I came crashing through the brush and slipped down the short bank, falling awkwardly on my hip, one leg flopping into the ice-cold water. She was cradling Hardy's head in her lap. His face was dead white and drawn, his curled fingers bluish. His legs dangled in the running stream. His eyes were closed and he looked peaceful, his fishing pole and creel neatly to one side of him. Nearby there were two fish on the rocks, one especially long fish that looked almost like an eel, and a shorter trout that was emerald green in color.

Penelope bent down to Hardy's face and placed her lips over his. Her cheeks billowed out and Hardy's chest swelled. She quickly switched to a kneeling position beside him and began to feel around on his chest with her fingers, found the spot she was looking for and placed the heel of one hand against it and then whipped her head around to me, her eyes wild and her face streaked with tears.

For fuck's sake, Walter, go call a fucking ambulance!

Then she turned back to Hardy and positioning herself over his body began to pump at his chest using both arms. His arms were splayed slightly to the sides, his legs swayed in the brisk current of the water, his toes bobbing in his rubber Wellingtons.

Walter, go back to the fucking house and get the mobile or the house phone and call a fucking ambulance!

I scrambled to my feet and using the roots of an old oak scaled the bank and began running up the trail, one foot squishing with cold water, my arms flailing and gasping for breath.

When I returned to the river Hardy was sitting up with Penelope supporting him. She was smoothing his thin crown of hair and murmuring to him. When I crashed down the bank again she merely glanced at me. I watched his face, holding my breath, until I saw his eyes flutter. Then I leaned over, supporting myself with a tree root, and quietly vomited on the smooth rocks, my face throbbing with every expulsion.

When the ambulance crew arrived it appeared that Hardy was going to be fine. A cardial infarction they said, a heart attack. Stopped his breathing for a bit but it appeared that he was revived quickly enough to spare him any brain damage or other lasting effects. We'd found him just in time. He was coughing and sputtering a bit as they loaded him into the ambulance, and he gazed at Penelope and me with a baleful look, the deeply sad and humiliated look of the recently returned to the living.

And then they were gone and we were alone at Hardy's house again, sitting at the kitchen table while Penelope wept loudly, her head in her hands. I sat next to her and rubbed her back and shoulders, all the while thinking that we had no time for this, that I had to get back to London.

You saved him, I said. You did a great thing.

But she just shook her head and sobbed wretchedly.

I rummaged around in Hardy's office and found another document case, a standard one, without any of the electronic environment controls, but it was better than carrying it around in my hands. By eleven o'clock we were at the Cambridge station waiting for our train to London. At the station Penelope seemed to pull herself together though she remained quiet and didn't seem to want to look at me. It was Guy Fawkes Day, November fifth.

We were nearly back to London, Penelope dozing fitfully in her seat, her head against the window, when I saw the tall African man from the British Library sitting a few rows ahead of me, across the aisle. I watched the side of his head as he read a magazine. He was wearing a white tracksuit with green piping down the arms and legs. It seemed about two sizes too small for him. He looked up and then turned his head around and looked directly at me and smiled. He put away his magazine and motioned toward the front of the car with his head, still looking at me. Then he stood and walked up the aisle to the door that led to the next car. When he reached the door he looked back and motioned with his head once more.

Before I knew what I was doing or thinking I was walking up the aisle and following him through the door. Everybody else in the entire train seemed to be asleep, heads jostling against shoulders, mouths agape like open drawers. We stopped in the small chamber that joined the two cars, both of us holding on to the bars that were posted into the walls, as the circular joint of the two cars made the floor swivel and twist beneath our feet. He stood with his feet planted far apart and regarded me with a sort of amused smile. The crest on his tracksuit said: "Ipswich Cricket Club."

What? I said. What is it?

He grinned, showing his long yellow teeth. There was a knot of something under the arm of his tracksuit.

I think, he said, you have something for me, yes?

I couldn't place his accent, something guttural and clacking, perhaps Nigerian or at least West African. He just kept on smiling.

Is it Oldcastle? I asked.

Oldcastle? he pronounced slowly.

He talked with elaborate precision, working all the way around the syllables. It was really annoying. I couldn't remember ever having wanted a physical confrontation so badly as at that moment. Twelve years ago in El Minya I was beaten rather severely by a small bearded man who apparently was after my jacket. He was a young man, though I was too then, and I certainly was the larger. I remember sitting on the edge of my bed back at my hotel, trying to figure out how it all happened, the darkened doorway of the cafe, the spinning fury of his fists, how I cowered in the dirty street. How he attacked me with such sudden and unrelenting fury. My beating by Alan the other night in his flat, how Gigantica subdued me so easily. Why was I lying down like that, without really trying? I'd been bullied from the beginning of this mess. I had bad knees and my back ached every morning when I woke up and I hadn't seen real physical exercise in more than ten years, if ever, but what was the point anyway? Why not when it usually all added up to a few brief seconds of terrific violence, a desperate swing, the awkward grab and kick, the thumb in the eye. The exertion of fear is complete and painless after all. Isn't it?

This guy had four inches and probably twenty pounds on me, maybe ten years my junior. There was no doubt that his build was athletic and there was about his movements the smooth quality of a man who can perform great feats of dexterity at blinding speed. But right then I thought: What the fuck?

Just tell me what you want, I said.

He stopped smiling and reached into his pocket. I gripped a support bar and balled my other hand into a fist. He took a step back and held up his other hand.

Wait, he said, and fished in his pocket and brought out a wallet. He held it up for me to see, as if showing me it was safe. Then using his other hand he opened the wallet and displayed some kind of identification card encased in plastic. It was embossed with a royal seal.

Dr. Rothschild, he said, my name is Christian Okonkwo. I'm with the Acquisitions and Security department of Her Majesty's Royal Properties.

Her Majesty's Royal Properties? Okonkwo? Definitely Nigerian. He drew out a small notebook and flipped it open. The train was rattling through a small rural station, pulling through the empty platform at great speed.

A few things we need to talk about, Dr. Rothschild. Starting with this small detail: Saturday, November first.

Okonkwo held the pad up at eye level.

You entered the British Library Rare Book room and departed illegally with a book. Joseph P. Thompson. *Egypt, Past and Present*. 1854, John P. Jewett and Company. First edition.

For a moment I thought I might hit him anyway. Christ, *the book* I accidentally took from the library! Where was it anyway? The last time I remembered seeing it was at Alan's flat, that night he came in and walloped me while I was sleeping. When I woke up I had nothing with me. The book was gone—Alan must have taken it.

The book, Okonkwo was saying, is valued at fourteen thousand pounds, so you can understand our concern when you left London. Do you have this volume with you at present?

No, no . . . I don't. You see, it was a mistake. I didn't mean to take it like that. I thought . . . you were looking at me . . . and sitting at Alan's desk, and then in line—

Alan?

Okonkwo flipped through his notebook.

Would that be one Alan Henry of 119 Great Russell Street? Born 1978, Broken River Reservation, South Dakota, 216 centimeters, 150 kilos? Also known by the name Michael Mannon?

Yes, I said. I mean, I'm not sure. I've never heard of Michael Mannon. How do you know him . . . his name?

I glanced back toward our car where Penelope was sleeping, head against the window. Okonkwo wasn't smiling anymore.

Mr. Alan Henry is a different situation altogether. Although related. You are a friend of his, Dr. Rothschild? An associate?

I suppose, I said. Sort of.

Do you have any information as to his present whereabouts?

None, I said, no idea.

Why were you looking for him? Okonkwo asked. Why were you surprised to see me at his normal desk?

Look, I said, at the library that day, you had a gun under your jacket. Why did you come up to me like that?

Okonkwo's face remained unsmiling, serene.

Dr. Rothschild, he said, you aren't exactly the most subtle character when it comes to stealing books from the British Library. You made it quite obvious, you know. There has been a ring of thieves operating in this very manner—

I said I didn't do it on purpose.

Relax, Dr. Rothschild. I believe you. After looking into your background, it seems obvious that a book like this would be of little value to a man like yourself, considering your work at the British Museum? Working with objects of much greater value?

I felt that searing heat in my groin again, the hot snake through my guts and up my throat. I thought Klein said he hadn't contacted the police.

Who did you talk to at the museum?

Okonkwo smiled grimly.

I want to trouble you, he said, as little as possible. I'd appreciate if you could also bring the book straightaway. We do not feel that you are involved with the ring I spoke of, though we feel you may have unwittingly contributed to their cause. A discreet number of manuscripts, mostly concerning ancient Egypt or certain types of experimental physics, have been stolen from the British Library in the last few months. We have to follow every lead, of course. I'm sure you will return everything to its proper place, Dr. Rothschild.

Thanks. I'm . . . working on it.

There will be a formal inquest into these matters, of course. We will have to investigate the serious claims listed against you. However, we would value your cooperation in terms of your friend Mr. Henry. We feel that he may be part of a larger operation that we have been tracking for some time now, working in the antiquities black market. If he has asked you for anything, or told you anything, about antiquities or books or anything else, we would like to know about it.

I held out my hands and shrugged, the international symbol for: *I have nothing of value.*

We would *greatly* appreciate, Okonkwo said, your help in this matter. Alan Henry is a potentially dangerous man. We would view your cooperation as an extension, to give you more time to locate the book and return it to the library, among other things? Perhaps erase all record of these issues? When will you see Mr. Henry next?

That was a good question. I hadn't been able to locate Alan all week, and I was pretty certain that the interview Okonkwo was talking about wouldn't be agreeable to Alan. Why did Alan just disappear like that? He must have seen it was me after he pummeled me into unconsciousness in his flat that night, and then stolen the book as well. So I figured I'd do what I thought seemed right—

Walter? What's going on?

There was a movement and the scent shifted, motes of air swirled, and Penelope stood in the doorway to our car, steadying herself against the rocking of the train. She seemed wide awake and stared brazenly at Okonkwo. I was happy to see her there. I trusted her completely, even if I didn't understand why she was helping me yet again.

I thought of Erin scampering behind the statues in the Egyptian Gallery in the early morning, drilling the lock to the storage closet, of her working at the British Library, doing "research," as Penelope put it; Hanif the writer; the Krishnas; the documents and items at Oldcastle's estate; the soft arc of Erin's eyes when we left her there, cradling Oldcastle's spotted skull in her lap; and Alan Henry waiting in the courtyard of the British Library for me at closing time, Alan Henry bursting into my flat, Alan Henry, the one man in London, or even the present world, for that matter, the one man who I thought I might call my friend. Wanted by the police, involved in the illegal acquisition and sale of antiquities. It seemed like I willingly aided these people, handing them blind trust and making it all so easy. So obvious. For the second time in a week, I was shot through with a hot current of shame and anger. I thought of my daughter waiting for me in London, standing along the dark Thames, cursing me, again. I had to find Alan.

Tomorrow, I said to Okonkwo. I should catch up with Alan tomorrow. He and I often meet at a pub off Oxford Street called the Spanish Bar. Around noon.

The Spanish Bar, Okonkwo said, I know it, yes. So, noon then?

Yes, noon, I said. We'll be there.

He grabbed my hand, which was still balled in a fist, and shook it firmly.

Good, good. This is good, Dr. Rothschild.

He pressed a business card in my other hand and then he was

zipping up his tracksuit, rolling his shoulders with a satisfied air and with another nod and grin at Penelope he lurched back into the car.

Walter?

I didn't say anything, but Penelope seemed to realize what I had done. My face felt leaden and sagging, a density like wet sand, pooling on my shoulders, and the bruise that extended across my forehead and around my eye began to beat slowly, in time with the clacking wheels of the train as we raced into London.

21:   TAKE A GUESS

BACK IN LONDON I called Zenobia's hotel. She wasn't in, but she left a message that she would be back in the early evening, and the clerk said she wasn't due to check out until tomorrow. It was Guy Fawkes Day, three in the afternoon. I had about forty-eight hours to solve the Stela.

I hadn't thought much about what I might do after this gig was up, I never did much contemplation on that subject while I was in the midst of a project. I saved my mental energy for the immediate problem. I didn't care much about what would happen afterward, whether I solved it or not, that wasn't the important thing to me. But this was different; it seemed like this could be the last project, the end of it all. What would I do then?

Mick looked upon this project as his chance to hit the antiquarian jackpot; he saw the Stela as a way to retire to Oxford, English-country-gentleman style, a publishing guarantee with a major press, a glossy manual in the museum bookstores, plus a small tour with speaking engagements and the conference circuit. But his contract was already extended because of the extra work he was doing for Klein; he could take his time and wait until I was out.

Of course Mick had all of his side projects, his other ways of making money, many of which Klein set up. I know that he supervised the Harrods renovation of the Egyptian stairway, reworking their hieroglyphic scripts and arranging the faux statues they had there. The text was total nonsense before, just random symbols put up because they looked interesting. Mick was brought in to make the signs actually say something—something that the Harrods people put together, about the owner of course, who apparently was of Egyptian descent. So Mick worked out the various proclamations and honorary phrases, and painted the symbols himself. Of course he was having his own sort of fun; the order in which the signs are to be read, from left to right or right to left, is indicated by the way the signs face. If anyone who could read ancient hieroglyphics were even to glance at the Harrods piece, they would recognize that the text could be read in several ways, although they might find the actual translation quite difficult. Mick arranged the text so that it could be read in columns as well. Essentially it said: *Sing the praise of those who sell food and clothing at such a price as to bring down the sun itself, those that populate these halls live in the bright light of everlasting greed and ignorance* . . . stuff like that. There wasn't much chance of discovery; maybe twenty people in the world could translate at that level of complexity, and there were maybe a dozen who could understand the full extent of Mick's jokes. I guess it was just window dressing anyway; people liked the way hieroglyphs looked, but they had little interest in what they said. Like graffiti, it is a sort of revenge, I suppose, a small, mean joke on a public who doesn't seem to care, who holds this art in little esteem, an unknown prank. I thought it all insulting and vulgar distortions of something truly grand and eloquent.

Dr. Klein's office was on the fourth floor of the west wing of the museum, a long room with a towering ceiling, one of the old eighteenth-century parlor rooms from the building's former duties.

His desk was stacked high with papers and mailing envelopes and tubes. There was a single plastic folding chair before the desk and there wasn't another piece of furniture in the room besides Klein's leather-backed chair. The walls were lined with wooden crates and boxes, packing materials spilling out onto the floor, creating a narrow path that led from the door to his desk. Klein stood behind the desk with his hands in his pockets.

Dr. Rothschild! he said. I knew it would all work out.

He took Hardy's document case from my hands and quickly removed the papyrus. He cleared a small section of his desk off and spread it out, using some ostracon and pottery sherds to weight the edges. He ran his fingers just over the surface, making little murmuring sounds to himself.

Looks like, he said, it's seen a little extra wear? Since last I saw it?

It was . . . unavoidable, I said.

He grinned at me, his lined face crinkling around the corners of his round eyeglasses.

Something of a story, eh? I'll bet. Love to hear all about it. Everything seems to be in order though.

Klein slipped the Song of Amun into a protective folder and sat back in his chair and motioned for me to take a seat. I didn't move. He folded his hands neatly on his lap. He seemed quite pleased with himself.

You told me, I said, that you weren't going to contact the authorities.

Klein flushed a bit, fiddling with some papers on his desk.

Well, then, he said, I suppose you've had a go at this? I'd like to hear what you came up with. Did you have some kind of accident, Dr. Rothschild?

I just stood there and watched the sky swirling in the light streaming through the tall windows that looked out over Russell Square. I was exhausted and hungry and I just wanted to step through an imaginary door and leave all of this. Where was the portal for my *ka* to escape, to find nourishment; where were my shabti? Where is the false door for those of us who are still alive?

I'm going down to the lab, I said.

I started walking to the door.

Ah, Klein said, getting up quickly, not a bad idea, I suppose, considering. Any new leads, Rothschild? The Amun papyrus give you some ideas?

I could hear him cat-footing it across the floor behind me, rustling through papers and squeaking on Styrofoam peanuts. I reached the door and passed through it without looking back.

Two more days, he called after me, better make the best of it. Let me know . . .

And then I was through the anteroom of his office and heading down the wide marble staircase that led to the main foyer of the museum. A man passed me on the way up, moving quickly, rippling the periphery, and for a moment I thought it might be one of the curators, Feynman or Witten, or both maybe, I didn't care. I seemed to have a sort of tunnel vision; the rest of the world was a telescoping swirl that rotated around the axis that lay right in front of me. I could tell that the main foyer was filled with the usual crowd of tourists, momentarily stunned by its sweeping grandeur. I pushed through them with my eyes on the floor, not wanting to meet their gaze. When I reached the service corridor to the basement I walked quickly down the stairs and through the hall, past the staring Impressionistic figures of Sue and Cindy, down into the lab.

It was immediately clear that I wasn't going to get any time alone with the Stela. Mick's form was hunkered over the stone; wearing the same clothes he was wearing two days ago, his hair in thick greasy clumps, no shoes, and still clutching a wad of papers in his mouth. The place smelled like an animal cage in the smoking section of a curry house. A formation of cigarette butts circled his feet. Mick didn't even seem to notice me when I came in. He'd obviously been working on it for the last two days.

There was a small pile of memos on my table, notes from some of the curators requesting certain things, asking some advice, other things that I normally just threw out. There was also a card in the pile, which turned out to be a "cheer up" sort of Hallmark affair from Cindy and Sue. I made a mental note to be nicer to those two, and to include them in my work in some way as soon as possible. Hell, I ought to just bring them in and let them take a look at the Stela. Their translation skills were quite rudimentary; I doubt they could tell the difference between a Late Middle Kingdom text and Late New Kingdom text, but perhaps their fresh eyes would notice something I was missing. Perhaps I ought to just trot the thing out on the sidewalk, just cart the entire Stela out on Great Russell Street and encourage the mobs that thronged the sidewalks to have a shot. Take a guess, everybody!

Mick wasn't moving. I could see over his shoulder that he had moved a couple of my colored markers that I had on the grid, corresponding to determinative possibilities. Even though I had them memorized, that irked me a bit.

In two days we would be separated, possibly forever. I would only be able to see the Stela in books or to come to the museum when they put it on display, ogling at it in a glass case like all the rest of the tourists. Not to have my hands on it, to feel the worn edges and the smooth writing surface, the slight indentations of the inscriptions, to trace them lightly with my fingernails. The possible profundity of meaning hidden in darkness, the impossibility of it, the frustration that oozed from it like a fog, the way it had managed to stymie all the greatest cryptographers in the world for all this time. I couldn't imagine not having the Stela with me, not having its implacable face to gaze upon, not being able to grip its worn edges in my hands, not being able to hold on.

I purposely made some noise with my stool and the papers on my desk. Mick didn't even flinch. His shirt back was soaked through with sweat.

Mick? I said.

Nothing.

Hey, Mick!

It is an understood rule that you never interrupt other translators when they are in the midst of working out something. Most of the time you have vast lines of text in your head that you are comparing to the text before you, with notations and lists of possibilities arranged in columns like extremely ornate sentence diagrams. Break your train of thought in the middle of that and it could all just evaporate. I walked over and touched him on the shoulder. He was bent slightly at the waist, leaning over the Stela with his hands clutching the sides for support.

Mick? You okay?

He lurched himself upright and staggered back a few steps. His eyes were closed, tightly pressed. He moaned and shuffled, still bent at the waist, over to his worktable, his eyes still shut. Mick climbed on the table with some considerable effort, pushing various stacks of papers, books, writing tools, clay tablets, rolls of papyrus, all clattering onto the floor. He stretched out on his back and promptly began to snore.

I turned back to the Stela and tried to figure out what Mick was doing. The colored tabs had been rearranged in a curious pattern, something I hadn't seen before. What he was doing was altering the already assumed translations of the vertical lines of text, something I had tried many times, but Mick had come up with a few interesting things. He was working with vertical lines 38–42, and in particular I was drawn to the expositions he developed from the opening invocations of the goddess Mut. We had assumed line 41 to read *the sun god illumines for all the power of Mut,* but Mick had played with the ideogram on the corresponding horizontal line 3 to change the phrase to *the sun god illumines for her the powers of Mut*. Her? It worked grammatically but the context was all wrong. Who was this *her?* If there was a her, then the focus of the delivery of the hymn to Mut was contorted; we had always taken it to be directed to a general audience, that of the gods and anyone else who would read it. But if the hymn was directed to a particular person, that would change things a bit.

I ran through some of the possibilities in the surrounding lines: vertical line 38 *great of strength in the presence of Mut the goddess of the moon,* could also be altered with horizontal line 2 *strength (her) eye, it illuminates,* to make vertical 38 read as *great of strength in her presence, your goddess of the moon, Mut . . .*

This was something. It complicated the issue by opening up more alternative readings of the two ways we already had. I would have to retranslate the entire text using Mick's transliteration of the vertical and horizontal lines. The epistolary format of the Song of Amun was the next thing. I would have to redo the grid, assigning a different determinative to the entire piece.

Working with Mick's alterations I moved through some other vertical lines.

Vertical 40: *He is illuminated by her beauty, and that is pleasing to her . . . the pure heart rides the waters in a settled boat . . . no sail is necessary, a pole to steer the way . . . Praise in heaven and on earth in the worn brow of her father . . .*

And the effect of horizontal 14: *She who is young rises behind the sun, over the east, wearing the two crowns . . . she shines as gold . . . the animals of the earth chatter, the apes make a song of her beauty . . . the beloved one, who has been exalted since before the time of the gods . . .*

The signifier of the apes, Thoth, the god of writing. The features of the text were moving in a much more personal manner, becoming less of a series of hymns or songs to Mut and Amun-Re, seeming to indicate another addressee, another figure, another person. Who? If not a god . . .

First I had to do something about Mick, not to mention the condition of the lab. It was really rank, a thick, full-throttled body stench, like an Algerian bus in August, so much so that I was having trouble concentrating, especially shuffling around ankle deep in curry containers and cigarette butts. Part of me hoped he had lapsed into a coma from which he would never return. I would need some help to get him out of here.

Of course Cindy and Sue were hovering right outside the door. They came into the lab like housecats creeping into a paper bag. Immediately they wrinkled their faces in disgust as the stench hit them, and they regarded with apparent horror the condition of the lab, floor littered with Styrofoam and papers, the walls covered with my charts, the Stela rising like an obelisk from the mess, and Mick's prostrate form stretched out on the table. I'm not sure what they expected to see, but they seemed a bit disappointed.

But they tackled the assigned task with great gusto: Cindy attacked the pile of trash while Sue helped me get Mick to his feet. We jammed a paper cup of hot coffee into his flaccid squirrel mouth. I figured that Sue and Cindy's coffee could make the dead walk a few blocks. We wrapped Mick in an old sheet that was covering a set of small statuettes that came from the temple of Amun at Karnak—more material that we hoped would have a connection to the Stela. I put an arm around Mick and his eyes flickered as Sue and Cindy's toxic potion hit his gut. I figured it would only last a few minutes; I had to hurry if I didn't want to carry him like a baby the four blocks back to our flat. They seemed even more shocked when I dropped the key to the lab into their hands.

Do what you can, I said. Or whatever you want. Including figuring out that fucking thing over there.

I gestured toward the Stela.

Thanks for the help.

They stared at me openmouthed, but as I carried Mick out the door I could hear them already rustling around, shuffling toward the Stela, the impossible density of its dark mass drawing them in.

We went out the east gate, Mick mumbling and shuffling his feet, leaning into me as I dragged him along. I was thankful that he was such a tiny guy, weighing no more than a hundred and twenty pounds or so, and so with my moderate bulk I was able to force him into movement. I supposed that we weren't an unfamiliar sight in London; many a man had to help his mate back from the pubs in this same fashion. However this was before noon, and with Mick, ghastly looking and wrapped up in a stained sheet, the crowds on the sidewalk on Great Russell Street cleared a path for us. We made the first block in fine fashion, but then Mick began to falter. He went limp as we crossed Museum Street and suddenly I was dragging him, his bare feet twisting on the concrete and gutter muck. I am not a strong man, and I certainly wasn't in the kind of shape to carry him all by myself, despite his small size. I spent the rest of my energy just dragging Mick across the street. I leaned him up against a mailbox and kept him upright by leaning into him. I was sweating profusely and the ground swam up in front of me. I was debating the possibilities of going for help, just leaving him there, or maybe attempting to hoist him over my shoulder, which would have surely destroyed me, when suddenly down the street there was a large smear of movement and Alan Henry came striding up out of the crowd, grinning, shining like the morning star of Horus, brother of Osiris, Seth, the defender of Egypt, the feared one.

22:   EXECRATION

ALAN STUFFED MICK INTO the little airplane bathroom in our flat, squirted some liquid dish soap over his prostrate form, turned the shower on full blast and closed the door. I made some tea in the kitchen and we sat at the tiny table with a couple of chipped mugs. Alan sipped from his tea, watching me warily.

I've been looking for you, I said.

I know. The building manager, Eddie, he told me.

Pause.

So where have you been? What've you been doing? I asked.

I've been around. I've been talking with an American scientist named Corner. From Ohio.

Alan Henry laced his fingers behind his barrel neck and leaned back in his chair, provoking a groaning sound that I was sure signaled the end of the kitchen furniture.

He consulted with the Canadian propulsion crew, Alan continued, for the moon-shot mission. It was his idea to use a single blast rather than a sustained charge, cutting-edge atomic physics. Corner had some interesting ideas that predicted the present discipline of superstring theory. To link up Einstein's general relativity and Newton's quantum mechanics? Planets and atoms, the big and the small? Both are understood and assumed to be correct, yet the laws of each make it impossible for *both* to be right. The kinda thing that physicists don't like to talk about much. The greatest scientific cover-up of the century. Corner was the one that first broke superstring theory, though of course he doesn't get the credit for it. He's the one who first supposed the idea that the smallest particles in existence are these loops of string that oscillate at different speeds and patterns, that in turn create the behavior of particles and create the laws of physics.

String? Little pieces of string make the universe?

Yeah, vibrating loops of string. Of course there are a lot of other variables—thickness, holes, Calabi-Yau space, between nine and thirteen dimensions. The tune they play determines whether they create hydrogen or a fruit bat. The winds of change blow through an aeolian universe.

That sounds . . . absurd.

Alan shrugged and yawned.

Matter of perspective I suppose. The position of the observer, as always, is the key to the resulting discovery.

Why did you punch me in the face like that? I said.

Alan checked his hands and scrutinized my face for a moment, as if by some indelible marking to either he might actually recall a beating he administered that escaped him at the moment.

What are you talking about?

Where's Hanif?

Why?

What do you know about Erin Kaluza? That girl we met a few nights ago at the Lupo Bar? The night Hanif was arrested?

Alan frowned and folded his arms across his massive chest.

Nothing. Don't know anything about her.

She's a thief. You're not telling me the truth. Hanif's a thief. I know all about it.

Alan stood up, jostling our cups and spilling tea all over the table.

What the *hell* are you talking about, Rothschild? Hanif's in the clink. *Prison.* The man's a bona fide political prisoner. Have you lost your mind?

This wasn't going the way I hoped it would; I didn't want to get Alan Henry all riled up and upset, because then it would be impossible to engage him in any sort of legitimate, rational conversation.

Look, I said, I'm starving. Let's go somewhere where I can get something to eat.

Alan followed me out the door, fuming under his breath, cracking his knuckles ominously.

We walked down Endell Street to the Rock and Sole Place Fish Shop. The lunch crowd was nearly gone and there was a small table open in the back. We squeezed in, Alan all but enveloping the table with his bulk. The place was crowded, full of Central London working stiffs, girls in executive-blazer outfits eating plates of chips with mushy peas, huddled together with gap-toothed dustmen, a wary Korean family who poked their hunks of fish nervously as if it might spring to fatty-fried life, fat-jowled cabbies with pork-chop sideburns, a couple of Greek men in leather jackets speaking Greek into their mobile phones at top volume, every other person sucking down entire cigarettes between bites. The windows steamed and the tabletops were slick with grease.

I got cod and chips, small order. Alan had a large skate, saveloy, battered sausage, chips and mushy peas. We crunched on our fish in silence. Pea-size beads of perspiration perched on Alan's upper lip, and I shivered as the sweat trickled down my back. I needed a shower badly. It often seems as if all of Central London is like this—like being in a chip shop, crowded, noisy, smelly, a bit greasy, the damp sheen of dirty sweat on your skin, the clumsy intimacy of strangers, the absurd variety of life crammed into one place, everyone sort of blandly pretending to enjoy their food and ignore their painfully hard chair, the stench of the man opposite, the churning intestinal strain, the teenagers screaming obscenities across the room, the shouting in four different languages that nobody understood, their tired eyes and aching knees, damp shoes, knowing that waiting at home for them was an empty room, if they were lucky, with a rusting hot pot and a miserably short mattress, the essential position of their lives at that moment. I was having trouble swallowing my fish and decided to quit trying.

What about the bail money? I asked Alan. The money Mick gave you?

Alan Henry was wiping his plate down with his last chip to gather all the smears of mushy peas and crumbs of fried material.

Okay, Alan said, Hanif got his barrister to hand it over to him in the pen, then blew it on a packet of methamphetamine another inmate cooked up in his sink. He got busted for that too, but the barrister says we should have him out this week.

Did you know that his girl Erin, that woman we met that night, that she stole something from the museum? Something extremely valuable?

Alan looked puzzled, delicately holding his half-eaten battered sausage in his hand like a conductor's baton.

What was she doing in the museum? When?

Never mind, I said. What happened to your stuff? In your room? Where are you staying?

Things got a little hot for me in there, Alan said.

He lowered his gaze and muttered toward the devastated skate carcass on his plate.

People were watching me and I couldn't trust it. Somebody broke in and was going through my things. I suspect agents from the CSA. I had an associate remove my belongings.

CSA?

Canadian Security Administration.

You're joking, I said.

We looked at each other for a few moments. This was exactly the kind of bullshit I was expecting. He wasn't going to come clean with me.

I've never heard of it, I said.

Exactly, Alan said. He raised his chin and widened his eyes knowingly.

It's not the first time they've sent operatives to check up on me. The CSA is nothing to trifle with. They built the mold, taught the NSA and the CIA all the tricks. I'm currently housed in an undisclosed location on the South Bank.

I always figured Alan was a little loose about certain things, but I was starting to doubt his basic foundations of reality.

Then what are you doing around *here?*

Alan looked shocked.

Why, I came to check up on you, Rothschild. I hadn't seen you around lately. And then our little friend Mick—

Remember the wrestlers from that night? The one called Gigantica? They're in on this too. Some kind of weird plot, and I'm all wrapped up in it. And the Krishnas. It seems so damn convenient, the night I meet Hanif everything starts to go crazy . . . I don't know what I'm saying. There's a guy looking for you, named Okonkwo. Did you know that? I first saw him sitting at your desk, and then he followed me all the way to Cambridge and back.

Alan pursed his lips and drank thoughtfully from his water glass. For the first time I saw panic flicker across his broad face as he tipped his glass up, his eyes searching the ceiling.

Okonkwo? he said. Rings a bell. A very faint one.

Why did you do it? I said. What possible interest do you have in Egyptian antiquities? What do the Krishnas want with it? Was it for Oldcastle? Is he paying you to do it?

Easy now, my good doctor, Alan said. Oldcastle? Never heard of 'em. As for Egyptian antiquities, well, you know that I respect your work, despite the fact that it seems dreadfully boring. Tell me about this guy Okonkwo again. Did he mention formal charges?

No, no. He saw me at the British Library. He was sitting at your normal desk. Then he was on the train from Cambridge. I didn't tell him anything. I left something in your flat, a book; that's what Okonkwo was after me for. Or at least following me for.

What kind of book?

Some old memoir of a journey through nineteenth-century Egypt. Brown leather binding. Nothing really special, I mean I only read the first couple of chapters. But the library seems to take it very seriously. It's pretty valuable.

Alan shrugged, his corded neck muscles rolling like snakes.

No idea, Rothschild, he said. I don't have any such book—wait, when the hell were *you* in my room?

What about that scarab ring on your hand? Where'd you get that?

Alan checked his hands.

You mean this?

He held out his fingers for me to inspect. There it was, the dull red stone, the roughly incised scarab. I felt foolish even considering the possibility that crept into my mind.

Hanif gave it to me, Alan said. What about it?

I felt the waters shift, an opportunity to switch paths, the other land. To possibly make it right. To defeat Seth you have to let him transform, let him assume the shape he wants. And like Horus, when Seth becomes a hippopotamus, roaring with animal fury, foaming the Nile with his gnashing jaws, you must become the hunter and spear him from the riverbank, you harpoon him and drag him onto dry land.

Look, I have to do some things tonight. Can you meet me tomorrow? At the Spanish Bar?

Alan Henry's eyes narrowed.

Let's resolve this tomorrow, I said. The Spanish Bar, at noon. Meet me there and we'll figure it all out.

I got up. Finally, I was getting to make my own exit, leaving Alan with his drawbridge mouth hanging open for once.

I gotta go, I said. I have to call my daughter. Tomorrow. Noon.

23: THE HEART SCARAB

I WALKED BACK UP to Great Russell then down Coptic Street to the Plough Pub. They had an upstairs room, a dining room, though I never saw anyone eating dinner or anything else up there. There were a few tables pushed up against the large lead-pane windows that look out on Little Russell Street and the Ruskin Hotel across the way. There was also a phone up there, a free local phone, an anomaly in London or pretty much anywhere in Europe for that matter. It was already ten after six so I rang up Zenobia's hotel. The clerk connected me with her room.

Back already? Zenobia said. So soon?

Her electronic distillation sounded agreeable, though a bit tense, as if there was someone else with her in the room.

I'm sorry about that, Zenobia, I mean it. Things got a little complicated. See, there was this guy Dr. Hardy—

Forget about it, she said, I don't care that much.

But he had a heart attack, in the river, and we had to resuscitate him and—

Wait, you *resuscitated* him?

Well, he was down, out. Dead. And then—

You brought him back to life?

Not really, I mean, Penelope did—

Penelope?

Yeah, she's the woman who was with me in Cambridge, we—she was there to help me—

Save it, Zenobia said, I don't have the time. I have to run to a meeting. Look, if you want to meet again, there's an international print-media reception at the South Bank Arts Center tonight. You know where that is? For Guy Fawkes Day. Show up around nine o'clock, and wear something nice. Not that old corduroy suit please.

Of course, I said, I'll be there. How long are you staying?

Oh, it'll last a couple hours I suppose. We'll watch the fireworks over Waterloo Bridge from the balcony and have some cocktails and things. Why, you have something else to do?

I meant in London, I said, how long will you be in London?

I'm due back in New York tomorrow.

Zenobia's voice softened for a moment, the electronic distillation wavered, the sound waves oscillating at a different frequency, the amperes sluggish, betraying a sensation of feeling. I felt like I was hanging on to the phone for dear life.

We got it back, I said. The stolen papyrus. It's a pretty interesting piece.

I bet it is. Are you still going to get fired?

Maybe. It doesn't matter though, my contract is up in two days. I'll have to leave anyway.

Where will you go?

I'm not sure.

I shifted my feet and the ancient floorboards creaked warmly.

Bring your friend, Zenobia said. I'd like to meet her. Like to meet the kind of woman that would . . . go with you to Cambridge to recover this stolen . . . thing.

We were both silent for a moment. I could hear her breathing lightly.

I'll put a slot on the list for your friend. It should be quite a crowd. They say Fergie is scheduled to make an appearance. Wouldn't want to miss that. Or do you know who she is? Seeing as she's actually still alive?

We were silent again.

Look, she said, I should go. I'll see you at nine. Just give them your name at the lobby and they'll find me. I'd like for you to come, because I . . . I have something I want to tell you. Some news. Something other than Mom remarrying. I didn't want to hit you with both at the same time.

I appreciate that, I said.

No problem, Zenobia said. And could you look presentable, please? Just do the best you can. Can you run out to the store or something? Or perhaps your friend Penelope can—

Zenobia, I said, I want to say something. I want you to know something. A lot of things have been happening lately, I don't think you understand the sort of pressure I'm under—

Please, she whispered harshly, please don't start with the "you don't understand" thing.

We were quiet for a moment and I just breathed, shallow and hot. I could hear the distant clink of glasses and wood from the bar below, the sounds of greetings and exchanges, the distant symphony of goodwill. Clearly, the English pub is the most welcoming and dreadfully lonely institution in the world.

See you at nine, she said. Right? Okay. Good-bye.

I stood by the empty bar with the phone pressed to my ear and watched the light fade over the dusky walls of the Ruskin Hotel. The leaded glass sagged slightly toward the bottom, giving the hotel facade a loose, drooping look. The skies were dark and beyond the sounds of the pub below I could hear the afternoon traffic warming up. I stood there and held on to the phone. The ancients had an understanding of the apocalypse; it was waiting around every corner. Every day was a preparation for the possible cataclysm, like the struggles of Osiris and the great serpent Aposis through the dark night of the underworld. Only preparation and vigilance brought the coming day into being. From *The Instruction of Amenemope:*

> Do not say: "Today is like tomorrow." How will this
> end? Come tomorrow, today has vanished, the deep has
> become the water's edge. Crocodiles are bared,
> hippopotami stranded, the fish crowded together. Jackals
> are sated, birds are in feast, the fishnets have been drained.
> But all the silent in the temple, They say: "Re's blessing is
> great." Cling to the silent, then you find life, your being
> will prosper upon earth.

The winds of catastrophe were building over my head, and I wanted nothing more than to withdraw to the temple steps and cling to the silent, the vast solemnity of the Stela.

I decided to ring Penelope to see if she wanted to go to the reception. I suppose I was more worried about how she was doing in general. She didn't pick up so I left the information on her mobile voice mail. I told her to meet me on the south end of Waterloo Bridge at nine and we'd go in together. I said I hoped she would come and that I was worried about her and I hoped she was sleeping off the effects of our trip.

The noise in the pub downstairs increased. The place was filling up; it was Guy Fawkes Day after all and the lads would be fueling up for a big night. The shadows on Little Russell Street were long and the light was going fast. I would have to work quickly.

I cleared off the table and taking out a felt pen I began to draw out my grid on the white tablecloth, setting up the coordinates in the new scheme. The wandering snake curling over the moon, the raised cobra and the bolt cloth, the illuminating sun, waterbird at rest, short sword, loaf, and offering hand, ripples of water, bundle of reeds, the all-seeing eye, seated woman under the moon . . . *strength, her eye, it illuminates . . . the Two Lands and the Otherworld . . . in the presence of the Sun God who . . . the Sun God illumines . . . the Sun-God illumines for her . . . She has illumined the Two Lands . . .*

The Two Lands and the Third Land are basking in her light . . . When she goes forth, all good plants and animals are born . . . She who rises early, existing in a multitude of forms, enduring mother . . .

My father never "saw the sights" per se; he never seemed too interested in that sort of thing. "Native structures," he called them, whatever indigenous items lay scattered in the landscape before the gaping maw of his machines. Back then I thought my father was right for the most part; I believed in his belligerent sense of progress at least. It was obvious to anyone that the dam was not only desirable, it was necessary. The Nile region could not exist on the ancient system of flood cycles, not if it wished to become a modern, thriving economy, leading North Africa into a new era.

My first chance to see the Great Temple of Abu Simbel came in 1962 after my father and I had been in Aswan for about six months, when the English archeologists finally persuaded my father to take a look at the temple. The group of English archeologists was from that charming old school of moneyed gents with a "sporting interest" in moving about and applying their particular intellectual acumen to those people and places who were obviously without the appropriate spotlight of civilized aesthetics. But you had to hand it to these guys, they worked vigorously and without much result, so steadfast was their resolve, and they had it in their collective minds to convince the important elements of the dam-building team to preserve certain Egyptian artifacts. By this time other British archeologists and officials had already bought or simply taken many of the available artifacts from the known ancient sites, often with the expressed consent or blessing of the Egyptian government, who seemed ready to open up the vaults of the ancient kings to any white man with money. These fellows didn't seem to be that sort. These were the high-minded Oxbridge set, men who stood doggedly by a set of intellectual values often so primitive and obtuse that they accomplished much by virtue of the sheer bewilderment of their opponents in these matters. Many of their acquisitions from that period are at the British Museum right now. The great British Empire of the Victorian period was built by this very sort of man, replaced later by the more rapacious progenitors of colonial capitalism.

They came round in the morning in a car, a half dozen of these sporting chaps, decked out in pressed linen three-button suits and hats and dusty satchels full of documents. My father received them in his makeshift study, a breezy tent on a little rise just behind the work trailers, wearing his usual chinos and white shirt with the sleeves rolled up. Trays of hot tea and fruit were laid out, and the men sat around the portable table for the good part of the morning, one of the Brits rising from time to time to pace, point vigorously at some sketch in a small book and declaim some sort of strident point. I was crouched in a dusty hole that Hakor and I had dug into the dry earth with a spade and then partially covered with a large plank to give us cover from the sun. It was situated just below the small rise to the tent, a place strategically chosen so that we might spy on my father as he convened with the Russians, assorted Egyptians, and now these Englishmen. Or I should say we were pretending to be spying; we knew my father was aware of our location. As was his custom when dealing with nondevelopment-related conversations, my father said very little, watching the men intently with a slight smile, his eyes trained on each of them as they spoke in turn. They pulled out sheets, drawings, photos, unrolled maps, sketched out diagrams, calculated figures, all of which my father perused very carefully, holding them in his fingers and reading them closely. From time to time he nodded and poured himself and the others more tea.

The archeologists went a few hours later, chatting as they left the yard. They seemed very positive as to the outcome of the meeting. My father stayed in the tent and summoned his two American assistants. They looked over some of the documents the Englishmen had left and talked for another hour. Later my father looked over to me and signaled it was time for lunch, sending Hakor scrambling out of the hole and running to the kitchen. I joined my father in the dining tent, squatting on a cushion and watching him as we ate, but I couldn't detect what he was thinking.

The next morning he called me into his tent. He had just finished a meeting with the head Soviet planners, who left muttering and smoking furiously. I noticed that some of the Englishmen's documents remained scattered on my father's worktable. But what my father wanted to talk about was the unfinished obelisk. Someone told him that I had been exploring the old quarry quite regularly. Quite simply, he wanted to know why. Why was that old piece of ruined stone so interesting that I would return to it day after day?

I was just a boy, what could I say? I think I just shrugged and gave the stock "I don't know" that young boys have used for eons to explain their illogical actions. I wish I had the chance to explain to him now.

Then my father showed me the diagrams of the Great Temple of Abu Simbel that the Brits left behind. He told me that they wanted to save the temple, to get my father to work with the Soviets and convince them to agree to move the massive structure. To transplant the whole thing to another site that was above the high mark of the coming waters. They also wanted to use the Soviets' equipment, delaying the construction of the dam and putting the machinery at further risk of damage or general wear. Against the wishes of the Soviets, who were opposed to the entire idea, my father agreed to go with the English to the site of the temple and see firsthand what exactly it was they wanted to save. Abu Simbel was past the first cataract, up into the southern reaches of lower Nubia. It would take several days to get there by boat, a steam-driven ferry that the Russians used for longer trips up and down the Nile. We would leave early the next morning.

I was thrilled at the prospect. I would get to travel with my father and discover something for the first time with him. I usually experienced such things alone. And I would also get to see Hakor's Nubian homeland, the place where his ancestors lived for more than a millennium. That night I rolled in my blankets for hours before I could sleep.

But we never got to Abu Simbel. Hakor shook me awake, holding my washing bowl in trembling hands, his wet eyes shining in the dark. When I sat up I saw my bags already packed and sitting next to the door. Sometime in the night the Soviet engineers received notice from Moscow to shut us down, to remove the western element from the process. The Egyptian government was revoking our visas, via instruction from Moscow. They knew what the British and my father were up to, and they did not want to reallocate the resources for archeological trips; it was slowing down construction and they were already way over budget. When I sat up on my pallet that morning, the sky still black and full of stars, Hakor crouched by my side, and I could see the tears making dark tracks down his cheeks. As I readied myself Hakor started saying things to me, like how my father was abandoning the Nubian people, leaving them to the Soviets who didn't seem to care if they lived or died. I said that we couldn't do anything else, that there was nothing my father could do. Hakor didn't accept that.

My father took it extremely well. He was down in his workshop, his drafting tools already packed, laughing and smoking with the Russian engineers who rubbed the back of their necks a lot and smiled sheepishly. They didn't want to see my father go; they had nothing to do with it. They were also embarrassed that they needed to go through his things to make sure he didn't take any plans or schematics with him, anything that might reveal the secrets of the Soviets' construction. He shook their hands in turn and they smiled at me and patted my head and then we were trundled off to the Land Rover for the drive to Luxor, where we'd catch a flight to Cairo and then Paris and then back to America.

As we were leaving, Hakor stood in the doorway and threw the money my father gave him at the truck, the coins clattering off the windshield. He swore at us in a Nubian dialect, something I didn't understand, but I suspect he was cursing me and my father for leaving, for giving up. His fury and flashing eyes froze my guts, and then with an anguished scream he went running down the dusty street toward the river.

The ride to Luxor was long and exhausting. We passed through the low hills, the eastern desert rising up into the sky, the Nile winding through canyons to our left. The road was mostly deserted excepting the occasional cluster of men walking on the dusty shoulder, often carrying large loads on their heads or backs. I didn't want to leave. I was just beginning to enjoy my explorations, becoming more confident in my forays. I had taken to hanging about the unfinished obelisk site, playing on its fractured surface until the evening call to prayer. I cried most of the way to Luxor, as quietly as I could, huddled in the backseat among our packing cases. My father chatted with the driver in front, laughing and sharing his cigarettes as we rattled down the road.

At one point my father reached into the deep pockets of his field jacket and showed me the feldspar scarab that the Russians had given him as a parting gift. He turned the scarab over in his rough hands and explained to me how the scarab figures in Egyptian mythology prominently as a symbol of the eternal aspect of nature because of the dung beetle's tendency to roll balls of dung away to a protected spot to lay their eggs in, just as the ball of the sun was rolled across the sky and the moon at night. I didn't tell him that I already knew this story.

The ancients, he said, often used this type of metaphor to explain and describe the natural phenomena of their world. We call it animism. It may seem silly to us now. But in a way it makes sense. It makes sense if you think in pictures. Do you understand what I mean?

Then he placed the scarab in my hand. It was cool and I rubbed it with my fingertips, exploring the crevices and fine lines of the rock. The green was slightly translucent, with hints of spidery shadows of fractures and veins just beneath the surface.

I wonder, my father said, now looking off toward the eastern desert, the scrub brush and baked sand lying flat and dead in the sun, I wonder if someday we will return to something like this. All of us. America even. Wouldn't that be something?

Then he took the scarab back from me and put it in his pocket.

How can we ensure that that doesn't happen? he asked me.

I knew the answer he wanted but said nothing.

All this, he said, the crumbling buildings, the decayed structures, all this is lying in the dust for a *reason*, you know.

Won't the Aswan dam fall apart too? I asked.

He laughed, tilting his tanned chin into the sun coming through the windows.

Yeah, I suppose it will eventually. Unless it is properly maintained. With solid design and careful construction it was possible to make something that would last a long time. The Egyptians did a better job than most, though they got a lot of help from the climate. But if you build something properly, there's no telling how long it could last, maybe forever. Of course forever means something different now. Time is different now.

I never saw that scarab again, not even after my father died during my first year at Berkeley, a few months before my wedding. He was on a site deep in the Amazon, living among natives, working on the design of a new set of hydroelectric bridge-dam hybrids that would later power most of southern Brazil. A stanchion perched on the soft earth wall of the river valley gave way and thirty tons of concrete and steel fell three hundred feet, burying my father and some workers by the river's edge. The amazing thing was that he was still alive; the rescue workers could hear him talking, tapping on steel girders. He was trapped in a tiny hollow of sorts, formed from steel drainage pipes and concrete. It took them eight hours to dig him out and by that time he had run out of air. They said his body was only slightly bruised.

They shipped him back in a box made from banana crates. When we opened the crate at the airport he looked like he had sprouted a dense coat of dark hair, from head to toe, obliterating his features altogether. It turns out he was covered by thousands of thick, furry spiders that had slipped into the casket and spent the long passage feasting and procreating on my father.

I flew back to the house in Syracuse with my poor, expressionless mother, so doped up with lithium or something else that she couldn't even begin to figure or express her grief. She held me dumbly in her thin arms, patting my back lightly like she'd done when I was a small boy. We sat quietly in the parlor for a few days and then I went back to San Francisco. My mother died a few years later.

From *The Book of the Dead*, Chapter 30B, "The Heart as Witness":

> Formula for not letting the heart of (?) oppose him in
> the necropolis. He shall say: O my heart of my mother, O
> my heart of my mother, O my heart of my being! Do not
> rise up against me as witness, do not oppose me in the
> tribunal, do not rebel against me before the guardian of the
> scales!

I sorted through his belongings, but he had almost nothing. Like me, my father traveled light and never accumulated much. A few

drawers of clothes, a shoe box of personal items, a few photos of finished projects, his degrees. This was a man who traveled all over the
world and never brought anything back. Instead he left his own huge
monuments, vast structures that would last a thousand years. I suppose he figured, why bring things *back* when you can *leave* massive
landscape- and culture-changing things there instead? That's exactly
the kind of thing he would say.

When I was a boy in Aswan, I had only a vague idea what animism was, and I wasn't sure what was implied by my father's desire to
return to this sort of storytelling, the metaphorical translation of science perhaps, into something more tangible and interesting, and
maybe even more satisfying. I mean, the story of the sun, the scientific explanation of it, a ball of gases, the earth in its pitiful circumference rotating around a lonely star, one speck in a handful of sand has
its own sense of majesty I suppose.

I think now that my father felt he could best express this idea by
building his own metaphors, his own soaring monuments to the glory
of man. The great pyramids, all the great structures of ancient Egypt,
are merely hieroglyphs on a much larger scale, a vast pictograph, a
metaphor. I like to think that he would appreciate this, what I'm doing and how it all worked out, even if I wasn't marking the landscape
in the same way that he did. I wish he could have met Zenobia, I wish
he could see her now, what I helped create.

A few years after we left Aswan, international pressure, notably
UNESCO, caused the Russians to save the Abu Simbel temple anyway; they cut the entire thing out of the rock and moved it up to a
neighboring mesa, out of reach of the floodwaters, an amazing feat of
engineering. I was able to visit the site sixteen years later, to watch
the setting sun spread its rays into the innermost chamber on October
twenty-second, watch it settle over the four gods. I must admit that I

felt then an odd sort of pride, that perhaps in part I played a role in all this. I also wished my father could have seen it for himself, put his hands into the finely chiseled symbols, felt the smooth granite of the Baboon of Thoth. Maybe he would have felt differently about the way things turned out for us in Egypt.

The saving of Abu Simbel got a lot of press, and people around the world supported UNESCO's efforts, and applauded when the project was finished. But a lot of other things, a lot of things nobody else knows about, smaller sites mostly, including several tombs, as well as a large chunk of lower Nubia, went under the azure waters of Lake Nasser. Some of the sites were examined by the English who did reams of tracings, sketches, etchings, trying to preserve what they could. There's no telling what might be buried under those waters; what even now is crumbling under the erosive and corrosive forces of water and silt. There could be another Rosetta Stone, something that might crack our understanding of the ancient world wide open. I'm sorry that I was there and that I wasn't able to do something about it. It seems highly unlikely to me now, but still I wish I had been able to convince my father, to get him to work with the English sooner, to convince the Soviets. I should have been more careful.

24: ABSTRACTIONS

WHEN I LOOKED UP again it was night, the lights on Coptic Street were winking through the lightly frosted windows and the noise downstairs had built to a roar of voices and music. The tablecloth was covered with my markings and my face throbbed with heat. It was eight-thirty. I took the tablecloth and folded it up into a parcel and stuck it under my jacket as I went downstairs. The pub was full of people celebrating the holiday, and I passed into the street quickly, also crowded with celebrants and tourists stamping their feet on the pavement in the cold. The sky was already black and faintly roiling. I wondered how the traditional bonfires and celebrations for Guy Fawkes Day would fare in an icy downpour. Probably just like everything else in England: grimly, gamely, sodden and dirty, but steadfast and determined to stick it out.

I turned down Museum Street to Holborn and then to St. Martin's Lane, each more progressively crowded, most people moving toward the Thames. It was now ten minutes till nine o'clock. I lost three hours in the pub. At this rate I would be late in meeting Penelope as well as Zenobia. At first I tried to find the cracks, to slip quickly through the opening gaps that closed like Arctic ice as quickly as they surfaced, until the press was too great and then I was merely carried along by the current, by the rippling tide of humanity down through Central London to the river.

The Victoria Embankment was already lined with people as far as I could see, along the Thames as it bent toward Blackfriars and to the south toward Lambeth Bridge and Vauxhall, all waiting for the fireworks to begin. It would take some doing getting across Waterloo Bridge to the South Bank Arts Center, and I had no idea how I was going to hook up with Penelope in all this mess. I was at the foot of the bridge before I realized that I was still wearing Hardy's clothes, rumpled and stained. I had no other choice, so I joined the bulky queue that formed at the water's edge, moving slowly across the river. The police closed off half the street across the bridge to allow for more pedestrians, though the crowd alternately surged into the lane of cars that sat idling, trapped now. Most of the people along the bridge were sharing bottles of champagne or the customary tall cans of lager, several of them wearing cheap glittery paper party hats, blowing plastic horns and talking loudly and expectantly. From the South Bank music was playing, echoing across the wet stones of the bridge, something sort of like rock and roll, something modern per-haps, and the crowds surged and swayed to the beat in their long black coats and mufflers. I was freezing, having left my mackintosh at Hardy's and lost my hat somewhere along the Cam. On the river a small tugboat-looking craft was turning in lazy circles on the oily black water between Waterloo and Blackfriars Bridge with some kind of rigged flamethrower on the flying bridge sending thick gouts of white flame into the night in regular patterns that appeared to be roughly synchronized with the music.

I was a quarter of the way across when I saw Penelope, about forty yards ahead, walking away from me, her hair piled high on her head, wearing fresh clothes and a gray overcoat, her neck wrapped thickly with a green scarf. I stuck to the outer edge of the crowd, and made my way across the bridge. The revelers smoked and chatted and swilled from their bottles and cans, checking their watches every few minutes and scanning the eastern reach of the river for any sign of fireworks. I watched the top of Penelope's hair as it bobbed through the mass of heads and hats. I was gaining some ground on her and when we were halfway across the bridge I shouted her name sharply.

Penelope!

She stopped and turned around, her face pale in the cold, her eyes wide as they searched for me in the crowd. Magnus, walking next to her, caught my eye almost immediately, looking at me with a little smirk nestled in the side of his mouth. She found me and smiled, raising her hand in a half salute. Then she said something to Magnus and he leaned over to reply into her ear. Magnus was dressed in a natty black suit and his hair was gelled into little spikes in the front like a crown. He had his arm around her waist, leading her to the side to allow people to pass. Magnus was talking to her; he appeared to be comforting her. Penelope looked like she might be crying. I was just a dozen yards away when I felt the quick stir of massive movement behind me and heard the shouts and protestations of people in the crowd.

Oi? Sod off! Ease off! Oi! What's this? What's this now?

I turned to see Gigantica shouldering his way through the crowd, stone faced, coming directly at me. The older Krishna fellow in saffron robes and graying topknot from Oldcastle's place was following in his wake, his pale dome of shaved skull gleaming dully in the street-lights on the bridge. I turned and pushed against the people in front of me, scrambling to move forward faster, roughly working my way past an American family in matching yellow raincoats, then trying to squirm between a small crowd of young barristers in trench coats, clutching tall cans of Old Peculier and cigarettes in their elegant, cold-reddened fingers. They formed an impenetrable wall of wool and houndstooth. I lowered my head to better burrow through. I pulled at the elbow of an angular fellow with long sideburns, jostling his beer.

Pardon me, I said, please, I must get through!

Foam squirted from his can of ale onto his cuffs and wrist as he pitched off balance.

Fockin' 'ell!

He shot his elbow back sharply and caught me just under the nose, jamming into my front teeth, crunching my glasses against my cheeks. Brilliant sparks of pain shot upward into my gums and up my nose and into my eyes and I shouted in anger. He looked over his shoulder at me, and I saw a moment of shock and recognition in his face when he realized he had struck me so directly. My eyes filled with tears and I had my hands over my mouth.

Aw, I'm sorry, mate! the barrister said. Sorry about that. You okay?

I turned to circumvent them, dizzy and half blind from tears and my cracked glasses, trying to find a weak spot in the press, when I felt something brush my shoulder. I cringed, pulling up my shoulders and raising my hands to protect my face against further damage.

Help me! I shouted, my voicing cracking, *somebody help me for god's sake!*

The crowd around me slowed their milling progress forward and quieted. I stretched on my toes and looked wildly around for Magnus and Penelope. I felt the warm, salty taste of blood in my mouth.

Then I was pulled from behind as Gigantica spun me around with a flick of his wrist. He went to one knee to examine my face. He was still wearing his white eye patch, and his other eyeball seemed to hang loosely in its socket, shot through with filaments of red. He held my shoulder tightly in his hand, squeezing lightly.

Calm down, Dr. Rothschild, he said. Get a hold of yourself!

Gigantica pulled a soggy red bandanna out of his back pocket. The crowd of barristers and others were reeling back now, trying to make space between them and the giant swabbing my face.

Look here, Gigantica said, you've hurt yourself. You're bleeding!

He pawed at my faced with the bandanna. I shrank back as far as I could, moving my head like a boxer to avoid his clumsy swipes. The Krishna stood at his elbow, studying me. I spat a huge wad of blood onto my own shoes. People began to mill about again, apparently convinced that no sort of interesting altercation was going to take place, or that whatever violence there was had already occurred and nothing more was to follow.

Dr. Rothschild, Gigantica said, we need you back at the estate. Look, we'll get you cleaned up and everything. We have a car waiting back on the Strand.

Gigantica began to pull me gently by the shoulder. I leaned away from him, trying to brace my feet.

I *can't*, I said, I have to go! You can have the money back!

He shifted his hand so it gripped my chin and cheeks and drew my face closer to his.

It's not about that. We just need you to come with us.

I can't, I gasped, I . . . I have an appointment. My daughter . . . she's waiting.

Gigantica gripped my chin more tightly, his fingers enveloping my entire lower face. He bowed his shaggy head for a moment. The Krishna in the saffron robes patted his shoulder as if to console him.

Oldcastle, he won't make it, Gigantica said. That's all over. Erin needs your help.

I tried to nod, but his hand held my face still. One side of my bent glasses was hanging down over my cheek, the other on my forehead. The world fell into an unfocused mix of muted color and dim light, the shapes of the two men before me still recognizable by silhouette, the rest of the world a moving mass of angles and rounded shades of black.

Come along back out to the house, Gigantica said, and Erin will straighten the whole thing out. She said you could finish it.

The man in the robes put his hand on Gigantica's arm and they looked at each other. I couldn't tell what was exchanged between them, what was on their faces. Everything was in motion, rotation around the circumference of our little fire circle. Without my glasses the outside world took on the sparkling, unfocused gleam of awakening from sleep, troops of shadows marching in even ranks, the flitting, hazy faces of strangers. Then the Krishna started speaking to me in Egyptian Arabic.

There is the matter of certain ceremonies, Dr. Rothschild. You have an obligation to this project. We found you again after all these years so that you could repay your debt, correct the wrong. This you know. You can finish the ritual in his place.

The voice surprised me, precise and clipped, vaguely familiar. Needs my help? With what? The Aten cult? The feminization of the human form, the change from the worship of Amun to the sun disk Aten? Oldcastle was somehow trying to resurrect this religious reform by acquiring appropriate texts and artifacts, by reshaping his entire body? Erin's automatic writings, the Order of the Golden Dawn, all the attempts to connect with the other world through some kind of bent space-time dimension were some kind of manufactured fantasy; it was impossible, it couldn't be done. And even if you could, why would you want to? I thought of that world, the cult of Aten, the restructuring of the principles of theology, the toppling of western conceptions, the true monotheism come to light. All I had was intellectual abstractions. The heart of it was a different matter, something *I* couldn't seem to tap into. I was the wrong person for the job. The ancient Egyptians knew the relative value of the brain and the heart. In the process of mummification, they pulled the brain through the nose by means of a long hook. The brain was useless in the afterlife, only the heart mattered.

Gigantica took his hand from my face and we both reached to straighten my glasses at the same time and succeeded in knocking them off, sending them clattering to the street. I bent down and nearly butted heads with the Krishna who kneeled to reach for them.

Look, Gigantica was saying, I'm sorry about what happened.

On my knees I looked up into the Krishna's face, a fleshy blur of head with two dark holes for eyes, inches from mine. His mouth was a thin, slightly curved line reaching around the lower part of his face, his nose bulging, like a snout. His ears sat low and small on his head and I caught the fuzzy impression of something simian, monkeylike. The Baboon of Thoth. I wanted to run.

I mean, Gigantica was saying, if I would have known it was *you* in that flat . . . why were you in that big Canadian kid's room anyway?

The Krishna handed me my glasses. On his hand was the hazy image of a scarlet scarab, burning on his middle finger.

I put my glasses on to get a better look at the ring. Then something shifted in the crowd, a palpable sensation or current of fear rippled through me and I clutched at my glasses quickly, slipping them on my face.

Walter! Watch out!

It was Penelope's voice behind me. I did what most people would do in that situation: I stood and looked back behind me for the source of the warning shout rather than looking to protect myself. Through a rent in the craning heads and shoulders I saw Penelope's face, her eyes wide and white as the sun. I saw Magnus next to her, pale and muttering something in her ear, begin backing up, tugging on Penelope's arm. Penelope wrestled free and pointed at me, behind me.

It was dark, you know? Gigantica was saying.

I turned back to Gigantica and the Krishna and right at the moment when things suddenly sprang into focus, the staring faces of the crowd, Gigantica's hairy mug and the serene, familiar baboon face of the Krishna standing there looking at me strangely, that's when I saw him, Alan Henry, coming from the north end of the bridge, barreling out of the crowd, bystanders rippling and falling in his wake, his brow lowered and his mouth set in a gaping howl that echoed off the dark waters of the Thames.

Gigantica must have seen it in my face because he quickly clamped his jaw and took his hand from my shoulder, turned swiftly with surprising agility, and bent his knees to absorb the blow. I fell back, feeling hands catching me as I toppled, watching the collision of these two behemoths. There was the scrape of shoes on gritty pavement, then the dull smack of flesh colliding at great speed. Alan Henry lowered his bull head and caught Gigantica in the sternum, locking his arms around Gigantica's torso and using momentum to pick the giant off the ground. Alan was roaring furiously, his face buried in the expansive chest of Gigantica, whose face was twisted with his own oaths of fury. Gigantica sledgehammered the back of Alan's head with both of his woolly forearms as Alan drove with his legs to keep his feet, forcing the two of them across the lane of road and onto the sidewalk and then crunching against the barrier on the edge of the bridge. The cement barrier cut into Gigantica's back as they slammed into it and he bellowed in pain and pounded on Alan's broad back with his fists.

The rest of the crowd was quickly receding in the face of this violence, people falling and pushing to get out of the way of the two men, the nucleus of the circle gradually spreading as people flailed away from this rather alarming tornado of violence. It's one thing to watch the safe entertainment of a short middle-aged man getting bludgeoned in the street, quite another to get sucked into a whirling maelstrom of titan punishment.

Alan's legs seemed to tremble and his yelling stopped. Gigantica's feet touched ground and he quickly slipped a hand under Alan's arm. Dipping at the knees, Gigantica turned Alan around with a subtle maneuver so that he was behind him, Alan's upper body hanging face first over the side of the bridge. There was a moment or two of tenacious gripping, fingers slipping on flesh, the low grunts of desperate action, and Alan's feet began to shift and slide. Gigantica leaned into him, twisting Alan's arm behind his back, pushing it up far between his shoulder blades, making it pop and crack like a falling tree. Alan had his other hand on the wall, trying to push off of it and away from the edge. Then Alan's feet began to come off the ground and Gigantica roared and jammed his arm farther up Alan's back and butted him in the back of the neck with his head, driving him over the edge. As Alan began to lift and topple, at the last second he twisted, his face coming around the bulk of Gigantica and into view, a look of anger and fear. His glasses were gone, and his hair twisted up into horns where Gigantica pawed at his head. Using his one free hand, Alan raked Gigantica's face, ripping off the eye patch, and grabbing a huge fistful of Gigantica's beard. The light from the streetlamps struck Gigantica's face as he turned, exposing a gory, wine-colored fissure where his eye should be.

Gigantica roared with rage and his head swung about and then Alan was falling and pulling him by his beard hard so as he fell he brought the big man over the side with him, Gigantica's face a mask of terror and surprise as he released Alan's arm and scraped at the wall with his fingers. Both of them levered over the side and hung for a moment, frozen in the moment of indecision, the speed of their bodies now only a reflection of their motion through time, every one of us standing still, watching the world pass us by.

At that moment they were suddenly lit up by the first exploding fireworks, like a thousand desert suns, bare figures on a stretch of white papyrus. I thought of the struggles of Seth, anarchy versus order, the protector of the badlands, the outlying territories, the defender of the endless sands of Egypt. I saw Alan Henry for the first time in his rightful place in the complete structure of things.

You couldn't hear the bodies hit the water.

Then the space in the crowd where the two men had fought, the space so earnestly vacated seconds before, was quickly filled with bodies and noise, the booming reports of the fireworks over the water, the shouts of people rushing to the edge, most looking over the edge and pointing, then police blowing whistles and yelling instructions. The Krishna had disappeared. I was lifted to my feet and pulled away as the fireworks pounded the air with concussive reports that muddled the sounds that all seemed to rush in like water into the gap. Magnus was pulling me out of the crowd and down the street toward the South Bank. I got my feet under me and staggered after him. Then Penelope had my other arm and we were out of the throng and running down the gentle slope of the bridge toward the arts center on the South Bank.

When we were clear I broke away from them and pushed my way through the wall of people at the edge of the bridge, looking over the side and down into the water. The fireworks exploded in shimmering reflections on the oily water, lighting up sections with intensely colored flashes. I didn't see anything, then a flash and a sound like thunder and a brilliant white charge lit up the water for an instant and I saw a broad form stroking awkwardly toward the North Bank. The small tugboat circled cautiously over toward the figure in the water, still discharging flame from the flying bridge, its pattern of lazy figure eights disrupted. The swimmer plodded through the water in the approximation of a heavy crawl stroke. I couldn't see anyone else in the water, though it was possible that the other part of the struggle had elected to swim to the bridge supports or possibly under the bridge.

In a moment the swimmer reached the wall of the Victoria Embankment, and someone on the bank dropped a collapsible ladder over the side. A small crowd gathered, including a cordon of policemen, as he clambered from the water, pulling himself heavily up the ladder, the water pouring off him in great torrents. I held my broken glasses to my face with both hands and leaned out over the bridge as far as I could, squinting. The rippling surface of the river was smooth and there was no one else visible in the water. Just as he reached the railing of the embankment, before he threw his first heavy leg over the rail, the swimmer looked back and regarded the water for a long moment. Through a chink in the phalanx of blue-capped bobbies that surrounded him, I could see the shaggy beard and brow of Gigantica, holding one hand over his missing eye. Below me the black current surged against the stone supports of the bridge, tracing white foam that eddied and slipped from the stanchions and was carried down the swiftly moving river under Waterloo Bridge, Guy Fawkes Day in London, November 5, 1997.

Alan, please forgive me.

25: THE MASK OF THOTH

PENELOPE AND MAGNUS LED me to the South Bank and down the stairs that led to the wide embankment walk under the bridge. Boats played searchlights over the water and the bobbies on the bridge were trying to clear the crowds, blowing whistles and shouting through their cupped hands, with the characteristic primitive utility of British law enforcement. Very quickly the milling crowd seemed willing to forgo their interest in the altercation and possible drowning and move once again in the direction of their Guy Fawkes revelry.

I sat on the edge of the seawall by the long tables of booksellers. Their wares were covered with sheets of rumpled opaque plastic and watched over by scowling Middle Eastern youths standing about with their hands stuffed in the pockets of their oversized American sports-team jackets. Penelope sat down next to me and Magnus trailed off into the crowd, apparently heading into the arts center pub on the ground floor, just beside the bridge. I mopped my face again with my sleeve, burrowing at my split lip with my tongue. Penelope put her arm around me and pulled me to her and I gratefully rested against her shoulder.

I'm glad you came, I said, I don't know what—

Did you know that man? she said. The other one that went over the side?

That . . . that was a friend of mine, I said. I think I made a horrible mistake.

We both turned and scanned the river for a moment, still lit up intermittently by the fireworks that echoed like gunshots in the steel canyon of the bridge's undercarriage. The water was now thick with small watercraft, circling the area under the bridge, illuminating the water with narrow columns of light from handheld torches.

I didn't see him come up, Penelope said. Can he swim?

I don't know, I said.

I felt with my fingers for a loose tooth, but everything seemed intact.

Why would they . . . what did they want?

They wanted me to come back to the estate, I said, back to Oldcastle's place. They need me to finish the project. I think Oldcastle's dead.

Walter, Penelope said, grabbing hold of my forearm, get out of here, back to America, somewhere. Look, before I forget—

She foraged around in her jacket for a moment and drew out an envelope.

Your money. Take it.

You should keep it.

No. It's ten thousand fucking pounds. Use it to get out of here. I did borrow a few hundred quid; I got sacked at the library, and my rent's overdue.

Why don't you just keep it all? It's my fault you lost your job.

First of all, she said, it's *your* fucking money! *Second,* I don't want to be connected to you or this anymore. The police have that big fucking bloke and he'll probably tell them the whole thing. You know what I mean?

She reached over to me and jammed the envelope into the inner pocket of Hardy's jacket, now smeared with my blood.

I was thinking about Erin in Oldcastle's ruined garden, off there in the indeterminate countryside outside Cambridge, standing in the shadow of the cantilevered obelisk, her hands folded over her chest, watching the path to the river. A small file of men in saffron robes trailed over the hill like a disappearing tail. Wrestlers piled in pickup trucks and gunned down a dirt track through the valley and into the woods. Oldcastle's body would be lying in the study, prostrate over his desk, on a bed of Erin's drug-induced scribblings, stiffening, turning the pale yellow of old papyrus, the crusted remnants of ostracon. Nobody was coming for him, or for Erin.

There's this event, I said to Penelope, my daughter's thing I called about? At the arts center tonight, it's right upstairs here; we could run in real quick—

Walter, Penelope said, I can't. You're crazy! You better get out of here!

She gazed off over the crowd. I felt her separating from me, the lands spreading, dividing. I looked back toward the bridge and the North Bank. I didn't see any bobbies heading toward this area; the cluster of police on the embankment had disappeared.

I don't think they're coming after me, I said. Maybe Alan swam away.

Dr. Hardy called me, Penelope said. He called me from the hospital this afternoon. I don't know how he got my number—

Wait a minute, I said, Hardy called you? How—

He wasn't calling to thank me, she said.

Suddenly Penelope slumped on my shoulder, sobbing. I put my hand on her head and watched Magnus returning, navigating through the crowd with a few glasses of something in his hands. I could feel the rain-dampened cement of the seawall soaking through my pants. Penelope snuffled and wiped her nose with her hand.

He called, Penelope said into my shoulder, to tell me that he wishes *we'd left him there!* On the banks of the river. He said that was the way he always *wanted* to die! All his life, he said, he wanted to die on the banks of the Cam, angling in the morning, the sun on his face. It was the way he always wanted to go.

Oh no, I said, Penelope—

He said he didn't feel a thing. He said it was beautiful. And then I *brought him back*. To this. To be *alone* again. Oh god. It's so awful.

Penelope's voice choked again with sobs. Magnus wove through knots of people, his arms outstretched holding drinks, a ridiculous grin on his face.

He said that he hates me for it, Penelope said. *He hates me for bringing him back.* Oh, Walter, he was so bitter, so angry. He cursed me for it!

There was a torrential rain of noise and light behind us over the river, the grand firework finale. The crowds along the bank under the bridge cheered lustily for the last explosions, the last displays. Then it was dark again and Penelope cried softly into my shoulder. *Cling to the silent, then you find life, your being will prosper upon earth.*

Magnus finally reached us, approaching shyly, handing each of us a glass of something warm and brown, with a short cinnamon stick and slice of lemon suspended in the amber liquid, smelling strongly of nutmeg and alcohol. Penelope snuffled and sat up, wiped her face with her scarf for a few moments while Magnus gazed off over the river, pretending to look at something, while I looked down at my wet and ruined brogans, one of them covered with a still glistening wad of my blood.

In my mind I shouted a prayer to any god who would listen, to see Alan Henry smiling and striding down Great Russell Street once again, to hear his booming welcome, his broad palm on my shoulder, to save all of us. I shook with the shame of what I had done.

With the fireworks gone and no place to focus their attention, the crowd began to direct their energies to the most serious task of the evening, the consumption of alcoholic beverages. Suddenly champagne corks began popping along the embankment, setting off a spontaneous volley of corks and toasts and shouts of *cheers* and scattered applause and the throaty chants of football songs.

Hot whiskey, Magnus said finally. For the chill, eh?

Penelope wiped her eyes and smiled and then we all clinked our glasses together solemnly.

Penelope gulped at her drink and because I realized how cold and damp I was, I did the same, taking a large swallow of the hot liquid that was apparently what it purported to be, hot whiskey and little else, though I had several ounces down my trachea before I realized this. Only by doubling over and putting my fist to my mouth and snorting loudly through my nose was I able to keep the burning liquid down, which of course resulted in the expulsion of a fine mist of whiskey and blood through my nasal passages, spray-painting the seawall with a circular pattern of reds and browns, an excruciating ordeal that made me yelp and curse, stamping on the cobblestones.

Penelope, amid her own gulpings, began to laugh and also snorted heavily, shooting whiskey out of her nose. Magnus started laughing then too, broad generous laughter, not the kind that I despise, the sort that comes at another's discomfort, but rather that large musical laughter of shared trial and experience. I looked over at Penelope, her face streaming again with tears, loosening the scarf from around her neck and exposing that delicate breastbone to the night air, and I smiled and sat back on the wall and sipped my drink again, finishing off the last bit, feeling the last of the hot liquid running flush through my body, feeling all my pores opening, the transpiration process initiating. As our laughter awkwardly subsided to sniffles and muffled snorts, her bare hand on my shoulder, eyes glimmering, Walter, she murmured, Walter, Walter, oh what are we going to do? And in that moment I felt the waves part and the tide receding, the fertile

ground left bare, dark rich soil in the sun, ripe for planting, the planting of eggs by the divine river birds, the beginning of a new season,
the floodplain exposed, the life-giving waters receded.

A moment later Magnus was gone and then reappearing through
the crowd, grinning grimly and bearing another round of drinks, more
double hot whiskeys, and this time we all toasted each other quietly
and with gratitude, gulping our drinks in the cold night air in the
midst of the gathering crowds. Then suddenly strangers were clapping me heartily on the back, grasping my waist with encircling arms,
pasty, frank English faces twisted in generous grimaces of goodwill,
and soon we were swigging on a bottle of warm champagne, caught up
in a dancing ring of young Brits, singing some sort of melodic anthem
that I'd never heard before, with words I didn't know, shedding our
coats and scarves, arms linked, moving clockwise in a large circle. The
circling throng ebbed and swayed and Magnus and another man in a
yellow slicker were in the middle now, doing a vigorous jig with Haps-
burg leaps and the hussar kick as hundreds cheered them on, the circle elongating and revolving, others in the middle now, cavorting
wildly, without form, Penelope next to me, her head thrown back,
eyes shut, singing with a full voice to the spiraling undercarriage of
the bridge. The framework of burnished steel reflected our movement with subtle flashes of color and light, then changed again, the
oval like an immense structural cartouche, the bodies in the middle
the signifying glyphs, the loose rendering of a symbol, a name. By tra-
dition ancient Egyptians chose names by drawing from the mother's
first words after her baby's birth. Consequently, many common Egyptians have names that mean things like "He is mine" or "The beautiful" or even "The pain is great." I watched the changing shape of our
reflection under the bridge, the nomen, the prenomen, waiting for it
to form, for the mother of this moment to speak. I could begin to see
the symbols lining up, the order becoming clear. It wasn't what I was
expecting. Not like that.

At that moment I felt someone or something pull on my arm from behind, and I dropped my drink glass, sending it shattering across the cobblestones. I stepped back for a second, frozen, afraid again, letting go of Penelope, and then she was borne off into the circle's vortex, and I was left in the outer ring as she rotated away from me. I was terribly dizzy, the shock of standing still after so much circular movement, and I staggered back to the seawall to steady myself. I felt suddenly sick; had I forgotten already that Alan Henry was probably drowned? That he died trying to save me? Looking back over the crowd, I noticed a high balcony, with people lining the railing, overseeing the melee. It was the South Bank Arts Center. They were all in various types of formal dress, drinking out of elegant wineglasses, watching and pointing into the fray of people along the embankment with great interest.

Zenobia's function! I checked my watch: I was over two hours late. I searched the file of people at the rail for Zenobia. There were several very statuesque women lining the rail, but not Zenobia. Penelope was now on the far side of the circle, dancing and singing along. Magnus was being tossed in the air on a blanket in the center, executing a rather alarming and impressive array of aerial maneuvers, grinning broadly as he was launched skyward, twisting his lithe little body into various shapes.

I made my way through the crowd toward the National Film Theatre, the first floor of the South Bank Arts Center. The National Film Theatre lobby housed a sort of combination pub and cafeteria, now jammed with damp Londoners trying to get warm, crowding the bright steel tables and stools that lined the broad windows facing the river. I found the elevator at the back and took it up to the Queen's Hall, where Zenobia's reception was taking place.

Alone in the elevator, I took a moment to regard myself in the mirrored walls. I was swaying a bit, holding on to the wall for what seemed to be an interminably long and bumpy ride, my face a purple-

and-crimson smear of bruise, blood, and crooked glasses. Hardy's coat was impossibly rumpled, my shirt soaked through the chest with dark rings of sweat, a crusty ring of dried blood on my neck and collar.

There was no real explanation for this. It would be clear to her that this was merely a segment in a long chain of such events, such predicaments that I involved myself in, by my own volition, for some unknown reason. She wouldn't believe that in fact I had never done anything like it in my life, that my time up till this week had been spent in the blissfully sweet, placid, and relatively predictable contemplation of ancient artifacts. It was a life ruled by order, the commonplace; the great events were only those that were contained in the passages I tried to decipher. No, it wouldn't do any good to explain.

I gave my name at the table that fronted the entrance to the hall and was given surprised looks and a name tag that was waiting for me: "Dr. Rothschild—Tripod Media." I assumed this was the parent company of Zenobia's magazine. A young man in a tuxedo made a movement to take my jacket, then after a look at my face declined and turned away with a wave of his hand, leaving me to enter the hall as I was.

It was immediately evident that the festivities were coming to a close, if not ended already, judging by the streams of people exiting the hall, most in tuxedos and formal wear. It was a slim, elegant, eminently fashionable crowd, narrow-hipped men in long, flat-front black trousers, form-fitting jackets with high lapels and at least four buttons, and the ladies in loose dresses with plunging necklines showing strangely tanned skin, delicate strapped shoes, minimal jewelry, straight hair hanging in limpid sheets or else frayed at the ends and mussed with purposeful negligence. This was the other side of London, the rich and the beautiful, so unlike their gnarled countrymen who stood in the rain without a coat and counted out pence in their horny palms for another pint and a sausage roll.

Inside, the ballroom was nearly empty. Oriental rugs covered wood floors and enormous oblong light fixtures swung from the ceiling. I stood to the side of the doorway for a moment, trying to get my bearings. Small knots of people clustered about the room, the quiet murmur of sophisticated conversation. I eased along the wall to a long bar that stretched the full length of the room. Two impressive-looking barmen were racking glasses and wiping down the polished wood with great vigor.

Excuse me, I said, leaning over the bar, but I was wondering if you—

Sorry, sir, a bartender said without even looking at me, the bar is closed for the evening.

I stood there and he glanced up at me. He had impossibly sharp cheekbones, cheeks that could open a letter.

No, I said, that's not what—

Bugger off, mate! he snarled. Bar's closed!

Now the other bartender set down his rack of glasses and joined his partner.

How'd you get in 'ere, anyway? he asked, looking me up and down.

No, I said, I just wanted to know—

By now the chisel-cheeked bartender had slipped over the bar and had me by my elbow.

Off we go! Out with you!

He started hustling me toward the exit, twisting my arm up behind my back.

Wait! Hold on a second!

I tried to struggle free. The barman worked my elbow like a ratchet, bringing my hand up to the back of my neck, doubling me over.

None of that, he said, just take it easy, mate.

We were at the door when there was a shout from across the room. The barman stopped. An impossibly tall woman separated from a group of people and began striding across the room. Her hair was pulled back tightly and she wore a long, loose, sheathlike sleeveless dress, her bare arms taut with muscle. She wore tall, thick-soled shoes with laces that zig-zagged up her calves. She covered the room in what seemed about four strides. Everyone in the entire place was watching her; the whole room grew quiet and still. It was an unbeliev-able sight, the athletic bounce of her step, the sheer physicality, the ropy musculature of her body, lithe and tense at the same time, ethe-real like a ballerina yet with a mass more dense than the sun. She looked ready to sprint lightly across the room or to possibly recline on the carpet and take a nap. People would have watched her in amaze-ment if she'd done either. I relaxed in the arms of the stunned bar-man.

It's okay, Zenobia said, waving him off, he's with me.

The barman's grip relaxed and then my arm was free and I had to stand under my own power. I took a few staggering steps, nursing my numb elbow. Zenobia grabbed me by the other arm and led off to a quiet corner of the hall. People moved out of her path, parting smoothly, trying to appear nonchalant, and when we stopped, they shuffled off to put some polite distance between us.

Thanks for showing up, Zenobia said. You look great. Are you alone?

Zenobia, I said, I'm so sorry. I have had a hell of a time these last few days.

Did you get beat up again?

No, no, not really. But there was an altercation. On the bridge.

Do you need some medical attention? Should I get a doctor?

No, no, I'll be okay.

Are you drunk? You stink like booze.

Not really.

Everything's *not really* with you. What happened to the friend you were supposed to bring?

She couldn't make it.

Are you dating this woman? Wait, don't answer that. C'mon, let's sit down.

Zenobia led me over to a low bench along the wall.

Wait here.

She walked back across the room to the bar. The barmen froze as she leaned over the bar and fished out a cloth napkin and a handful of ice. She was smiling when she came back, chuckling a bit.

I'll tell you what, Dr. Rothschild, you surprise me. This kind of shit. Amazing. And I thought I was the one with the exciting life, the bearer of radical news.

It's not like this normally. Not at all. It's been an extraordinary few days.

She folded up the ice in the rag and held it up against my upper lip.

Ouch!

Don't be such a wuss. You've got blood all over your shirt. What'd you do, pull these clothes off a bum on your way over here?

I took the rag from her hand and held it to the side of my head. My first injury, the Africa-shaped welt, was beginning to throb in time with my pulsing lip. The room was emptying out, people stealing glances in our direction as they left.

A friend gave these clothes to me, I said. He just loaned them actually.

Good god. Do you need some more money?

I would've given them back but then he died.

What?

The man I told you about on the phone. It's okay; he's alive again. But he's pretty angry about it.

You're seriously drunk.

Possibly. Then I was ... . attacked on the bridge on the way over here.

Is that what all the police were doing out there?

Yeah. Though they were also looking for my friend. He fell off the bridge. He was trying to protect me.

Fell off Waterloo Bridge. Did they find him?

I don't think so. I do have money though, and I want to pay you back for that loan the other day, hold on a second . . .

I brought the blood-stained envelope out and fumbled with the stack of bills, but my fingers wouldn't cooperate.

Jesus! Put that away! I don't want any money.

Sorry.

Where the hell did that come from? Who carries around wads of money in envelopes? Is that your blood?

It was for a job.

A *job?* What'd you do, translate something for some gangsters?

Um, possibly.

Who?

A strange old Englishman. But I think he died.

Oh. But he's alive again, right?

No, I think he's still dead. He's the one I hope is dead. Too many people around me are dying, or almost dying, I don't understand it. I'm sorry I'm late. I'm sorry I . . . I'm sorry for embarrassing you here in front of your friends.

Zenobia sighed and slung her long arms onto her knees and leaned forward, relaxing her back and eyeing the diminishing crowd wearily.

These people aren't my friends, she said. They're just . . . whatever.

The lights in the ballroom faded to dark and then back again, twice, the polite signal to leave. The hall was now empty save the bartenders who were covering the bars with plastic, and other caterers pushing dollies stacked with glasses and bottles. The only thing left was the large flower display set on a small circular stand in the center of the room.

Should we leave? I said.

No. Fuck it—we paid enough for this place. And I'm not embarrassed. I don't get embarrassed. Something I learned from you.

From me?

Maybe. But nobody knows it.

What do you mean? I'm—

Forget it, Zenobia said. At least you made it here. It's not like . . .

She raised herself, her back straight, and turned to me. She has this thing about looking you directly in the eye. Very disconcerting. I held the ice rag over my forehead.

Remember, Zenobia said, when I told you I had another important thing to tell you?

Oh. Yes, on the phone.

I glanced at her from under the folds of the cloth. She was still looking at me very intently. The lights in the ballroom dimmed again, three discreet pulses of light.

Not exactly the best timing. Do you want to hear it?

I nodded.

I'm going to have a baby.

I took the rag away from my eyes. We were alone in the room, and as she sat there with her hands in her lap she suddenly reminded me of that young girl, the teenager who came to visit me in Egypt, weeping on the edge of the bed in that hotel room, having just witnessed a savage public beating, the dusk sunlight filtering through dirty curtains, the sounds of the market. Just a young girl, but even then a girl who was not very easily shaken. How hard it must have been for her. Yet she rose up like a titan and now held the world by the throat, unafraid and unashamed, despite what I did to her and her mother. How did she do it? I naturally looked at her midsection for some indication.

I'm only ten weeks, Zenobia said, so you can't tell yet.

She smiled at me. Her hands went to her stomach, tucked tightly in the sheath dress. I could tell she didn't know she was doing it. Helen used to do the very same thing.

Did . . . did you get married?

Zenobia tossed her head back and smiled at the ceiling, dimples forming in her tall cheeks.

Ugh. I figured you'd ask that. No, I'm not. And I'm not planning on getting married anytime soon.

So . . . who's . . . the—

The father? He's in New York. His name is Stanford. I met him when I was at Columbia. He's a consultant to fund managers, sort of like an actuary. He also teaches at the NYU math labs. We've got it all sorted out, the money, custody, all that bit. We've got legal documents drawn up. Neither of us wants to get married, not yet anyway. We have the financial capability, and since he works from home, he'll be doing most of the actual at-home stuff, from our loft in Brooklyn Heights. It works out well.

I'm . . . glad, I said. That's amazing news.

The first image that came to my mind was a scarab pushing his burden up the dune to his simple home. A small ball of nutrients in the warm burrow of my daughter's stomach, that would one day come forth into the world, sprouting green and golden, and continue the cycle. The chain of reverberative events, that spiraling helix, bending sweetly like a wounded elm, touched earth again, leaving a smudge, a dark stain, a human trace.

Look, Zenobia was saying, I'll write you and let you know how it goes. But I'm not sure how much . . . maybe after she's grown a bit you can visit. But I want to bring this baby up in a world she can trust. You understand?

I heard a strange music, echoing in the empty room, the odd sound of one's own voice, amplified, repeated, almost like through the telephone, like the distillation of one's true sound. I felt Zenobia's hand on my shoulder. To look at her beautiful face, her forehead creased with concern, touching my face with her hands. Then all the lights went out in the room and it was like the darkness brought some kind of relief and I heard myself crying; I was sobbing in my daughter's hands. I tried to cry quietly so as not to disturb anyone, even though I knew there was no one there. But she was, my daughter, her arms around my shoulders, her cheek resting on the top of my head, my daughter held me there in the dark.

26:   REGRET

IT WAS ALMOST THREE in the morning when I started back across Waterloo Bridge back to Bloomsbury. The sky was the color of old coffee, diffused with the multitude of lights that sprinkled about the heights of London. Saint Paul's dome shone dully in the gloaming, wrapped in a lacework of scaffolding, dutiful and sad, alone in its rotund glory. The perpetual tall building cranes hung over the skyline like crooked scarecrows, towering structures of metal grids, tapering to a bowed arm, and a lone cable that hung over the city, a hook to hoist something into the dizzying heights. The bridge was deserted now, the police cordons gone. A few cars whisked over the damp pavement on their way to some early-morning destination, the drivers themselves gazing through their mottled windshields like sleepwalkers. I walked along the sidewalk, which was almost uniformly covered with the flattened remains of various sorts of drinks receptacles, broken glass, newspapers, party hats. I stopped from time to time to look over the rail into the dark water. I tried to find the spot where Alan and Gigantica went over the rail, the exact place they toppled, but couldn't, the scale of it was all off without the crowds.

The river ran fast by the angled stone bridge supports, surging and making traces of shimmering foam that stretched out like long fingers of white, then dissipating, the water the color of the sky. Along the North Bank of the river the walls of the Victoria Embankment loomed, making its dark way toward Northumberland and on to Saint Martin's Lane. The stone-and-mortar walls of the embankment were built in the nineteenth century to control the flooding of the Thames—"Strand" is in fact an old Anglo-Saxon word for beach—the tides used to bring the waters all the way up past Fleet Street. Not anymore. The tides of the Thames were almost inconsequential; it would never flood again. At low tide the river exposed a pitiful bank of mud, pocked with refuse. At high tide the water remained safe a dozen feet from the top of the wall, just the right level to sit and gaze across.

I watched the Thames run along and bend out of sight toward Tower Bridge and then Greenwich, then to the Thames Barrier at Woolwich, the massive set of steel dams that span the river and protect the upper reaches from flood. Then out to sea. I figured that if you could see the river meet the horizon then the two of them would blend and reverse places, as if the sky were pouring through this tract that ran through the city, through this land, the very way the ancient Egyptians would have seen it, the road to the otherworld.

The West End was silent at last. I picked my way past the dark theaters and cafes, heading north to Great Russell. Saint Martin's Lane was deserted of people and cars, but it was a sea of champagne bottles, the sidewalks and gutters filled, overflowing onto the streets, a graveyard of green glass, an emerald river, and I had to pick my steps carefully.

When I got back to my building Eddie was standing in the hallway, trying to affix a piece of paper to the door of my flat with some tape. When I approached he turned and thrust the paper into my hands, scowling. His bloodshot eyes rolled thickly in his head and he reeked of beer.

'Ere, mate, they've been trying to get a hold of you all day now, the two birds from the museum, yeah? Ringin' the board an' such. The little one in'a spot of trouble. *Right*, off I go. UEFA, innit.

Eddie trundled back down the six flights of stairs to his desk post and his telly and his football and Old Peculier brew.

The note said:

> Dr. Rothschild—
>
> Dr. Wheelhouse is deadly ill and at the Euston
> Hospital on Hampstead Road. The doctors say he had a
> sort of stroke or seizure. He has been unconscious for
> most of the day. The situation is very grave. Dr. Klein
> also wants to see you right away. Please advise us as to
> what we should do.
>
> Sue & Cindy

A few minutes later I was back on Great Russell Street. The Euston Hospital was six blocks away. I walked with my head down, my face throbbing, freezing in my damp clothes, cursing with every step.

The nurse at the front desk assumed I needed medical attention myself, and it took me some time to explain that I was here to see someone else. I stood in the otherwise empty lobby while she riffled through some files to find Mick's room.

As I stood there I heard the faint *ting* of the elevator bell. Across the room the door opened and an ancient man in a hospital gown inched out, trailing a rack with bags of IV fluids hanging like distended fruit and a small rolling metal table with the sharp, slivered ends of some kind of surgical instruments peeking out from under a white cloth. As I watched he made his way slowly to the front doors, his paper slippers schussing on the tile floor, the table and IV rack jerking along behind him, the trailing lines of clear tubing slightly discolored with percolating liquids. The automatic doors opened and the old man stepped out into the night.

The nurse gave a quick shout and when I turned around she was grinning at me proudly, waving Mick's room number on a piece of paper.

Mick lay in the hospital bed like a sewing needle, his shoulder bones poking out of the wide neck of the hospital gown. The nurse at the floor station said he was in and out of consciousness all day, and his vital signs were weak but steady. They had him on several stabilizing agents that should keep him from having another stroke. They weren't sure how well he would recover, if at all. There was a possibility of brain damage.

Mick's eyes were closed, his pallid blue lips parted slightly, and for a few moments I was afraid he was dead. Or not necessarily afraid. Actually, there was something like relief to see him there, stretched out, finally knocked down, incapacitated. I know that part of it was the knowledge that he would never solve the Stela of Paser now. I was momentarily ashamed of this, but I knew Mick had something dark inside him, something small and hard and sour like a crab apple, hanging, rattling in his rickety rib cage. This was precisely the same kind of fate he would have desired for me.

Mick was clutching his carved ear votive in his white-knuckled hand. Even in his sleep his fingers worked the ancient wood nervously. I wonder if he prayed in his dreams, praying for his salvation. More likely cursing his innumerable enemies. The light from the hallway fell across his pinched face. When I looked up I saw my reflection in the window opposite, now beaded and dripping with rain.

Standing in the doorway, half under the white neon hallway light, I looked a rough figure. My hair was plastered to my head in sweaty strands, my glasses cracked and crooked, my coat and pants soaked through and mottled with various stains. My lips were dry and scabbed, and my facial bruise boomed deeply in my skull. After a few moments I realized Mick's eyes were open, glassy, and staring at me. He shuffled in the sheets a bit, and brought the hand clutching the votive up to his mouth, and began whispering something to it, watching me all the while. I instinctively wished to grip my own votive, lost the night of my beating in Alan's room. The right side of Mick's face was completely slack. His lips drooped and his right eye was hooded by loose skin. He seemed to have trouble keeping his eye open.

Nonsense, Mick muttered, fabrications. Bollocks.

What?

Song of Amun, he said. The glyphs. Not without the transliteration. Grammatical constructions.

He spoke out of one side of his mouth. Half of his face was worked into a fierce expression of anger. The other merely sagged.

I never told you my translation, I said. How do you know what I came up with?

Doesn't matter, Mick said, I know what you think. You're wrong. About the Stela too.

This was just the kind of thing from Mick that I was expecting all along. I just couldn't believe that he had waited till now to say it.

Really? I said, then why don't you tell me what I'm doing wrong?

What do we know, Mick said, about the Stela? Rather pedestrian hymn. Mut. Who has no importance in the Twentieth Dynasty. Or Intermediate period pantheon. The whole thing is bollocks. You know it. Five thousand years of transmogrification. Transmutation. Absorption. In the end all these gods and goddess. Distill down into the same few iconic figures. The Stela of Paser is a prayer. But it isn't the fucking Rosetta Stone.

He winced and his thin lips drew tight over his teeth in a strange smile.

There isn't, he said, even any real cryptography anyway. The third way is all shite. Klein knew you'd go for it.

You don't know what you are talking about, I said. The top register—

I know what it fuckin' says. You stupid cunt.

Well I don't agree with you, Mick.

Ah, fuck the whole fucking load of it, Mick hissed. I wish I'd never seen it.

Mick brought his hand with the votive up to his face, stroked his paralyzed cheek with the ear and began to murmur into the rough whorls of wood. I wanted him dead, deader than anything in the entire British Museum.

Hey, Mick, you know a man named Oldcastle? Up at Cambridge? He said he knew you. He mentioned your name.

What'd he say? Mick murmured.

Well, it's difficult to say. I think he said he was going to kill you. Get yourself involved in something?

Mick shivered, his bony shoulders shaking.

Kill me. Done it for 'im, eh?

It's not *my* fault you're in here.

That cunt Alan Henry. That Paki writer. All of you. You did it.

That's not true, Mick. We didn't do anything. You got sick.

The pills, Mick said. Those fucking pills. You were supposed to take them too.

I don't see what you mean. The pills that Hanif gave you?

Oldcastle, Mick wheezed. Invocations. Bugger.

It wasn't Alan, I said. I know that. He tried to help me.

His face suddenly cleared like the face of a child. For a brief moment I thought I saw something inside, some kind of hint of something.

You know, Mick said, you know what you could do? Something actually useful?

The dark pools of his eyes flexed and flowered, his skin blanched, then reddened. Then he collapsed, letting his eyelids fall. The hospital was impossibly silent, and I found myself wondering where all the commotion was, all the machines, the nurses, doctors, the patients, where was all the noise, the work of medicine, curing ailments, fixing the broken, since when was caring for the ill such silent work?

The Song of Amun, Mick said. It's just one man . . . a letter. Even Klein knows it.

I think there's more to it than that, I said.

It's not going to change anything, Mick said, whatever it is. Won't change a thing.

A murmur of voices from down the hall, a flash of light, the rolling sound of a gurney behind me in the hallway, ushered along by two low, murmuring voices. Mick held his hand over his drooping eye.

My eyes, Mick said, it fucking hurts to open my eyes, Rothschild. The pain . . . it hurts fucking bad . . . so fucking bad . . .

Mick held his hand over his eyes and began groaning into his ear votive, no longer a prayer of words but something far more plaintive and awful. In the reflection of the window I saw the gurney come past the doorway, a single man pushing a form draped under a sheet, both of them hooded in shadow, continuing past down the hall and then receding into the distance and it was quiet again. I walked a little closer to Mick's bed and watched his narrow chest rise and fall under the sheet. He stopped murmuring and his hands relaxed and fell to his sides. His face looked like a death mask, waxy and gray. His hand fell open and the worn wooden ear votive, damp with sweat, a dull lump of hardwood three thousand years old, lay cradled in his thin palm. His chest still moved. I stood and listened again for a moment, but heard nothing.

I left Mick there, lying in the dark. I hurried along the pale corridors of the hospital, gripping his votive in my hand. He didn't stir, not the slightest bit, when I took it from him, regarding me with one drooping, half-open eye.

As I left the hospital, the sky was clearing finally, clouds breaking over London, the wind cold and cutting. A woman sat in a wheelchair by the curb of the emergency room, clutching a flannel nightgown about her tightly, sitting half in the streetlight and half in the dark, her shoulders shaking as she wept. I began walking quickly down the street, vaguely in the direction of my flat. The morning sky through the buildings seemed distant. I put my hands into my pockets and for the first time in a long while I wished I was back in America.

27: GRAVITY

ZENOBIA WAS JUST OVER three years old when I left.

I remember the night clearly. I woke up from a dream. I had been standing before Anubis, holding my heart in my hand, bloody and dripping. He prepared the scales, holding the feather against which my heart would be weighed, while the slathering, long-fanged, doglike creature squatted at his feet, ready to devour my heart. We were in the desert, like the eastern desert outside Aswan, and in the distance, the realm of coming into being, just over the edge of the horizon, a light was shining, a suffused glow like the rising sun. But the sun was already in the sky. When I looked back to Anubis, he had transformed into a much larger figure, broad shouldered and clutching an ankh in one hand, in his other hand, outstretched, my heart. It was Seth, defender of Egypt. I turned and ran away from him, toward the light on the horizon, but as I started up the first dune the sky went dark and the dune stretched on upward into the sky like a towering mountain.

It was a damp November night in San Francisco, much like the weather in London. The rain was lightly tamping on the windows, I remember because the sound woke me from my dream. Helen lay at my side, curled tightly in the sheets and blanket, her face shadowed from the pale streetlight through the window. I had one hand resting on her waist, moving slightly with her breathing. When I awoke I could still smell the burnt, salty air of the western desert, the Sahara, mixed with the delicate shades of vanilla and sandalwood, the smell of my wife. I shifted closer to her, to see her face in the shadow of the curtain. Her breath slipped through her slightly parted lips, her face relaxed, her eyelids smooth. Helen's book lay open on the night table, the clean lines marred only by a single underlining, a few lines that she marked deeply with pencil:

Mozart lies somewhere in a pauper's pit, a communal grave in Vienna. His own wife was unable to find his body the day after he died.

I slipped out of bed and walked down the short hall to Zenobia's room. She lay curled in her crib, much in the same position as Helen. She clutched her blankets tightly, but her face was soft and calm. On the nightstand was a New Kingdom amulet, inscribed with a crocodile and a short spell to protect a child from bad dreams and sickness: *Spell for a knot for a child, a fledgling: Are you hot in the nest? Are you burning in the bush? Your mother is not with you? Lay still, child, and know that you are always safe in your father's house!*

I gathered her up in my arms, her warm body nestling into my neck and chest with barely a murmur. Even then she was solid, the weight of her was surprising, the density of her small form. I carried her back into our room and stood at the edge of the bed looking down at my wife as she slept. Something about her shape, the rounded curve of her back, the hands clutched in front of her face, the form of the draped sheets, struck me deeply, and I shivered, holding Zenobia, my daughter, curled against me, like lead in my arms.

I lay Zenobia down next to her mother, her arms seeking out and finding Helen's neck and clutching there, burrowing her forehead into her mother's chest. The depression that Helen made in the bed made a shallow crater that Zenobia slipped easily into, the gentle circumference of her form. I was standing on the outside, somehow free from the pull. I wasn't standing on the floor anymore, or in that house in California, or anywhere on earth, anywhere that I could recognize. I was on a vast, endless grid, the horizon curving out of sight; I could feel the mass of my wife and child, their gravity softly curling the line of space downward. I was on the edge of a spinning galaxy, moving at terrifying speeds, where all the universe seems to be moving past one fixed point, the point of reference, the way to measure time. It was the two of them, Helen moving her head slightly to accommodate this new body, her cheek nestling on Zenobia's tousled head. But there was another pull, coming from the dark space over the horizon.

When I looked at those two sleeping forms, their dear shapes that I can draw in the air with my fingertips even now, as I watched them breathe I felt for my heart in my chest and what I found was a dark rock, a pyramid of stone.

I went into the kitchen to have a glass of water. The water was ice cold and metallic in my mouth. I set the glass in the sink, quietly, and stared at the dull shine of the fixtures for a few moments, gripping the counter. Through the window the staggered peaks of the rooftops of North Beach fell away to the low sections of San Francisco and the sea. The rain had ceased and the moon hung just above a layer of low clouds moving like a gentle stream. I felt the moon's cold light on my hands and face. I heard a furtive scuttle on the floor and when I turned a fat beetle scurried across the square of moonlight etched on the linoleum.

The truth is I could see it even then, that night, in the drops of water that beaded on the window; the forming image of it, the abstraction, the symbol, delicately positioned. *This body is my only tomb, this mind the black land, the only fertile ground.*

28:   THE LAST FLOOD

THE LAB WAS IN excellent shape; Sue and Cindy had done a remarkably thorough job. They also had the foresight not to disturb any of
our materials, regardless of where they lay. So the worktable was still a
jumble of Mick's notes and scratchings, his shaved papyrus quills,
scraps of ostracon dusting the table. My notes, Stewart's translations,
my grid alterations were scattered around the Stela in a semicircle,
right where I dropped them. The museum was dead quiet. I sat on
the table and watched the Stela, trying to hold my gaze on the black
stone without wavering. I had at least forty hours left, my last hours
with the Stela. Darkness closed around me like a cloak. As always, it
seemed like there was plenty of time. But I was wrong about that too.
I sat in that lab and let the world pass me by. I thought about what
Alan Henry once told me: Because all vantage points become the
same in the light of physics, *all observers, regardless of their state of motion, may proclaim that they are in fact stationary and the rest of the world is
moving by them* . . .

✤

I was conscious of being awake for several minutes before I actually was. I know that I was dreaming something about Sekmet, the lioness goddess. There were hundreds of black granite images of her in her common seated position, holding the flail and ankh across her chest, lined across a windy hillside, the sky mackerel gray and rolling. I was walking away from them; like most of my dreams I seemed on the verge of fleeing, but I was afraid to run, afraid to turn around, because I knew I'd see them coming after me. Usually in this sort of dream I would cower and curl up on the ground and wait for consciousness to rescue me, which it always seemed to do. But this time I just stood there.

I knew I was awake because I could sense that Klein was in the lab, I distinctly felt that he had used his key and was now standing over me, even though I hadn't opened my eyes yet. I could feel his image, like the spirit of a man, the *ka*, the ethereal form that returned from the underworld through the false door to recover his shabti, foodstuff, and other items provided for him in the tomb.

I could smell the strong coffee he was holding in his hand. I flicked my eyes open dramatically, just to see him jump. Which he did, letting out a *whoof!* and hopping backward with both feet together, coffee slopping out of the mug he was holding.

Whoa! Wakey wakey, Dr. Rothschild!

I sat up and regarded him. I never really looked at the man too closely before. I enjoyed how he visibly squirmed in my gaze. Strangely enough, I felt extremely well rested and my facial injuries merely hummed a small tune of discomfort.

What? I said.

He shrugged, spilling more coffee on the floor.

Just wanted to see, eh, how things are coming along. Your time here coming to a close, as you know. I'm glad to see you working hard till the end! I brought you some coffee.

He handed me the mug. I could tell by the smell it was Sue and Cindy's work. I felt I owed it to them to gulp some down. I tried a sip. I swear the lights brightened and my auditory powers sharpened a bit.

What time is it?

A little after one o'clock.

I didn't even remember falling asleep. I'd planned on staying up through the morning. It was my last day with the Stela. I had wasted all that time.

You know, Klein said, I certainly wouldn't sleep in the museum, especially down here in the basements. Lots of, restless spirits, the bodies . . . no, not for—

I have to go, I said, hopping off the table.

How's that final report coming together?

I haven't really started it.

But, you have something at least? For the next man to work with perhaps?

What next man?

Klein sipped his coffee and shrugged.

Too bad about Wheelhouse, eh? What a shame. Just when I think he was getting—

I have to go.

As I started toward the door, Klein stepped into my path to block my exit, still with that tight grin on his face. I swerved and purposely hit him sharply with my shoulder. He staggered back into a pile of shabti, ostracon, and Mick's writing tools. Grabbing for something to stop him from falling, he ripped a large mock-up of Gardiner's tables off the wall, ending up on his ass in the corner, his face livid and eyes bulging.

Rothschild! he roared. You are still under contract!

As I stood over him I felt a thrilling rush of power. I wanted to throttle him with my bare hands, or at least make some kind of bold gesture. I was riding a tide of something monumental, some sort of great discovery. But it had little to do with Klein.

Sue and Cindy were waiting expectantly at their desk in the hallway. They looked so freshly scrubbed and attentive, I suddenly felt terrible for how I had been treating them. I stopped at the desk and hoisted the mug over my head.

This, I said, is *excellent fucking coffee!*

I reached over and grabbed the pot on the hot plate and poured myself another full cup. Their mouths gaped open. They began to stand up.

Rothschild!

Klein stood awkwardly in the door of the lab, clutching the door frame with both hands, his face an impossible shade of purple. I saw Sue's and Cindy's faces begin to curl, to fold into themselves, their hands held at their throats.

Don't worry, I said to them, it's okay. Sit down, all is well. I'll talk to you guys later.

I ran down the hall and to our private side entrance, coffee sloshing out of the cup onto my pants, wrenching myself up the stairs and out the door onto Montague Street, the sidewalks already full of people milling about with folding maps and suitcases, bumping into one another as they craned their necks to catch the street names posted on the buildings high above them.

The door to my flat was open. Eddie was in the kitchen poking around in the refrigerator. When I walked in he stood up holding one of Mick's frozen sausage rolls in his hairy fist.

Aye, Dr. Rothschild. Just checking on your situation 'ere. Feelin' a bit peckish.

Eddie tossed the sausage roll back in the fridge with a thud and clapped his hands together.

You are aware, Dr. Rothschild, Eddie said, that you have to be cleared out tomorrow, all the bits and pieces, the whole kit, yeah?

Yes, I said, I'm aware of that. I haven't really started packing. And you know Mick's in the hospital.

Right. Poor little bugger. Well, you have to be out by half twelve tomorrow, yeah? Another bloke comin' in.

No problem.

Right then. Gotta take a slash—mind if I use ya crapper?

After Eddie left I splashed some cold water on my face and flattened my hair with my hands. The swelling on my face was down, though my split lip was still a ruby knob. Through the bedroom window I could hear the men rattling about the scaffolding, apparently working on the logistics for some kind of construction and cursing the very soul of the idiot who sent them up there to do it. I recognized the loopy turns of the Rastafarian who normally woke me in the mornings with his tapping and whacking. The sweet smell of marijuana filled the room.

I phoned Penelope and got her answering machine. I left a message saying that I wanted to see her before I left town. I figured I'd try Magnus as well, in case she was with him. She wasn't, but I ascertained from Magnus that Penelope was in fact at her flat. He asserted very seriously that she didn't want to be disturbed, no, she did not want to see or hear from anyone, but he cheerfully gave me her address in Highgate and even directions via bus or tube.

As I came down the stairs I heard one of those deliberately muffled conversations going on in the lobby, the kind that men have in public rooms when they are trying to discuss a dodgy matter. It was Eddie, for one, and after hovering for a moment on the last flight I caught the clacking tones of Okonkwo. And there were a few others. So I did what seemed appropriate: I went back up to my room and locked the door and paced around the bed saying *fuck fuck fuck* under my breath for a bit, then put on my jacket and made a rather wobbly attempt to climb out the window onto the construction scaffolding, startling the two construction workers sitting just under the sill.

Whoa! You comin' out 'ere, man?

My dreadlocked friend was crouched there in his baggy trousers and quilted jacket, sharing a joint longer and thicker than my finger with a dusty, stubble-faced chappie with cheap tattoos across his hands and who in fact seemed not at all surprised to see me there. I was clinging to the window sash, one foot planted on the wobbly and splintered board that they sat upon.

Listen, I said, it's . . . eh . . . an emergency. I need to get down.

The Rastafarian shook his dreadlocks and winked at me as he drew on the weed.

Now howya gonna get down from 'ere, man? Only way 'a down is you gotta climb. You tink you up for dat?

The wind was terrific out there at that height, whistling through the pipes and boards, making the whole setup sway slightly from side to side, as if giving the building a good scratch. I kept one leg inside the window for balance, which was a good thing because the first pipe I grasped for support came loose in my hand with a squeaking wrench.

Oi! Mate!

Now it was Tattoo Hands addressing me. His brow was rippled with fury.

I fink ya betta get a' fuck back inna window before ya bring the whole fucking fing down, yeah?

Ah, give eem ah break, man! 'E can do it!

I handed Tattoo Hands the section of pipe I'd removed from the scaffolding. It was six floors down, and leaning out a bit more to look over the edge almost made me sick with fear. A police van was parked at the curb.

Sorry about the . . . pipe there, fellas.

I climbed back inside and closed the window and shut the curtains. I considered the balance of elements, the possibilities. I paced and cursed a bit more. Then I started down the stairs, building my momentum and speed on the last flight, and sprinted through the entranceway, past the surprised Okonkwo, Eddie, and a couple of bobbies who stood around Eddie's desk, the television flickering in the back room. I took a skipping right out the door and ran down Great Russell Street, weaving through the usual afternoon museum tourists, making my way toward Tottenham Court Road. When I reached the intersection I looked back down Great Russell to see Okonkwo chugging through the crowded sidewalk, head and shoulders above the crowd, pumping his arms like an Olympic sprinter, his long knobby legs slashing at the ground. There was no way I was going to outrun him; my hope was to flag down a cab on Tottenham and disappear, but there was no time for that either. The pedestrian traffic light in front of the Sainsbury's on Tottenham Court was just changing red to yellow, so I ran across the street ahead of the surge of traffic, dodging a few motorcycles and bicyclists who jumped the light, then started running north. A bus was just pulling away from the Goodge Street stop, the 73, where it runs I have no idea, but at a flat run I was able to catch it and hop on the back landing to the bemusement of the ticket taker. As the bus gathered speed I looked back again but didn't see Okonkwo or any other police in the crowds along the sidewalk. I figured I needed to change methods of transportation in case they saw me getting on the bus so after a few blocks I hopped off the back again.

Unfortunately I wasn't paying attention and the bus was still moving at a decent rate of speed when I jumped. When I hit the ground my feet flew out from underneath me and I turned a few furious somersaults on the sidewalk, eventually crashing into a filthy man with a sleeping bag over his shoulder eating a bag of crisps. He shouted as I cut his legs out from under him like a scythe. I rolled to a stop, seemingly unhurt. The homeless man was sitting up, extracting crumbs of chips from his stained shirtfront.

Sorry about that, I said. I'm sorry. Sorry.

I reached in my pocket and took out the envelope of bills. My wrist screamed with pain as I riffled through the money. My jacket sleeve was shredded—Hardy's jacket. I thrust a few hundred pounds in his face. He looked at the fluttering bills with rheumy eyes for a moment, then snatched them like a cobra. I turned and ran for it.

Fucking scumbag Americans! he yelled after me.

I reached the Euston stop just as the 134 bus pulled up, which I boarded along with a raft of young mothers struggling with baby strollers apparently containing freshly born infants covered in clear plastic sheets. I climbed the stairs and took a seat in the back of the upper deck, craning my head around to check for Okonkwo, breathing hard. In the seat in front of me two Albanian men talked conspiratorially into the collars of their leather jackets, one side of their upper lips packed with some kind of snuff tobacco. The upper deck of the bus was stocked with preteen girls in baby blue skirts and jumpers with their school crest emblazoned on their narrow chests. They were kneeling on the seats and screaming nearly incomprehensible obscenities of remarkable vulgarity at each other.

The bus wound its way toward Camden, weaving a figure-eight pattern down the road past pedestrian islands and cars parked illegally in the bus lane and I watched London hurl itself into the afternoon. On the sidewalk an old fellow in a tweed coat and cane was speedily helped out of a cafe to the curb by his elderly wife, where he smoothly vomited a gray geyser of fluid, careful not to lose his hat or get any on his trousers. A Muslim woman in a headscarf pulled a small boy along the sidewalk on a makeshift sled, the lower half of his body in a cast. He lay on his stomach, facing forward, just a few inches off the ground, stuffing crisps into his mouth from a packet of Walker's. He seemed to be enjoying himself.

It isn't just the dogged resilience of these people; it is their ability to exist in the midst of a blatant contradiction that amazes me. The urban world of London seems so entirely bound up in the consumption and acquisition of things, yet the bulk of Londoners exist on so little. It seems to be part of their psyche—to long for what they cannot have—to exist in a constant state of dissatisfaction. So they draw their pleasures in small doses: a packet of crisps, four channels of BBC telly, a pint of lager, a tiny, rocky plot of garden worked tirelessly for a few withered aubergines, the harbored fag in the evening, a plate of gherkins, the favorite pants worn four days a week. This exists as well in other countries, including the United States, in some form, but not to this degree; citizens of most nations seem to come to a level of peaceful acceptance of the limits of their financial circumstances, condition, existence. Not so with Londoners. Which possibly explains all the dodgy hucksters, crooked shysters, con-men, petty thieves, grubbing schemers, betting shops and casino parlors, the omnipresent video poker and fruit machines in the pubs, lottery mania, get-rich-quick schemes, the fanatical worship of popular entertainment figures, royalty even. It is a sad, sad world, filled with so much disappointment. So many go unfulfilled, so many dream of something better, something so impossible that it can't hurt to desire it with a hunger that makes you spit on the sidewalk outside the newsagent's and curse your tired feet. It is an empire recently fallen, humbled and forgotten, yet stubbornly proud, maybe something like the end of the Ptolemaic era or the Late New Kingdom in Egypt, the diminishing light, the beacon for the civilized world kneeling before the crushing weight of its own greatness. And perhaps this is why I love London more than any other place in the western world; it is the only place in which I have felt completely a part of the pattern, the ordering equation, where the quiet heart, the tree in the garden, seems to have its moment in the sun.

In Kentish Town I got off and remembering the envelope of money in my pocket, flagged down a black cab and bundled in, my lungs wheezing, cradling my wrist. I gave the driver Penelope's address and I was off, the cab doggedly climbing through the hills of North London.

Penelope lived in a basement flat under a tailor's shop on Archway Road, Highgate. It was a typical London storefront with a faded red awning that read simply: "Marcos Tailors." To the side was an alcove with a row of buzzers and the door that led to the flats. "P. Otter." I rang Penelope's bell and waited. After a moment she materialized behind me, making me lurch with fear. She had been in the tailor shop and seen me come out of the cab.

Christ, Walter, she said, whatcha doing here? What now?

Penelope was almost unrecognizable, so long had I spent with her in different shades of disarray that her current state of ordered cleanliness was shocking. She was wearing a heavy cotton sweatshirt and fresh-looking jeans, her face scrubbed and shining as much as her English pallor would allow. Her hair was pulled into the Victorian knot, neatly arranged. But her eyes looked tired.

A fireplug of a woman came out of the tailor shop in an apron, thick glasses perched on the end of her nose. She addressed a stream of fiery Greek at Penelope.

It's okay, Penelope said, making calming motions with her arms. It's all right. He's a friend of mine.

The little Greek woman eyed me for a moment, then seemed satisfied: *okay okay bye bye bye!* and went back into the shop.

My landlady, Penelope said.

Penelope's flat was actually just a single room, even smaller than the one Mick and I shared, with a half fridge sitting in the old fireplace, a small sink and toylike oven perched in one corner, a telephone booth–size bathroom and a portable closet. The back window did look out on to the back garden, a rather weedy plot with a rusted barbecue grill beside a leaning wall of ancient brick. Penelope boiled some water in her electric kettle and made us a quick cup of tea while I sat in the only chair at the table that was obviously more of a desk. It was covered with large glossy books on nineteenth-century painting, a few assorted paperback novels. *London Fields, The Black Album, Mid-*

night's Children. A crooked stack of printed sheets marked up with pencil, and underneath it all a laptop computer.

I would've cleaned up, Penelope said, if I knew I was going to have company.

She handed me a cup of tea.

And don't start, Walter.

She walked over and lightly smacked my hand that was apparently paging through one of the novels. I guess I was hoping to see some of her notes in the margins.

Every time, she said, you walk into a fucking room you immediately start reading or deciphering whatever's laying about. Gets on my tits, you know?

I'm sorry, I said. I called earlier but you didn't answer.

Penelope leaned on the sink. I realized for the second time that she really didn't seem too happy to see me.

Don't worry, I said, I won't stay long.

How'd you find out where I live? Go back to the library and ask some other girl this time, yeah?

Magnus told me. But he told me not to come. It was my idea, my fault.

Magnus, Penelope muttered, *the sod*.

I think I'm in trouble. Still.

There's a fuckin' surprise.

Penelope chucked her tea into the sink and rinsed out the cup. She put her hands on her hips.

Well, she said, let's get out of here anyway. I've been in all day and I need to get out. We'll go for a walk on the heath.

We walked in silence up the gentle slope to the Highgate High Road and through Pond Square, past the cemetery and onto Merton Street, which wound back down the hill, threaded with grand homes and walled estates, ending in the east end of Hampstead Heath. Penelope had her hands thrust into her mackintosh pockets and stomped her way along the gravel path that sloped down toward a series of lakes and then wound back up and over a large hump of grassy hill-side worked with footpaths.

We walked between the large duck pond and the men's bathing pond where a few hardy men climbed gingerly down frozen dock lad-ders and splashed about the green water in crude, crawling strokes, annoying a half dozen scrawny swans. A few people sat on campstools at the water's edge and watched their fishing floats bobbing in the film of algae, white buckets beside them boiling with tiny slivers of fish. Papers posted on the surrounding fence, bordered with skulls and crossbones, told of bacterial infections, fungus growth, inhalation dan-gers. It was a beautiful London afternoon, the clouds breaking up and the damp chill swept clean by high winds and fresh leaves.

We carried on along a narrow tamped-grass path straight up a high mounded hill topped with a lone oak tree. Penelope veered off under the tree toward a wooden bench. An inscription carved into the back read: *For my dear husband, Harry, who always loved the Heath. 1909–1991*. All across the hillside packs of dogs roamed at the ankles of solitary long-skirted women with walking sticks, rambling about the women's epicenters in widening gyres. The bench faced south, and we could see London shrouded in its veil, church spires giving way to steel towers, the Thames a narrow rut, a ditch, a faint depres-sion in a field of stone. Some kind of flying insects were waging a des-perate war in the dirt at our feet. Penelope shrugged her delicate chin into the collar of her coat and gazed steadily at the city skyline.

I had that sickening feeling, the sensation that the consistency of my world had been shaken beyond repair. The harsh reality of the formative cycles, changing seasons, the great floods, were only regu-lated by the strictest of attention, only by the unflinching gaze. But it wasn't enough: The gods were infallible; we are to blame for our own sufferings. Hathor, Sekhmet, Mut, born from their father's brow into the world, they would wreak havoc upon the lands until their anger was satisfied, until their father was able to contend with the enormity of what he had done, to come to them in humility and offer his bare neck. Only then was order restored.

I felt Penelope take my hand, her eyes following the traces of birds that arched across the tight bowl of the sky, competing with absurd kites that fluttered gamely in the light breeze, kites shaped like planes, stacked boxes, pentagons, pyramids, an outstretched hand. I shut my eyes and held on to her. Solitary dogs called from the deep woods. This would be different, I thought, this would be the other thing, this would be the Third Land.

How can you make your way back once the floodwaters have receded and you return to your village to find the grain stores washed away, the house in splinters, your family drowned? The touch of another human was the spark of destruction, the chaos unleashed, flung into the black river that spins at the edge of time.

Walter? Penelope said.

I don't know how long we had been sitting there; time had compressed itself again, the casual trick of concentration. Or was it absentminded reverie? Either way, I wanted to go back, to stay in it, at least for a bit more. Penelope looked so sad and so young. She was too young to be this sad, and too beautiful.

I loved her then. I loved her life more than my own. But then I watched this too slip by.

She nodded her chin slightly down the hill.

Okonkwo, his long form looking regal in his dark suit, was trudging through the grass at the foot of the hill, still several hundred yards away, flanked by two pairs of policemen who began to angle out from him up the hill like a pair of wings. Okonkwo circumvented one of the roving packs of dog and long-skirted woman with stick, stooping for a moment to pat a skinny mongrel affectionately on the head.

Good-bye, Walter, Penelope said.

And then she got up, brushed off her coat, and walked away, behind me, down the backside of the hill toward the line of trees that crept across the valley of grass. When she was out of sight over the crest of the hill and into the woods I turned and stood up and waved to Okonkwo, who stopped and waved back. I watched the kites working their shapes against the cold blue of space, working their way through the circular dimensions that Alan Henry had dreamed of, the very dimensions of time. The light, fresh wind on my face cooled the heat of my bruises.

If the fabric of space is made up of strings, tiny vibrating strings, forming looped dimensions that shimmer with the music of eternity, then we must walk through eternity at every step. This need to return, to follow the line of linear history to try and reel it back, gasping and flopping in the boat, desperate under the knife of the present; it still can only be understood in terms of the relative position of the observer as the entire world moves past him. History is so much like physics in this manner. But my position was no longer stationary; I had allowed myself to be caught up in the currents of the great river. The third way was a solution that could not be translated, at least to anyone else. I would have it in my heart, alone.

The wind that moves the hair of a crooked old woman bundled in scarves outside the Virgin record store on Oxford Street holds the essence of pharaohs in its tightly curled tendrils. Why is that not enough? Why is that never enough?

I took a last glance at the kites making their way over London, then began to walk down the hill toward the line of people who were coming up to meet me.

EPILOGUE: A LETTER

I GOT A POSTCARD from my daughter the other day. Zenobia's living in Connecticut, commuting into New York. Apparently the baby is doing well, now nearly two years old. Helen is great, Zenobia says, still in San Francisco, happily married, giving lessons to kids and playing music. Zenobia wanted to let me know that she named her daughter Marie. It was just a postcard, so that's really all there was to it. The picture on the front was of a New England farmhouse, blanketed in snow.

I'm currently splitting time between Aswan and Deir el-Medina. The new Berlin Museum is desperate for material and I'm supervising a few different digs and collection archives. Klein helped set it up through his contacts in Berlin in return for a promise to turn over my notes and a new translation for the Stela of Paser. He has no idea how long he may have to wait. I haven't the heart yet to tell him. I think in truth he really just wants me to remain quiet, to go away and never be heard from again. This is something I have always been able to do.

The wall of my apartment building in Aswan actually has a

Ptolemaic Stela fragment built into the cornerstone. It has some nice ligatures and a decent example of figurative hieroglyphs. There is something to this land, where the rudest building might be laced with two-thousand-year-old prayers and the words of gods. I can put my fingers into them, tracing along their curves and angles as I stand in the street, my body in two eras at once.

I heard from Klein that Mick recovered from his mysterious illness and moved in with his mother in Slough. A few weeks later he killed himself in the bathroom stall of a High Street kebab shop. He sliced his wrists with a paring knife, clutching a handful of votives and shabti on his lap. I suppose he didn't want to do it in his mother's house.

After I heard about Mick's suicide I took the ear votive I'd stolen from him that night in the hospital and threw it into the Nile. I don't know what Mick was praying for, what he was whispering into those votives, but I feel now that it was probably something similar to what I was thinking on those same lonely nights.

Every month I send a check to Mick's mother to cover his outstanding loans. The government arranged a payment plan. I sent her the rest of the money that Oldcastle gave me as well, but I don't think she even knows who I am or why I'm doing it and I haven't got the heart to tell her.

Hanif got out of jail and wrote a scathing, controversial political play that is currently playing the West End, something about the corrupt legal system and promiscuous British girls preying upon innocent foreigners. I also read that a group of American wrestlers were deported under murky circumstances. Apparently one of them had a rare book from the British Library on his person when they raided his flat. A group of Krishnas was also detained in connection with the wrestlers, and they turned out not to be Hindus at all but Saudi and Egyptian Muslims operating some kind of stolen-artifacts ring to support extremist groups. It seems the wrestlers were acting under the orders of the Saudi oil magnate who owned their contracts and the cable channel that broadcast their shows. The desperate political conditions led some of these revolutionary groups to attempt to tap into the ancient powers of their ancestors—and this, I suppose, is where Oldcastle came in.

Mick implied to me at the hospital that it was Alan Henry who had orchestrated the whole thing, or at least my involvement in it, but I know that isn't true. The fact was Mick couldn't solve the Stela, and trying almost killed him. Everything was so easy for him and when he tried to bend his mind around the possible third way it broke him. He was bitter and resentful of me. Klein planted the seed of the third way to be sure, but that is where his responsibility ends. Mick couldn't see it like I did, and he drove himself mad trying, just like Oldcastle. I thought I had entered into the poetic imagination of the ancient scribes; in fact I had made the third way into a false reality, a fabric of truth where before there was only conjecture, and madness. All along it was only my own, and for this phantom I left my family behind.

I never saw anything in the papers about the death of Oldcastle. They never were able to find the body of the man called Alan Henry, and I never heard anything else about his book or the CSA, but I have to admit I didn't look too closely. There was no mention of a woman called Erin Kaluza.

I also got a letter from Penelope recently. We've been corresponding for some time now. She tells me that I write like an Englishman, that my diction and syntax sound oddly British. I told her that I suppose that is because I learned how to read and write from reading history books mostly written by Englishmen.

Penelope says she's been working on a novel. It's going to be about us, about what happened to us that last week in London. She dumped the dissertation about the painters and got a stewardship job at the British Museum, working during special events, serving cocktails, trying to keep the wealthy donors from touching the artifacts, things like that. She says it's a great job because it's mostly at night, flexible hours for writing, and she meets famous people all the time. She wrote that just last month in the Parthenon Sculpture Hall she got to tell Princess Margaret to put out her cigarette.

For about three months Dr. Hardy sent Penelope awful letters, full of hate for what she did. She said it almost broke her. He was hospitalized again and called Penelope every day for a week, until he finally passed away. She says she threw away her answering machine after his first message. I told her that that was a good idea. She says she thinks of him a lot and is definitely going to put him in the book she's writing, write him as a nice old guy to even things out a bit, if that's possible.

Penelope's also been asking me to write down everything I know or remember and to send it to her. I can't visit as I'm not allowed in the UK for another twenty years because of my involvement in the theft of the Song of Amun and the book from the British Library. Penelope knows the phone is out of the question. I told her I miss London terribly, the most wonderful city in the world, something I understand now that I am no longer there. I told her to work with her own recollections for her novel; I have little doubt that it will be much more sensible and vivid and true than my own.

In her last letter she said she came up with the perfect plan for me:

> Look, if you really wanted to preserve your body after
> death and all that, to stay fresh for future generations,
> I've got a better idea. Get yourself embalmed, in the
> modern manner, everything intact, and put into a tank of
> preserving solution, then encased in a solid sphere of
> lead, to a thickness of at least eighteen inches for
> radiation shielding. Situate this in the nose end of a
> cylinder made of high-grade titanium, another twelve

inches of thermal-rated steel, with radio-controlled angling planes and a tracking system. Take it out on a trawler in the Sea of Japan and drop it into the Marianas Trench, the deepest part of the ocean. Get your mates on the ship to drop it overboard and to steer your body into the deepest point possible. The bottom there is covered with about another four hundred feet of soft silt. You'd go right through it like butter.

And the best part of it is, not only would you be assured of surviving whatever catastrophic events happen here on the surface, including nuclear annihilation, melting polar ice caps, whatever, but you'd also be closer to the center of the earth than anyone else ever! With any luck, because of the proximity of seismic activity, you'd be subducted into viscous magma of the mantle! Maybe even the earth's core! Wouldn't that be something? And if anyone ever did find you, imagine what sort of cosmic events would have to take place for you to be dredged up! You might even survive long enough to make the final party, the implosion of the universe, the reverse of the big bang, the end of time, when everything finally comes home to stay.

She's quite an inventive girl. I sent her a small wedjat emblem, the eye of Horus, inset with a deep green slice of feldspar and rimmed in gold. I told her that the falcon eye of Horus is the eye of truth and wisdom, something she will need if she wishes to be a chronicler of events, a great scribe. I inscribed a short hymn on the back, with a cryptographic representation of writing and truth, a hymn to Thoth, the baboon, the original "True of Voice," asking for wisdom and grace. Then I also inscribed in hieratic script a short prayer to no god at all. The prayer is that she will only write the truth, though I didn't tell her about that part. She says she keeps it on her writing table.

I listen to music all the time now, all kinds, everything I can get my hands on. I spend most of my days down at the dig sites or at the Aswan antiquities archives, and most of my nights listening to music in my flat. I have a little stereo CD player with headphones so I can play it as loud as I want. I also found an old record player, and you'd be surprised by the number of secondhand records floating around Aswan. Now I have all sorts of records, CDs, tapes, all kinds of stuff. Classical, jazz, rock and roll, blues, country, opera, everything. I particularly like country and western, such poignant, simple stories, so clear and honest.

It's still a mystery to me how it happens, how music works, like something moves inside you, something that you can't see or even know, not even slightly, like the most subtle stirrings of the universe. I feel this way particularly when I listen to Bach's cello suites, when I think of Helen, playing the cello in a room, but not an empty room, a room full of people and laughter and noise. And there are times when I'll think about Penelope, typing away in some little studio flat in Highgate, looking out her window into a rainy garden, her pale forehead furrowed with effort. I'll sit here in my armchair and listen to music all night long. I have a lot of catching up to do.

It's midday and the market is in full swing. Standing on the high Aswan parapet, I shade my eyes from the glaring sun with my hand. The Valley of the Kings stretches out to the north, and the Nile winds its way along to the east. The massy brown stone of the High Dam looms to the south, the great spreading pool of Lake Nasser just beyond, glittering in the sun. The Nile dips to the east into the semicircle stretch of sandstone cliffs that ring the great tombs. At dusk the sun drops like a white stone into the broad curve of the river, much like the hieroglyph for the same expression. It looks remarkably like the figurative symbol for "go forth," the phonemic sign of the snake leaving a hole. I know that figurative orthography was designed to make dead pictoral metaphors alive once again. Pyramids, tombs, temples, all the vast structures that rework land are expressions of language on a vast scale; the entire landscape is a finely sculpted symbol, carved from the unforgiving rock by countless hands. It's the sense of scale that matters. My father had that part right; he just had it the other way around. These days his image is worn and quiet, like the faint tracing of reed quills over ancient paper, like the watermarks in submerged caverns, buried deep.

I can still see the Stela when I close my eyes. Now I see it down in the farther reaches of the museum, the sub-storage rooms, its implacable face covered with canvas, the words sitting in darkness. I don't mind. You have to let it go on by itself, let it walk over the hill and into the sun. The place where everything comes into being. We have to let the story go on without us.

AUTHOR'S NOTE ON
THE HISTORY OF THE STELA OF PASER

I came across the Stela of Paser in 1999 while wandering the corridors of the British Museum. I was born in London at the time to teach undergraduates about Shakespeare and Modern English Literature and I spent many off hours in the museum, just down the street from where I lived on Great Russell Street. I pored over the majestic Rosetta Stone many times, and I loved to let my fingers hover just inches over the ancient sections of naked granite inscribed with hieroglyphs in the English galleries. I was drawn to these scripts more than the mummies or other more exotic fare.

On this particular fall afternoon, the British Museum was celebrating the bicentenary of the discovery of the Rosetta Stone with a special exhibition: "Cracking Codes: The Rosetta Stone and Decipherment." The remaining fragment of the Stela of Paser was just one of many objects on display, all of which presented particular problems of translation or decipherment. Nearly all of them, like the Stela of Paser, normally remained out of sight and mind in the storage rooms of the museum basement. I found it fascinating that these scripts had not been solved for several thousand years, even when we are able to fully translate ancient Egyptian languages. I had little understanding of hieroglyphs at the time, but I was drawn to the particular problem of the Stela of Paser: that these symbols placed in a grid could be read horizontally and vertically, giving different variations on the same hymn, and that a mysterious "third way," as mentioned in the reading instructions, was yet to be discovered. It seemed a preposterous task, and I immediately thought of what sort of person would dedicate their lives to such a thing. What would it be like to hover over this impenetrable text and extract meaning that has remained hidden for nearly three thousand years? When the Stela of Paser was returned to storage after the exhibition was over, who would be there, huddled in the dark reaches of the basement, waiting for it?

I bought the book produced by the British Museum to accompany the exhibit, *Cracking Codes: The Rosetta Stone and Decipherment* by Richard Parkinson. After this I began assembling a modest library of Egyptology books, but none was as important as Parkinson's as it lays out the essential groundwork of cryptography in ancient scripts.

I returned to London several times, and in 2002 I was able to secure a job at the museum that allowed me access to the various nether regions, as well as to the staff and curators who worked with the actual objects. One October day I arranged to see the Stela of Paser, back in storage, with an Egyptology curator. We walked through rooms stacked high with statuary and pottery, an immense wealth of antiquities. After a bit of searching we found the Stela simply leaning against the rough stone wall, a small marker, E.A. 194 (E.A. = Egyptian Antiquities), designating the bin number. My Egyptologist guide simply shrugged when I asked about the "third way" mentioned in the script. I had already begun the novel by this time and it was just as I had hoped: It was still a mystery. What if unlocking the "third way" could open up some kind of new understanding of ancient hieroglyphs or even of the Egyptian culture and people? What if the Stela of Paser is some kind of new Rosetta Stone? This is the premise I created that drives my protagonist, Dr. Walter Rothschild.

The Stela of Paser is a badly damaged piece; like most stelae, it was originally in the classic tombstone shape. Most of the top rounded section is now lost, as well as some of the edges and the bottom fourth. A large fissure runs from bottom left to top right, splitting the Stela into two pieces. The mystery of the Stela of Paser comes from the top horizontal line of text, which is a Middle Kingdom Egyptian hymn to the goddess Mut, and also contains directions on how to read the Stela: *As for this writing, it is to be read three times. Its like has not been seen before, or heard since the time of the god. It is set up in the temple of Mut, Lady of Isheru, for eternity like the sun, for all time.* It has been suggested that the third way would be to read the outer edges, but the piece is too damaged to undertake this possibility. The Stela can be read vertically and horizontally because of the sort of verbal wordplay employed by some Egyptian scribes. They utilized stylistic devices, such as syllabic orthography (sequences of consonant and vowel combinations), and figurative hieroglyphs that are created by the scribe to evoke a new metaphorical understanding of the symbols. As these elements create a "coded" effect, they often fall under the rubric of cryptology.

I figured that in order to solve these kinds of puzzles, you would need to have a special gift that went above and beyond what is known about hieroglyphs. That is why Dr. Walter Rothschild believes in another level of meaning, something I've called "poetic interpretation," that uses the established elements of cryptography as well as something more that only he and a handful of others in the world can do. I created this new understanding of hieroglyphs so that I might apply what I intuit about the translations and the way Dr. Rothschild might see them.

I became more intrigued by the "third way" concept the more I delved into Egyptology. The concept of the "Third Land" shows up repeatedly in ancient Egyptian writing, mostly as a sought-after destination. This has to do with the Egyptian understanding of the "Two Lands," which refers to the divided kingdoms of the upper and lower Nile valley. It was the goal of nearly every king to unite the two lands, creating the "Third Land." In this way, the Third Land became a metaphor for a sort of promised land, a place that integrates the two known ways of living and makes a third, perfect way. It is similar to the way we might say we wish we could meld the separate aspects of our modern lives, the living and dead, or to walk in the past and future at the same time. This ancient Egyptian concept takes the most basic binaries established by western philosophy—positive and negative, truth and falsehood, good and evil—and struggles to reconcile this with the Eastern conceptions of organic unity, such as the yin and yang, striving to seek oneness, wholeness. The third way is the middle path, the perfect solution, the dream of reconciliation with all that is right and wrong in this world and in ourselves.

—MATT BONDURANT
SEPTEMBER 2004

ACKNOWLEDGMENTS

I am in great debt to Jane Springer, Seth Tucker, Mike Mannon, and Jason Corner, my friends, peers, and inspiration. Thanks to Adam Johnson, Elizabeth Stucky-French, and Bob Shacochis for their guidance. Cheers to the international program at Florida State University, Dr. Eugene Crook, and Mary Balthrop, for so generously allowing me to live and teach (twice) in the very epicenter of London, the city of my heart.

I am indebted to Richard Parkinson's *Cracking Codes: The Rosetta Stone and Decipherment*, which was my central resource for ancient cryptographic puzzles and the Stela of Paser, and also a great source of inspiration. Other important works included *The British Museum Book of Ancient Egypt; The Hieroglyphs of Ancient Egypt;* and *The ABC of Hieroglyphs* by the Ashmolean Museum in Oxford, which served as a great elementary primer. Other sources included Umberto Eco's *The Search for the Perfect Language*, Miriam Lichtheim's *Late Egyptian Wisdom Literature in the International Context* and *Ancient Egyptian Literature: A Book of Readings*. Also Jan Assmann's *Egyptian Solar Religion in the New Kingdom:*

Re, Amun and the Crisis of Polytheism, Lana Troy's *Mut Enthroned*, Herman te Velde's work on the gods Seth and Mut, the classic works of E. A. Budge, and H. M. Stewart's *A Crossword Hymn to Mut*, the most complete true translation of the Stela of Paser.

Physics works consulted include Brian Greene's fascinating *The Elegant Universe*, and I also drew inspiration from reading *Billions & Billions, Broca's Brain*, and the many other wonderful works of the great Carl Sagan.

Cheers to Don Adams, Judy Lindsay, my fellow stewards, and the rest of the corporate services staff at the British Museum for their generosity and general goodwill.

Some of the principal elements of this book were conceived in the upstairs room in the Plough Pub, WC1 London. Too many others to name here, so cheers to all the pubs of London, may you never change.

I am grateful for the faith and spirit of my agent, Alex Glass, who has been with me since the beginning, and the folks at Trident Media Group. And thanks to my editor Peternelle van Arsdale, whom I trust implicitly, and all the great people at Hyperion Books.

This book owes plenty to the writing program faculty at Florida State, and in particular to my mentor, Mark Winegardner.

I would also like to thank my mother and father, and all of my family, for their love and support always.

And thanks to Stacy Lowe, my dearest friend and companion.

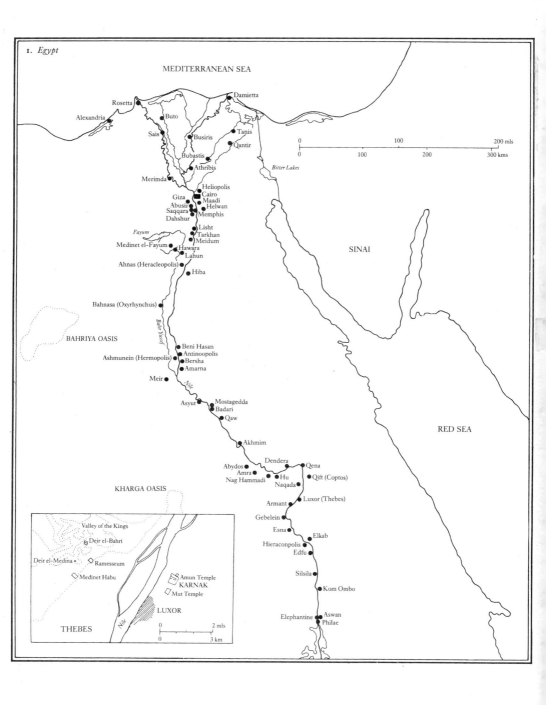

1. *Egypt*

MEDITERRANEAN SEA

Rosetta
Damietta
Alexandria
Buto
Sais
Busiris
Tanis
Bubastis
Qantir
Athribis
Bitter Lakes
Merimda
Heliopolis
Cairo
Giza
Maadi
Abusir
Helwan
Saqqara
Memphis
Dahshur
Lisht
Fayum
Tarkhan
Meidum
Medinet el-Fayum
Hawara
Lahun
Ahnas (Heracleopolis)
Hiba

SINAI

Bahnasa (Oxyrhynchus)

Bahr Yusuf

BAHRIYA OASIS
Beni Hasan
Antinoopolis
Ashmunein (Hermopolis)
Bersha
Amarna
Meir
Nile
Asyut
Mostagedda
Badari
Qaw
Akhmim

RED SEA

Dendera
Qena
Abydos
Amra
Qift (Coptos)
Nag Hammadi
Hu
Naqada
KHARGA OASIS
Armant
Luxor (Thebes)
Gebelein
Esna
Elkab
Hieraconpolis
Edfu
Silsila
Kom Ombo
Elephantine
Aswan
Philae

Valley of the Kings
Deir el-Bahri
Deir el-Medina
Ramesseum
Amun Temple
Medinet Habu
KARNAK
Mut Temple
LUXOR
THEBES

0   100   200 mls
0   100   200   300 kms

0   2 mls
0   3 km